PRAISE FOR ALYSSA PALOMBO

"Handsome. Intriguing. Dangerous. Seductive. [This] is everything you want in a book—it's a romance, a page-turner, and a ride deep into the sumptuous and tumultuous time of Renaissance Italy."

—Crystal King, author of *The Chef's Secret*, on *The Borgia Confessions*

"Alyssa Palombo's deft and delicate prose makes a gorgeous contrast against the visceral and cutthroat world of the Borgias. Dark and decadent, *The Borgia Confessions* is mesmerizing from start to finish."

—Meghan Masterson, author of *The Wardrobe Mistress*

"Palombo has crafted a sweeping and surprisingly sympathetic portrait of Cesare Borgia, one of history's most notorious 'bad boys,' and the world surrounding him. [A] dark Renaissance parable about the intertwining of lust and power. If you're as fascinated with all things Borgia as I am, you won't want to miss this one!"

—Kris Waldherr, author of *The Lost History of Dreams* and *Bad Princess*, on *The Borgia Confessions*

"Under Palombo's skillful hand, the entangled world of the Borgias comes vividly to life, exposing the dark facets of class structure and the all-consuming greed that comes with ambition—and love. I was utterly engrossed from page one. A colorful and suspenseful novel, *The Borgia Confessions* is packed with complex characters and political intrigue, and will leave readers hungry for more."

—Heather Webb, internationally bestselling author of *Last Christmas in Paris* and *Meet Me in Monaco*

"Marrying forbidden love, devoted friendship, and the supernatural with Palombo's signature passion for music, storytelling, and heartbreaking choices, *The Spellbook of Katrina Van Tassel* enchants with a concoction of love, longing, and loss plucked from the bones of one of our most enduring and haunting legends."

—Erin Lindsay McCabe, *USA Today* bestselling author of *I Shall Be Near to You*

"Strikingly feminist . . . a compelling narrative that is difficult to put down."

—*Publishers Weekly* on *The Most Beautiful Woman in Florence*

"Palombo skillfully blends historical facts with innovative and colorful fiction, creating a delightful, fast-paced romance that is sure to please music lovers and romance readers alike."

—*Shelf Awareness* on *The Violinist of Venice*

ALSO BY ALYSSA PALOMBO

The Spellbook of Katrina Van Tassel

The Most Beautiful Woman in Florence

The Violinist of Venice

The BORGIA CONFESSIONS

Alyssa
Palombo

St. Martin's Griffin • *New York*

This is a work of fiction. All of the characters, organizations, and events portrayed in this novel are either products of the author's imagination or are used fictitiously.

First published in the United States by St. Martin's Griffin, an imprint of the St. Martin's Publishing Group

www.stmartins.com

Library of Congress Cataloging-in-Publication Data

Names: Palombo, Alyssa, author.
Title: The Borgia confessions / Alyssa Palombo.
Description: First edition. | New York : St. Martin's Griffin, 2020.
Identifiers: LCCN 2019035016 | ISBN 9781250191205 (trade paperback) | ISBN 9781250621863 (hardcover) | ISBN 9781250191212 (ebook)
Subjects: LCSH: Borgia family—Fiction. | Italy—History—1492–1559—Fiction. | GSAFD: Historical fiction.
Classification: LCC PS3616.A3563 B67 2020 | DDC 813/.6—dc23
LC record available at https://lccn.loc.gov/2019035016

First Edition: February 2020

10 9 8 7 6 5 4 3 2 1

For Lindsay Fowler, who has been listening to me talk about this story in one form or another for years now.
Thank you for everything, always.

Prologue

CESARE

Rome, August 1484

The day I learned of my father's plans for me, I was but nine years old. In many ways, it was my first memory to take firm root. I remember other days, ones in the nursery with my younger siblings: countless mock sword fights with Juan, who always cried to our nurse when he lost; little Lucrezia showing me each of her dolls; and lessons, endless lessons in endless languages, as well as in mathematics, philosophy, history, politics, and geography. However, these memories do not hold the same cold, cutting clarity.

From then on, the memories of my childhood would take on a different cast, as though viewed in a darkened room. That day was the first memory of a young man who was no longer a boy.

It may be telling that this crucial piece of information was gained by subterfuge. I had gotten into the custom of eavesdropping on my parents during my father's visits; after coming to see us in the nursery, he would adjourn to one of the sitting rooms in my mother's palazzo, where she would have a meal laid out, and they would have a long, private conversation. Eager to hear what was said about me, I had begun to secretly listen in, only to be disappointed: most of their talk was idle gossip about people in Roman society whom I did not know or talk of Vatican politics I did not yet understand. (Though I did ascertain that several very favorable reports of my progress in lessons were given to my father, much to his approval and my secret pride.) But on the day in question, I finally heard something of interest. And I would almost instantly regret it.

I tried to steal quietly out of the nursery to follow my parents, but Lucrezia—even at the age of four—missed nothing. "Cesare," she called, poking her head out into the hallway. "Where are you going?"

"Shhh," I hushed her. "I am going to follow Father and Mother."

She stepped out into the hall, clutching one of her ever-present dolls tightly. Her golden ringlets fell unrestrained past her shoulders. "Why?"

I sighed. "I want to hear what news Father has," I said.

"I want to hear, too!" she answered immediately, her eyes shining. She adored our father without reserve.

I sighed again, knowing that taking a four-year-old on what I considered a daring espionage mission would not aid me in remaining undetected. Yet I could deny my little sister nothing. "Very well, if you promise to be very, very quiet!"

She nodded vigorously, her curls bouncing.

I took her hand and led her through the halls to the sitting room where our parents usually closeted themselves. My mother, Vannozza, was no longer Cardinal Borgia's mistress by this time—the meaning of which I was only beginning to grasp—and was rather happily married to Giorgio di Croce, a secretary to His Holiness Pope Sixtus IV. But my parents maintained an easy and affectionate friendship and were firmly united in their ideas of how their children ought to be raised.

As we approached the door, I could hear my mother's low voice, my father's louder rumble. "He cannot last much longer," my father was saying.

Turning to Lucrezia, I put my finger to my lips. She nodded again, minding her promise. I crept closer to the door, and she pressed close behind me.

". . . if you think you can," I heard my mother say.

"I mean to become pope at this conclave, Vannozza," my father said. The words took me by surprise, though they should not have. I was no fool, and my penchant for eavesdropping meant that most of my father's ambitions were known to me. But the finality, the conviction in his words, made me understand in a way I never had before: my father could become the pope, the leader of all Christendom, the sacred and somewhat distant figurehead of Rome.

I stole a glance at Lucrezia; her large gray-blue eyes were wide with wonder, but bless her, she made not a sound.

"I have been waiting for this moment for years," my father went on. "I must not fail."

"And what of della Rovere?" my mother asked. "If he has enough support to block your election?"

"I must not fail," he repeated. "I will win della Rovere's supporters to my side, whatever the cost."

"And yet if he—"

There was a loud, sharp sound, as though the cardinal had slapped his large hand down on the lacquered wooden tabletop. "There can be no 'if,' Vannozza," he said.

"Even so," she said, her voice soft yet firm. "It does not do to underestimate one's enemies and thus be caught unawares and unprepared."

"To plan for failure is to admit it is a possibility, and once you have done that, you are undone," my father said, his voice louder than before. "Everything depends on this, everything! You would plan less than the best for our children?"

"Surely there are other ways for you to give them what you dream, even if—"

"No," he bit out. "It is for them as much as for myself that I must succeed. You know what must happen, Vannozza. I will become pope; Cesare shall follow me into the Church; Juan shall wield the military might of the Holy See; and Lucrezia will marry to the best advantage of the family. We will become the first and greatest family in all of Italy, and no one shall dare spit on the name of Borgia ever again."

My mother made some reply, but I did not hear it, nor did I care to. My father's words rang loudly in my ears. *Cesare shall follow me into the Church . . .*

The words were like a death sentence to a boy who loved to ride, to wrestle, to play at sword fighting; a boy who devoured his lessons in military history like life-giving nectar. I had always loved the tales of that great Roman conqueror, Giulio Cesare, whose name I shared. In my mind, to be a soldier, a conqueror, was the finest occupation for a man. I was aware of the considerable power my father wielded as a man of the Church, yet it was a different sort of power altogether, and not what I would have chosen for myself.

And to make a soldier, a general, out of that weakling Juan! It was too much to be borne. In one foolish moment—the culmination of my shock and anger and envy—I found myself pushing open the heavy wooden doors of the room and barging in.

"Cesare," my father said in surprise.

"Father, please . . . tell me it isn't true!" I cried. "You don't truly mean to send me to the Church, do you?"

"Cesare, for shame!" my mother scolded. "Were you listening at the door? That sort of behavior is fit for servants, not a young nobleman!"

I ignored her, knowing punishment would come no matter what. Keeping my gaze fixed on my father, I pressed on. "I don't want to be a priest, Father! Make Juan go into the Church, and let me be your general! I can do it, I know I can!"

"Cesare, get back to the nursery this instant!" my mother said, advancing on me. "It is not your place to—"

Finally my father spoke, causing her to break off mid-sentence. "This was decided long before you could even speak," he said. His tone was not angry; rather, it was perfectly even. He was stating a fact, not presenting an argument. "I shall become pope, and you shall someday become pope after me." He stared hard at me, his usual jovial good nature gone. "Do you not wish to become a man to whom others turn for counsel, a man who accomplishes great things on behalf of Holy Mother Church? Do you not wish to make your family great?"

When he spoke, it was as a man speaks to another man, not

as a man to a child. I had never been spoken to in such a way before, and it did much to soothe my impetuous anger. I stood a little straighter. "I do."

"Good. Trust me when I say I know what's best for our family." A note of condescension had slipped back into his voice, but it did not break his spell over me. "Now, get yourself back to the nursery." His stern countenance slipped as a smile tugged at the corners of his mouth. "And take your sister with you."

I jerked my head back toward the doorway, but Lucrezia was not to be seen. She must have darted out of sight. I nodded, turned, and left the room, closing the door behind me.

"Mother is angry with you," Lucrezia pointed out from her hiding place against the wall.

"Yes, I know."

She took a couple of steps toward me. "Are you going to be punished?"

"I don't know, Crezia." I started in the direction of the nursery, as I'd been bidden, my sister trailing behind.

"Cesare," she said, after a few silent seconds had passed, "why are you so sad? Because you have to become a cardinal?"

"Yes, I suppose." The spell my father had cast had yet to fully wear off, but the sense of disappointment was still palpable. I considered the machinations of my nine-year-old brain far too advanced for little Lucrezia, however, so I didn't elaborate.

"And I must be married?" she asked. "That's what Papa said?"

"Yes."

"Like Mama and Signor di Croce?"

"Yes, only . . ." I trailed off as I considered Lucrezia's fate. More dread curdled my insides. "Only Papa will choose your husband, and you will go live with him."

Lucrezia's angelic face looked troubled at this, and I regretted causing her worry. "Papa would never let me go away, would he?" she asked. "I don't want to live anywhere without him and you and Mama and Juan and Jofre."

"You're a girl, Crezia," I said, the best explanation I could muster. "Girls are supposed to marry."

She considered this. "Can I marry you, Cesare?" she asked eagerly. "Then I wouldn't have to leave you!"

I couldn't help but look down at her and grin, despite my strange haze of disappointment mingled with pride. My first marriage proposal. "No, Crezia," I said patiently, taking her hand. "Brothers and sisters cannot marry. It is against God's law. Besides," I added, "if I am to be a cardinal, I may not marry anyone."

She frowned in concentration as she thought this through. Joy dawned on her face as another idea quickly formed. "We could switch!" she announced triumphantly. "I shall become a cardinal in your place, and you can marry!"

I laughed aloud, and impulsively bent down to hug her. "Oh, sister. They do not let women become cardinals. They must be men, like Father." I squeezed her tightly. "Though I'm sure that you are clever enough to be a cardinal, if you were allowed."

Lucrezia hugged me back without reservation. "I love you, Cesare," she said in my ear. "I don't ever want to leave you."

I pulled away so I could see her face. With all the confidence and arrogance of a privileged young boy, I made her a promise that would haunt me mercilessly in the years to come. "I'll never allow you to be sent away," I vowed, "husband or no. I swear, by the Holy Virgin herself."

Already a pious child, Lucrezia's eyes widened at this oath. "Then we must pray to her, Cesare," she whispered almost fearfully. "Pray to her to never let us be parted."

She took my hand and dragged me to the small chapel within the palazzo. Once there, she threw herself onto her knees, crossed herself, squeezed her eyes shut, and began to pray in earnest. I knelt beside her, moved by her fervent devotion, and tried to pray myself.

God, and Holy Mother Mary, whoever is listening . . . help me keep my promise to my sister. And please, try to change my father's mind. It's not that I don't wish to serve you, I added hastily, fearful of offending some holy personage on high. *But I can do so better as a soldier, leading armies in Your name.*

I could think of nothing else to add, so I sat back and watched Lucrezia finish her prayers, her lips moving silently, her brow furrowed in deep thought. Finally, she opened her eyes and smiled at me. "The Virgin shall hear our prayers," she said confidently. "Don't worry, Cesare."

I smiled at her innocent, childish devotion. "If you say so, it must be true."

PART ONE

The HOUSE OF BORGIA

Rome, August 1492–October 1493

Chapter 1

MADDALENA

Rome, August 1492

The bells of St. Peter's—indeed, all of Rome—tolled incessantly to announce the death of the pope. Pope Innocent's death was not unexpected; far from it. The Holy Father had been very ill of late, and the sweltering summer certainly had taken its toll on him—as well as on the people in the crowded streets of Rome, God bless them.

I hadn't attended to His Holiness directly—not a lowly maid like me—but everyone in the Vatican knew it had been a hard illness of many days, a violent and unrelenting fever. And we knew the rumors, the claims that the Holy Father believed drinking the blood of young boys would restore him to health, and that his physician had procured such for him. No one could say whether the story was true, but His Holiness's physician had been observed carrying a goblet of something into his master's bedchamber every night for a week.

Still, guilty of such a ghastly deed or no, he had been the pope, and it wasn't for me to question the doings of Christ's vicar on earth. On hearing the bells I went directly into the servants' chapel to pray for him, that he might be greeted at the pearly gates by his predecessor San Pietro with a welcome worthy of God's highest servant.

Upon leaving the chapel, I ran into Federico Lucci, the footman whom I counted as my closest friend among the other servants. He was kind to me, helping me learn my duties and my way around the vast palazzo when I first arrived, and told me all the gossip. He thought I didn't know he made eyes at me when I wasn't looking, but he had very fine and handsome light brown eyes, so I couldn't say I minded. "May as well come with me," he said by way of greeting.

"Oh? To where?" I asked, falling into step beside him.

"The Sistine Chapel. It's got to be cleaned and made ready for conclave. I've been told to round up any servants I see for the task."

Joy sparked in my heart. I would be in the palace for the next conclave. I would be in the same building when the next pope was chosen. When history was made. And I would be a witness to it. What more could I have hoped for in coming to the Holy City?

My dear uncle Cristiano, God rest his soul, had often told me: *God's will shall always find a way.* A priest himself, he would have been proud to see me serving in the Holy Father's house. I wished I could tell him that I would be present—in a fashion—for the election of the next pope. Perhaps, then, it was God's will that had brought me to Rome after all, that I might bear witness to His workings through His Church—no matter what my mother had said about my coming here.

Surely a prideful thought, to believe that God himself had brought me to the bosom of His Church. I quickly crossed myself and returned my attention to Federico.

"A large task, then?" I asked. "Readying the chapel?"

Federico whistled through his teeth. "Indeed. All those cardinals will be shut up in there for days, weeks even, though they'll all likely bring their favorite furniture and trappings and such. All of them sleeping and eating and shitting in the same place until they can agree on a new pope."

I crossed myself at the blasphemy. "But surely God comes to them, to guide them," I said as we reached the heavy wooden doors that led to the chapel. "They are not *agreeing* on a new pope; they are listening and waiting for God to make His will known to them, *sì?* And the man God chooses is the man they must all cast their votes for."

As we stepped into chapel, astonishment overtook me. I had never been inside before. Paintings more beautiful and colorful than any I had ever seen lined the walls. They depicted scenes from the Bible, but with people so lifelike I thought they might step right down from the wall and begin to converse with us. The simple village church where I'd attended Mass growing up certainly had nothing like this; and since coming to the Vatican I had not had opportunity to be in any of the truly fine rooms. Even if I had, never would I dare to linger to look at paintings or any of the cardinals' fine things. Yet now I had a moment I might take advantage of. I stepped as close as I dared to one of the scenes, depicting the temptation of Christ. He stood with the devil atop a temple in the center of the image, looking down at the throngs of people below that he might rule over. I marveled at the way the robes of the people in the crowd appeared to fold and tumble about them like real cloth; at the detail of the gold embroidery on the robes of the priest; at the texture of hair and skin, so real I wanted to touch it to see if it was truly naught but paint; at the lifelike angles of heads and limbs; at the way all the many figures in the painting seemed to be moving, somehow. Looking up, I found the blue ceiling was dotted with painted gold stars, as though to represent the very heavens themselves.

A few paces away, Federico was shaking his head at me, albeit with a smile. "The man God chooses," he repeated, and I was pulled back to our conversation. "I forgot you haven't been in Rome very long, *mia dolce* Maddalena. You'll learn how the Vatican really works soon enough."

Chapter 2

CESARE

Rome, September 1492

The archbishop's purple velvet mantle and robes of purple silk were damnably uncomfortable in the Roman heat. Even sitting in the shade of the loggia in my mother's lush courtyard, I felt as though I were roasting in hellfire—as well I may, for being as I was and daring to wear an archbishop's robes anyway. If the Almighty takes issue with me for such, I would beg him to lay the blame at my illustrious father's door, I thought crossly, pulling the collar irritably away from my neck. He had not wasted much time after his elevation to the throne of St. Peter in bestowing upon me his old archbishopric, and as such I was now the Archbishop of Valencia.

Yet hypocrisy amongst His servants did not seem to bother God in the least, judging by all I had observed in my years in Rome and elsewhere in Italy. Were He to set about smiting them, He would have a very long list to attend to before reaching me.

As my mind ranged over these dark musings, a pair of cool hands covered my eyes. "Lucrezia," I said, smiling as I heard her telltale giggle. I seized her arm, tugging her around me and into my lap.

"Cesare, *germà*," she said in the Catalan we always spoke when we were alone as a family, kissing my cheek. "Perhaps it is just as well that you are not a warrior, for I was able to sneak up behind you quite unnoticed!"

The same words from our brother Juan would have set my fingers itching for my dagger, that I might cut out his tongue, but from my sister they made me laugh. "Ah, but even the greatest of warriors shall always be bested by woman's wit and cunning," I said, my tongue sliding into Catalan as well, still familiar after all those years of speaking only Italian and Latin at school.

She giggled again. "I have taken the liberty of sending for some chilled wine, if it pleases Your Excellency," she said.

I groaned. "None of this 'Excellency' business from you of all people, Crezia," I said. "Though the wine will please me well enough."

She wrinkled her nose. "Donna Adriana has taken to reminding me of proper addresses and courtesies," she said. "She says I need them now that Father is the pope." We both crossed ourselves at this mention of the change in our family's fortunes. "Summer is the time for making popes, it seems," she added.

"It seems so, indeed," I agreed.

One of the servants came bearing a tray with a decanter of wine and two glasses. Lucrezia poured the straw-colored liquid herself, first mine, then hers. I took a grateful sip and closed my eyes, letting the sweet, cool liquid roll over my tongue.

"And so it seems everything Father planned has come to pass," Lucrezia said, leaning back in her chair with the listless grace of a young girl. "Soon he can make you a cardinal, and he will send me off to marry."

I remained silent, not sharing the rumor that was making the rounds of Rome: supposedly our father had offered Lucrezia's hand as a bride to the family of the cardinal who had brought him the most votes in conclave. No one knew for sure which cardinal this was, but the consensus seemed to be that Ascanio Sforza, the younger brother of Ludovico Sforza of Milan, had been the one to tip the scales. Sforza was still rather young for a prince of the Church, and that he had been promoted to the post of Vice-Chancellor of the Curia—my father's old post, and the most important and lucrative after the throne of St. Peter itself—just after the conclave, over the heads of older and perhaps better qualified candidates—such as Cardinal Giuliano della Rovere, my father's old enemy—spoke volumes.

Technically Lucrezia was betrothed to a Spanish nobleman from Valencia—our family's place of origin and my new archbishopric—but such a contract could and would be easily set aside. There would be much higher targets, much more prominent and profitable matches, for the daughter of a pope as opposed to the daughter of a cardinal.

The very thought of my dear sister being used as a bargaining chip in the tawdry game of politics was enough to make me want to do my father injury, sin though it was to raise a hand against one's father. And raising a hand to the Holy Father was a sin that no doubt Lucifer himself would hesitate to contemplate.

"And has His Holiness spoken to you of your marriage yet?" I asked casually.

My sister shook her head, her gold curls tumbling about her shoulders. "No," she said. "His Holiness has, I believe, had much more pressing matters on his mind. Perhaps soon, once he has become accustomed to his new station."

Our father had had much to preoccupy him since his ascent, but I knew him better than Lucrezia did if she thought her marriage was not a pressing matter to him.

It galled me that I had been in Rome two weeks already and still had not been summoned to the Vatican. After his election, I had been rousted from Siena, where I'd been preparing a horse to race in the Palio, and sent to our family's castle in Spoleto, an old and out-of-the-way place where nothing ever happened, to bide my time until I was needed. Yet now I had been sent for, ordered to return to Rome, and still I had not seen my father. I should not be forced to speculate about his doings; I should be by his side, his right hand, helping him and our family to greatness. I understood why I was not: Roman gossips and Vatican power mongers alike would be quick with accusations of nepotism should the new Holy

Father show too much favor to his family too quickly. Pope Alexander would know best how to proceed; yet knowing this did not make the waiting easier.

And as to Lucrezia's marriage, that was a subject on which I would have much to say, whether His Holiness asked for my opinion or not.

"It is all in God's hands," Lucrezia added.

I held my tongue. My pious sister could not begin to imagine how little of God was to be found in the running of His Church. No doubt she would learn someday, and the day Lucrezia lost her faith would be a dark one for us all.

"But while we wait," I said, "let us enjoy the sunshine, and this delicious wine you have been so good as to pour for us." I raised my glass in a toast. "You shall win the day no matter what His Holiness decides for you," I said, "for you will always be the most beautiful woman in Rome."

She giggled, and drank along with me.

Our talk turned to other things: Lucrezia's complaints about Madonna Adriana, our father's cousin and her governess, and how our mother's temper grew ever shorter in the Roman heat. I regaled her with stories of my time in Pisa and Siena that had not made it into my frequent letters to her and assured her the castle at Spoleto was as dingy and boring as ever.

Soon our pleasant afternoon was quite spoiled by the arrival of our brother Juan, the Duke of Gandia, a Spanish title our father had seen bestowed upon him several years back. Even in the heat, Juan was dressed in his usual outlandish costume: bright yellow leggings with a yellow and crimson striped doublet. His black hat sported a large white feather, and he wore a codpiece so enormous that it was only a matter of time before some whore he patronized accused him of making false promises.

"Sister," he said, sweeping a bow over Lucrezia's hand and kissing it. He turned and bowed to me as well, this time with mockery in every movement of his muscles. "Your most esteemed Excellency."

I ignored him.

"Wine, *germà?*" Lucrezia said, signaling to a servant, who waited just out of sight. "I shall send for another glass."

"You know me too well," he said, flopping down into the chair on Lucrezia's other side. "My mother's house is always the coolest and most pleasurable oasis in all of Rome."

"The whores will be surprised to hear it," I sniped. "No doubt since you have taken your leave of them, they are flooding the churches to offer thanks for their deliverance."

Petulant anger crossed Juan's face. "Jealousy is unbecoming to a man of the cloth, brother," he said. "Just because you do not know how to use what is under those archbishop's skirts of yours—"

Lucrezia took both of our hands. "Please!" she cried. "Be at peace! It is far too hot for such petty quarrels. Can you two ever be together without arguing?"

Chastened, I fell silent and turned my attention back to my wine. I would never enjoy Juan's company, but the last thing I wanted was to upset Lucrezia.

"It has been damnably difficult to see Father since the coronation," Juan said, idly spinning the stem of his wineglass between his thumb and forefinger. "I do not suppose you have had any luck, Cesare? I would speak with him."

In debt again, are you? I nearly asked. "His Holiness is no doubt quite busy with the affairs of Holy Mother Church," I answered instead. I would be damned if I would admit to Juan that I had not seen our father since being summoned home, though he likely knew. "He has much less time for family matters."

"It sounds as though you do not know our father as well as I, Cesare," Juan said, smirking. "Has he not told us all these years that it is precisely for the family's benefit that he must rise to the throne of St. Peter? The business of the family and the business of Holy Mother Church are one and the same, I think."

"Of course," I snapped, losing patience. "It is all a matter of appearances, fool. He must be seen to serve the Church first, and his family second."

"Ah, well," Juan said, still grinning. "This is why Father made you the cleric. Men of action like me have no head for politics."

"Even so, a brain in your head would not go amiss," I grumbled.

"You two agreed not to fight!" Lucrezia cried in a petulant tone I did not often hear. She must be upset indeed for her persona of the poised, elegant Roman lady, for which she strived so hard, to slip.

I sighed. "*Perdó, germana,*" I said.

"We shall behave ourselves, if only to see our little sister smile," Juan added, and at his words a small smile bloomed on her lips.

"Juan! Cesare!" a high voice exclaimed, and a small boy crashed into me, wrapping his arms around my shoulders. I laughed and ruffled my youngest brother's hair. "Jofre," I said. "I have missed you!"

"I missed you, too!" he cried. He ran around me to hug Juan, who pulled him into his lap.

"Why, I only saw you a few days ago, and I swear by the Virgin you have grown since then!" Juan said.

"Like a weed, that one is," said a low, throaty feminine voice, and I immediately rose from my chair to face my mother. I swept her a bow and kissed her hand. "*Madre,*" I said, switching to Italian. Though her years with Rodrigo Borgia—and his children—had taught her much of the Catalan tongue, she still preferred her native Italian.

"Cesare," she said, kissing my cheek. "Welcome home, *figlio mio.*" She smiled as she appraised my attire. "Or as I should rightly say, 'Welcome home, Your Excellency.'"

"My mother can address me however she pleases," I said.

Vannozza dei Cattanei was a handsome woman, with a dark Roman complexion and rich auburn hair that had yet to show signs of silver. It was easy to see how she had caught—and kept—Cardinal Borgia's eye for all those years. Now she seemed quite comfortable in her palazzo—purchased for her by her old lover—with Carlo Canale, her new husband. Canale had also been procured for her by our father, who had also seen to it that he had the post of Governor of the Torre di Nona, the city prison, so he might keep his wife in the style to which she was accustomed.

She went to kiss Lucrezia, then Juan, before taking a seat at the table, and Juan poured her a glass of wine. "I hope you will all stay for dinner," she said. "It has been some time since I had all my children about me." She smiled at each of us in turn.

"I would be honored," I said.

"Indeed, Mother," Juan said. "I can think of no place I would rather be."

Juan patted Jofre on the back and shifted him off his lap. "Run and fetch the chess board, little brother," he said. "I must see how far you have progressed since we last played."

Jofre ran to do as he was bidden, and the five of us spent a pleasant evening together in the garden as the shadows lengthened and the air cooled. Even Juan and I managed to be civil to each other, a rare feat. Our mother provided us with a simple meal of cold soup, bread, cheese, and some cured meats—the perfect light fare for a hot summer evening.

As the sun began to set, Mother asked me to see Lucrezia home, saying a young noble girl can never have too many guards on the streets of Rome.

"Even the pope's daughter can never be too safe," she said. She shivered as she reached up to brush a long strand of unruly hair away from my face. "Nor can the pope's sons, for that matter. I worry about you, Cesare," she said, lowering her voice so the others could not hear. "I worry about you all, now that we are the first family of Rome." She glanced back to the table, where Juan and Jofre were engaged in an arm wrestling contest for the last sugared plum; Juan, in a great show of being overpowered, yielded to our brother, who squealed with delight before presenting his prize to Lucrezia.

My mother looked back up at me. "I used to miss the power that being Rodrigo's mistress gave me," she said. "All those petitioners lined up at my door, bringing me gifts and promises in hopes I might whisper their desires in his ear. All the women in Rome scorning me yet craning their necks to see me so they might copy whatever I was wearing. And yet God has blessed me doubly," she went on, "in that I now enjoy a simple life, as a simple gentlewoman with her husband." She sighed. "Rodrigo would think I had taken leave of my senses to hear me say it, but it is this simpler life that I would wish for my children, if it were within my power to wish anything for them."

I embraced my mother tightly. "It is a mother's prerogative to make wishes for her children," I said.

She smiled. "I know you do not believe me, Cesare. But I think the day will come when you will remember my words and realize I was right. Mothers usually are," she teased.

I laughed and kissed the top of her head—when had she become so small, and I so tall? I glanced over at my brothers and sister, and for a moment I understood what she was saying—and yet I would never be free of my ambition, even if it did not align completely with my father's. Who would I be, if I were a simple gentleman, and not Cesare Borgia? I did not know, and I would never be given the chance to find out.

Chapter 3

MADDALENA

Not much changed for those of us in service at the Vatican Palace when the new pope took over. There were still the same tasks to see to, the same rooms to be cleaned, the same floors to be scrubbed, and the same laundry to be washed. The Holy Father was to be obeyed whoever he was, and his earthly house was to be kept clean and running smoothly so he could attend to far more lofty matters.

One morning I was returning to the kitchens with an empty tray from one of the cardinals' rooms—the new Vice-Chancellor, Ascanio Sforza by name—when I passed a man heading for the

Holy Father's audience chamber. He was rather garishly dressed, in brightly colored hose and tunic with a huge codpiece, and wearing a hat with a large feather in it. He winked and leered at me as I passed, and I cast my eyes down. Surely such a man was not fit for an audience with the Holy Father?

I caught up with one of the other maids, Fabrizia, at the end of the hallway. "Fabrizia," I murmured, my voice low so my words would not echo off the marble floors and walls, "who is that man?" I jerked my chin toward the man's retreating back.

She snickered. "That's Juan Borgia. The pope's son," she confided.

I gasped. All of Rome knew of the existence of Cardinal Borgia's children—Pope Alexander, I corrected myself. It was no secret that many of the other cardinals had mistresses and bastard children as well. But for a pope to acknowledge such children . . . "He brings his children into the Vatican?" I asked, shocked. "He allows them to be known as such, even now that he has been made pope?"

Fabrizia nodded. "It is unusual, indeed. No referring to them as his nephews or nieces, as popes usually do. And you know he keeps a mistress, yes?"

I gasped again. I had heard the whisperings, but I tried my best to close my ears to such things. Gossip—especially gossip about the Holy Father—was a sin.

Yet my curiosity rose, despite my pangs of guilt. I shall confess this sin after Mass on Sunday, I promised myself. "I . . . he does?" I asked.

Fabrizia's eyes gleamed, and she drew me into a small alcove. She was well and truly settled in to gossip. "Oh, yes. Honestly, Maddalena, even for a country bumpkin you seem altogether too innocent sometimes—and you a widow, no less. Her name is Giulia Farnese and she is the most beautiful woman in Rome. He keeps her with his cousin, Adriana, and his daughter, Lucrezia. Can you imagine? And La Bella Farnese is married to Adriana's own son! They were just married when Giulia La Bella caught Cardinal Borgia's eye, and so Donna Adriana banished her son to the country estates to get him out of the way—before the cuckold's horns were even properly affixed to his head, they say." She snickered. "If the stories are true, Cardinal Borgia—Pope Alexander—has rewarded Adriana and her family richly, including the poor cuckolded son, which is exactly what she was hoping for." She leaned closer and lowered her voice further. "He is said to be moving them to the palace of Santa Maria in Portico. He wants La Bella Farnese nearer to him—they say there is a secret passage that connects the Vatican Palace to that one, so he can visit her in secret."

I crossed myself automatically. "God forgive him," I said. "He has been led astray by a harlot." Immediately I regretted my words—he was the Holy Father; he could do no wrong. Who was I to criticize, when I could not understand the ways in which God spoke to His representative on earth? "But that is not for us to say," I added hastily.

Fabrizia rolled her eyes. "Indeed," she said. "All I know is men do what they want, whether they wear hose or a cardinal's robes. Or a pope's, even. I don't know that God has much to say about it. But his son, that Juan . . ." She nodded in the direction from which we'd come. "They say Pope Alexander has big plans for him, and for his other son, Cesare. He'll not let his children fade into the background, not the Borgia pope."

It was some weeks before I saw the other son, Cesare. It was late evening, and he looked to be heading in the direction of the pope's private rooms. I curtsied to him as he passed in the darkened hallway in his purple archbishop's robes. I felt his eyes on me as I curtsied, and when I rose our eyes met briefly. Goodness, but he was handsome, with his head of thick, dark curls under his cap and his dark eyes and the stubble lining his cheeks and chin, which looked like they belonged on a statue in the Vatican gardens. He was much more handsome than his fop of a brother, that was for certain. His eyes turned away, forward once more.

My cheeks burned with shame as I continued on, back to my cot in the bowels of the palace where I shared a room with three other maids. Cesare Borgia was a man of God, an archbishop, no less—it was not meet that I should think him comely or attractive.

I crossed myself, whispering a silent prayer of forgiveness. Back in my room, I bent over the handkerchief I was embroidering, squinting at it in the dim light, and recited a prayer with each few stitches to keep my thoughts from wandering where they did not belong.

Chapter 4

CESARE

My father had sent for me at last, late in the evening, as though he did not wish anyone to see me. I stewed over this on my ride to the Vatican. Juan strolled in and out of the palace as though he were master of it, in broad daylight, wearing his ridiculous clothes. Yet I, the son our father had chosen to follow in his footsteps—*the worthy son*—waited weeks on his pleasure and came to the palace only under cover of darkness.

I made my way directly to his personal chambers, where he had indicated I would find him—lest he have to greet me in full view of anyone at the papal court, I thought bitterly.

"I am His Excellency, the Archbishop of Valencia," I said curtly to the guard beside my father's door. "His Holiness has sent for me."

The guard nodded once and swung the door open. "God give you good evening, Your Excellency," he said.

I stepped in, the light within as dim as it had been in the hall. As the door shut behind me, my eyes adjusted further, and I saw my father standing by the fire, for the evenings had gotten cooler. It was the only source of light in the room.

At the sight of him, head bare and dressed in a simple white robe, all the anger and frustration I harbored melted away. Here was Rodrigo Borgia, the father I knew from my childhood, the father I had always sought to impress and whose regard I craved above all others, save perhaps Lucrezia.

Yet now he was the pope. He was not just a man, but God. Not just my father, but the father of all the Church.

I approached him and dropped to my knees, kissing the Fisherman's ring on the hand he extended to me. "Holy Father," I murmured, the awe in my voice genuine.

He placed a hand on my head in blessing. "Rise, my son," he said, and my heart lifted at the warmth in his voice. I stood and beheld his smile of pride before he embraced me tightly.

"The archbishop's robes look well on you," he said as he drew back. "I am proud, Cesare."

I bit back the urge to grin like an idiot.

He gestured toward the two chairs in front of the fire. "Sit, sit. Have some wine."

I obeyed and poured us both a glass of blood-colored wine from the decanter on the table between us, first into his gold-and-ruby-encrusted goblet, then mine. I drank deeply, feeling both body and mind relax. I was in my rightful place at last—at my father's side, if only for a few hours.

I wanted to ask his purpose in sending for me, but with a patience that was hard-won I schooled myself to wait. There was no point in acting like a schoolboy impatient for his dinner.

"I trust you were not disappointed to have your studies interrupted," my father said after a moment. "But I needed all our family in place for this momentous occasion. And now I need you by my side."

"Not disappointed at all, Holy Father," I said, all but glowing at his words. "I learned much in my time there, but I agree I shall be more useful here with you."

"Indeed." He leaned toward me. "I have need of your sharp mind, Cesare, as I always anticipated. The Curia is a den of snakes, as I have long known, but it all takes on quite a different cast when one is the head viper in the nest." He wore a sardonic smile as he lifted his goblet to his lips.

I wondered at his metaphor, verging on blasphemy in its conjuring the image of the serpent in the Garden of Eden and Eve's temptation. Yet it was something my father would have said before he ascended to St. Peter's throne, and so, blasphemous or not, it went no small way in putting me further at ease.

"What troubles have emerged thus far?" I asked, taking another sip.

He sighed, and I could see how weary he was. He was older than the last time I had seen him, I reminded myself, and though still possessed of his legendary energy and vigor, I could see his first weeks on the papal throne had not been easy. "Claims I bought the election, of course," he said. "Della Rovere's voice is the loudest among them, as we might expect. Such rumors are nothing new following a papal election, but they stick more firmly since I am a Catalan, not an Italian like the rest. Corruption is all par for the course when their own countrymen do it." He chuckled, but turned a serious gaze on me. "They see us as outsiders, Cesare. Never forget that."

There was a note of anger in my voice as I spoke. "But you are the pope, and so they must respect our family. We will be greater than any of them."

"Yes, we shall, but until that day comes, until we have shown them what we are capable of, be cautious and circumspect, Cesare. Rise above the pettiness and hatred but never be ignorant of it."

I snorted. "You may wish to impart such wisdom to Juan, then," I said, unable to stop myself. "Rumor has it he fought a duel with a man in some tavern in Trastevere for scorning the name of Borgia."

"I have spoken to Juan, and he well knows what is expected of him," my father said, his voice cold. "Do not worry about your brother's actions. You are neither his keeper nor his judge."

"But his actions reflect on all of us, and I will not have—"

"Silence," my father said, his voice booming, and like a child I obeyed. "It is not for you to say what you will or will not have, Cesare.

Mind you do not forget that. I am head of this family, and head of the Church. You owe your full obedience to me."

I remained silent, inwardly seething but knowing I could not argue with him, which only made me angrier.

"We need Juan to fulfill our military ambitions," my father said. He had lapsed into the plural *we*, and I could not tell if he was using it as popes customarily did—to refer to himself and the Almighty God who spoke through him—or if he meant the house of Borgia. Perhaps there was no longer a difference. "The lords of the Romagna owe us their allegiance and their tribute, as Rome is their overlord, but they have been neglectful of this duty, using their funds and men to engage in petty border squabbles with one another. That ends now. We will demand that we are paid what we are rightfully owed, and if they do not give it to us we will take it with fire and steel."

I nodded my agreement. The Romagna and its collection of small city-states surrounding Rome proper was a lawless, unruly place, ruled by brutal warlords and petty princes who abused and exploited their people for their own gain. The pope was their temporal lord as well as their spiritual one, but the Holy See did not often have the money or the men to enforce its rule via military strength. This, my father wanted dearly to change.

That was to be Juan's role, though I doubted mightily he would succeed. "And what of Lucrezia?" I asked to change the subject, though not without trepidation.

My father's entire countenance softened at the mention of his only daughter. If Juan was his favorite son, certainly Lucrezia was a favorite as well, in the way that only a daughter of an indulgent father can be. And where does that leave me? I wondered sulkily. Yet I loved Lucrezia as much as our father did, if not more.

"Lucrezia," he sighed. "She must be married, of course. I wish that it need not be for a few years yet, but we will need the support her marriage can bring us, both political and military. We must continue to strengthen the alliances that have brought us to St. Peter's throne."

"The Sforzas," I said. The rumors were true.

My father raised his eyebrows. "You are well informed, my son."

"I make it my business to be."

He nodded. "Good. Yes, the Sforzas. Ludovico is already married—damnably unfortunate, that. So is his nephew, the true duke, though Ludovico is the real power in Milan, however ill-gotten that power. I don't trust him and his scheming ways, so it would have been well to bring him into the fold. Alas, we must find another Sforza relation for our Lucrezia. God and all the saints know there are enough of them." He took another long drink.

I stared into the fire. It was just as well that Lucrezia would not be packed off to Milan. Perhaps there was a lesser, more pliable Sforza lord she could marry who might be convinced to stay in Rome. Yet that would mean he had no land or estates of his own, and thus he would not be a grand enough match for Lucrezia Borgia, the pope's daughter.

I'll never allow you to be sent away, husband or no. I swear, by the Holy Virgin herself.

I had never forgotten the vow I had sworn to Lucrezia when we were children. We had never discussed it again, but I was sure she remembered. I had meant it then and I meant it now.

How might I broach my unwillingness to see Lucrezia sent away, good of the family or no?

But my father spoke again. "You have not yet asked the question I have been expecting."

I looked up, puzzled. "What question is that, Holy Father?"

He waved a hand at me. "In private you may call me simply Father, Cesare. I am surprised that you have not asked of my plans for you."

I went still. "I believe I know your plans, Father," I said evenly. "You will make me a cardinal, as you have always wanted. I will be your ally inside the Church. And I trust whatever other plans you have will be revealed in good time."

He laughed. "Always sharp, and ready with a diplomatic answer when needed," he said. "You are quite right. You will be made a cardinal as soon as I can prudently do so. You'll not be the only one. I don't have nearly enough men in the College of Cardinals who are beholden to me. And then, though I will not live to see it, you shall be pope after me, in time." His eyes gleamed with ambition. "We shall create a Borgia dynasty so great that all will be beholden to us. Nothing will be done in Italy without our knowledge and consent. They will all look to us, Cesare. To us."

I took a long pause before speaking again. "You know this was not what I wanted," I said softly. "It is not what I would have chosen for myself. But I will serve our family as best I may."

"You certainly will. For the politics of the Church, Cesare, your intellect is needed most. That is why I chose you to follow in my footsteps. You, and not Juan or Jofre. You, the most brilliant of my children." He smiled. "With the possible exception of Lucrezia. The College of Cardinals is lucky indeed that she cannot be among their number, for she would put them to shame."

I laughed, knowing he was right, but I sobered quickly. "Father . . . would not my intellect be well needed, and well used, on the battlefield? Is not military strategy as—"

"No, Cesare. This is as I wish it to be. This is as it must be. I allowed you to question me when you were a boy, but no longer. I expect you to do your duty without complaint."

Before I could respond, he picked up a small bell and rang it, summoning a serving man from an adjoining room. "Send to the kitchens for more wine for myself and His Excellency," he ordered. The man bowed and left the room.

Finally I spoke again. "I will, Father," I said, schooling my voice carefully so he did not hear my resignation. "I will do as you think is best. I want only to make you proud." This, at least, was true.

"I've no doubt you shall." He leaned back into his chair. "You are what, seventeen? Still scarcely more than a boy. Your temper and passions are high. I remember that age well. But you were born a Borgia, as I was, and so much is expected of you. You must rise above your desires and toward greatness."

We were interrupted by the door opening, and to my surprise a maidservant came in bearing a tray with a new decanter of wine. It was usually a footman or serving man sent in to attend to the Holy Father; but the hour was quite late, so perhaps she was the nearest servant to be found. I smiled at her as she briefly caught my eye. I had passed her in the hall; she was a pretty thing, and not easy to forget: creamy pale skin, and dark reddish-brown hair. Her wide, striking amber eyes went wider at my smile, and she dropped both of us a curtsy. She carefully placed the decanter on the table between us and removed the empty one. "Would you like me to pour for you and His Excellency, Your Holiness?" she said, a slight quaver in her voice. She spoke with a noticeable accent—she came from somewhere in the Romagna, no doubt.

My father smiled benevolently. "By all means, my child," he said. She served him first, then me, and dropped another curtsy. "God give you good night," he added, turning his attention back to me before she had gone and closed the door behind her. "I have every faith you will live up to my expectations, Cesare," he said, taking a sip of wine, and resuming our conversation as though it had never ceased.

I acknowledged this in silence, sipping from my own goblet. But what if I could not live up to the expectations I had for myself?

Chapter 5

MADDALENA

"*Buon giorno,* Federico," I called in greeting one afternoon as I passed him in the immense courtyard. He was leaning against the cool stone wall of the palazzo in the heat of the day, reading a bit of parchment. "What have you got there?"

He smiled at the sight of me, a bright, wide smile. "Well met, Maddalena. Just a letter from home." He held up the parchment.

"Good news, I hope?" I said, drawing closer.

"Nothing out of the ordinary," he said. "My father expects a fine harvest this year, despite the heat. He is a winemaker, you see," he added.

"Indeed? And will you return to the vineyard someday to assume the running of it yourself?"

He made a face. "No, not I, for I am the second son, and content to be so. I have no head for numbers and no true desire to make wine, so it is just as well that my elder brother, Samuele, does. I have a taste for the city life, for adventure, so I struck out on my own to Rome."

I smiled, pleased that Federico had shared this with me. We'd never spoken much of our lives beyond our work in the Vatican Palace—only the barest of details.

"And what of you, Maddalena?" he asked. "Is there no one where you come from to write to you?"

My smile floundered. "No," I said, casting my eyes down at the dusty cobblestones. "My husband is dead, as you know, and I have only my mother left." A mirthless laugh escaped my lips. "And even if she could write, she would have no desire to write to me."

I jumped as Federico placed a hand on my shoulder, for I had not noticed him draw nearer. "Ah, poor Maddalena," he said softly. "How can it be that so beautiful and bright a star is not missed?"

I looked away from his earnest eyes. I could never repeat the ugly words my mother had spat at me when I decided to come to Rome after Ernesto's death, to get away from her and her spite before she could arrange another loveless marriage for me: *You are a worthless* puttana, *a handmaid of Satan himself, that you would leave your mother all alone. There is nothing in a city like Rome but sin and depravity for a woman alone. And what will you do for work, sell yourself? If you leave, do not come back, not with such sins as you'll find there to stain your soul.*

I had no desire to ever go back. Her words haunted me—the promise of sin and corruption and evil—but I had yet to find myself embroiled in any such things. After all, I worked in the house of the pope. Where on earth could possibly be safer for my soul?

"It is a long story," I said at last, meeting his eyes.

I do not know what he saw in my gaze, but his expression softened. "I understand, I think," he said. "I hope you know I've a ready ear if you ever decide to tell it."

"I thank you for that, *amico mio*," I said softly.

"And in the meantime," he said, his voice louder and more jovial, "I shall write you notes, Maddalena, and have them delivered to you, that you might know the joy of correspondence." He paused and looked at me anxiously. "You can read, yes?"

I smiled. "I can. I was lucky to have an uncle who was a priest. He taught me to read and write." Another gift from Uncle Cristiano, who had had the time and love for me that my father never did in his brief life. Uncle Cristiano would have written to me.

Perhaps Federico would have to do.

Federico's expression cleared. "*Eccellente*. You may expect messages from me in the future."

I laughed. "I shall look forward to it."

He swept me a bow and kissed my hand gallantly. "And if the lady would do me the favor of writing back, why, I may even faint dead away from the honor."

"Your correspondence must first prove its worth," I teased.

He tucked his letter from home into his pocket. "I shall give it all due thought and consideration," he said gravely. "Now I must be off—there is a new horse just arrived in the stables, a Spanish mount, and if I'm to get a look at him before I must be back to work it needs to be now." With one last bow and a wink, he turned and crossed the courtyard toward the stables. Federico had a great love of horses and spent all his free time hanging about the stables, chatting with the grooms.

I remained where I was, smiling after him like a fool. Federico was as handsome as they came, tall and well-muscled with merry eyes and a head full of sandy curls. And for all his flirtation, could such a man see me as more than an acquaintance, a friend? What had just passed suggested he might. I could certainly find no better catch in Rome, not a young widow of my station. Yet . . . did I want to marry again?

My features twisted into a scowl as I remembered Ernesto. He had owned a farm larger than ours, and though he was a widower over twenty years my senior, my mother had arranged the match when I was just fifteen—rather a young age to marry, in our village at least. "The sooner I've not got to worry about your mouth to feed, the better," she'd said when I'd protested. So I'd married Ernesto, having had only one conversation with him prior to our wedding day.

I hadn't loved him, nor had he loved me. He largely ignored my presence in his house, unless something was not to his liking, or he wanted to engage in the marriage act, which was often. I bit back my dislike of the act, for his hefty weight on me, his member inside my body. I knew it was a wife's duty. I endured it—and the other acts he directed me to perform for his pleasure—without complaint, even if I knew I was not always successful at hiding my distaste. It did nothing to further endear me to him. I tried always to keep Uncle Cristiano's advice in mind—*Matrimony is a holy state, Maddalena, and the one God wishes for his flock*—but my marriage had been miserable. Uncle Cristiano's death of a fever, a few months after he performed my marriage ceremony, had only darkened my life further.

But as luck—and I crossed myself at the thought, at the sin of finding relief in another's death—would have it, my sour marriage had lasted only a year. He had inadvertently strayed onto the lands of some lord or other while hunting. The lord and his men, assuming he'd been poaching, had tied him up and shot him full of arrows as punishment. Even bearing no love for Ernesto, I had been horrified to hear how he'd met his end. Yet I shed no tears, not when the news was brought to me, nor when I washed and prepared his body for burial, or even during his funeral Mass.

His death left me without a penny, for his son by his first wife—who was my age—inherited the farm, farmhouse, and everything else Ernesto had to his name. There was nothing left for me. But I was free.

I was free, and I thanked God for it every day, even on those nights when I was too exhausted from my duties to work on my embroidery. I had charge of myself, as much as any woman ever could, and I would never be sorry for it.

And if Federico did want to make me his wife, I could say yes or no as I pleased. I could not help but feel the marriage act would be rather different with a man like him.

Enough, Maddalena, I counseled myself. The man wished to write me some notes, not propose marriage.

But even so, the smile was back on my face.

Chapter 6

CESARE

"Cesare!" Lucrezia whirled around as her footman announced me. Trunks of clothing, hairpieces, jewelry, bedding, and linens surrounded her. "Oh, you should have come later, *germà*! We are in quite a tizzy of unpacking at the moment." She started toward me, a perceptive maid whisking a small case of jewels out of her path so she would not trip.

"Is that any way to greet your favorite brother?" I teased as she kissed my cheek.

"It's best Juan didn't hear you say that," she said, but I noted, with childish glee, that she didn't correct me. "Oh, dear, I can send for some wine or food if you like, but much of the palazzo is still in disarray." She waved her hand at the chaos of her bedroom.

The Holy Father had moved his women—Lucrezia, Giulia Farnese, and Adriana de Mila—to the Palazzo Santa Maria in Portico, so he might make use of the secret underground tunnel connecting it to the Vatican Palace.

"Do not trouble yourself," I said. "I came to see how you were settling in, but it seems that is still a work in progress."

I had wanted to assure myself Lucrezia was well and pleased with the move. And despite her flustered words, there was a flush of pleasure in her cheeks and a smile in her eyes as she surveyed her new rooms, with their marble floors and plush carpet and cheerful frescoes of frolicking nymphs. The change in her status completely agreed with her.

"Is there anything I can do to help?" I asked.

The exasperated look she turned on me was one only a thirteen-year-old girl could give to her brother who knows nothing of women's matters. "Indeed there is not, Cesare," she said. "I love you dearly, but I do not trust you to see that my gowns are unpacked and put away properly."

I laughed. "You are wise to withhold your trust in that regard, I think. Very well." I leaned down and kissed her cheek. "I shall away, and hope you invite me to supper once you are settled."

"I surely shall!" she said, turning and flouncing back to a trunk full of dresses.

I shook my head and chuckled as I left. Dear Lucrezia.

I left the palace and swung back up onto my horse to head home, but hesitated. Perhaps I might stop in a tavern for a drink. Since I'd only been going to see Lucrezia, I hadn't dressed in my archbishop's robes, so there would be little danger of my being recognized. I turned my horse sharply down an alley, a shortcut that would take me to a favorite tavern.

It happened so quickly, but still I cursed myself for not being more aware. A dagger whirred past my head, so close my hair moved in the breeze it created. I immediately flung myself from the saddle and slapped my horse's rump. "Home!" I commanded him in one loud, terse voice, and he ran. He was a well-trained beast and would not stop until he reached his stable. I drew my dagger from where it was sheathed at my hip and spun to face my attacker.

He was almost upon me, another dagger in his hand. "Here, let's have your purse, m'lord," he growled, swiping at me.

I dodged his blade easily and attacked, but though he was

clumsy in wielding his weapon, he was quick. What manner of footpad robs a nobleman in broad daylight? I wondered even as I fought him off.

I heard the whir of another dagger behind me, and leapt out of the way, spinning to see yet another man at the mouth of the alley. Well. This grew more interesting by the second.

In the split second I took to decide whether or not I would charge at him, thus eliminating his range and to hell with the first man, a sword suddenly protruded through the man's chest. His eyes went wide with shock as he looked down at the blade, as though he could not believe what he was seeing.

Meanwhile, the first man, unaware of his companion's fate, took advantage of my hesitation and seized me from behind, reaching up—he was rather smaller than I—to cut my throat. I spun in his grip, grabbing his arm and bending it at an unnatural angle, and drove my dagger into his heart, twisting it as it found its mark. Blood bubbled onto his lips, and I ripped out the dagger and let him fall to the dirty cobblestones to breathe his last.

Breathing hard, I raised my eyes to the mouth of the alley, where I found a slender man of medium height cleaning his sword in an unconcerned manner, as though he stabbed would-be thieves in alleyways all the time—and perhaps he did. "It seems I owe you a debt of thanks, my good man," I said, eyeing him carefully, hoping he would prove friend and not foe.

"I've no doubt you would have handled them on your own, signore," he said casually. I was surprised to hear a slight Valencian accent. A fellow Spaniard. I relaxed slightly. "I merely hurried the process along." He sheathed his sword and looked up at me meaningfully. "Or should I say, 'Your Excellency'?"

"Ah," I said. "It seems my lack of ecclesiastical garb is not quite the disguise I had hoped."

"More people know you in this city than you realize, Your Excellency," he said. "The same is true of your brothers and sister."

My entire body tensed at these words. "Is that a threat?" I demanded.

"Not at all," he replied. "I am merely stating facts. There is great interest in the city in the doings of your family since Pope Alexander's election."

I searched his face for honesty. "That is true enough," I said carefully. "Including our friends here." I motioned to the two bodies now lying on the filthy ground of the alley.

The man snorted. "Indeed," he said. "I'm sure a man as astute as Your Excellency is reputed to be realizes this was no mere robbery."

"I suspected as much," I said. "But you speak as though you have certain knowledge of their motives."

"I suppose I do. They've been tailing you since you left Santa Maria in Portico."

That stopped me cold. As clumsy as they'd been, I had not noticed. My mind had been wandering, intent on a drink.

Clearly these brigands knew where I'd come from, that my sister was now housed within the palace. Such moves did not occur without much of Rome being aware. Could she have been their target?

No, they'd followed me, after all. And Lucrezia and Giulia Farnese were protected as well as the pope himself. I need not worry myself overmuch for them.

Myself, on the other hand . . . bold as it was to attack an archbishop—and the pope's son—in broad daylight, I knew that I had likely become an attractive target. Perhaps these brigands had been hoping to ransom me back to Pope Alexander. Perhaps others would try to do the same in the coming weeks, months, and years.

I glanced up at the man and saw he had been watching me think all this over. "What is your name?" I asked.

He bowed. "Miguel da Corella, Your Excellency. Known to my friends and comrades as Michelotto."

"A Valencian, as I'd thought," I said. "You must be in Rome to work for my father."

"I'm a recent member of his personal guard, yes, my lord."

"Why are you here and not guarding him, then?"

"Day off," Michelotto said. "Lucky for you that it is."

Another nobleman, jealous of his pride—like my brother Juan—would have taken offense, but I only laughed. I wanted this

Michelotto on my side. "Indeed," I said. "It would seem I need another pair of eyes to watch my back. In that case, I'll give you another thirty percent of whatever you make now to serve as my personal bodyguard."

A look of surprise crossed Michelotto's face, but he quickly masked it. "Generous of you, my lord," he said. "But how do you know you can trust me? Might I not be in league with your attackers?"

"If you were, I doubt you'd confess such to me right as I've offered to hire you," I said.

He grinned broadly. "You and I will get on splendidly, my lord. I accept."

I stepped over the body of the man he'd slain and shook his hand. "Good," I said. "Accompany me to my palace in the Borgo and we'll see about getting you some livery, and a room."

Michelotto nodded agreeably and fell into step beside me. Even as we walked, his eyes were everywhere, scanning for potential threats. It appeared to be something he did naturally, without thinking.

I had chosen well.

Chapter 7

MADDALENA

It was early evening, and I'd just left His Holiness's chambers, where I'd delivered some fresh linens. Ever since I had served the pope and his son the first time, simply because there was no other servant handy at the time, I was often sent to perform tasks for His

Holiness himself. I had no idea why, but I took great pride in each task. It almost—almost—made me long to see my mother, that I might tell her of the privilege. *Not the task God would send a whore or a dire sinner, is it,* Madre?

I was so lost in my prideful thoughts that I did not see the man coming toward me until he was almost upon me. "Oh," I said, my face burning. I dipped a curtsy, eyes cast down. "Excuse me, signore."

Yet he did not step past me, but stopped entirely. Fearful at having caused offense to some important personage, I peeped up through my lashes.

At once I recognized the pope's second son, Juan, the Duke of Gandia. Rather than looking upset, he had a wide smile on his handsome face—handsome, yes, but features more watered down than his brother's, somehow. I could not help but notice his weak chin.

"You may put yourself in my way any time you like," he said with a leer. Instantly uneasy, I curtsied again and made to move around him, but he stopped me with a hand on my chin, lifting my face up so he might see it better. "I've seen you before," he said. "You're a pretty thing. Very pretty. What's your name?"

"Maddalena," I said.

"Maddalena," he repeated, his tongue curling obscenely around my name. "Just like the companion of Our Lord. Tell me, Maddalena, are you as free with your favors as she was?"

My heart began to pound. "No, my lord," I said softly, but hoping he could hear the steel behind my words.

"No? More's the pity." Before I knew what was happening, he had seized my arm and tugged me into a narrow, dark hallway, where he pressed me against the wall, my body trapped beneath his. "But women are so fickle . . . no doubt you can be convinced . . ."

He put his mouth over mine, and I froze in shock and horror. He took it for acquiescence, pressing his body flush with mine, and I could feel his arousal prodding against me. I tried to push him away, but he was too strong and kept me firmly in place against the wall. I went still again, hoping not to encourage him further.

He broke away, and I found a moment of relief before he reached down and began to lift my skirts. "No!" I cried out, looking frantically up and down the hall for help. But then I had a horrible thought—even if someone did see, who would have the nerve to gainsay the pope's son?

"Now, now," he said, running a hand up my thigh. "You'll enjoy this, I promise."

"No!" I cried again, struggling against his grip. "Please, my lord!"

"Yes, say it again," he said, fumbling with the laces of his codpiece and breeches. "I'd like to hear you beg me."

Rage tore through me. *I survived a horrid mother, an inconsiderate and lustful husband, and came all the way to Rome where I serve the Holy Father himself, only to be raped in a hallway by this . . . this bastard? I think not.*

As Juan's attention turned to shoving down his breeches, I raised my knee and drove it as hard as I could into his balls.

He let out a scream, one of shock as much as of pain, and I tried to shove past him and run. My heart sank as his hand closed on my wrist with a roar of fury. *I'll do whatever it takes . . . he will not violate me, I swear it . . . even if I have to kill him with my bare hands . . .*

"Why, you little . . ." he growled, shoving me up against the wall again.

"Juan."

The one cold, terse syllable stopped him in his tracks. He hurriedly hiked up his breeches and stepped back, still breathing hard and doubled over. Weak with terror and dread and anger, I collapsed to my knees, hands pressed over my mouth to muffle a sob of relief. I glanced up to see my savior and found none other than the Archbishop of Valencia.

"Why must you spoil my fun, Cesare?" Juan complained.

"It did not look as though the lady was having fun," his brother said, genuine fury filling his voice. A scornful smile crossed his lips as he surveyed his brother's posture. "Nor, perhaps, would you have, by the time she was through with you."

Juan scoffed. "She is no lady, brother. Just a serving girl."

"Be that as it may," the archbishop said, his disgust for his brother evident in his voice, "I hardly think it appropriate for you to rape one of His Holiness's servants in his very palace."

The Duke of Gandia rolled his eyes. "Come, come, Cesare," he said languidly. "Surely you find pleasure in subduing a reluctant woman every now and then?"

An involuntary shudder worked its way through my body. Men like this were the reason women could not walk safely in the streets at night.

"I do not," the archbishop replied sharply. "Personally I much prefer a woman who will gladly devote herself to pleasing me. But," he added coldly, "I am not a coward who must prey upon defenseless women to prove I am a man."

"You dare," the duke snarled, stepping forward, hand on the hilt of his dagger.

"I say only what I see in front of me," the archbishop said. He reached out a hand to help me to my feet, and I took it. "Now, you'd best be off and not trouble me further. I am late for a meeting with His Holiness as it is."

"Not before I've spoken to him," the duke protested, and suddenly I had been forgotten.

"He summoned me, and I doubt he'd thank you for keeping him waiting."

The duke scowled, remaining where he was standing, yet his expression was uncertain.

"Get out, Juan," the archbishop said, sounding almost bored. "There are plenty of whores in Rome who will be happy to take your coin."

The duke spat on the marble floor at his brother's feet, spun on his heel, and walked away.

Once he was out of sight, the archbishop turned his attention to me. "Are you all right?" he asked, his face filled with concern.

"Yes, I . . . I think so," I said.

"He didn't manage to . . . ?"

"No," I answered. "No, he . . . he didn't. I . . . I injured him somewhat, and . . ."

He smiled. "Praise be to God. Yes, I gathered the, ah, nature of his injury. Quick thinking. You may not have needed my assistance at all, in the end." He sighed, his face looking drawn suddenly. "I cannot apologize enough for my brother. He does not conduct himself as a man should, let alone one of his station. His actions are inexcusable."

"You . . . you need not apologize, Your Excellency," I said. "His sin is not yours. And I must thank you for coming to my aid."

"I could do nothing else." He studied me, my face growing warm under his scrutiny. As I relaxed somewhat, I was struck anew at how handsome he was. "I have seen you before, serving His Holiness," he said finally. "What is your name?"

It was nearly the same thing his brother had said, but the words bore not the slightest trace of threat. How strange, that the same words could so differ in their meaning when spoken by two different men. "Maddalena, Your Excellency," I said, a genuine smile spreading across my face. "Maddalena Moretti."

"A lovely name," he said, brow furrowed. "Unfortunately, after I've succeeded in embarrassing my brother so, I think he may seek you out again."

Bile rose in my throat.

"It would be best if you could be out of his way," he mused.

He has rescued me only to tell me I am dismissed, I thought dismally, so that I might not further tempt his brother.

"I have an idea, if you are agreeable," the archbishop went on, and I grasped at his words hopefully. "I can see to it you are given a place in the household of my sister, Lucrezia, and her chaperone, Adriana de Mila. You would be responsible for serving them, as well as Adriana's daughter-in-law, Giulia Farnese."

"Truly, Your Excellency?" I asked. "You could arrange that?"

"Of course, if you wish."

It had been a very long time since anyone had asked me what I wished. "But what of my duties here?" I would miss waiting on the pope, but if I did not need to fear further advances from Juan Borgia, that would be compensation enough, and more.

Even if I would be serving the pope's mistress.

He waved a hand casually at this. "There are plenty of servants here, are there not? And someone else can always be hired if need be."

We are all the same to them, I thought crossly. But I swiftly shoved aside my annoyance. He had done me a good turn and sought to do me another. Gratitude was what was in order here. "In that case, I accept." I curtsied. "Your Excellency is most kind."

"It is no trouble," he said. "I will send the chamberlain at the Palazzo Santa Maria in Portico a message letting him know to expect you. Report there tomorrow morning. I will see that your wages are the same as here—with perhaps a little extra for the inconvenience of taking a new position."

"I . . . I cannot thank you enough, Your Excellency," I said.

"As I said, it is nothing. And you will like working for my sister." A tender smile came over his face, succeeding at making him even more handsome. "She is hardly a harsh taskmistress."

"I am sure I shall like it very much," I said, already curious, in spite of the tawdry nature of the situation, for my first glance at the pope's famous daughter and his even more famous mistress.

"Yes." He rested his eyes on me once more. "Well. *Buona fortuna* in your new position, Maddalena." With that, he turned and continued back up the hallway, headed for the pope's private chambers.

That night when I returned to my room, I immediately fell to my knees and thanked God for delivering me from the Duke of Gandia, and for sending the Archbishop of Valencia.

Chapter 8

CESARE

When I finally arrived at my father's rooms, he rose impatiently upon my entrance. "Cesare," he said sourly. "You are late."

His words sparked my anger at Juan anew. "Apologies, Holy Father," I said stiffly. "I had to prevent His Grace the Duke of Gandia from violating one of Your Holiness's servant girls."

My father was taken aback straightaway. "May God forgive him," he sighed, crossing himself. "I will speak to Juan."

Yet almost immediately, we left the subject of Juan's outrages against women. "Sit, my son, sit, and have some wine. I have something of great import to discuss with you."

I sat, but did not drink. I was still too angry with Juan, and my father for so casually brushing his actions aside. "What would that be?"

My father's next words chased all thoughts of Juan and the poor servant girl—Maddalena, her name was Maddalena—from my mind. "Lucrezia's marriage," he said. "I have decided on a suitable bridegroom."

I sat up straighter. "You have? Who?" I demanded. I had expected to be consulted, to be able to advocate for the man who would be likely to keep Lucrezia in Rome, or at least nearby. Yet I had not so much as heard the name of any man being considered, and here my father was telling me he had already decided.

"Giovanni Sforza, Lord of Pesaro," my father said with satisfaction.

Immediately I sorted through the information I possessed about this man, admittedly not much. He was a cousin of Ludovico and Ascanio, if I was not mistaken—not of the main branch of the Sforza family. And Pesaro was a small city of little import. "Giovanni Sforza?" I repeated, incredulously. "He is married already, is he not?"

"Widowed," my father said. "The marriage would make Lucrezia Countess of Pesaro, as well as strengthen our ties with the Sforzas of Milan."

"Holy Father, you cannot be serious." The words were out of my mouth before I had time to think better of it.

His expression darkened. "I assure you I am," he said, irritated. "And I wonder that you have the nerve to speak to me in such a tone."

"I assumed you brought me here so that I might offer my opinion," I said, trying to sound as calm and reasonable as possible.

His scowl softened slightly. "I did," he conceded. "Now explain to me what possible objections you can have."

"Giovanni Sforza is hardly the most wealthy or prestigious match that could be found for the pope's daughter," I began. "He brings a connection to the Sforzas of Milan, yet he is but a cousin—and a relatively poor one at that. Pesaro and its title are of little importance to those on the Italian peninsula. And he must be at least twice her age, no?" I could not add my final and perhaps most strenuous objection, one that would carry little weight here: I promised Lucrezia she would never be made to leave us. To leave me.

"Is there a more prestigious Sforza relative for her to wed that you are hiding from me?" my father demanded. "Any connection to them will benefit us, and we owe them a boon after Ascanio's support of me in conclave. The boon they wish for is to be more closely connected to the Holy Father."

"The vice-chancellorship is not enough for Ascanio, I see," I said scornfully. I had never much liked the man; he had a face like a rat, and his ambition knew no bounds. I wondered how far he would take this sense of obligation Pope Alexander felt toward him, and how far the pope would allow it to go.

My father looked at me with a faint glare. "We owe them a boon," he repeated. "And what is more, Giovanni Sforza is a noted condottiere, as I'm sure you know yet left out of your accounting of him. We can call upon his military strength and his numbers whenever we have need."

Referring to the man as a "noted" condottiere was rather generous, but I held my tongue. In truth, that Giovanni Sforza could bring military aid to us was perhaps the only advantage of the match, so far as I could see. We would need his troops and more to bring the Romagna firmly under control. "Surely there are even more advantageous matches, from a military perspective," I argued. "One of the Orsini or Colonna, even . . ."

"And how to repay the Sforzas, then?" my father asked impatiently.

"Why must it be Lucrezia who marries into their Godforsaken family?" I demanded. "Why not get a Sforza bride for Juan or Jofre?"

"I have other plans for Juan," he said. He meant bigger plans, better plans. Nothing but the best for his favorite son, no matter how little deserved. "And Jofre is too young for marriage as yet. We need this alliance now."

Jofre was not that much younger than Lucrezia. "I do not trust the Sforzas," I said. "Ludovico has all but stolen the ducal crown, and Ascanio—"

"All the more reason to align ourselves with them, and keep them close," my father interrupted. "And you know as well as I do that we need an alliance with a notable Italian family as soon as possible. The Italian nobles do not trust our Catalan blood."

He was right, but I still couldn't bear the thought of Lucrezia marrying into that family, of this being her future. "Do you think Lucrezia could love him?" I asked at last.

My father waved this away. "Young girls fall in and out of love as easily as they change their gowns," he said. "Political alliances are not made on the basis of love. You should understand this by now, Cesare."

"But this is Lucrezia," I protested, finally making the emotional plea. "Your only daughter, my only sister. Do you not want her to be happy?"

His face softened. "Of course I want her to be happy. And I expect doing her duty to her family will make her happy."

I angrily picked up the goblet of wine and finally took a sip. A long one.

"Lucrezia is a prize as a bride," my father went on. "Giovanni Sforza will know this and will know how he is being honored with her hand. He will have no reason not to treat her like the princess she is."

"I shall make certain he does," I said, through gritted teeth. "For if he does not, I will make him pay."

My father chuckled. "Ever you are a loyal brother, Cesare," he said. "I mark it well and appreciate your loyalty. We will have much need of it in the days to come." He picked up his glass from the table between us. "Then we are decided?"

I took up my own glass, clinked it against his, and drank, though I did not speak. I could not bear to give words to my acquiescence.

Chapter 9

MADDALENA

Reluctant as I had been to give up my service to the pope—which only served to make me more resentful of Juan Borgia—I soon found that a place in his daughter's household was just as delightful, if not more so. The tasks were light; there were other maids already employed to see to the scrubbing and the laundry, so I was responsible only for such things as bringing trays up from the kitchens, mending, and seeing that Madonna Lucrezia's room was always in good order and her clothes properly put away, though she had two other maids to help her with dressing, her hair, and bathing. The heaviest task was hauling hot water up from the kitchens when Madonna Lucrezia took her weekly bath, which also involved washing her long, thick, pale golden hair. I'd never seen someone with such an obsessive need for cleanliness, but it was not for me to say what was right for a noblewoman of her standing.

My new position suited me perfectly, and with the extra wages I was able to purchase even finer thread for my embroidery, which I now had more time for. I certainly owed His Excellency the Archbishop of Valencia a debt, though how the likes of me could ever repay someone like him I had no idea. I only knew I was grateful.

My biggest regret was that I missed seeing Federico regularly. A part of me wished I might have had more time to discover how he truly felt about me, and in turn, how I felt about him. Yet I was strangely relieved I would likely not find out his true feelings and have to make a difficult decision.

I sent him a note to tell him of the change in my position—hoping he had not simply enjoyed flirting with me as a passing amusement—but the messenger returned without a reply, saying Federico had not been in his room. As time passed, and I never heard from him, I meant to send another note, but I grew accustomed to my new life and it slipped my mind. Surely if he missed me he would have sought me out, no? Perhaps that in and of itself was answer enough to my questions.

Since I'd come to the Palazzo Santa Maria in Portico, wisps of rumor about the lady Lucrezia's marriage had gathered into the certainty of a rain cloud overhead, though I had yet to hear the name of a groom confirmed. I was rather wistful at the thought of losing so fine a mistress, but maybe she'd bring me to her married house. Or, barring that, I could still serve Giulia Farnese and Adriana de Mila, who were not much more trouble.

Giulia Farnese was as beautiful as everyone said, with her heart-shaped face, long gold hair that fell almost to her ankles, and a figure that was by turns slender and fleshy in all the right places. I had been brought up to believe the pope was more divine than man—though living and working in the house of two popes had showed me how human they truly were—and so should be above such earthly temptations, but La Bella Farnese could truly tempt a saint. And very few men were in fact saints.

Initially I had tried to keep my distance from her; after all, how did one properly interact with a woman committing such grave sin? But not only was Giulia beautiful, she was kind to a fault, and never failed to thank the servants or give us a quick smile. It was impossible not to warm to her, whether you were a man or a woman.

One day I brought a requested tray of pastries and cakes from the kitchen into the second floor sitting room, where I found Lucrezia and Giulia giggling with their heads together, and Adriana nowhere in sight. "Oh, come, Giulia, you must tell me," Lucrezia wheedled.

"I wish I could," the older girl said, laughing, "but I cannot."

"Then who will?"

"Surely that is the duty of Madonna Vannozza, your mother."

"I should far rather have you explain such a thing to me!"

I set down the tray on the table before them, curtsied, and made to withdraw. But Lucrezia glanced up then. "Oh, Maddalena," she said, waving a hand at me. "We are gossiping of women's things, so you must tell us. Are you married?"

"Widowed, Madonna," I said, surprised she should ask. Most women in domestic service were either unmarried or widowed, yet a young lady from a wealthy family would have no reason to know what was usual for the poor and working classes. I had an uncomfortable idea of where this conversation was going.

"Oh!" Her hands flew to her pale cheeks, surprised. "And at such a young age, too! Why, you cannot be older than my brother Cesare!"

"No, Madonna," I said, for gossip had informed me we were the same age. "It was a brief marriage, as my husband met with a . . . fatal misfortune." I did not wish to go into the horrifying details in front of these fine ladies.

"You poor thing! To have had a taste of wedded bliss, only to have it snatched away," Lucrezia cried. She crossed herself. "May God have mercy on his soul. I shall light a candle for him when next I go to Mass."

Giulia crossed herself as well.

My heart warmed even further toward the pope's daughter. *Blessed Virgin, keep her happy and innocent as long as you can,* I prayed silently. May she never know anything but wedded bliss, hard as it may be for many women to find. "You are very kind, Madonna," I said, smiling.

"Well," she began, eyes sparkling anew as she returned to the topic at hand. "Perhaps you can tell me, since our lovely Giulia is so reluctant . . ." She trailed off, raising her eyebrows at her friend before turning her gaze back to me. "What, precisely, takes place in the marriage bed between husband and wife?"

My face flushed, though I had been expecting this question. "Madonna, I . . . it . . . it is not my place to tell you such things," I stammered. May God and all the saints strike me down if I were to explain such a thing to the pope's daughter, soon to be married or no!

"Oh, *per favore*, Maddalena?" she cajoled, reaching out to take my hands. "I am nearly a woman grown, and yet no one will tell me anything!"

How sad, that in our world thirteen years of age should be nearly a woman grown. "It would not be proper, Madonna," I said, lowering my eyes and carefully withdrawing my hands from her smooth ones. "The task of revealing such information must fall to your lady mother."

Lucrezia sat back with a huff. "Oh, you are terrible, the two of you!" she said, looking between Giulia and I, but merriment was in her eyes. "Never you mind. I shall find out, soon enough!"

"Indeed you shall, but no sooner than you need to," Giulia said, soothing her.

Sensing I was no longer needed, I curtsied once more and left the room, still smiling to myself. I wished only the best for Lucrezia Borgia in her marriage—and surely the daughter of the pope had a far happier, more exalted marriage to look forward to than a poor country girl like me had.

One afternoon, as I was bent over a table in the sitting room, returning the dirtied dishes and linens to the kitchen tray, my handkerchief—the one I'd finished embroidering weeks ago—slipped from my sleeve and fluttered to the floor. I stooped further to pick it up, but Madonna Lucrezia noticed first and scooped it up. "What it this, Maddalena?" she asked, the teasing note I'd already grown to know so well in her voice. "A token from a lover, perhaps?"

I smiled. "No, Madonna. Only my handkerchief, I'm afraid."

She made to hand it back to me, but her eyes caught on the embroidery. "My, this is exquisite work," she said, spreading out the cloth so she could examine it more closely. She traced the patterns of flowers along the edge, all emanating from a cross in one of the corners. "Beautiful. Some of the finest work I have seen anywhere. Where did you get it?"

"I made it, Madonna," I said. "That is, I had the scrap of cloth from an old dress, and I did the embroidery myself."

She looked up at me, astonished. "You? Indeed?"

"*Sì*, Madonna. I can make lace as well."

"Wherever did you learn how to do work so fine?" She passed the handkerchief to Donna Adriana, who was seated beside her. Adriana bent over it, murmuring noises of surprise and approval.

"My grandmother, Madonna. She was educated at a convent school, and one of the sisters there taught her." My mother's mother. She had lived with us until her death when I was ten. I missed her dearly, not least because she had not been there to protect me from my mother's cruelty. It was highly unusual for women of her station—and mine—to learn such fine embroidery, as such was the province of noble ladies, and she'd managed to make a good income for herself—and us—while she lived. She had been lucky to receive such tutelage from a nun who was the daughter of a wealthy family, and who recognized a gift for needlework when she saw one. I was lucky to have inherited her gift.

"You have quite a gift for this work," Lucrezia said, echoing my thoughts. She gave the handkerchief one last look before taking it from Adriana and passing it back to me. "I wonder," she said, tapping a fingertip against her lips, "if you could be persuaded to embroider some items for my trousseau."

My head snapped up. "I . . . truly, Madonna?"

"Yes, indeed. Some small items, methinks; handkerchiefs and other linens, perhaps a few petticoats. Oh!" She clapped her hands as another idea occurred to her. "And I have an old gown that must be made over, since I have grown—some new panels added. Perhaps you could do some embroidery on that as well? And add some lace?" She turned to her guardian. "Do you not think?"

"It is certainly fine work," Donna Adriana said. "You are old enough now to choose your own embroiderers and seamstresses, if you like their work."

"Please do say yes, Maddalena!" Lucrezia said, clasping her

hands together and looking the very picture of an earnest child begging for sweets.

"It would be my honor, Madonna Lucrezia," I said, trying to bite back a wide grin at the thought of doing such work—if it could even be called work, as it was something I loved doing so!

"Wonderful!" she exclaimed. "I shall see a little bit is added to your wages."

"You honor me, Madonna," I said, curtsying. I had sold some pieces back in the village—the only reason Mother had tolerated my "fool stitchery"—but there were few there with the money or appreciation for fine work. To be paid to take on these tasks for a noble lady like Lucrezia was more than I had ever dared dream of.

And perhaps . . . perhaps the experience, as well as the extra money, might help me someday achieve the thing I desired most: to support myself as a seamstress. It would not be easy, not when men controlled the guilds and such independent craftswomen were usually widows carrying on their husbands' business, but maybe if I could win the confidence of the pope's own daughter . . . maybe . . .

"No doubt we have maids enough to take care of these other tasks while you are working on the lady Lucrezia's things," Donna Adriana broke into my reverie, gesturing toward the tray I was still in the process of clearing.

"I am happy to serve in any way I can," I said quickly.

With that, I gathered the rest of the dishes and whisked them away, at last letting my smile have free rein. Oh, what fortune was mine in this house!

Chapter 10

CESARE

Rome, February 1493

By January, all of Rome knew Lucrezia was due to marry Giovanni Sforza, Lord of Pesaro, and by early February the betrothal was signed, sealed, and had been executed by proxy. All that was left was for the groom to come to Rome for a wedding as lavish as the pope could muster—which would no doubt make it the most lavish the Eternal City had ever seen.

"We must call to mind the splendor and pomp of ancient Rome," Pope Alexander declared at the start of the wedding planning. It had been a small meeting, that first one: just myself, Johannes Burchard, the master of ceremonies, and Vice-Chancellor Ascanio Sforza, who beamed throughout (and throughout all the arrangements that followed) as though he were a proud papa. As well he might, I thought darkly, for he has managed to marry off his obscure cousin to the daughter of the pope. "Romans love a spectacle; they always have. We must give them one. And we must show that the Borgias are an empire unto themselves. It shall reflect our glory."

Burchard—a pompous, pious little German whom I couldn't help but like for his constant dry manner—paused, his quill ceasing scratching, and intoned, "You mean it shall reflect the glory of God's kingdom on earth, Your Holiness, surely?"

My father waved his hand at Burchard good-naturedly. "Yes,

yes, of course," he said. "And Lucrezia's gown, of course, is of the utmost import . . . it must be a setting suitable for the crowning jewel that she is . . ."

Cardinal Sforza chortled. "You are asking the wrong group of people for advice on gowns, Your Holiness."

"Yes, perhaps Madonna Giulia Farnese would be of more assistance in this area," Burchard said coolly.

"An excellent idea, Burchard," I said, ignoring his barb. "There is no one in Rome more fashionable than La Bella Farnese. I am sure she can advise."

Sforza rolled his eyes at me, but I stared stonily back.

"Yes, yes, indeed," my father said distractedly. "Perhaps I get ahead of myself there. What I really wished to speak to you gentleman about was the guest list . . ."

And so it began, and went on for months. One would have thought we were planning large-scale conquest rather than a wedding.

And a wedding to so undeserving a groom. It still pricked at me, like a thorn caught in the folds of my archbishop's robes.

To make matters worse, tension was growing between Milan and Naples. The French were again making noise about enforcing their ancestral claim to the Kingdom of Naples, which was hotly disputed by—along with the Neapolitans themselves—King Ferdinand of Aragon, whose relatives reigned in Naples and who was furthermore a friend of my father's. Indeed, as a cardinal, my father had helped broker the near-impossible match between Ferdinand and Isabella of Castile, uniting their two kingdoms on the Iberian Peninsula.

Ludovico Sforza, still insecure in the ducal crown he'd all but stolen from his nephew, was in a difficult spot politically: Venice nibbled at the edges of Milanese territory every chance they got, always waiting for their opportunity to take even bigger bites and add to their Adriatic empire; Naples was increasingly hostile given that King Ferrante's granddaughter, Isabella, was married to the rightful duke; both Florence and the powerful Roman clan of the Orsini were friendly with Naples; and could Ludovico Sforza, even with a cousin marrying the pope's daughter, be sure of the support of a Spanish pope against that nation's interests? As such, he had been braying about how he would support the French if they chose to press their claim to Naples, no doubt wanting whatever scraps of protection he could get from a major European power. There were fears that the promise of free passage through the duchy of Milan would be enough to tempt the French king to come to Italy with his armies, though how likely that would be was difficult to say. But the question in my mind was: should war come, should the French come, did Pope Alexander really wish to find himself more closely allied with Milan, and against his natural allies in the Spanish king and queen?

I broached this subject with my father privately one night after the betrothal ceremony had already taken place. I was not altogether surprised that his outlook was more optimistic than mine. "Milan is a long way from Naples," he reminded me. "Free passage through one duchy is not likely to offset the expense of such a campaign, especially when the French king does not yet know what resistance he would encounter from the rest of the Italian peninsula, particularly Venice."

"But if King Charles does come?" I pressed.

"Cesare, do you think I have not thought of this?" he said. "If Ludovico Sforza invites the French into Italy, none of the rest of Italy will stand with him. It is a political position that would hardly be worth it for him. And Giovanni Sforza is bound by the marriage contract to provide his army when and where I call for it. His first loyalty will be to us."

I remained silent.

"In any case," he went on, "the betrothal has been set. They are as good as married now."

In late May, I went to see Lucrezia as I did every week, if not more. With the wedding drawing nearer I had the sense she must be getting nervous. Could she possibly be excited? Perhaps young girls looked on their marriage with some combination of the two emotions.

I was shown into her sitting room, where she was chatting with Giulia Farnese. "Cesare!" Lucrezia cried excitedly as I entered, getting to her feet. Giulia rose and swept me a curtsy. "Your Excellency," she murmured. "I shall leave you two to speak in private." She swept out of the room, and a maid who'd been sitting off to one side, head bent over her embroidery, rose to leave as well. It was a moment before I recognized her—*Maddalena*. I smiled at her, and a pretty blush crept up her cheeks. She curtsied in my direction and left, taking her embroidery with her.

"Is Maddalena serving you well?" I asked my sister, switching to our native Catalan.

"Oh, yes!" Lucrezia enthused. "Thank you for sending her to me, *germà*. I discovered she is a most gifted seamstress and can do wonders with embroidery and lace. She is working on some items for my trousseau."

"Ah," I said. "I am glad. And tell me, how are you feeling with the wedding so soon approaching?"

Her face took on a contemplative look. "I am a bit nervous, of course," she said. "I hope I will like my bridegroom, and that I shall be pleasing to him as well."

"How could you be anything but pleasing?" I asked with a smile.

"I can only hope he thinks so!" she said. "I hope he is kind, and handsome, and that we shall come to love each other. Surely we shall, we must, for why else would God be bringing us together?"

"Indeed," I said softly. My sister was wiser in the ways of the world than many other girls her age, but in some ways, she was still so innocent. If she believed all marriages were blissful gifts from God, I did not have it in my heart to disillusion her.

"But I . . . I am sure I shall be happy," she said resolutely, but I could hear her uncertainty plain as day. "I am doing my part to help our family secure our place in the world and am honored to do so."

This was so close an echo of the words our father had spoken when he'd told me about the Sforza match that I had no doubt he had repeated them to my sister. Yet she seemed to believe them, or was trying to.

How I wished I could have changed all this for her and found her a handsome prince out of some old heroic story to win her love, rather than this cold arrangement of contracts and armies and alliances and favors owed.

But my promise was not broken yet. Perhaps the groom could be persuaded to keep his bride in Rome. For no matter what Lucrezia—or our father—said, it was Giovanni Sforza who was advancing in the world with this match, not the Borgia family.

"I certainly pray you shall be happy," I said aloud. I took one of her hands and brought it to my lips. "I pray for it every day."

She threw her arms around me. "I know you do, dearest Cesare. You are the most beloved to me, I think, of any person in the world."

"And you to me," I said, holding her tightly.

Our talk soon turned to other things: how Mother was upset (but not surprised, protocol being what it was) to have not been invited to Lucrezia's wedding, and the astonishing number of callers Giulia had been receiving, ones bringing her gifts and bribes in the hopes that she might advocate for them to the pope as they lay in bed together. "It is quite ridiculous, for it is not as if she needs any more costly cloth or jewelry or fine wines," Lucrezia said. "Papa gives her all that she could possibly want."

"Ah, but that is how the game is played, Crezia," I said.

As I was leaving later that afternoon, I passed the maid, Maddalena, in the hallway. "Wait," I said, and she stopped, startled. "Maddalena."

"Your Excellency," she said, dipping down in a curtsy.

"I will not keep you," I said. "I only wished to know how you are finding your new position."

Her eyes sparkled as they met mine, and I noticed anew what an extraordinary amber color they were. "I like it very much, Your Excellency," she said, genuine contentment in her voice. "I am doing some embroidery for the lady Lucrezia, which is my favorite art to practice. I cannot thank you enough."

"You need not mention it. And you are safer here, yes?"

"Oh, yes," she said, her eyes darkening slightly at the allusion to our first meeting.

"*Eccellente*. I am pleased to hear it. My sister was speaking to me of your fine work, and since you have made her happy, it is I who owe you thanks."

She smiled once more, and I was surprised to realize I had been trying to bring forth that exact expression again. "You are a fine man, Your Excellency. If you don't mind my saying so."

I was taken aback by her words. "I thank you," I said. "I shall endeavor to be worthy of such praise."

And as I took my leave, I found I truly did want to be worthy.

Chapter 11

CESARE

Rome, June 1493

The week before the wedding, Father summoned Giovanni Sforza to a private audience.

A private audience with the Holy Father was never truly so, of course, for those who were not family. I was present, as was Burchard, Ascanio Sforza, and my father's chamberlain. Michelotto waited outside, within shouting distance if there was trouble. I did not expect any, but Michelotto was always expecting trouble on my behalf. It was what made him so eminently well suited for his job.

Giovanni Sforza entered the throne room, flanked by an attendant, and bowed. Standing to my father's right, I wondered at the formal setting. Private audiences were occasionally held in the throne room, but oftentimes in the Holy Father's own rooms. Surely a meeting with his soon-to-be son-in-law was more suited for a smaller, private chamber?

It would seem, whatever it was Father wanted to discuss with Sforza, he wanted to remind the Lord of Pesaro who truly wielded the power here. I was a bit miffed I did not know why Father had summoned Sforza. But I was present in the room, standing at his right hand, and I would be informed in due course.

"Signor Sforza," my father said as Giovanni approached, kneeling and kissing the papal ring and slipper. "Rise. I trust your esteemed cousin in Milan is not planning on causing us any trouble, *sì?*"

Giovanni rose stiffly. "I cannot speak for my cousin Ludovico, nor his actions," he said, and it was all I could do not to laugh aloud at such a clumsy answer. "But I—"

"My brother Ludovico wants only to be in the good graces of Your Holiness, and to enjoy as close a relationship with the Holy See as possible," Ascanio cut in smoothly. "There is nothing as dear to his heart, being a man of true piety as he is."

I could not resist a soft snort. I failed to see how a man of true piety would keep his nephew, the true duke of Milan, all but a prisoner while usurping the powers that belonged, by rights, only to the duke. I caught the glare Ascanio sent my way, but I ignored him. At the side of the room, Burchard's eyebrows were raised, but he merely continued to studiously take notes.

"Of course," my father replied, no hint of irony in his voice. He focused his attention on Giovanni. "And I trust you are still finding your accommodations quite comfortable?"

"Very much so," Giovanni said. "Your Holiness is most generous."

"Indeed," my father said. "Your rooms in Santa Maria in Portico are being prepared as we speak, so you might live with your wife after the wedding."

"I thank Your Holiness."

"Not at all. A man must be near to his wife, of course. And you will be free to take her back to Pesaro with you as soon as travel arrangements can be made. However, we are very fond of our daughter and would not encourage you to make haste."

"I am eager to show her my home, Holiness," Giovanni said. I was astonished to hear a note of petulance in his voice, that he would dare show even a trace of ungratefulness before the Holy Father. "And the people of Pesaro are eager to meet their new countess."

"Indeed," my father said, his voice cooling. "Yet surely there is no rush. You've a lifetime of wedded bliss to introduce your wife to Pesaro. As she is still so young, we would not wish to see her unduly homesick. Some time for her to adjust to married life in the comforts of her own home is warranted."

I marked the look of frustration Giovanni sent to his cousin the cardinal. He opened his mouth to protest, but Ascanio shot him a quelling look. "Of course, Your Holiness," he said tightly. "As you say."

"We are glad we're in accord. Which brings us to the other matter we wished to raise." Father paused, steepling his fingers and peering at Giovanni over them. "As you are well aware, Lucrezia is of a tender age. In the interest of cementing the alliance between our two families in such . . . uncertain times, the marriage will be proceeding anyway. However, we have one additional condition. It is regarding the consummation of the marriage." He paused again.

The pope remained silent for so long that Giovanni was prompted to speak. "Yes, Your Holiness?" he asked. "What of it?"

"It is our desire that the marriage not be consummated immediately."

I saw my own surprise reflected on Giovanni's face, though I was certain I hid it better than he did. "Oh?"

"Yes," Father continued. "As we said, she is of a young age still, and out of respect for such an innocent state we think the consummation could be left off for some time. Say, until November of this year, at which time we can revisit the issue."

I could not resist a slight smile of satisfaction. Not only was I pleased my little sister would not need to bed this man just yet, but I could not help but feel perhaps my father had come around to my way of thinking on this marriage. For if the marriage had never been consummated, it could be put aside without any difficulty at all, if political circumstances should warrant such.

Both Sforzas, Giovanni and his cousin the cardinal, had obviously come to the same conclusion. "This is most irregular," Giovanni sputtered.

"But important, and hopefully understandable given the circumstances," my father replied good-naturedly.

"Holiness, surely this is not necessary," Ascanio interjected. "Your daughter is a fine and obedient young woman, and pious, too, from what I hear. Surely she will understand her duty to her husband as ordained by God, and wish to perform that duty."

"And so she does," Father said, his good humor not slipping for an instant. "I ask only that you indulge a doting, loving father."

It was a masterstroke, and they both knew it. The marriage was going ahead and would be legally binding; the alliance between Borgia and Sforza would be complete. Yet it gave the pope a way out should he need it, and these men could hardly argue with a tenderhearted father—especially not one who was also the pope and to whom they both owed obedience.

Cardinal Sforza, at least, was wise enough to recognize when he had been outmaneuvered. He bowed his head and said simply, "Of course, Your Holiness. As you wish."

Giovanni, however, did not seem to know he was beaten. "This . . . restriction was not listed in the marriage contract," he pointed out.

"Indeed it was not," my father said. He rose from his throne, indicating the audience was at a close. "We did not think it needed to be included, certain as we are that you are a man of his word who does not need such a clause to pay your bride the respect she is owed, by virtue of who she is and who her father is." He stared levelly down at Giovanni. "We trust we are in agreement, then?"

The implied threat was nevertheless clear. Giovanni had no choice but to bow his head and reply, "Yes, Your Holiness."

Chapter 12

MADDALENA

"You, girl," Adriana de Mila called to me, poking her head out of Lucrezia's dressing room. "Come. We need your help."

I rose from my usual chair where I was adding some embroidery to one of Lucrezia's shifts and hurried toward her. "Of course, Madonna Adriana."

Lucrezia was within, being dressed for her wedding, to take place that very day. I had seen much of her wedding gear over the past week—the gown, its elaborate sleeves, the new silk shoes dyed to match, some new pieces of jewelry. Yet I was unprepared for the true vision that my mistress made. When I stepped into her dressing room, I gasped.

She stood in front of a tall Venetian glass mirror, with Adriana, Giulia, and two maids standing around her. Her gown was of the palest blue and trimmed with gold: gold lace at the bodice and hem, gold embroidery down the front panel, and gold ribbons on the sleeves, which were slashed to reveal a cloth-of-gold chemise beneath. A gold chain set with pearls wound around her head, crossing her brow and disappearing into her elaborate coiffure, where the chain was woven through the strands of her pale hair. A gold necklace set with an enormous diamond encircled her throat, along with gold rings on various fingers, and dangling diamond earrings.

She was breathtaking, and all who set eyes on her would

think her an angel. Her eyes moved to me as I entered and, set off by the gown as they were, seemed almost impossibly blue. Their troubled expression widened into one of relief when she saw me. "Oh, Maddalena," she said. "Thank goodness. Come here, please, quickly."

I crossed the room to her and bobbed a curtsy. "How may I serve you, Madonna?"

"There is a tear," she said, her lip trembling as though she were trying not to cry, "in the hem of the dress." She pointed down, and I saw where the gold lace had likely been stepped on and come away from the hem.

"Honestly, Lucrezia, if you had just stopped fidgeting like I told you to . . ." Adriana began to complain, but she was silenced by a sharp, irritated gesture from her young charge.

"Yes, I am well aware," Lucrezia said testily. "But what's done is done, and it must be fixed." She turned her beseeching eyes back to me. "You can fix it, can't you, Maddalena? You are the most gifted seamstress I know, and if you cannot fix it . . ."

That was all? A bit of lace torn away from the hem? Tension leaked from my body. I smiled with relief, hoping to put her more at ease. "This is easily fixed, Madonna," I said. "Have no fear. I'll only need you to stand in place while I mend it."

Lucrezia's delicate body sagged with relief. "Thank the Blessed Virgin," she murmured. "Yes, of course, I shall stand for however long it takes, and be grateful for it. Zia Adriana, please get Maddalena whatever she needs."

I knelt to examine the lace and the hem. I looked up at Donna Adriana. "I can fetch my needles from my bag in the next room; I have one fine enough for this work," I said. "But I shall need gold thread."

"We have some, somewhere," Lucrezia said. "Zia Adriana, please find it, and fetch Maddalena's sewing bag as well."

"No, no, Madonna, I can—"

But Adriana was already off, gone to fetch my bag and to hunt for the gold thread. As a bride, Lucrezia was indeed queen for a day, and it seemed all would do her bidding, even if her bidding was to fetch and carry for a lowly maid like myself. I allowed myself a bit of satisfaction with this turn of events. I was saving the wedding dress and, in a way, the wedding! I would need to confess this sin of pride later, but for now I allowed myself to revel in it.

Within minutes Donna Adriana returned with my sewing bag and a spool of gold thread, and I got to work.

I was not permitted to attend the wedding ceremony, of course, nor the banquet that followed; but, as everyone I served was in attendance, there was no one to stop me from sneaking into the Vatican Palace to have a look at the revelry. And, I thought rather mischievously, perhaps I would seek out Federico and pass some of the evening in his company. It had been far too long since I had beheld his handsome face.

But oh, what a sight the wedding banquet made! Well worth the scolding I would receive if I were caught, though I knew Lucrezia wouldn't mind if she saw me there.

The room was a glorious sight: an elaborate glass chandelier overhead blazed with candles, and more candles lit the room from sconces all around the walls and on the tables. Fine velvet and satin hangings, in the Borgia colors and stitched with the crest of the Borgia bull, adorned the marble walls, along with intricate tapestries depicting biblical scenes such as the Wedding at Cana and the Sermon on the Mount. The many tables in the huge hall were covered with cloth of gold, and gold plates and cutlery still remained on some of the tables as the servants worked to clear the remains of the feast—a feast comprised of enough food to have fed my village for a month, by the looks of it.

And the guests! They were nearly more dazzling than the room. Ladies wore gowns of every color, in the finest fabrics, and with jewels to match. The men wore clothes nearly as vibrant, and gold and silver stitching glinted from many a doublet. Even the cardinals in attendance, in their bright red robes and caps, had added lace to their sleeves and wore their largest jeweled crosses for the occasion.

The wealth on display was unbelievable. I had seen evidence of great wealth in the Vatican Palace, certainly, and the treasures in Madonna Lucrezia's house, yet this was something else altogether. The excess was brilliant to look at, but was not such pride and vanity and waste a sin? Especially while people starved in the streets and villages outside?

Quickly I crossed myself. This was the pope's palace, and his daughter's wedding, I reminded myself. Many of these people served God and His Church. If God in his wisdom had seen fit to bestow such wealth upon them, it was not for me to question or judge. Surely it was right for God to reward His holy servants so.

I positioned myself behind one of the wall draperies, to watch as the dancing began. The pope sat at the head table beside Giulia Farnese, both watching approvingly as Lucrezia was led out by her bridegroom. I started a bit at the sight, so discordant a pair did they make: she, blushing and glowing radiantly in her extravagant gown, and he, dour and with a tight smile on his lips. He was not yet thirty—still much older than his teenaged bride—but already his drab brown hair was beginning to thin and he had developed a paunch around his middle, which his fine doublet did nothing to hide. He had a short beard that looked to hide a weak chin, and his small eyes darted nervously around the room, as though he were a rabbit in a room full of foxes and was hoping they had not noticed him yet, that he could still slip away unscathed.

He bowed to her and took her hand, and as the musicians in the corner struck up a lively tune, they began to dance. He was clumsy and awkward on his feet, and several times Lucrezia had to step gracefully out of the way, lest he tread on her toes. Still, her bright smile did not slip for so much as an instant, even as she tried to make conversation with her new husband, and he replied with no more than a word or two. No doubt he needed to direct his full concentration toward the dance, I thought, feeling somewhat irritated on my mistress's behalf.

After what seemed a painfully long time, the bride and groom's dance ended, and other couples rose to take a spot on the floor. The pope rose from his seat at the dais and spoke in his booming voice.

"Cesare," he called, "lead the bride in a dance, won't you? Let's have a Spanish dance."

All heads turned toward where Cesare Borgia rose from his seat. I blinked once, almost disbelievingly; I hadn't recognized him without his archbishop's robes. He was dressed as a nobleman, wearing a doublet of midnight blue trimmed with silver and silver hose—beautiful clothes, and finely made, but not nearly as ostentatious as what was worn by many others in the room. He wore only his large archbishop's ring on his left hand; no other jewelry or adornment. His hair flowed freely in dark curls to his shoulders, without his bishop's cap to hold it back. He was the handsomest man I had ever seen; handsomer even than Federico.

I may not have recognized Cesare Borgia when I'd first slipped into the room, but once I did, I did not know how I had missed him. Or how to look away. He inclined his head to his father in agreement and walked out onto the floor, where the other dancers waited for him to take his place. He took Lucrezia's hand and kissed it, and she beamed, a smile that eclipsed any she had thus far given her bridegroom. She was no doubt relieved to be dancing with someone as familiar as her brother. Giovanni Sforza stood awkwardly behind the pair; then, as though only just realizing he had been dismissed, walked stiffly off the dance floor and back to his seat. A slight scowl twisted his features, and I wondered if anyone else noticed, and what they made of it if they did.

"Very good!" the pope called out and clapped his hands. "Begin!"

On his cue, the musicians struck up a lively dance, and Lucrezia and Cesare began to move. The other couples had returned to their seats, as it seemed they were not familiar with this Spanish dance.

And what a striking pair they made. If one did not know they were brother and sister, it would not be easy to guess: him dark and tall, she slight and golden. They were each beautiful in their own way, though, and therefore alike even as they were different.

The dance was a quick, vigorous one, yet it managed to be sensual all the same, with the dancers holding each other's gaze and pressing together quickly before again moving apart. It was slightly shocking to me that a brother and sister should dance it together, yet the Holy Father was beaming approvingly from his seat on the dais, clapping along with the quick beat.

A glance at the other attendees, however, showed I was not the only one mildly scandalized. A few other guests, some of them cardinals, raised their eyebrows as they watched the Borgia siblings. Others exchanged shocked glances. And Giovanni Sforza wore a scowl that only deepened as the dance went on. Only Juan Borgia, sitting beside Cesare's empty seat, seemed indifferent, his attention fully focused on his wine goblet. I pressed myself closer to the wall, praying the Blessed Mother would keep his gaze from falling on me, this night or any other.

Once the dance ended, all those in attendance clapped heartily, and the two dancers bowed in acknowledgement. Juan rose to take his turn dancing with the bride, and Cesare escorted a smiling Giulia Farnese to a place among the other couples who had returned to the floor. And the bridegroom, amidst all the splendor put on for his sake, remained sullenly in his seat.

I could not help but pity Lucrezia while watching the sneer of distaste beginning to curl his lip. She was so young and full of life, too much so to be saddled with a husband who could take no pleasure in the things that brought her joy. If anyone would know that, it was I.

And as I watched the dancing continue on into the night, my eyes were drawn back again and again to Cesare Borgia, in his elegant and understated clothing. A true prince, in both looks and dignity, I thought, watching him charm his dance partner of the moment, a lady I did not know. A pity a man more like him could not have been found for young Lucrezia.

Chapter 13

CESARE

The wedding banquet had begun to come to a close, and the bride and groom would be retiring soon. I knew what was not supposed to happen behind the doors of their marital chamber, and I wanted to make certain Giovanni Sforza remembered it as well.

He had been sitting sullenly at his place most of the night, dancing only once more with Lucrezia after their first dance. He had also been drinking heavily, and from the scowl on his face, I highly doubted he'd forgotten his conversation with the Holy Father. Yet on the off chance he was drinking to get his courage up for disregarding the pope's wishes, I decided it was best that he and I have a chat.

He rose from the table, no doubt intending to go fetch his bride, but I was already at his side. "Brother-in-law," I said, clapping a hand on his shoulder. I smiled widely. "A word with you, if I might."

"Very well." He met my eyes, waiting.

My smile never slipped as I said, "I just wanted to ensure that you remember what was discussed in your audience with His Holiness last week."

He laughed mirthlessly. "As if I could forget."

My fingers tightened their grip, digging into his shoulder. "Good," I said. "Make certain you don't."

"Let go of me, Borgia," he snarled, forgetting all titles and courtesy in his frustrated drunkenness. "I'm not some Borgia dog to be commanded as your family wills it. She is my wife and if I choose to exercise my right as her husband, then I—"

He broke off as I tightened my grip, pressing my thumb into the spot above his collarbone that would cause the most pain. "I think you'll find that you *are* to be commanded as we will it," I said smoothly. "That is what you agreed to when you signed the marriage contract. And as such, you will not lay a finger on my sister. Is that understood?"

"Take your hand off me, bastard."

Icy rage flared in me, but I tamped it down. "Be careful who you insult, Sforza. You will not touch my sister."

"And if I do? There is not a court in the land that would find me guilty of anything for fucking my own wife."

Michelotto stepped from the shadows to stand behind me, one hand on the hilt of his sword. "Is there a problem here, my lord?" he asked calmly.

Sforza's face went white. Michelotto had quickly become known throughout Rome as my bodyguard and hired blade. Just as I had intended when I'd dropped the story of the would-be assailants into the right ears.

"*Non lo so,* Michelotto." I looked back at Giovanni, my grip not loosening at all. "Is there, Sforza?"

"No," he bit out. "No, there isn't."

"Good." I released him, and he stumbled slightly. "I have made myself clear, then?"

"Yes."

"I didn't quite hear you."

"Yes!" he all but shouted. "You and your father were very clear."

"Excellent. I do so wish you a good night." I grinned at him, more a baring of the teeth than anything. "You will no doubt find it a restful one."

With that, I left the dais, and Michelotto faded back into the shadows. I had a servant bring me another glass of wine, well satisfied with my work that evening.

Chapter 14

MADDALENA

When I slipped back into my tiny chamber after the wedding banquet—shared with my friend Isabella, who mostly served Donna Adriana—I stripped down to my shift and climbed into bed. As I laid my head on the pillow, the crinkling of parchment startled me. I sat up quickly. Frowning, I unfolded the parchment and got up, walking to the small window to try to make out the words by moonlight.

The hand was one I did not recognize, the letters bold and spiky. I glanced at the bottom of the missive and smiled at the name scrawled there: *Federico.*

In my tiredness I had forgotten my plan to seek him out; but it mattered not. Apparently he had also been thinking of me this night. That had to be a sign of some kind, surely?

Squinting in the dim light, I pressed closer to the window and began to read.

Mia amica Maddalena—

I trust you will forgive the tardiness of this missive. It was some time ago indeed that I promised to write you. The Duke of Gandia sent me from Rome with several of the grooms to secure some fine horseflesh for him, having heard I've an eye for such things, and in the meantime you were given a new position. I did not receive your missive until my return, and I did not know anyone in your household whom I might have persuaded to carry a message for me.

I flinched at the mention of the Duke of Gandia, but my grin returned as I pored over Federico's words. He must have slipped in, knowing everyone would be busy with Lucrezia's wedding. No doubt Isabella, at the sight of his handsome face, had directed him to where he might leave his letter.

I have missed your company, even in our brief encounters in the courtyard or the hallways. I flatter myself that you have not forgotten me—though surely such a beauty has all the men of Rome at her feet—and that you think fondly of me from time to time. If this is the case, perhaps I could persuade you to take a stroll with me tomorrow night, in the cool of evening. I will be waiting beside the gates of Santa Maria in Portico at twilight if you are so inclined. If you've another suitor who has swept you off your feet since last we spoke, I completely understand and can only envy the lucky man.

Yours,
Federico

I shut my eyes and clutched the paper to my chest.

Lucrezia Borgia had been required to make a marriage that was arranged for her, as I once had. Yet for the first time I pitied her, for it was I who might—just maybe—have a chance at falling in love.

The following evening, I slipped from the palazzo as the sky began to darken. I pulled the pins from my hair, letting it fall loosely over my shoulders. My heartbeat quickened when I saw him leaning against the marble wall. Federico, as handsome as ever. His wide smile matched my own as I placed my hand on his arm, and we set off into the Roman dusk. I did not ask where we were going, for it did not matter; I was content for Federico to lead me anywhere.

May this be the first of many such nights, I thought.

My fears that my life and position would change greatly after Lucrezia's wedding proved futile. The new bride returned to her rooms in Santa Maria in Portico, and though her husband now had rooms in the palazzo as well, I rarely saw him—nor did she see him more often. She often dined with him, I knew, sometimes in the company of her brothers and father; yet other than that, she passed her days much as she had before: gossiping and giggling with Giulia Farnese, enduring lessons in deportment and history with Donna Adriana, and attending Mass or praying in the palazzo's private chapel.

I often wondered how she found her new husband, and if she had come to love him. I was surprised to realize I had grown protective of her, as though she were the younger sibling I never had. This feeling was far more familiar than a servant should feel toward her mistress. But I could not help it. Something about Lucrezia's glowing innocence, her guileless charm and kindness, inspired such caring in me.

I wished I could ask if she was happy. That was all I wanted to know. Yet as the days passed, I had my answer: she was much the same as she had always been, full of life and spirit and with joy in her eyes. And why not? She was the favored daughter of the pope and had made a fine marriage, after all, one that would benefit her family and his. Surely she had little to be unhappy about.

It was not until a few weeks after the wedding that I came to see the ways in which I had misunderstood Lucrezia's situation.

I was in the corner of the sitting room, working on some mending Donna Adriana had dumped at my feet: a gown, some chemises. Nothing arduous. As such, my attention wandered as I stitched, almost hoping one of the ladies would summon me to perform some task—the reason I did my work in the sitting room and not in the servants' quarters.

My afternoon was certainly about to be livened up. As I worked, Lucrezia stormed into the room, Giulia on her heels. "Hunting! Again!" she cried. "I have hardly seen my husband since we were married! What sort of husband is he? And what sort of wife am I?"

Giulia sought to soothe her. "You have seen your husband much more since your marriage than I have seen mine," she said, attempting a joke. The state of affairs between her and her cuckolded husband—who still languished at one of the Orsini country estates—was by then well-known to all of Rome.

Lucrezia, who would normally have giggled at such a scandalous joke, merely gave Giulia an exasperated look. She was not in the mood.

I kept my head lowered over the mending and my ears open.

"He is only getting settled," Giulia said, trying again. "Imagine how different Rome must feel to him, after such a little place like Pesaro. He is overwhelmed, no doubt, and getting his bearings. Hunting is obviously something he enjoys, and so . . ."

"Is he such a country duck, then?" Lucrezia demanded. "Why would my father marry me to a man so . . . so provincial?"

"I am not privy to all of His Holiness's decisions."

"Psh!" Lucrezia scoffed. "You know his mind better than anyone, methinks. You and my brother Cesare."

I could not help raising my head at the mention of the Archbishop of Valencia, but I looked down quickly, lest they notice my interest.

"His Holiness thought this an advantageous match for many reasons," Giulia said, sounding uncomfortable. Clearly she did indeed know more about it than she was telling Lucrezia. "You know that."

Lucrezia sighed loudly, and dramatically flopped down onto their usual couch in a most undignified way. "I just don't know why Giovanni does not wish to spend time with me," she wailed. "He is not what I pictured, I'll admit, but I want to be a good wife to him. Yet he won't let me!"

"Marriage is not easy," Giulia said, sitting beside the younger girl. "And each marriage is different."

"Oh, what would you know!" Lucrezia burst out petulantly, rising from her seat and pacing the room. "But since you claim to be so wise, tell me this: why has my husband not come to my bed yet?"

My head shot up at this. Luckily, neither woman noticed.

"He still has not?" Giulia asked neutrally.

"No!" Lucrezia cried, anguished. "I know what to expect, what he will do—my mother told me, since you weren't any help." She shot a look in my direction at this, too. "And my husband has never so much as entered my bedchamber. He kisses me on the forehead each night as we retire—rather stiffly, too, as though I were his sister and not his wife. Then he goes off to his chambers, or God knows where." She flopped back on the couch in a huff. "What is wrong with me, Giulia? What can be so wrong with me that my own husband does not wish to lie with me?"

"Nothing is wrong with you, *cara*," Giulia assured her, wrapping her long arms around the younger girl's shoulders. "Why, you are one of the loveliest women in Rome."

"Then why? Why won't he lie with me?"

"That I cannot say," Giulia said, a look of calculation in her eyes. She knew something. But what? I found myself leaning forward in expectation. "But do not despair, Lucrezia. Perhaps this is a good thing. If he does not come to your bed, you shall be spared the dangers of childbirth for some time yet."

"I suppose. But it is my duty to give my lord and husband an heir."

"Indeed it is. But you are so young yet, *cara*. Your father needed to make this marriage, yes, but it is not such a bad thing to retain your innocence for a bit longer," she said, with a trace of wistfulness in her voice. Perhaps she spoke from her heart more than Lucrezia realized.

"I do not want to be a child anymore," Lucrezia protested.

"I understand. Believe me, I do. But sex does not necessarily make one a woman, either, no matter what many would have you believe. And sometimes it is more trouble than it is worth, for women especially."

Lucrezia glanced sideways at her. "You seem to enjoy it well enough," she pointed out.

Giulia giggled. "I surely do," she admitted. "It can be most pleasurable, especially with a man who knows how to treat a woman in bed." She blushed, as though remembering she was speaking to her lover's daughter. "But it is not all that is important in a relationship between a man and a woman, Lucrezia. Get to know your husband, talk to him, spend time with him. Perhaps he is merely being considerate of your young age. When the time is right, he will come to your bed. And if you are lucky, by then you will love him."

"I want to love him," Lucrezia whispered. "But I do not know if he wants to love me."

Giulia gave her a quick hug. "Of course he does. Who would not love you?"

With Lucrezia reassured, their talk turned to other things. Yet my mind continued to turn over what I had heard.

I had never heard of a marriage not being consummated immediately—unless the man was unable to perform, of course. Could that be the case? But, no—he was a widower, and I'd heard his first wife had died in childbed, though perhaps I was mistaken on that count.

I did not know well the ways of the wealthy—maybe this was more customary than I knew. Yet if that were so, why was Lucrezia so upset?

The more I thought about it, the less sense it made. It was possible Sforza was simply being considerate of her age—she was rather younger than most brides. Yet it would seem to me that a marriage to cement a political alliance would need to be consummated as quickly as possible. A marriage that was never consummated was not valid.

I bit back a gasp. Yes, by the laws of God and man, Lucrezia's marriage was not truly valid. Why had the pope not directed her husband to come to her bed posthaste?

My fingers stopped on my needlework as my mind whirled, going further than it should have dared. Yes, in an important alliance the pope would have made certain everything was legal and irrevocable. He was no fool, far from it. Could it be . . . was it possible . . . ?

I crossed myself quickly and returned to my work. I did not want to think that the Holy Father might be sabotaging his daughter's marriage for some hidden political purpose. He would not do that—after all, the very God with whose voice he spoke prescribed the roles of husband and wife.

He wouldn't do that. Would he?

That evening, released for my duties for supper, I met Federico by the servants' entrance, as we always did on nights when we had arranged to see each other. He grinned widely when he saw me, and my heart fluttered at the sight of his handsome face. Smiling, I took his arm, as I always did, like we were a grand lord and lady out for a stroll without a care in the world.

We headed in the direction of the market, to get some fresh bread and cheese for dinner, and no doubt some wine. For someone who claimed he had no interest in winemaking, Federico certainly could wax poetic about the types of grapes and what sort of soil they had been grown in. I enjoyed listening to him, for I always learned something.

"What gossip from the domain of the lady Lucrezia?" Federico asked, when we were far enough from the palazzo.

I smiled tightly. I often shared small tidbits of gossip with Federico—a temper tantrum Donna Adriana had thrown over a poorly prepared meal; an extravagant gift Giulia Farnese had received from a favor seeker; Lucrezia insisting upon bathing twice in one week. He was always amused, and I liked that I could make him laugh in the telling of such simple, silly stories.

Yet what I had heard that day felt very different. This was no small, passing amusement. Whether I was right in my suspicions about Lucrezia's marriage or not, it was not something of which to speak lightly. She would be mortified to know something that caused her such hurt and embarrassment was the talk of her servants. I owed the lady Lucrezia a great deal, and my loyalty was an easy enough place to start.

I looked up and smiled at Federico. "La Bella Farnese misplaced her favorite headpiece when she was summoned to dinner with the Holy Father," I reported instead. It was true; it had happened the night before. "She was in a right state."

Federico laughed. "Surely Giulia La Bella has more headpieces to choose from than she could possibly count."

I giggled. "She surely does. But this one frames and flatters her face like no other, or so she claims. I think she looks equally as beautiful with anything or nothing on."

Federico's eyes gleamed. "I'm sure Pope Alexander agrees."

My face flushed—honestly, how could I still be so squeamish, working for these women as I did? "Indeed. Nevertheless, she had nearly all the maids in the palazzo searching high and low for it until it was found. She kept the Holy Father waiting at dinner! Imagine!"

He chuckled. "Beauty's privilege. One you could exercise as flagrantly, if you so chose."

I blushed again. "Surely you do not put me in the same class as La Bella Farnese, when you speak of beauty."

Federico stopped walking and took my face in his hands. "You are a class all your own, Maddalena Moretti," he said, in a voice very different from the one he usually used. "You could stand right beside Giulia Farnese and I would have eyes only for you."

My heart began to pound wildly, both at his touch and at the affection in his eyes. Never before had a man looked at me like that, as though I were truly the only woman in the world he had eyes for. As though his pretty words matched what was in his heart.

I thought he might kiss me then, and I leaned forward, lips parted ever so slightly, but he dropped his hands and drew away.

"So," he said, after a moment had passed. "Where was La Farnese's glorious headpiece finally found?"

I smiled, somehow both relieved and saddened by the return to our usual banter. "Why, in the chest where it was supposed to be all along, of course. She'd simply put it in the wrong spot within it."

Federico laughed outright at this, and his reaction made me giggle in turn as we reached the market. Such a silly story, in truth. Yet everything, I was finding, was more enjoyable with him beside me.

That night, back in my tiny room at Palazzo Santa Maria in Portico, I had a dream.

I had never had a dream like it before. Perhaps I had never had reason to. I had never truly known the sin of lust before.

I was back in the marital chamber I had once shared with Ernesto, but it was not my husband in bed with me—it was Federico. I was in his arms, and he was kissing me, passionately, his tongue tangling with mine, and I responded in kind, wantonly pressing myself against him. At some point I realized that we were both unclothed, though I could not remember either of us removing our clothing. It simply was, in the strange way of dreams.

He had shifted his body atop mine, moving himself between my legs. Some small corner of my mind—a part nearer wakefulness than the rest—protested, telling me something was wrong, that this couldn't, shouldn't, be happening. But the rest of my mind pushed this aside and clung to him eagerly.

"Maddalena," he whispered, the word a statement and a question, a request for permission.

"Yes," I gasped, shamelessly opening my legs for him. "Yes."

And as he entered me, I threw my head back with a cry of pleasure, such as I had never uttered before, and opened my eyes to see it was no longer Federico with me, inside of me.

It was Cesare Borgia, the Archbishop of Valencia.

"Maddalena," he said softly with another thrust, his voice penetrating to my very core as his brown eyes met mine.

I let out another cry—of pleasure or surprise, I could not be sure—and I awoke, sweating and panting, in my narrow bed in Santa Maria in Portico.

I sat up quickly—too quickly—and was struck with a wave of dizziness, my head spinning so that I nearly toppled to the floor. I closed my eyes and tried to catch my breath.

The shift I slept in was soaked, clinging to my skin, and my heart was pounding as though I had been engaging in some physical exertion—as though, I thought, flushing anew, the dream had been real. Even as my heart pounded in my chest, so too was there a throbbing between my legs. The dream might not have been real, but the desire—and therefore the sin—very much was.

I rose from my pallet and blindly opened my trunk to pull out my cloak. I needed fresh air and did not want to risk waking Isabella by fiddling around in the dark for clothes. Instead I simply threw my cloak on and stole into the hallway, and out one of the servants' entrances into the cool night air. From there, I wandered into the maze of hedges and flowers that was the palazzo's garden.

It mortified me to remember the particulars of the dream, but I could not stop thinking about it. Bad enough I should dream something so shameful about one man; about Federico, someone I counted as a friend. But to dream about a second man, an archbishop, a man of God no less . . . I crossed myself, whispering the Pater Noster under my breath as I walked.

Yet the feeling of the heat of skin against skin, of being touched in love, in passion, stayed with me. I was no virgin, but that was something I had never known. The throbbing between my legs had lessened only somewhat; it was an ache waiting to be soothed.

But which man was I imagining touching me? Which did I desire?

One was above desire. To even think it was a grave sin.

I turned and went back into the palazzo, moving swiftly but silently into the chapel. A single candle burned on the altar at this hour, but I did not need more. I knelt on the hard stone and began to pray for forgiveness and that I might be washed clean of such desires.

I remembered something that Uncle Cristiano had once told me. *There are seven deadly sins, Maddalena, but lust is the deadliest,* he'd explained as I was on the brink of womanhood. *All other sins flow from it: lust for power, for money, for recognition, and yes, for another person. For pleasures of the flesh.* I'd blushed furiously at this, uncomfortable to be discussing such a thing when I barely knew what pleasures of the flesh involved. Nevertheless, despite my squirming and my crimson countenance he had forged on. *If you can avoid one sin only, let it be this one. Being free of lust will save you much pain, much heartache, and many a stain on your soul. Remember this.*

I prayed until the sky outside began to lighten, and when I rose from my knees and left the chapel to dress and ready for the day, I was more at peace. I would go to confession later that day and be absolved, doing my penance gladly.

And if, somehow, that ache still remained—for love, tenderness, passion—the answer was not far to seek. Federico enjoyed my company, that much was plain. Perhaps, as I had once fancied, he would soon find himself in want of a wife. I could say yes and have those things I ached for within the sanctity of marriage, where they were blessed by God.

I could have what I wanted, what no doubt God wanted for me, and I could forget I had ever looked with desire upon the Archbishop of Valencia.

I would be washed clean.

Chapter 15

CESARE

My father was in a fine mood. That he had something he was eager to share was obvious. He beamed at all of us from the head of the table: myself, Juan, Giulia Farnese, Lucrezia, and Giovanni Sforza. Even the latter was not exempt from Father's good cheer. Sforza never looked truly relaxed in our company, but tonight was the closest I had ever seen him. I'm sure we had the wine, some of the finest vintages from His Holiness's cellars, to thank for that.

"I'm delighted to have you all here tonight," Father said after the main course had been cleared away. He spoke in Italian rather than Catalan, in deference to Giulia and Giovanni. "I have been in negotiations with Their Most Catholic Majesties, Queen Isabella and King Ferdinand of our native Spain," he said. Instantly my mind flew back over the past few weeks, trying to remember any conversation I'd had with the pope about Spain, and what we may need or want from them or vice versa. The last in-depth conversation concerning Spain we had had was shortly after he was elected, when Isabella and Ferdinand had issued their edict expelling all Jews from their kingdom. They had wanted the Holy Father to forbid the Jewish refugees entry into Rome, but Alexander had refused. Whether this arose from any ideal of mercy, or more so from his desire to welcome the wealth those formerly prominent Spanish Jews brought with them into Rome's economy, I could only guess. Perhaps it was both.

But I could not remember anything more recent. I had seen the Spanish ambassador around the Vatican of late, but he was one of many. And I was not present at all of the Holy Father's audiences, much as I may have wanted to be.

He continued. "I am most pleased to announce another marriage for our family, one that will do our name much honor. Their Catholic Majesties have invited our son Juan to the court of Spain, where he shall marry one Maria Enriquez, a cousin of King Ferdinand himself."

There were delighted, surprised gasps from the ladies. Juan leaned back in his chair, arms crossed over his chest and with a look of smug self-satisfaction on his face.

Anger swept over me. He had already known. Certainly our father would share with Juan news that directly affected him, but still. Why had I, once again, not been brought into his confidence? Why had I not shared in the negotiations with the Spanish royals?

"This is a great honor for the family of Borgia, that we may be respected both in Italy and in our native Spain and beyond, as is our due," the pope went on. "I trust Juan will behave admirably and in keeping with what his family expects of him, and do us proud."

He shot a warning glance in Juan's direction. It gave me some petty glee to observe. Juan did not seem to notice, however; he merely took another long swig of his wine, basking in the admiration of those at the table.

Though not that of Giovanni Sforza. The only emotion on Sforza's face seemed to be one of relief. Interesting indeed, but I had more pressing things to consider.

"And what have Their Catholic Majesties asked of us in return, for so honoring our brother Juan?" I asked, looking at our father.

"Only that which is most certainly in our power to give," he replied, reaching for his wine. "Spain and Portugal are in dispute over sovereignty of these new lands to the west, the ones that Genoan—what is his name, Colombo?—has found. I am happy to decide the matter in Spain's favor, seeing as Ferdinand and Isabella financed his expedition, after all. They also wish for our support regarding their claims to the throne of Naples; that the house of Aragon, as

King Ferdinand's own relations, should be allowed to continue to rule there."

This at last got Giovanni Sforza's attention. He went rigid in his seat, his face pale. As well it might: it was his worthless cousin Ludovico who kept threatening to invite the French into Italy to enforce their ancestral claim to Naples. This marriage of Juan's could put him in a very difficult spot.

I glanced at my sister, who was certainly astute enough to grasp the politics of the situation as well as, if not better than, her husband. Yet she wore only a smile. "Blessings on you, brother, and on your upcoming marriage," she said to Juan. "Though I shall miss having you in Rome."

He turned to her, a softer smile graving his face. "And I shall miss you, dear sister," he said.

"Do promise me you will write often," she said taking his hand.

"Of course," he said. "I have ever been a poor correspondent, but I shall seek to rectify that habit for my only sister."

I scowled, even as I knew both spoke in earnest. For all Juan's faults—and God knew they were countless—he had only ever been kind and loving toward Lucrezia.

"Yes, we shall expect you to become a better correspondent indeed, *figlio*," Father said, directing a stern look at Juan. "We expect to be kept apprised of your doings and of the news from the Spanish court."

Juan would make a poor spy indeed, if Father sought information on political matters. Juan would pay scarce attention to anything but his own pleasure, whether he be in Rome or Spain.

If I were the soldier, the one who was free to marry, it would have been me on my way to a royal Spanish bride. And my eyes and ears would be open the entire time. Yet another task I was far more suited to than Juan.

"In this and in all things, I shall obey you as a loving and dutiful son," Juan said, smirk firmly back in place. He turned to direct it at me. My fist clenched around the stem of my goblet, but I said nothing.

"We know you shall. And so, a toast." Father rose, lifting his goblet high. "To our beloved son Juan, Duke of Gandia. We must put aside our sorrow at his departure as he leaves to make great the name of Borgia, and so elevate us all."

We rose and lifted our glasses. "To Juan," everyone said. No one noticed my half-hearted mumbling of the words.

After the meal was over, Juan left, citing an appointment with Prince Djem. Juan had become close with the brother of the Turkish sultan, kept in the Vatican as a hostage for the sultan's good behavior—and to ensure Djem could not usurp his brother's throne. Djem and Juan had become notorious for combing the streets of Rome at night, drinking and gambling and visiting whores. Juan even at times adopted a Turkish costume in the same style as Djem's, and the pair made quite a sight. And when his antics made it back to our father—a fight in a tavern, broken windows, a dispute over a bill—the pope only scolded him fondly and sent him on his way. One might think Juan would have a care for his new station, but I did not hold out any true hope.

I offered to escort Lucrezia back to Santa Maria in Portico—and if I wished for a glimpse of the pretty Maddalena, that was my own business. But Lucrezia waved me away with a smile. "I have my husband to escort me back, brother," she said, practically hanging on Sforza's arm. He stood stiffly all the while, and it made my blood boil to see him so unworthy of her, and to see her want to please him anyway.

"Of course. Take good care of her, brother-in-law," I said, knowing he would hear the warning.

I called Michelotto over as the pair departed. "Follow them back, just to ensure Lucrezia is safe," I murmured. "And make sure Sforza catches a glimpse of you, that he might remember his promise."

Michelotto nodded. "Very good, my lord. And you?"

"I would speak with His Holiness. Return here after your errand and perhaps we shall have some entertainment this night as well." Juan wasn't the only one who enjoyed a drink and a woman.

At least I managed to be discreet. There was a new courtesan in one of the finer houses in the city, a Florentine woman called Fiammetta with flame-red hair. She seemed to enjoy my company, and there was a dark-haired Spanish woman in the same house whom Michelotto delighted in visiting.

He grinned, understanding my meaning perfectly. "I'd like that very much, my lord."

He took his leave, and I returned to the dining room, where my father still lounged at the head of the table. Giulia sat on his lap as they whispered to one another, and his hand lazily reached into her bodice to toy with her breasts.

"Your Holiness," I said, clearing my throat. "I would have a word, before you retire."

He sighed heavily, but got to his feet even so, Giulia sliding from his lap. "I thought you might," he said. He turned to Giulia. "Go on, *mio tesoro,* and wait in the bedchamber. I shall be along shortly."

She left the room, a coy smile playing about her lips.

"Come, let's go to the private audience chamber," he said, leading me out of the dining room.

I followed him upstairs to his private suite of rooms. We would not meet in his sitting room tonight, not with Giulia waiting next door. Though the pope used his rooms, evidence of the work still being done on them was all over, notably the frescos he had commissioned from the painter Pinturicchio. Drapes, knives, and paintbrushes were collected at the edges of the room, along with wooden scaffolding, waiting for the painter and his assistants to return in the morning.

The richer furniture had been removed for the time being, so my father settled himself onto one of the stone benches cut into the window alcove and motioned for me to take the one across from him. "Let us hear it," he said wearily.

His tone should have made me more cautious—he already knew what I wanted to say and was not looking forward to it—but it only served to make me more irate. "I simply wish to know more as to your strategy here," I said.

"My strategy regarding what, precisely? Speak plainly, Cesare."

"Regarding the political situation in Europe," I said tersely. "You marry Lucrezia to a Sforza when they are all but allied with France over dominion of Naples, and next send Juan to the Spanish court in a sign that you favor the Aragonese claim. How long do you think you can play both sides?"

"I do not know that I am," he said. "Lucrezia's marriage was a sop to the Sforzas, as you well know. Giovanni Sforza will command his armies as we instruct him to when it comes down to it. None of the Sforzas are in any position to defy the pope, least of all the man who is the pope's son-in-law. Juan's marriage will bring us closer to the court of Spain, which is our natural alliance as a family. No one in Europe would expect anything different."

"I think Ludovico Sforza and his brother Ascanio expect something different."

"Ascanio's first loyalty is to me, and he knows his job is to keep his brother in line," Father snapped. "I have repaid that debt, and they know it well and shall not forget it."

"So Spain and Naples are meant to take heart at Juan's marriage, yet France and Milan are not supposed to read it as opposition?"

"I shall marry my children off as best suits our political needs, as princes all over Europe do, and as both the French king and Ludovico Sforza will surely understand," he bit out. "The political situation is delicate, yes, but we must go about our business here."

"I understand that," I said through gritted teeth. "But Sforza went rigid as a beam tonight when you announced Juan's marriage. You can see what a position this puts him in, and by extension Lucrezia."

"Lucrezia is a Borgia first and foremost. We protect our own."

This was the most encouraging thing I'd heard all night. "Agreed. And yet I cannot see how sending Juan to Spain will not aggravate the French—"

"I have been dealing in international politics since before you were born, Cesare. I would pray you remember that," the pope said, his voice low and dangerous. "You would be a fool to think I have not thought through all the implications of what I do, including those of which you cannot possibly have any knowledge."

I was silent, for he was right. "Granted," I said at last. "And yet you have consigned me to the Church because you claim you need my sharp mind and insight to advise you. Why then do you disregard my counsel when I speak?"

He sighed. "I do not disregard it. I do rely on you and shall continue to do so. But believe me, I know what is best."

It seemed there was nothing left to say.

The pope rose from his seat. "I am for my bed, then, and bid you goodnight, my son."

"Yes," I said, rising. "Goodnight, Father."

I left him to his bed—and the woman in it—and made my way to the front entrance hall of the palace where Michelotto waited. "All is well with Lucrezia?" I asked as I approached.

"Indeed. She did not know I was there, though her husband did."

"Perfect." We stepped out into the evening air, walking toward our preferred brothel without needing to discuss it. "Let us enjoy ourselves tonight, Michelotto. Lord knows I could use some amusement."

On August 6, Juan departed for Spain with great fanfare. His baggage train consisted of hundreds of carts, with hundreds of servants to accompany him. He was dressed in hose made of cloth of gold, and a red doublet trimmed with the same. The bridle and saddle of his horse were encrusted with jewels, as were the hilts of the dagger and sword he carried at his waist. The nobles of Spain would be either impressed by the display, or simply blinded.

Juan and his party took leave of the Holy Father on the steps of the Vatican. As he knelt for our father's blessing, those watching could plainly see the pope had tears in his eyes as he placed his hands on the head of his favorite son. "May God watch over you and help you to do His work in the kingdom of Their Most Catholic Majesties," the pope intoned, "and may those worthy monarchs welcome and treat you like their own son. We send to them our greatest gift and treasure this day." He closed his eyes, and a tear rolled down his cheek. "God ride with you, Your Grace, and may our Lord and Savior Jesus Christ protect you from all evil."

With that, Juan rose, and the assembled company—the rest of our family, prominent Roman nobles, and the cardinals and bishops who were in the Holy City—crossed themselves before applauding. Juan waved to the crowd and jauntily swung himself up into his saddle, looking—I ground my teeth as I thought it—like a very knight errant out of some old chivalrous tale. Lucrezia wiped away tears of her own, and a dejected look fell across Prince Djem's face—upset at losing his carousing partner, no doubt. Juan spurred his horse and rode for the exit of the piazza, his companions, grooms, servants, and luggage carts falling into place behind him.

It took over an hour for Juan's entire entourage to filter out onto the road, but the Holy Father waited until the last mule and cart had left the square, and so too was the gathered crowd required to wait. It was a brutally hot day, and I was sweating profusely beneath my silk archbishop's robes. One elderly cardinal fainted dead away from the heat. Yet none of us could leave until finally the Holy Father turned to go inside, signaling that everyone else could disperse.

I stepped gratefully into the cool stone halls of the Vatican, glad the day's ceremonies were over, and gladder still that Juan was gone. Perhaps without Juan blocking his view of me, Father would be able to see me for the man I truly was and realize the full potential he had thus far not allowed me to reach. This was my chance to convince him the Church was not where I could be most useful to him.

Maybe we could let Juan rot in Spain, and I could fulfill our family's military ambitions in Italy. God knew I could do it, for had He not given me the intellect, the strength, the courage?

"I am looking into arranging a marriage for Jofre, and I would know your thoughts," Father said to me several nights later, having summoned me to his private apartments.

I took a sip of chilled *vino blanco* a servant had poured for me, buying myself a moment to consider this. Jofre was only twelve years old. Old enough to be betrothed, certainly. A marriage for a young man at that age was not unheard of, but was rather unusual. Still, Rodrigo Borgia was an unusual man with more than the usual ambition. "Indeed?" I said. "And to what corner of Europe do we look for Jofre's future bride?"

"Where else but to Naples?" he said pleasantly.

I was struck speechless. I had not considered a move this bold.

"Think of it, Cesare," he said, sensing my surprise. "Such a match will signal to Europe our support for Naples and the Aragonese line. It will also assure Ferdinand and Isabella of our continued goodwill."

"While thumbing our noses at Ludovico Sforza in Milan," I added.

"While sending a message to the Sforzas of Milan," Father corrected. "I have no further patience for Ludovico Sforza threatening to bring the French down on our heads, and I want him to know it."

"What does Ascanio say of such a match?"

"I have not told him that I am considering it," Father replied. "But he will do as I say and not challenge me—not too much, anyway. He holds the post of Vice-Chancellor of the Curia at my pleasure, and he would do well to remember that. He has already made himself quite rich off the post, and he will not do anything to jeopardize the source of his wealth."

"Indeed. His brother thinks nothing of how his actions might damage the rest of Italy; only of his own gain."

Father snorted. "No different than any of the other Italian princelings. And why should it be? None of them have each other's interests at heart. They are all separate nations."

"But imagine a united Italy," I pressed. "At least, a more united Italy. If the Papal States, Florence, Milan, Naples, and Venice all stood together, who would come against us?"

"You dream a lofty dream, my son," Father said, sipping his wine. "I will settle for bringing the Papal States firmly under the control of Rome once more."

I said nothing further on the subject, but the vision my words had conjured lingered behind my eyes. If the Italian peninsula were united, we would be a match for the great powers of Europe. No more would they seek to divide us, conquer us, use us as bargaining chips for their own power or pleasure.

If I had the right army, I could do it. Through military force and political negotiations and cunning, I could bring together the biggest powers of the peninsula. I could be another Giulio Cesare and become worthy of my name.

I was so lost in this most potent of daydreams that I barely noticed my father had started to speak again. "Do you not want to know who I am considering for your brother's bride?"

I blinked, pulling myself back into the present and the matter at hand. I had, I realized, lost my chance to share my vision with him. There will be other chances, I consoled myself. "Who is the fortunate lady?" I asked.

"One Sancia of Aragon, natural daughter of Alfonso, the crown prince," Father said.

A bastard, then, just as Jofre was. As we all were. Still, such a marriage for a younger son was not without its advantages. She was, after all, the granddaughter of King Ferrante, the current ruler. "I recognize the name, but cannot call to mind much of anything about the lady," I admitted. "What do we know of her?"

"Her mother is Alfonso's favorite mistress, and much in favor at court," Father said. "Sancia has an elder brother, also Alfonso, in addition to her half siblings by her father's wife. Sancia is apparently much beloved of King Ferrante—as much as that man can love anyone, I expect. He offered her for Juan, which was not possible, but I am thinking we might still be able to accept his proposal for Jofre. Old Ferrante and his son will no doubt be overjoyed to have any tie to the Vatican in these uncertain times."

"Let us hope she is not as bloodthirsty as her grandsire, at least," I quipped, only half joking. King Ferrante was notoriously ruthless, quashing any hint of rebellion or trouble in his kingdom with an iron first. Rumor had it that he kept what he called a museum, containing the preserved bodies of enemies whom he had killed. Everything I had heard led me to believe the rumor was quite true.

The pope chuckled and crossed himself. "God forbid," he said. "But by all accounts she is a very spirited lady, and quite beautiful, in that dark, Aragonese sort of way."

"Hopefully Jofre can handle her."

"She may be a bit much for him," Father conceded, "but no doubt as he grows into a man Jofre shall learn to tame her. Indeed, it may be that he needs a woman like her to make him a man."

Jofre, as the youngest, had long been coddled by our mother and mostly ignored by our father as he tended to the needs—and uses—of his eldest children. But Jofre's childhood was over and he, too, must take up the mantle of duty for the Borgia family.

"It seems a fine match," I said aloud. "It shall serve the needs of the family quite well, and I'm sure Jofre will not object to a beautiful wife."

"I believe you are correct on both counts," Father said, and we tapped our wineglasses together in accord.

Chapter 16

MADDALENA

As had become our custom, Isabella promised to make my excuses and attend to Madonna Lucrezia should she call for me. She gave me a lusty wink as I left. "Off to see that handsome footman, I'll warrant," Isabella said. "Don't hurry back, and *don't* behave yourself."

I blushed at her words but could not help a wide smile all the same. "*Grazie,* Isabella," I said, slipping out the back door and into the late summer twilight.

The first time I had gone walking with Federico after my lustful dream had been a bit awkward; I couldn't quite meet his eye. Yet he engaged me in conversation as usual, making me laugh as only he could, and my embarrassment soon left. I had confessed my sin of lust—not to Federico, of course—and was given a week of eating only bread and water as penance. I obeyed gladly.

Our meeting had been hastily arranged, via a message from Federico saying that he had something he urgently wished to tell me. As such, I walked swiftly to the market, but not without some trepidation. Federico's note had said to meet him at the stall where we usually shared a meal of bread and cheese. I had treated myself to a slice of beef last time we'd met, what with the increase in my wages that Lucrezia had given me for my embroidery work. My stomach growled at the memory.

My footsteps quickened when I saw Federico, and a smile spread across my face. Yet when he turned and saw me approaching, his face remained solemn.

"Federico," I said, smile fading as I neared him. "I . . . I am glad to see you. You do not look as if you are glad to see me, though."

He sighed, running a hand through his sandy hair. "I am thrilled to see you, *bella* Maddalena, as always," he said. "It is just . . ."

When he did not finish, I pressed him. "What is wrong?" I asked. Fear clutched at my heart.

He did not answer immediately. "Do you mind waiting a bit for our supper?" he asked. "Will you walk with me first? Perhaps share a glass of wine with me?"

"Of course," I said, puzzled but no less alarmed. I relaxed only slightly when he offered me his arm as always. I took it, and we made our way through the throngs and out of the market. We strolled along the edge of a grassy field, where a few cows grazed—I still marveled that even within the Eternal City, there were such patches of countryside. But perhaps it was no wonder, when one considered the disrepair into which the city had fallen since the days of the mighty Roman empire, most especially when the popes had removed to Avignon. Only of late was Rome returning to its former glory, with the popes undertaking building projects and encouraging the cardinals and other wealthy citizens to do the same.

"Whatever is the matter, Federico?" I asked, when he still did not speak.

"I have had some bad news from home," he said at last.

"What news? Your parents?"

"My elder brother, Samuele," he said heavily. "He is dead."

I gasped, pressing my free hand to my mouth. "Oh, Federico," I said. I crossed myself. "May he rest in peace, and may God have mercy upon him. I shall light a candle for him and pray for his soul."

Federico smiled—a genuine, if wan, smile. "You are the sweetest and best of women, Maddalena," he said. "I thank you for your prayers and condolences. Samuele was a good man, and I have no doubt he rests with our Lord Jesus."

"Surely he does," I said, though I had never met the man. Federico said that he was a fine man; that was enough for me.

By then, we had reached a wine shop we had visited before, as a friend of Federico's owned it. Soon enough we had two glasses of a fine red, with the proprietor waving away payment and showing us to a table by the window.

"Did some misfortune befall him?" I asked, when Federico did not continue. "Your brother?"

He shook his head. "A fever," he said. "Though I suppose that is misfortune enough. Why an illness should take him, young and strong as he was, I do not know. That is only for God to say."

He took another swig of his wine and stared through the window, his eyes vacant.

I laid a hand on his arm. "I am truly sorry, Federico. Is there anything I can do? To help ease your sorrow?"

He looked over at me and seemed to come back to himself. "In truth, there was something I wanted to ask you. You see, while I shall miss my brother very much, I have another cause for sorrow at his death, though it seems selfish to speak it aloud."

"You can tell me," I said. "I shall not judge you. Only God in his wisdom can do so."

"I can only hope God does not find me wanting." He took another long swig of wine. "My brother and I are the only sons of our family. Thus my father has summoned me home, so I might learn the vineyard business. My sister's husband has no desire to take over, and Father would rather leave it to his own son in any case."

My heart seized at this. "You . . . you are leaving Rome?" I whispered.

He turned sorrowful eyes on me. "Eventually, yes. My father said I might stay on a bit longer if I choose, but within a year or two I must return home and stay there."

Silently I bowed my head, trying to blink back the tears that had formed in my eyes. Federico's sorrow for the loss of his brother was far greater than my own, yet I could not help but be sad at the thought I would soon never see him again. His companionship—and his letters and sweet compliments and bright smiles—had made my life all the better. My days would be dimmer without him.

"Running a vineyard is not the life I envisioned, as you know," he went on. "I wanted an adventure, to see as much of Italy as I could. To work in Rome for a bit, then move on somewhere else, and somewhere else after that. Yet that is not to be. I must not abandon my family, nor turn my back on what they expect of me."

"I am sorry, Federico," I murmured. "So often our lives do not go the way that we wish. I certainly understand that." I thought of my unhappy marriage, and of Madonna Lucrezia's and how it had disappointed her, and the hopes she had had.

"Yet it need not be all bad. You see, I have a hope of something that may make my life in the country more palatable. Even pleasurable."

"Oh?" I asked. "And what is that?"

He set his now-empty wine cup down on the table and took my hand in his. "I cannot help but hope you would consent to become my wife," he said softly, his eyes warm with hope and tenderness as they gazed into mine. "And that when I leave Rome, you will come with me. With you by my side, I think any life shall be a paradise."

I was struck speechless by his proposal. I had anticipated it, but now that it had come, I did not know what to say.

I should give no answer but yes, I knew that. But was I really eager to enter into another marriage, even with so kind and good a man as Federico? Did I want to marry again? When I finally had a measure of independence, a life to call my own?

As though reading my thoughts, Federico went on. "You have not spoken much of your marriage, or your late husband, but I have gleaned the marriage was not a happy one, nor was it of your choice. I understand any hesitation you might have. But in this, you do have a choice, dearest Maddalena. And I would be most honored if you would choose me as your husband."

I had to say something. "Federico, I . . ."

He hurried on, as if afraid I was about to refuse. "I am not a man of great wealth and never will be, but you would be mistress of a farm and vineyard. You would never need to serve anyone else ever again. You could devote more time to your embroidery, which I know you enjoy, for your own pleasure. And no one in my family has ever gone hungry."

I could picture it all. I could. I would run Federico's household, see to the making of cheese and bread, and oversee the storage of meat for the winter. He would take charge of the vineyard, the planting, the winemaking, the purchase and slaughter of livestock. Our days would be quiet and simple. Maybe eventually there would be children to care for, though I had never conceived with Ernesto. And our nights . . .

Our nights would be spent in our marriage bed, where he could exert his husbandly privilege whenever he wished. Where we might perhaps get those children, if God willed. The act would be so different with Federico than with Ernesto. Enjoyable. Warmth flooded between my legs, and I blushed. I had dreamed of that, had I not?

"You are quiet, Maddalena," Federico said anxiously, when I did not speak. "What say you?"

I shook my head slightly to clear it. I knew marriage to him would be so different from my marriage to Ernesto. And yet . . .

"I . . . I find I do not know what to say, Federico," I said at last. "You are right, my first marriage was not a pleasant one, and so I hope you understand why I hesitate."

"I do," he assured me. "I do. If you need time to think, I shall wait for you to come to a decision. Please know, I promise to treat you with naught but respect and love for all our days."

Love. It was the first time the word had passed his lips.

I remembered my dream anew, my desire for love and affection and even passion. Here was the opportunity for me to have those things, within a marriage blessed by God. Where else would I find that? With what better man than Federico?

I appreciated his willingness to give me time to think, yet what would be the point? My situation would not change. Nor his. I was not ready to leave Rome just yet, but there was no reason for me to not give him his answer.

"No need," I said. "I know my answer. Yes. Yes, Federico Lucci, I will marry you. I will be your wife."

He let out a shout of joy and leapt up from his seat, pulling me up and into his embrace. He was laughing as he began to dance me about the room. "Did you hear that?" he cried to the other patrons. "This beautiful woman is going to be my wife!" There were some whistles and shouts of congratulations as Federico picked me up and swung me about. Laughing, I implored him to put me down, which he eventually did. "We will not leave Rome just yet?" I asked, looking up at him.

"Not if you do not want to, my beauty," he said, still beaming. "I am inclined to stay on a bit myself before returning. We shall stay as long as you like. Although," he said with a heavy sigh, "that shall delay our wedding. My parents would never forgive us if we did not marry in our village church."

"I believe Scripture counsels patience at moments such as this," I teased.

"But did any of the writers of Scripture ever have so beautiful a woman in their arms?" he asked. With that, he cupped my face in his hands and bent his head to kiss me. It was a chaste enough kiss at first, but soon his tongue gently parted my lips and slid into my mouth. I returned the kiss as best I could, uncomfortably aware of the whistles from the other patrons. I tried to relax the stiffness of my body as his tongue wetly explored my mouth, but found I could not.

I tried to push away the quiet but insistent voice asking if perhaps I was making a mistake.

Chapter 17

CESARE

The negotiations for Jofre's marriage were swift ones. King Ferrante and Crown Prince Alfonso were most eager to gain a close connection to the pope, so they enthusiastically accepted the pope's terms and dowered Sancia richly. Mere weeks after Father had first raised the possibility of the match, Sancia and Jofre were married by proxy. Arrangements were made for Jofre to travel south to Naples, where the bride and groom would be married in person and be invested with their new titles by King Ferrante: they were to be Prince and Princess of Squillace.

"Do you think she will like me, brother?" Jofre asked me one night. I had gone to dine at our mother's house, where Jofre still lived for the time being. "I have heard she is very beautiful. Will she think me handsome enough?"

I felt a twinge in my chest at the earnestness in my little brother's eyes. Only twelve years old—thirteen by the time he met his bride in person—and he was concerned with pleasing a wife, who was three or so years older than he. Why can we not let children be children in this family? I asked myself angrily. Yet Father was only doing what needed to be done, for the good of the family. "I am not acquainted with the lady Sancia, and so I cannot speak to her beauty or character," I told Jofre, "but she has been raised a princess of the Neapolitan court. I am sure she is a true lady in all respects. You are growing into a fine and handsome young man, Jofre. I am certain she shall be nothing but pleased when she sees you."

He smiled at me, looking not yet a young man. "You are always right, Cesare. I am sure you shall be this time as well."

He was much more certain of my words than I. For Jofre's sake, I wanted to be right.

"Your Excellency. A word, if I might."

I turned to see Ascanio Sforza coming toward me in the hallway, where I was returning from a meeting with the Neapolitan ambassador about Jofre's journey to Naples. The pope was entrusting me with many of the details, a fact in which I took great pride.

"Cardinal Sforza. How may I be of assistance?" I asked.

He began to walk slowly alongside me. I matched my pace to his, curious as to what business the Vice-Chancellor of the Curia had with me. "I wonder if you might give me a bit of insight into His Holiness's mind," Cardinal Sforza began.

"I? It was my understanding that you and he work most closely together, Cardinal Sforza," I said, more than a little smug.

"That we do," he replied, smiling what he no doubt hoped was a winning smile. "Yet it is plain no one knows his mind quite like you do. Close as he and I have become over the years, they say he trusts no one so much as yourself."

"I suppose," I said, with mock humility. "And what is it you would seek to know? Of course I shall assist such a loyal servant of His Holiness as you in any way I can."

"I appreciate that. I wonder if you might reassure me on a certain point."

"If it is in my power to do so, I shall."

"Indeed. It is my hope that His Holiness remains well disposed toward my native city of Milan, and toward my brother Ludovico as its ruler."

I stopped walking, turning to Cardinal Sforza in mock confusion. "Can there be any doubt, Your Eminence? Especially when your cousin remains married to my sister?" I emphasized the word *remains* ever so slightly and left off the words *for now.*

"I do not think so, no," Cardinal Sforza hurriedly assured me. "I seek merely to assure my brother, you see. He was a bit . . . troubled at the departure of the Duke of Gandia for Spain, and was further distressed by the news of your younger brother's marriage to a Neapolitan princess."

I shrugged. "Sancia of Aragon is only Prince Alfonso's natural daughter, not a legitimate one," I pointed out casually. "She is no nearer the throne of Naples than you or I. It is a fine match for a boy such as Jofre."

"Yes, of course. It just seems the pope is aligning himself very firmly with the current ruling family of Naples, and therefore with Spain."

"Indeed he is," I agreed. "And can you blame him, being from the Iberian Peninsula as he is? I'm certain you know he helped broker the marriage between Their Most Catholic Majesties as well."

"A brilliant piece of statecraft, such as only His Holiness could accomplish," he said. "And of course he is and shall remain most sympathetic toward his native land; that is only to be expected. But is it not—"

"If I recall, you supported Jofre's marriage to Sancia of Aragon in consistory," I said. Not being a cardinal, I had not been present, but I had heard about it. "Why did you not voice your doubts to His Holiness then?"

"I . . . ah. Well. As Your Excellency is so well informed, you no doubt know Cardinal della Rovere voiced very strenuous opposition to the match. I felt His Holiness would benefit from my support."

"Ah." I let the syllable hang there between us. "So you were not completely honest with His Holiness?"

"No, no, that is not the case at all. You mistake my meaning, I fear. I agree it is a fine match for your brother. I do certainly feel that way. What I would like to know, if you would be so good as to assure me, is that His Holiness is still well disposed toward Milan and views my brother Ludovico as a staunch ally among his many allies throughout Christendom. And if you could remind His Holiness of Milan's desire to be viewed as such . . ."

Oh, I was enjoying this immensely. "His Holiness is as well disposed toward Milan as Milan is toward His Holiness and the interests of the Holy See," I said. "Now, if you would excuse me, Your Eminence, I have promised to luncheon with my sister, Lucrezia, and it would not do to keep that excellent lady waiting. I bid you good day."

With that, I bowed to Cardinal Sforza and continued on my way. I did not look back, but knew he was likely staring after me with a mixture of anger and worry.

Chapter 18

MADDALENA

I assisted in serving lunch to Madonna Lucrezia and her brother, the Archbishop of Valencia. As ever, they were happy to be in each other's company, and it made me glad to see their obvious, easy affection. Some things in the world could still be simple. Being in their presence was the first time I had felt my confused, muddled thoughts of Federico quiet and recede in my mind.

Unfortunately, these thoughts were replaced by flashes of that damnable dream. Cesare Borgia above me . . . his eyes looking down into mine as he . . .

Stop it, Maddalena, I scolded, lowering my gaze in the hopes of hiding my reddening cheeks. I did not want another week of only bread and water as penance, now, did I?

If I must think such lustful thoughts, they should be of Federico. He would soon be my husband, and any such imaginings would be easily forgiven.

Yet my eyes continually strayed to the archbishop whenever I thought he would not notice. He was impossibly handsome, and so kind and loving toward his sister. A fine man indeed, as I had been so bold to tell him once.

At one point I stole a glance at him, only to find him already looking back at me, seeming to study me. I blushed as our eyes locked, and he gave me a warm smile and a nod. I quickly looked away, embarrassed to have been caught but elated that he had been looking at me.

After the meal, I removed the dishes and assisted with their washing as Madonna Lucrezia and her brother adjourned to another room to continue their conversation. Once everything in the kitchen was back in order, I made my way upstairs to continue my mending tasks for that day. As I approached the sitting room where I usually worked, I came upon the archbishop leaving that very room. I curtsied, eyes cast down as I murmured, "Your Excellency."

I expected him to merely pass me by, but instead he stopped before me. "Rise, *per favore*," he said. "I was coming to find you, Maddalena."

My heart began to pound inordinately fast. "You . . . you were?"

"Indeed. I've a . . . rather delicate question to ask. Please walk with me, if you would. I would not want my sister to overhear."

My breath caught in my throat as I followed him. What delicate matter could the Archbishop of Valencia have to discuss with the likes of me?

I knew well what wealthy and powerful men—even churchmen—often asked of their female servants, but His Excellency did not seem the type. Yet what other "delicate matter" could he possibly have in mind? My heart pounded even faster, and though I tried to tell myself it was with fear, it did not feel true.

He paused within the entryway of the palazzo and glanced quickly about. "I shall not keep you from your duties long," he said. "I hoped you might answer a question for me. It may be you do not know the answer, in which case I beg you to simply be truthful."

Perhaps my initial guess had been wrong. "I shall assist however I can, Your Excellency."

"Good." He lowered his voice and stepped closer. I shivered slightly at his nearness. "I would know whether or not Giovanni Sforza has consummated his marriage to my sister."

I sagged at his words and told myself it was from relief and not disappointment. "He has not, Your Excellency, though I do not know why," I said. "It has been a source of great distress to Madonna Lucrezia."

The archbishop closed his eyes briefly in relief. "Good. That is what I had hoped to hear."

Suddenly I remembered my previous puzzled reasoning: a marriage can be easily put aside if it was never consummated. Oh, dear. It seemed that was indeed what the archbishop—and by extension, surely, His Holiness—had planned for my mistress. How I wished I did not know!

"Say nothing to Lucrezia of this," the archbishop advised me. "I do thank you profusely for your information." He slipped a gold coin into my hand.

Even as I slid the coin into the pocket of my apron, the words were out of my mouth before I could stop them. "I thank you for your generosity, Your Excellency. But Madonna Lucrezia puts her trust in me, and in future I would not wish to jeopardize that trust by spying on her and her affairs for anyone. Not," I added boldly, "even her own brother."

He paused and scrutinized me, his gaze impassable. I met his gaze evenly, but inwardly I was already regretting my words. Surely I would be dismissed, and Federico and I would leave Rome forthwith.

But I owed Lucrezia Borgia a great deal, and grand lady or no, pope's daughter or no, she was entitled to keep private her personal business.

Yet I was surprised to see a wide grin spread over the archbishop's face. He chuckled, shaking his head. "I admire your loyalty, Maddalena," he said. "I was right to send you to serve my sister, and she is well served by you indeed." He donned his bishop's cap and nodded to me. "I shall take your wishes into account in the future, as much as I am able. And I thank you for your service, both to Lucrezia and to me."

With that, he turned and left, and I could only gape after him, marveling at my good fortune and at the odd mixture of relief and regret roiling in my belly.

I tried to put the Archbishop of Valencia from my mind after that. I found the reaction I had to his presence disturbing, and it would do no good to dwell on it. I did not want to have to confess any more sinful dreams. Once had been embarrassing enough.

Yet when I succeeded in banishing Cesare Borgia from my mind, my thoughts returned to Federico—a proper topic, as he was my betrothed. But I found such thoughts no less troubling, for reasons I could not quite identify. So I focused on my embroidery, began stealing even more time to work on it—new handkerchiefs, even a fine set of sleeves for myself. I'd work late into the night, dreading the moment I would lay down to sleep and all my confusion and uncertainty would come rushing back. Even this made me feel guilty. Should I not meet these disquietudes head on, push through them, and emerge to the other side, at peace with my decision?

Was there any way through this thicket of doubt?

Federico and I continued to meet as often as our respective duties permitted. I still enjoyed his company, found him charming and amusing and handsome. Yet I found myself wishing I had accepted his offer for time to consider his proposal. Why had I been so hasty?

I knew deep down there was no reason to say no. I cared for Federico, and he for me. Marriage was a most desirable state according to the Church, especially for a woman. Upon my marriage to Ernesto, Uncle Cristiano told me, *Matrimony is a holy state, Maddalena, and the one that God wishes for his flock.* I knew this to be true. I also knew the marriage bed was the one place I could satisfy my desires without sin.

And yet.

Chapter 19

CESARE

Rome, September 1493

The two papal bulls sat on the table in front of me. I let my eyes listlessly wander over the Latin text, though I knew what they said. I'd always known this day was coming, had known it since my father was elected pope—since before then. This was what he had always wanted for me, and he was only a step away from making it so.

The first bull declared me the legitimate son of Vannozza dei Cattanei and Domenico da Rignano, my mother's husband at the time I was born—a necessary fiction for me to be made a cardinal. Illegitimate sons are not eligible to receive a red hat.

The second bull, to be issued in secret but no less official, countered the first one, naming me the son of Rodrigo Borgia and Vannozza dei Cattanei. My father, proud man that he was, could not bear the thought of issuing a proclamation that I was not his son without correcting it, even if no one would know the latter had been issued and everyone knew the former for the falsehood it was.

Foolish, really—could not a man such as my father see that the means are irrelevant if the end is in sight? But apparently, in this, he did not. It was all done, and in consistory a few days hence he would name me a cardinal, along with several other men who would be beholden to him for their investiture and therefore keep Borgia interests close to their hearts.

I could feel my father beaming across the table from me. "Soon it shall be done," he said. "You are staring your future full in the face, Cesare. How does it feel? Does it not feel glorious?"

Slowly I raised my head and looked at him. I had fought a long, raging, anguished battle with myself over what I was going to say at this meeting, ever since he had told me last week that the bulls were being drawn up. I did not want to enrage him or alienate him when he was finally beginning to fully trust in and rely on me. Yet this was my last chance, futile though it might be, to convince him he was wrong, that this was not what was best for me or for our family. All too soon there would be no going back.

"It does not feel glorious," I said slowly. "It cannot, when I am on a path contrary to the one in my heart."

Instantly Father's good humor vanished. His face set like one of the marble statues in the basilica. "What is in your heart is of no use to me, nor to this family," he said coldly. "It is what is in your mind that will serve us, and what I intend to make use of within the Curia."

"Do you not think a mind is needed to serve us on the battlefield? To create strategy and tactics and to run an army?" I demanded. I laughed shortly. "You must not think so, if your hopes for a general are pinned on Juan."

Father slammed his hand down on the table, and though I was startled I remained still, staring back at him impassively.

"We have been over this again and again since you were a boy, Cesare," he growled. "And you are still a boy, clearly. Which is why I make the decisions for this family, and you obey, as a good son should."

"Do you not see that I am not suited for a cleric's life?" I asked, raising my arms as if to draw his attention to my purple robes. "My strengths do not reside in quill and parchment and whispered negotiations in back hallways. I—"

"You speak as if I mean to make you a parish priest, burying plague victims and hearing villagers' confessions," he spat. "I am placing you on a path to power, to true power, to the most respected power in Europe."

"Is Rome really so?" I shot back. "How can we be without an army? If Charles of France decides to come, he can lay waste to all of Italy with his troops and weaponry, let alone Rome. True power is won at the point of a sword—"

"You speak like a foolish child," he said, derision dripping from every syllable. "Like a boy who knows nothing of the world, nor of how battles are really won. You will learn. I will teach you, and despite your fantasies of becoming the next Giulio Cesare, someday you will be the third Borgia pope. My uncle Pope Calixtus III made me a cardinal, and I as a pope do the same for you. Someday you will sit on St. Peter's Throne, and make a son or nephew a cardinal. And so it shall go on throughout history, and the Borgia family will have our own dynasty within the Church."

"But my talents would—"

"Your talents are much the same as mine, for the politics and negotiations you show so much disdain for," he snapped. "I need you here. This is where you will be of most use to me."

"It seems you do not know my true talents," I said. "And why should that surprise me, when you insist on seeing myriad talents in Juan when he possesses none."

"If you were still a child I would send you to your nursemaid to be thrashed," he snapped. "I've half a mind to do it myself. You'll not speak ill of your brother, and you will not forget that it is I who sits on St. Peter's throne."

Silence. My face burned with shame and anger at his words, at his condescension. I would always be naught but a boy to him, someone to be lectured and taught the error of his ways. He claimed to value my counsel, but when it most mattered—when it most mattered to me—he would not hear it.

"Do I get no say in my own future?" I asked at last, my voice soft.

"No." The single word was low and terse. "You will do what is best for your family, as we all do. As I did, when I went into the Church, and when my uncle made me a cardinal. And you will come to see in time that I was right."

There was so much more I wanted to say, but all of it was ill-advised. Instead I turned and left his chambers without another word or waiting for him to give me leave. He did not call me back.

On September 20, my elevation was put to a vote in consistory. And thus—over the loud objections of Giuliano della Rovere—I would be a cardinal.

"Credo in unum Deum, Patrem omnipotentem."

I spoke the words softly—almost as softly as I was able—in unison with the men on either side of me, all of us dressed in new crimson robes, our heads bare. We knelt before the altar of St. Peter's Basilica, reciting the Creed and professing our faith in God the Father, the Son, and the Holy Ghost. I kept my eyes cast down in a show of piety so no one would see the misery on my face.

When the prayer ended, we rose, and I caught sight of my father, seated on the papal throne and wearing the immense papal tiara. Tears of pride had sprung in his eyes. The ugly words we had exchanged a month ago had been forgotten, by him, at least. But he could afford to forgive me. He was getting what he wanted.

Eventually I would silence this voice within me that screamed for a different fate. I would become resigned to this life, this life of quietly wielding power. I would come to revel in it. I would perhaps even come to love it.

But that day had not come yet, and I both yearned for and dreaded it.

We recited the oath of obedience to Pope Alexander VI and his successors, and then, one by one, each man stepped forward and had his biretta—the three-cornered red hat—placed upon his head by the Holy Father.

I was somewhere in the middle, no doubt to draw the least amount of attention to the fact that Pope Alexander's eighteen-year-old son was being made a cardinal. I stepped forward and knelt, and the hat was placed on my head. When I rose, I was a cardinal.

I met my father's eyes. They had gone cold, calculating. Pride was there still, but also a determination to finally wield this weapon that he had forged in ways only he could know.

I stepped back into my place in line, now Cardinal Borgia, and kept my eyes locked on his until the next man stepped forward and his attention shifted.

I would forge my own weapons, whatever weapons I could. And by God and the devil, I would learn to wield them.

PART TWO

ANGELS *of the* APOCALYPSE

Romagna and Rome, July 1494–July 1495

Chapter 20

CESARE

Vicovaro, July 1494

King Charles was coming. And far too few in Italy were inclined to try to stop him. And, unfortunately, the ones who *were* so inclined seemed to be underestimating the threat facing us.

"And Your Highness thinks this plan will work?" I asked the King of Naples, not bothering to hide my skepticism.

I could feel my father's disapproving glance from where he sat beside me, at the head of the table. Across from me, King Alfonso of Naples merely stared at me, his upper lip curling in displeasure. He had taken the crown a few months earlier, upon the ill-timed death of his father Ferrante—the scourge of popes, even at the end—and this, coupled with Ludovico Sforza's enthusiastic invitation, finally prompted King Charles of France to announce his invasion of Italy.

"Does Your Eminence have a better idea?" Virginio Orsini asked from beside the king.

I exhaled slowly, thinking carefully before I spoke. Despite my years of study of military history and strategy, and of the geography of the Italian peninsula, I could not hold a candle to the tested battle experience of Virginio Orsini, one of the most noted of the many condottieri on the Italian peninsula, who currently had a condotta to serve under King Alfonso as general-in-chief of the army of

Naples. I had to tread carefully here; we needed to keep him on our side, and yet I was determined to have my say. I had something of value to contribute, and wanted these men to know it.

"I certainly understand His Serene Highness's desire to keep the bulk of the Neapolitan forces around the city of Naples," I said, nodding to King Alfonso. "It is the obvious choice, given that the kingdom and more specifically its capital is the French king's aim. Yet why wait until they get that far? Have Prince Ferrantino," I went on, referring to Alfonso's eldest son and heir to the throne, who was to command the Neapolitan forces, "bring his troops into the northernmost part of the Romagna to see if they can halt the French advance before ever nearing Naples. His force should be able to close the Apennine pass to the French."

Silence fell as my proposal was considered.

"And," I added, "this strategy has the added benefit of being near enough to Milan's territory that Ludovico Sforza should feel sufficiently threatened, which is all to the good."

The silence continued until Virginio Orsini finally spoke. "His Eminence is right," he said. "This makes more sense. And then Prince Ferrantino will be near in case Prince Federigo needs aid in his assault on Genoa."

This last piece was key; King Alfonso's brother Prince Federigo would need to take and hold the port city of Genoa on the west coast to ensure the French could not access it to resupply and reinforce their army.

Virginio looked from the pope to King Alfonso. "I am in accord, so long as Your Holiness and Your Highness are as well."

King Alfonso nodded, and his face relaxed somewhat—I had yet to see him smile, and he did not seem like the sort of man who did so often, if at all. "I shall keep a guard around the city, of course," he said, "but I agree that Cardinal Borgia's plan is sound. If we can stop the French farther from my kingdom, all the better."

My father's eyes rested on me, and I basked in the approval I saw there. "We concur. Cardinal Borgia proves most sound in his judgments."

"When shall we deploy?" Virginio asked.

"As soon as possible," I said, before my father could speak. "Charles announced his intention to invade four months ago. He could be crossing the Alps as we speak. We don't have any time to waste."

King Alfonso snorted. "We would know if he were that close," he said. "We will need more time to prepare."

"It is a large force we are mustering," Virginio said, looking to the pope. "We shall need time, as His Highness says, and I believe we have more than His Eminence suggests."

My father considered this carefully. "We are inclined to agree," he said at last. "But it is also true there is little time to spare. Let us be ready as soon as is possible."

The pope rose, and everyone else followed. "We have done all we can here, my lords," he continued. "Tomorrow let us return to our respective homes and begin our work."

The pope left the room, and I trailed after him, with King Alfonso not far behind. Virginio lingered in the large room, and I wondered if he was as low on optimism as I.

As the sun was setting later that evening, I found my father up on the ramparts of the Orsini stronghold in which we had gathered to meet. Forgoing the formality of a greeting, I asked, "And what is your assessment of what has been accomplished here today? Do you think we shall hold off the French invasion?"

"We shall prevail," Pope Alexander said without hesitation. "God is on our side, for our cause is righteous. Alfonso is Ferrante's son and heir—God rest his soul—and should by rights sit the throne of Naples. Our Lord sees this and shall give us victory."

"And what is the size of Our Lord's army?" I inquired. "If He would be so good as to let us know, we could refine our strategy, and sleep easier in the coming nights."

My father clucked his disapproval. "Blasphemy, Cesare."

I bit down on my tongue to keep from replying. Who could guess at what a pope who kept a mistress and made his son a cardinal might actually find blasphemous?

"The Lord will give us victory," he said again. "And our strategy is a good one, thanks in part to you," he went on. "Prince Ferrantino is a fine commander, and there is none better than Virginio Orsini. We've Florence on our side and shall send for Giovanni Sforza and his force from Pesaro as well. He shall meet Ferrantino's force in the northern Romagna and add to their numbers."

"Florence shall be of no help to us militarily," I said bluntly. "You know that."

"They can refuse Charles passage through their lands, should he take the route through Tuscany."

"And how will they stop him? When Charles does not turn around and take his army back to France after being asked politely, what shall that fool Piero de' Medici do?"

Father sighed. "I accept that Florence will likely not be able to halt them, but they are on our side politically at least, which is more than we can say for the rest of Italy." He closed his eyes briefly. "Would that Lorenzo de' Medici were still alive. I should dearly like to have his aid in this."

I nodded my agreement. The late Lorenzo, whom many called Il Magnifico, had been an unparalleled statesman. Had he been alive to help us, no doubt this situation would not seem quite so dire. Florence had long been friendly with France, but I doubted Lorenzo de' Medici would have desired for them to be meddling too closely in the affairs of Italy. His successor, his eldest son Piero, was by all accounts mismanaging the business of Florence, from his family's bank to the government. One of Lorenzo's younger sons was a cardinal now, and while he showed similar political savvy to his father, he was still young and untried, and too unknown in Florence—having been given to the Church at a young age—to make him a plausible rallying point for the people there.

In the years following Lorenzo's death, a preacher had risen to prominence in Florence, a Dominican friar by the name of Girolamo Savonarola. He railed against the excesses of the Medici family and, lately, of Holy Mother Church itself. Father had been keeping a close eye on the situation, and we'd received word that Savonarola's sermons throughout Lent this past year had been largely concerned with a scourge that was coming to Italy to sweep away all the corruption and make the peninsula pleasing to God once more. Some of his militaristic language strongly suggested he considered King Charles VIII of France to be this very scourge.

"That said, I might trade a living Lorenzo de' Medici for a Venice willing to involve herself rather than remain neutral," I said, somewhat bitterly. Venice had enough might—both financial and military—that had she declared herself opposed to Charles's coming invasion, he likely would have been given pause. But Venice kept herself above the conflict embroiling the Italian peninsula, as she always did unless there was something in it for her.

Once again I could not help but dream of a united Italy, one strong enough that foreign invaders could not pick her apart at will. If only all the petty princelings and lords could put aside their differences and join together. But they would never come to it on their own. They needed a strong leader to unite them, one as mighty as Giulio Cesare had been.

Father chuckled, bringing me back to our conversation. "Agreed."

We looked out over the vast countryside spread before the castle before he spoke again. "But you, Cesare," he said, turning to me. "What think you of our chances? You did well today," he added. "Your plan is a sound one, and has aided us greatly, I daresay."

I kept my smile of pride to myself. "I do not know as we can stop them," I said bluntly. "I do not think our entire force together—Naples, Orsini, and the few papal troops we have—is enough to repel them. Their numbers are greater, and I have heard of a new kind of siege gun they have, one that shoots iron instead of stone, and can easily be maneuvered and transported. If that is true, I do not know how any force in Italy can stand against them. And," I added, "we are starting too late. As I said, they could be nearer than we know. We may be too late to stop them."

Father frowned. "The odds are not good, but I do not think defeat is inevitable. You forget Giovanni Sforza's force in your tally. I will write to him as soon as we return to Rome, and he will bring his army directly."

I laughed outright. "Giovanni Sforza's force is hardly enough to tip the scale," I said. "Even if he brings it. He has no desire to find himself on the opposite side of a battlefield from his cousin Ludovico." And Ascanio, I thought silently. The Milanese snake. In consistory in March, when the pope announced he favored the claim of Alfonso of Naples after the death of King Ferrante, Ascanio had sided with his brother and come out in support of the French claim, showing his true colors at last. He had, however, spoken harshly against Giuliano della Rovere's push to form a council to depose Pope Alexander, and if anything could save him from the pope's wrath after this conflict was over—if we survived it—it would be this.

"He will bring it," Father said. "If he knows what's good for him."

"I really and truly do not think he does." At least he had gotten Lucrezia out of harm's way. In February he had finally insisted on taking her to Pesaro, and the pope, out of reasons to forbid it, had acquiesced. I had tried to stop it, sure the coming conflict would prove that Lucrezia's husband must be set aside, and in his own castle he would surely consummate the marriage—but I was, as was so often the case, overruled. I had suffered many a sleepless night of shame that I had not been able to keep my promise to her.

But with the French on their way, I was glad that Lucrezia was out of the way in Pesaro, a place of no interest to King Charles. Rome would soon become unsafe for us all, let alone a woman as young and precious as my sister.

I wondered, fleetingly, if she had taken pretty Maddalena with her. Since Lucrezia's departure I had sadly had no occasion to visit the Palazzo Santa Maria in Portico.

"And," Father went on, "you forget what is perhaps our best card to play, beyond armies and military strategy. Only the Pope of Rome can invest a man with the crown of Naples. Charles cannot afford to alienate and make an enemy of me. He must stay in my good graces."

"Giuliano della Rovere has a solution to that," I said darkly. "He means for Charles to depose you and make him pope, and he shall invest the French king with the crown."

"Della Rovere overreaches," Father said, irritated but not worried. "It is no small feat to depose a pope. Even a king would hesitate before doing so. I am God's chosen, remember."

He said these last words without a hint of irony, and I wondered if he had come to believe them; if he truly believed now that God had set him on St. Peter's throne rather than his own wealth and politics and political maneuvering.

Yet it did not matter. Nothing did. We might not even survive the next few months. "I do not think this will end well for us," I said, turning to go back into the castle. "And no matter what happens, it certainly will not end well for Italy."

Chapter 21

MADDALENA

Rome, September 1494

Palazzo Santa Maria in Portico was quiet without Madonna Lucrezia. The same crowds of visitors came to see Giulia Farnese, but the halls and rooms seemed emptier, somehow, less full of life.

I had been sorry to see her go, but thrilled at the joy and hope I saw in her eyes. Once they were away from Rome and her powerful family, perhaps this would be a new chance for her and her husband. "I wish I could take you with me to Pesaro, Maddalena," she'd said regretfully when she had told me she was leaving. "But my lord husband has said there are more than enough servants there, and so I am taking only a few of my ladies and my maid Pantasilea. You shall remain here and serve Adriana and Giulia. I am certain they have enough mending to keep you busy."

I had curtsied. "I am glad to keep my position, Madonna, but sorry to see you go."

She smiled at me. "You are too sweet, Maddalena! But never fear, we shall return to Rome often to see Father and Cesare, and perhaps even live here some months. I must arrange it all with my lord, of course."

And so she had ridden off one rainy February morning, bound for her husband's northern castle. No doubt she would find it very different from Rome, but I hoped she would like it.

I was still contemplating my return to country life. Federico had returned home not long after his proposal for his brother's burial, but had come back to Rome soon after, bringing me the greetings of his parents.

"They are delighted I have found a good woman to make my wife," he said as we went for a stroll one night, his eyes alight with joy and pride. "I spoke often of your beauty, your piety, your skill with a needle, and all the rest. They are very eager to meet you, Maddalena *mia*. You are welcome at my home at any time."

I had smiled, genuinely touched by the affection his parents had for me without ever having met me, but it only served to make me all the more guilty for my reluctance. "I am eager to meet them as well," I'd replied, "but we shall stay some time yet, *sì*? I am quite fond of Rome."

Federico had stopped and kissed me right there in the street. "Of course, we shall wait as long as you need," he said. "I am not ready to return home yet, either. We shall go when we are good and ready."

Yet it became quite apparent to me I would likely never be ready to leave Rome. And Federico was beginning to sense my reluctance. When Lucrezia had departed for Pesaro, he had assumed we could leave Rome soon, for I no longer had anything keeping me there. But I continued to put him off, saying Adriana and Giulia had more need of me than ever before now that some of the staff was gone. Federico had accepted this readily, but of late he was beginning to grow impatient.

"Donna Lucrezia has yet to return to Rome," he had said the night before. "I understand that you liked serving her. But she no longer lives here. What then is keeping you at Santa Maria in Portico? Surely Adriana de Mila and Giulia Farnese can find another maid."

"Surely they can," I agreed, "but I wish to save more money yet. I want to bring something to our marriage. I have no dowry, only what I can earn for myself." That much was true, if not the whole truth.

I spent hours in prayer in the chapel, begging God to give me clarity. Yet the only answer I received was Uncle Cristiano's words, reminding me that marriage was the state that God most desired for his flock.

It was clear what God wished for me to do. That much was most plain. So why did something in my heart rebel?

If I truly did not wish to marry Federico, I owed him the honesty of telling him so. Yet the thought of turning him away caused my heart to constrict painfully. I did not want to lose him; indeed, I could not imagine my life without his warm eyes and jokes and the way he was always interested in how I had spent my day. Who knew such a man could exist?

Then why was I not eager to marry him? Was it really only that I loved my life of independence? Or was it something more?

I found myself thinking of Uncle Cristiano's other words, how lust was the root of all sin. Was it my lust for independence, my pride in my own small accomplishments, that kept me from returning to marriage, as a good woman should? Perhaps. And so I prayed for forgiveness for that sin, prayed for it to be taken from my heart. But I remained as confused and conflicted as ever.

What do you want, Maddalena?

Yet dire news from up north had quelled thoughts of marriage and the future temporarily. Word had arrived just last week that the French army, led by King Charles VIII, had crossed the Alps and entered Italy.

No further news had come since—save the gossip of visitors and what we servants picked up in the streets—yet the ladies I served could discuss little else.

"How can you eat at a time like this?" Donna Adriana fretted, pacing about the room as Giulia helped herself to the plate of sweetmeats I'd served.

La Bella arched one of her perfect eyebrows. "Are we not to eat until the French have left the Italian peninsula, then?" she queried.

"Oh, you know that's not what I mean," Adriana said, finally sitting down beside Giulia. "I've had a letter from one of my cousins. They say the army Charles has brought with him is bigger than anything we've seen in years. Certainly in my lifetime."

This sent a chill through me. A bigger army than those possessed by the lords and princelings of Italy? Bigger than the armies that clashed throughout the countryside at each and every perceived slight, trampling anyone and anything that stood in their way?

"His Holiness has a plan and is confident," Giulia said sedately. "If his fighting men cannot do it, he will stop the French with the power of the Holy See."

"Rodrigo is the most intelligent and canny of men," Adriana said, her agitation plain in the way she slipped in referring to the Holy Father by his Christian name, rather than any of the proper addresses about which she was so careful. "If anyone can save us, it is he. But there is such opposition . . ."

The ladies continued on—if Giulia knew any details of the strategy of the papal-Neapolitan forces, she did not share them—but my mind strayed from their chatter while I mended in my nearby chair.

They were worried about their families, their politics, whether they would retain their prominence and power—and rightfully so, no doubt; had I any of those things, I would surely be frightened of losing them as well. Yet there were so many who stood to lose much more: their livelihoods, their homes, and their very lives.

When I was a girl of twelve or so, two of the neighboring lords had taken it into their heads to fight. No doubt over borders and land, as much of the conflict in the Romagna was. One of their armies had ridden through our village, and though the people there had no cause to meddle in the politics of lords, we were not spared. The soldiers stole food from storehouses—food that families had been counting on to see them through the winter—and torched the buildings and farms of any who dared resist. Any woman on the street, no matter her age, was raped, and any man who tried to intervene was cut down where they stood.

Mother and I had huddled within our cottage, united, for once, in our terror, unable to do more than simply pray that the ruffians would pass us by. Miraculously, they did, only stealing our one horse and the pig we had been about to slaughter for meat. It made for a lean winter, but we counted our blessings nothing worse had befallen us. Many of our neighbors were not so lucky.

And now people from the Alps to Naples lay in the path of this French king and his massive invading army. Were they any better or more merciful than the petty princelings of the Romagna? Surely a king conducted himself with more honor and saw to it his soldiers did as well.

But Rome had shown me that a man's station was not necessarily a guarantee of his character, much as the priests and nobles wanted to assure us it was otherwise. I wanted to believe the people in villages like mine would be safe, but I found I could not.

That night, after being dismissed, I went to the chapel and spent several hours in prayer. Not for myself this time—for in the coming conflict I was as safe as Adriana and Giulia were, which was likely as safe as anyone in Italy—but for the common people who were in the way of the armies that would meet in battle. If God did not watch over them, no one would.

Chapter 22

CESARE

Rome, November 1494

It was a good plan, the plan that we'd made at Vicovaro. Yet—as I'd known—we'd put it into action too late.

"He had one job, the fool!" Father snarled, tossing the letter to the floor. He whirled away from me and paced the floor. "Piero de' Medici had one task and he, worthless fool that he is, couldn't even do that. Oh, Lorenzo is rolling in his grave, make no mistake." He stalked to the window and peered out as though he expected the French to be at the gates of the Vatican. "All the idiotic boy had to do was block the roads into Tuscany—easy enough from a military standpoint—and he could not manage it."

I warned you thus was upon my tongue, fighting to be let out, but I held back. "Piero de' Medici is not much of a military strategist. Or much of a strategist about anything, for that matter."

If Father heard me, he paid no heed. "If he had accomplished this one minor thing, we would not have the French breathing down our necks, and our army scrambling to catch up."

"Charles surely knew we would put the bulk of the army in the Romagna, and he gambled that Florence would yield easily," I said. "A rather certain gamble, given the state of their army and the intelligence of their leader."

"Piero is paying for his sins, that much is certain," Father said, sitting heavily in a gold-painted chair. He waved at the letter, and I bent to pick it up. "Read it. The Florentines have risen up against him and driven the Medici from the city."

That I had not expected. "Lorenzo is indeed rolling in his grave," I said, scanning the rest of the letter. "And so the madman Savonarola rules in Florence now."

Father nodded grimly. "More or less. And if he thinks he shall last the year, he is more deluded than I thought. The Florentines shall miss the Medici before too long."

We had learned that Savonarola had met with Charles, in Genoa. He had hailed the French king as "an emblem of divine justice," who had "been sent by God to chastise the tyrants of Italy," and predicted total success for the king's endeavor. With much of the Florentine government and populace under the sway of such a man, we could expect no help from Florence.

I kept reading. "God's teeth," I swore. "Charles is declaring a crusade? He has proclaimed that his possession of the Kingdom of Naples is key to reclaiming the Holy Land?"

Father sighed impatiently. "Outrageous, of course. He thinks that declaring a crusade—of sorts—will force me to let him proceed. But he is wrong."

"And so?" I asked, folding the letter and handing it to him. He snatched it back, his irritation showing in the movement.

"We have already recalled the bulk of our forces back to Rome, to defend the city," Father said. "Giovanni Sforza, damn him, has not responded. I sent another letter last week, and still no word."

Sforza was never going to come. *Who could have predicted this?* I wanted to say sarcastically. Instead I simply asked, "But what do we do now?"

He turned to me with an expression I had never seen on his face: haunted, almost defeated. "Now we wait."

"But—"

"We wait," he repeated, as though he were trying to convince himself as much as me. "There is nothing else we can do."

Another message came two days later, this one from the French king himself. "Father," I said, arriving in his bedroom late that night, still dressed in my red robes and cap. He was alone, only a servant present to help him undress for bed. He waved the man away impatiently when I entered. "What is it, my son?" he asked.

I lifted the letter in my hand. I had intercepted the messenger, who had dared not defy a cardinal—being a prince of the Church did have some advantages—in order to bring the news to the pope myself. "Another message. This one from King Charles."

Father closed his eyes as though praying—and perhaps he was, for a moment later he crossed himself and opened his eyes. "Tell me what it says, Cesare," he said, sitting in a chair beside his bed.

I dropped my eyes to the Latin words on the page, though they had no doubt imprinted themselves in my mind. "Charles repeats his proclamation that he shall mount a crusade to reclaim the Holy Land, and to do so he needs control of the Kingdom of Naples. He demands that His Holiness, Pope Alexander VI, grant him free passage through the Papal States."

"No. We will do no such thing."

I admired his resolve even as I understood it was not wise. "The College of Cardinals will not like it," I warned reluctantly. "Nor will the people of Rome."

Father snorted. "The College of Cardinals, indeed. Half of them are traitors. Why, della Rovere rides with the French king, though why that surprises me I could not say."

He rose and began to pace. "As for the people of Rome . . ." He trailed off. "Their lives are in my hands," he said, more to himself than me. "We must pray I can keep them safe."

Touched by the genuine emotion in his voice, I nodded. "Indeed, Holy Father," I said. "I will pray for that very thing."

And I would. I would pray that the Holy Father could guide us all through, even though our army and weaponry were no match for the French; even though all of Italy wished to simply hand Naples over to the French and be done with it; even though the Colonna family had already raised the French flag over the fortress of Ostia at the mouth of the Tiber. I would pray for the Holy

Father to lead us through this, as he was the only one who cared to try.

And though I could not imagine how he could possibly best the French, I knew that if anyone could, it was Rodrigo Borgia.

A few days later, we got a sample of the forces ranged against us.

The pope received the envoys of the Duke of Ferrara, who had arrived some days ago and were clamoring for an audience. Apparently their master had some advice he wished to impart to the Holy Father. Duke Ercole was a seasoned old condottiere who thought much of himself and his whole noble d'Este family, so I had no doubt his advice would be as pompous and arrogant as possible.

Father received the envoys in his audience chamber, where I was present, as were a number of cardinals who had not (yet) fled the Holy City before the French advance. And, of course, Burchard.

I eyed the red-robed prelates where they were seated at the sides of the room, like a mass of birds waiting to see if the branch on which they sat would prove sturdy. Which of you shall prove loyal, in the end? I wondered savagely.

I stood to my father's right, watching impassively as the two men approached the papal throne, bowed, and kissed both the Fisherman's ring and the pope's slipper. "We greet you well, Your Excellencies," Father said, as jovial as ever. "I trust your journey from Ferrara was not too arduous, and that your accommodations here in the Vatican have been to your liking."

"Your Holiness's hospitality is second to none, as always," one of the men replied smoothly.

"However, the journey was not as relaxed as we might have liked," the other man spoke up. "These are troubled and dangerous times."

Father sighed heavily. "Indeed. No doubt this brings us to the matter you wish to discuss."

"We thank you profusely, Holy Father, for granting us this audience, and wish to extend the greetings of our most illustrious master Ercole d'Este, Duke of Ferrara," the first man went on. "It is indeed regarding the French invasion that he has sent us, that he may offer Your Holiness some counsel in these difficult times."

"Indeed." Father waved a hand lazily. "Well, let us hear it."

"Duke Ercole is most upset at the French king's presumption to the Italian peninsula," the first man began. "He has no desire to bow before a French king."

"Indeed?" I said aloud, causing both men to turn toward me in surprise. When the pope did not interject, I continued, noticing the slight look of irritation on both men's faces when they realized they must listen respectfully to the bastard son, the upstart cardinal. "If that is so, why does His Grace the duke not join his troops to ours, that we might successfully drive the French from Italy?"

"Quite right, Cardinal Borgia," Father said, turning back to the envoys. "Why does Duke Ercole not come to our aid? A man of his military renown and expertise would be of great assistance in this crisis."

"His Grace regrets that he cannot offer military aid, as much as he may want to," the first man said. "He has his own people and their interests to think of before his own."

"He has his Holy Father to think of as well," the pope reminded them.

An awkward silence fell. "Of course! There is no one dearer to Duke Ercole's heart than Your Holiness," the second man finally chimed in. "This is why he has sent us to tender his advice."

"Yes, yes. We are most eager to hear this advice."

"Duke Ercole knows that Your Holiness has troops assembled together with Virginio Orsini and with King Alfonso and his son, the crown prince," the second envoy went on. "He knows, too, that such a force—mighty as it is—likely cannot withstand or repel the French."

"Is that so?" Father said, a slight smile on his face. "We keep hearing of the wonders of this French army and their cannon, and yet we do not know as they have been truly tested yet. The north of Italy thus far has proven more than willing to lie on her back for these invaders."

Another heavy silence filled the room. The second man cleared his throat. "That is neither here nor there, Holiness," he said. "Duke Ercole would encourage you to save your sacred person and flee Rome."

"And what becomes of Rome then, Excellency? What becomes of our people?"

"Holiness, the Spanish house of Aragon is not an ally worth supporting," the second man went on. "They cannot withstand the French, who do have a claim on the throne of Naples, and there is no need for you—and the rest of Italy—to fall with the Aragonese. His Grace feels it is best if we let the French king have what he came for, in the hope of preserving as many lives and as much territory as we can. Soon enough he will go back to France, and—"

Father held up a hand, and the man broke off. "When we said, 'our people,' Your Excellency," Father said, "rest assured we meant the people of Rome. Not those of Spain or Spanish descent, which is how you seem to have taken my words."

"Apologies, Holiness, I only meant—"

"Mark my words, gentlemen," Father went on. "My first concern is only ever, first and foremost, for the security of the Italian peninsula. My thoughts and desires are quite aligned with your master's in that. I would sooner give up St. Peter's throne, and my very life, before I would bend the knee and become the creature of the King of France."

I felt a chill encompass my body at the power of these words, at the absolute conviction with which they were spoken. This time the silence that overcame the room was stunned. And the pope continued to speak, his voice ringing off the marble walls and floor of the audience chamber as he continued to drop the plural pronoun in favor of the singular. "I might be a Spaniard by birth, but Italy is my home now, and I love it no less for it not being the place of my birth. And God the Father and his Blessed Son together forbid that I should see the Italian peninsula in the hands of anyone but Italians, so long as I may live in His service." He paused, and the silence in the room remained absolute. "This is why we will not yield to the French king, Your Excellencies. We trust you can convey our feelings on this matter to His Grace Duke Ercole."

After a long pause, the first envoy raised his head. I saw a glimmer of moisture in his eyes. "Your Holiness speaks very powerfully," he said at last. "I understand completely and will be honored to report your words and feelings to His Grace."

"See that you do," Father replied. "We would have His Grace understand our position with perfect clarity."

"We will see to it," the second man said. They bowed before the papal throne before backing out of the room, the audience at an end.

I leaned closer to my father as the gathered cardinals turned to one another and began murmuring. "Impressive, Father," I said softly. "I wonder what King Charles will make of such words, should he hear of them."

He glanced at me impassively. "He may make whatever he likes of them," he said. "They are true."

Chapter 23

MADDALENA

Rome, December 1494

Palazzo Santa Maria in Portico was in an uproar. The French were approaching the Holy City, and we had just received word from the pope that Adriana and Giulia were to pack up their valuables and move into the Castel Sant' Angelo with their household for their protection. Servants were scrambling about, making sure the ladies' trunks were packed and all their fine clothing and jewelry accounted for. The stewards were seeing to the transport of the more expensive furnishings and artwork, so we maids did not need to worry about that; yet it still contributed to the chaotic scene as furniture was moved about while we were trying to locate personal effects and take trunks downstairs for transport.

It took us three days to pack and send everything off. All that was left were the beds we were sleeping in and clothes to put on the next day. First thing in the morning, we would move into the Castel, the massive, squat, round fortress that loomed over the Tiber.

That day, before we were to depart, I prepared to slip out. "I am going out for a bit," I whispered to Isabella as we passed in the kitchen. "Everything is about done here, but if I am missed, make some excuse for me, I pray you."

She nodded quickly. "Off to see your man?" she asked, a slight smile curling her lips.

"Yes," I said. "I must tell him where I will be."

"Surely he knows. Surely all of Rome has heard by now, what with all the racket in here."

"No doubt, but I must tell him myself." And convince him to come if I could. My entire body rebelled at the thought of entering the mighty stone walls of the Castel Sant' Angelo without Federico, him alone and vulnerable as the French army bore down.

I left and moved quickly through the streets, filled with people going about their business, as usual. The anxiety in the streets was nearly palpable. The people of Rome knew what was coming for us. And yet families still had to be fed, clothes mended, work done, wages earned. Adriana and Giulia and the pope himself could hide away from it behind fortress walls, but the people out here could not.

God watch over them, I prayed as I pushed through the throngs toward the Vatican, still full of guilt that I could hide away in the safest place in the city. Not that my own fate in this was certain. Anything could happen. And when powerful men took it into their heads to claim what was not theirs, anything did.

God watch over us all.

I slipped into the courtyard of the Vatican Palace and made directly for the stables. If Federico was not there already, someone would know where to find him. The low wooden building was a hive of activity, not unlike Santa Maria in Portico in the last few days. Horses were being fed, brushed, outfitted in their tack, and led outside. I peered into each stall in search of Federico, trying to remain unobtrusive, though a few stable hands whistled at me as I passed. I did my best to ignore them, but their regard made me nervous. If I did not find Federico very soon, I would need to leave.

Then I spotted him, heading into a stall. "Federico!" I called, just as he ducked out of sight.

He stepped back at the sound of my voice, a surprised expression on his face. "Maddalena?" he asked. He came toward me, wiping dirty hands on his breeches. "What are you doing here? You shouldn't have come by yourself—"

"I had to see you," I said. "I had to talk to you. I—"

"Come outside," he interrupted, taking my arm and steering me outdoors and to the back of the building, where it was quiet. When we were alone, he asked. "What is it? Not that I am not glad to see you, but it will be dark soon, and—"

"I came as soon as I could get away," I cut him off. "You must have heard—Adriana and Giulia's household is moving into the Castel Sant' Angelo."

"I heard," he said. "They are taking all their servants, yes?"

"Yes. I—"

"Then you will be safe."

"Yes," I said. "As safe as anyone can be with an invading army bearing down."

He smiled, placing his hands on my shoulders. "I shall thank God for that tonight. One small blessing, at least."

He looked as though he was about to kiss me, but I leaned back slightly. "Federico," I said urgently. "You must come with me."

He laughed. "What? How?"

"Come to the Castel Sant' Angelo with me. Slip inside when the rest of us are entering. Everyone will think you are another groom or steward or guard or what have you. There will be so much commotion, no one will think twice."

"With you and all the women of the household?"

"There will be men there as well," I said. "For goodness' sake, there are soldiers stationed at the Castel. No one will even notice you are there."

He drew back. "I cannot, Maddalena. I am needed here."

"Surely you will not be missed—"

"We are taking some of the horses to one of the papal houses in the countryside, to hopefully hide them from the French," he said. "I am needed here."

I grasped his arms in desperation. "Federico, I cannot wait safe inside a fortress and wonder what has become of you outside!"

"The French aren't going to raze the Holy City. Even I know that the French king needs to remain in the good graces of the pope."

"You don't know that. You don't know that they won't."

"If we had left Rome when I wanted to leave, we would be away in the countryside right now! Together!" he exploded suddenly.

It was as if he had driven a knife right through the chink in my armor. The only reason we were still in Rome was because I had insisted we stay; he was right. "I . . . I didn't . . ."

He sighed, immediately contrite, and pulled me into his arms. "Forgive me, Maddalena. I did not mean that."

"Didn't you?" I asked, my voice muffled against his chest.

"Not really, no. In truth we may well be safer here in Rome, close to the Holy Father, than out in the countryside where there is no one to stop the French soldiers from taking whatever they want." He drew away slightly to look upon my face. "And you will be safe in an impregnable fortress. That is what is important."

"I do not want to be safe without you," I said, nearly sobbing.

"All shall be well," he said, drawing me against him once more.

"When this is over, and the French are gone," I said, "when we are reunited, we will leave Rome. At once. We shall go to your house in the countryside and marry immediately. I am sorry, Federico. So terribly sorry I delayed us this long."

He bent his head and kissed me soundly, passionately. I still could not sink into his kisses as I longed to; could not melt into his arms with abandon as I had in that damned dream of so long ago.

But it would come. With love and tenderness and marriage, the passion would come.

"When we are reunited," he repeated as he drew away. "I shall hold you to that, Maddalena. I shall dream of it throughout the coming days. You shall be my strength, as though you are the Madonna herself."

I tried to laugh around the tears that had begun to choke me. "Such blasphemy," I chided.

"Then God shall have to punish me for it, because it is true," he said. He kissed me again, and for an instant I felt a tingle of desire, something so largely unknown to me, and I pressed closer to him hungrily, eager. But all too soon, he drew away. "I must go," he said. "I am sorry, my love. But I will be missed, and you soon will be, too. Hurry back before it gets dark."

"I will see you soon," I called to him as he turned toward the stables.

He spun to face me one more time. "And soon I will make you my bride, but not soon enough!" he said. He waved to me once, a smile on his face, as if we were saying but a brief goodbye and he would be taking me for a stroll the next night.

As though we had any idea of when we might see each other again.

I shivered, suddenly mindful of the cold, and turned to make my way back to Santa Maria in Portico in the falling dusk.

Chapter 24

CESARE

"Your Holiness." A weary and rumpled Ferrantino of Aragon knelt before the pope, still dressed in his armor from the hard ride to Rome. "My army is here and at your service, at the service of our common cause."

"Arise, Your Highness," the pope said. "We are indeed glad you are here and thank God for your army's safe and timely arrival."

"Your Holiness is kind," Ferrantino said, his exhaustion evident as he stood. He was obviously ready to dispense with the formalities. "And not a moment too soon. The French will be upon us any day."

Father's face was grim. "Yes. We are hopeful our allies among the Orsini family can hold them off north of the city."

"You may hope, Holy Father, and pray for it, but unless God grants us a miracle, I do not think it likely," Ferrantino said bluntly. "This French force is like nothing Italy has ever seen, not in recent memory."

"Does Charles fancy himself a new Caesar, then?"

Ferrantino shook his head. "I know not. But he wants my home and my crown and my birthright, and I shall die before I let him have it."

Father nodded and rose from his chair in the audience chamber. "Come. Dine with us—your generals as well. We have much to discuss."

I followed after the pair. Ferrantino's arrival filled my father with more hope than it did me. His Holiness was of the mind that if the Neapolitan force was already in Rome, Charles might be inclined to avoid the city altogether. But as far as I could see, the French were bound here no matter what.

As we stepped out into the hall, Michelotto moved silently to my side. "I intercepted the messenger," he said, handing me a letter. "I knew you'd want this directly."

I opened the letter and scanned it quickly, my eyes delighting in Lucrezia's careful, lovely hand. "She is safe," I said. "The French have not been near. They will simply pass by Pesaro, as we guessed."

"Good news, then."

I read the rest of the missive before crumpling it in my fist. "Not entirely. Her worthless husband still has not stirred forth with his army. He has not even mustered a force. He will not be coming to our aid, just as I expected."

Michelotto snorted. "What use is he, then?"

I scowled. "No use at all."

Though I had not truly expected Sforza to come, it would have been a welcome surprise, and I found myself further disheartened. Prince Ferrantino was better off taking his force home, to defend Naples as best he could. It seemed as if there was no hope of saving Rome.

A week after the arrival of Ferrantino and his army, the Orsini betrayed us and surrendered all their holdings—including the key fortress of Bracciano, north of Rome—to the French. There now lay nothing between the Eternal City and King Charles's force, Ferrantino and his men being camped south of the city. Our last bulwark, our last hope, was gone.

"The traitorous, cowardly, sinful bastards!" my father roared. He toppled a heavy brocaded chair in his rage, upending it and sending it crashing into the wall with the force of his strong arms, still powerful, even at his age. The messenger narrowly missed being struck, his eyes wide with fear.

"You are dismissed," I said curtly. The messenger wasted no time in making a hasty bow and fleeing.

My father, in his rage—so rarely aroused to this extent—did not notice. "How dare they! Virginio Orsini, who holds a contract with the King of Naples, with the royal house of Aragon, invited us into his castle and plotted strategy with us, only to betray us all! His employer, and his liege lord and spiritual father the pope!" He sent another chair flying. "Judas Iscariot himself would blush with shame at such treachery!"

This was the same sort of blasphemy Father was wont to scold me for, but I knew better than to remark upon it. "And yet Virginio rides south to Naples, to continue his employment for King Alfonso," I said, shaking my head. "These petty lords and princelings of Italy are a faithless lot."

"They are faithful to their coffers only," Father bellowed, "to their coffers and to their own damned skins. What a fool I was to expect anything better. What a fool Virginio has made of me!"

I remained silent. I had not expected the Orsini to be able to beat back the French, but neither had I expected this. I had thought Virginio's *condotta* with King Alfonso would keep the Orsini family firmly arrayed against the French, but in this I, too, had been mistaken. It was not the first time an Italian warlord had behaved in such a manner, nor would it be the last.

Father had calmed down slightly, though he was pacing the room like an agitated bull, stalking up and down its length, his ire visible in every stride. "This changes everything," he muttered to himself. "But once we get through this, oh how those Orsini will pay . . ."

I cleared my throat, reminding him of my presence. "We must ride for Naples," I said. "We must leave for Naples with Ferrantino's army and regroup there."

"To what end?" he demanded.

"To what end?" I repeated incredulously. "To save our skins, that's what! The French are at our gates. If we have any hope of seeing this through, we must go to Naples and confer with King Alfonso."

"Think about what you are proposing, Cesare," Father snapped. "You would have me flee the Vatican and leave Rome to Charles to do with as he will. And with St. Peter's throne vacant, do you really think della Rovere will not seize it for himself?"

"He would not dare."

"Who would stop him, if Charles holds Rome? And once made pope, he would have the authority to crown Charles King of Naples. No, fleeing Rome would play right into their hands. If I stay, I force Charles to contend with me." With the departure of his fury came the return of his cool calculation, the political acumen for which he was renowned.

He was right, and I cursed myself for a fool for not seeing it. I just felt such an urgent need to do something.

"And furthermore," Father went on, "if I were to go to Naples, I have no doubt I would be a guest at the king's pleasure, however long that might last. They would keep me there however long they needed to legitimize Alfonso's claim. I would be obliged to do whatever they asked of me."

"I know. You are correct," I said. I slammed a hand down on the arm of my chair in frustration and rose, beginning to pace myself. "I do not know what else to do, that is all. Are we to simply sit here and wait? Wait to see if Charles invades Rome by force? Wait to see if we survive? Wait to be taken prisoner? There must be some action we can take!"

"Charles—even with della Rovere at his side—would not dare capture the Holy Father in the Vatican itself," Father said.

"You sound awfully sure of that."

"I am as sure as I can reasonably be. It would be a great deal less trouble for him to persuade me to do as he wishes than to depose me, no matter what he may have promised della Rovere. Deposing a pope is a messy business. No, he will wait to see if I admit him to the city before he tries to enter by force. He will want to meet with me."

"And what will you do?"

He did not answer for a long time. "I cannot refuse him for long, not with the army he brings. I have the people of Rome to think of. They look to me for safety and protection." He cursed again. "Damn the Orsini, damn them!"

"So you would admit an invading army to prey upon them?"

"It will go much better for the people if I allow them entrance than if they force their way in."

That was likely true.

"But yes, Cesare," he continued after a pause. "Difficult though I know it is for you and me, we must wait. There is nothing else we can do."

Both armies, the Neapolitan and the French, waited at His Holiness's pleasure. The Roman people waited at his pleasure. Charles had sent a messenger to the pope asking that the gates of Rome be opened, and he and his army admitted. The pope sought to delay as long as possible, but the situation was untenable. Charles sent another message, saying he was loath to enter the Holy City by force, but he would do so if necessary.

Ferrantino was spoiling for a fight, but to pitch such a battle here and now would be suicide. "His Holiness cannot truly be considering letting the bastards in," he snarled to me as we left a meeting in the Vatican.

I raised an eyebrow. "What would you have him do, Your Highness? Allow Rome to be sacked before they ride south to conquer your kingdom? I do not like it any more than you, but our resources here are limited."

Ferrantino growled in response but did not reply.

I tried to persuade Father to flee to the Castel Sant' Angelo for safety, where he had already sent Giulia Farnese and cousin Adriana and their household. "No," he said firmly. "When the French ride into this city, they will find me on St. Peter's throne, not hiding behind fortress walls."

He had said when the French ride in, not if.

On Christmas Day, instead of celebrating the coming of a savior,

Pope Alexander announced that he would admit the French king and his army into Rome.

There was no savior coming for us.

There was nothing left for Ferrantino to do but ride for Naples with his army and hope to defend it as best he could. "It was a good plan, Your Eminence, thanks in large part to you," Ferrantino said as I rode beside him through the streets of Rome, the army in retreat. "We just couldn't execute it quickly enough. And perhaps even then we did not have enough men."

"I wish things had turned out differently," I said helplessly.

"It's not over yet. I will fight every moment there is breath in my body." He swore and spat. "Better I should be dead than see my kingdom in the hands of the French."

As we reached the Lateran gate, he turned to me before we parted. "What does he have planned?" he asked, nodding back in the direction from which we'd come. "His Holiness? How does he mean to avoid giving all of Italy over to the French king yet keep his tiara at the same time?"

The question grated on me, for I had wondered the same thing, and despite being at the pope's right hand throughout this crisis, I still had no idea. "I do not know," I was forced to respond. "I wish I did. But I would have faith in no man in this situation but Pope Alexander."

Ferrantino snorted bitterly. "You are a good sort, Cardinal Borgia," he said. "You are wasted in the Curia. I could use a man like you on the battlefield." He reached over and clasped my hand. "Godspeed, my friend. May you come through this in one piece."

"And you and yours," I said. With a certain bitterness, I turned and rode back to the Vatican Palace, while the Neapolitan army streamed out of Rome and toward their homeland.

Chapter 25

MADDALENA

On the last day of December I found myself on the very upper terrace of the Castel Sant' Angelo—the Terrazzo dell' Angelo—along with Giulia and Adriana and the rest of their household. We stood below the great statue of St. Michael the Archangel sheathing his sword, promising protection from evil to all the children of God. It was cold and clear out as—with dread in our hearts—we watched the French army ride into Rome.

Pope Alexander had opened the gates and allowed them admittance. They were not sacking the city. And yet we understood Rome and its people would not escape unscathed. Not when an entire army of French soldiers and Swiss mercenaries were within its walls.

People would suffer.

Not Giulia Farnese or Adriana de Mila, of course. Anyone with the wealth to do so had already fled Rome, taking their valuables with them. And the pope's women had access to his very own fortress. It was only by the grace of God that I was safely ensconced with them. I thanked Him on my knees every day in the fortress's chapel. Why he had chosen to spare me from this threat, I likely would never know.

Because the people out there in the streets of Rome—the merchants and shopkeepers and peddlers and craftspeople and artists and servants whose masters did not care enough to save them, the elderly and the children and the sick—would be living in a state of fear today, of soldiers who might strip them of their livelihoods and perhaps even their lives. Who was watching out for them? Who was praying for them, except me?

I'd had no word from Federico since we had parted outside the Vatican stables, and I could hardly sleep for fear. Was he safe? Would he remain safe, now that the French were within the city walls?

The only thing I could do was wait, and pray.

Yet waiting was difficult in these days. There was not much cleaning to do, not in the small suite of rooms we occupied, and there were no dinners or fetes to ready the ladies for, and certainly no visitors. I could not recall ever having quite so much free time, and I did not know what to do with it. For the very first time in my life, embroidery did not serve to distract me; instead of focusing on the stitches, the pattern, my mind worried over what would become of us, of Rome, of Federico.

A few paces away, Giulia and Adriana were chattering nervously, worrying about His Holiness and what this would mean for him, and about their own palazzo, and whether it would be spared.

I heard their talk, but I could not listen to it. I liked my mistresses, and all the saints knew they treated me well. But they were worried about the wrong things. I could only hope that God would reveal their error to them in His own time.

I thought of the soldiers that had come through my village those years ago, the harm and evil they had wreaked. Long instructed that all sin was punished, I had always assumed God had punished them somehow, in some way.

Yet this was the army of an anointed king who held his throne only because God had blessed him and placed him there. So how could the evils committed by this king's army—for evils were certain—be punished?

When God's chosen vicar on earth was in opposition to an anointed king, who could emerge victorious?

And what would become of the innocent people caught between them?

Dear God, protect Federico, and keep him safe, I prayed as I watched the soldiers stream into the Eternal City. *If you do this one thing, I shall never ask for anything else, ever again. Please. I beg of you.*

We stayed on the terrace into the night, unable to look away. We stayed until the entire army had made its way inside the city. The sounds of fighting, of screams, rose up from the streets below and across the city as spots of fire lit the dark sky.

It was as if we were watching the apocalypse.

That night, on my narrow pallet in a room next to Donna Giulia's chamber, I had a dream—a premonition, I hoped.

The statue of St. Michael atop the fortress came to life and stepped from his pedestal. He drew his sword, preparing to spread his wings over the city of Rome to save it, to drive out the French invaders and protect his people from the evil that waited to befall them. I fell to my knees before him, weeping in relief and gratitude, mumbling prayers of thanks. And when I gazed up into the light emanating from him, I saw he wore the face of Cesare Borgia, Cardinal of Valencia.

Chapter 26

CESARE

The French messenger approached the throne, kneeling to kiss the pope's ring and slipper. Good—the French king was respecting the honor and reverence due the pope. For now, at least.

Father tersely bid the messenger rise. "What demands does His Highness King Charles have for us?" he asked.

The messenger blanched slightly. "Not demands, Holiness; certainly not. His Royal Highness King Charles understands that he is Your Holiness's humble servant and can make no demands, only requests."

I rolled my eyes, not caring if the messenger saw.

Father snorted. "Indeed. Let us hear it, then."

Only myself, four other cardinals, and Burchard remained in the Vatican with the pope at that point, and all were present for this reception of King Charles's messenger. We held a collective breath as we waited to hear what Charles would have the gall to demand—or whatever word he wanted to use for it—of Christ's vicar on earth. Ever since the French king had installed himself in style in the Palazzo Venezia a few days earlier, we had known his terms were coming. Now there was a sense of relief that the moment had finally come. At least now we would know what he wanted, what he expected us to part with. What, if anything, we might be able to retain or gain.

"His Highness asks Your Holiness to turn over the Castel Sant' Angelo to him, that he may properly defend the city, and prepare for his Holy Crusade," the messenger began, reading from a scroll of parchment.

Not even a breath disturbed the stillness of the audience chamber. My father's grip on the arms of his throne tightened so that his knuckles paled, but he did not speak.

"He also requests that Your Holiness give into his custody the infidel Prince Djem, as a token of Your Holiness's good will."

So Charles can receive the payments for Djem's keep from the Sultan, more like. My father merely raised his eyebrows at the messenger.

"Finally," the messenger went on, and here he hesitated briefly, "His Royal Highness requests, as yet a further token of Your Holiness's good will, that Cardinal Cesare Borgia ride with his expedition to Naples."

Rage exploded behind my eyes, but I fought to keep my expression impassive. No good would come of me showing my true feelings at this juncture.

But the nerve of him, the absolute gall, to ask to take me as a hostage! He wanted the Castel Sant' Angelo *and* the pope's son, a prince of the Church?

A hostage. Father would never agree to it.

Would he?

"Is that all?" Father inquired mildly.

The messenger rolled up his scroll and bowed. "It is. I trust Your Holiness does not find these things too much to ask, given the circumstances."

"The circumstances, as I see them," Father said, speaking softly but with underlying steel, "are that King Charles has pushed his way into the Holy City and demanded these boons from me, the Pope of Rome and Vicar of Christ, in my own city, when I hold the crown of Naples in my keeping. I wonder that he feels owed anything at all."

The messenger gaped at him.

The pope rose suddenly. "You are dismissed," he said curtly. "This audience is at an end."

"But . . . I . . . what shall I tell his Highness?" the messenger babbled.

"Tell him no." With that, the pope swept out of the room, and I followed closely behind.

Father was of the opinion that Charles, while he would no doubt be enraged, would still not deem it politic to use force against the pope or the Vatican. Yet with della Rovere whispering poison into the French king's ear, there was no telling what they might attempt. So, that very night, Father and I, along with Burchard and the four cardinals still present, took our most necessary belongings and escaped to the Castel Sant' Angelo via the secret tunnel between the fortress and the Vatican. If we were going to wait out Charles, best to do it from behind impenetrable walls.

Chapter 27

MADDALENA

I arose early one January morning and climbed up to the Terrazzo dell' Angelo, to watch the sun rise over Rome and to pray in sight of the statue of Saint Michael. Since he had come to me in my dream, this had become my custom. It was as much comfort as I could find in these uncertain times.

I had yet to hear from Federico, though I had begun to hope he would find a way to get a message to me, or even come to the Castel after all. His was the face that now haunted my dreams, his fate the one I worried over most. The guilt that had slid into my heart with deadly aim that day outside the stables continued to fester. Federico and I might both be safe and together had I not been so selfish, so full of sin.

That is my fault. My fault. And there was nothing I could do but pray.

When I reached the terrace, I was surprised to find I was not alone; someone stood in my usual spot, gazing out over the Eternal City. When the figure turned to me, it was as though my dream had come to life in earnest, for before me stood Cardinal Cesare Borgia.

All thoughts fled as I stared at him in dumbfounded surprise, our eyes locked, before I knelt hastily. "Your Eminence," I murmured, eyes cast down on the stone walkway beneath me. My heart pounded, racing with joy and delight. He was here! We were saved. "Forgive me; I did not expect to see you here." But I had, hadn't I?

"Rise, Maddalena," he said, his voice low and intimate in the early dawn light. When I met his gaze again, he was smiling slightly. "You did not expect to see me up so early, or you did not expect to see me at the Castel Sant' Angelo at all?"

"Both," I replied. "I have been coming here many a morning, for quiet reflection and prayer. I have yet to find anyone else doing the same. And I thought . . . I assumed Your Eminence would remain at the Vatican with His Holiness."

"His Holiness is here as well," he said. "We arrived late last night."

"And have you come to—" I broke off, embarrassed. *Have you come to tell us we are saved, and can return to Santa Maria in Portico?* I wanted to ask. But that was a silly question. The Pope of Rome and his son the cardinal need not come to the Castel Sant' Angelo in person to tell the pope's women they might go home.

But surely they—surely Cardinal Borgia—were here to liberate us?

My face flushed, and the cardinal looked at me expectantly. "Yes?" he prompted. "You may speak freely."

My face heated even more. "I . . . I only meant to say . . . to ask if you have come to tell us we are saved," I said at last. "Surely the pope has reprimanded the French king, and he will be leaving Rome soon?"

Cesare sighed heavily. "Would that that were the case, Maddalena," he said. "No, sadly, we have come for no such happy purpose. The French king is as much ensconced in Rome, and in Italy, as he was before. His Holiness and I are now inmates of the fortress as well."

I could feel my face fall, though I tried not to show my disappointment. How had my dream so misled me? Were not such dreams sent by the saints to guide us?

And had not Cardinal Borgia proven to be my savior before?

Listen to yourself, Maddalena, a small yet caustic voice within me chided—a voice suspiciously like my mother's. The saints sent a heavenly portent in a dream to you, so lowly and unworthy a woman?

Cesare Borgia was only a man, after all, not an avenging angel. I would do well to remember that.

He seemed to correctly interpret my crestfallen expression, for he hastened to explain. "We have not given up," he tried to assure me. "Neither I nor His Holiness nor Naples. We shall not let the French have Italy. This is simply a more . . . defensible and strategic position."

He hesitated as he spoke the last words, almost as if he did not believe them. Yet I was more astounded that he felt any need to explain himself.

"Of course," I said, hurrying to reassure him in my own fashion. "I understand. His Holiness is guided by God and Christ Jesus, and so will only do what is best for his people. For all his people."

"Yes," the cardinal said, though he sounded even less sure. "But I am glad to see you, Maddalena," he said, changing the subject. "I had hoped you were safe with Adriana and Donna Giulia. You are looking well."

Warmth spread within me at the realization he had been thinking about me, anxious over my welfare. "I thank you, Your Eminence. I am as well as anyone can be, under the circumstances."

A smile, albeit brief, broke across his handsome face, and it dazzled me more than the sun then rising over the buildings and churches and fields of the Eternal City. For a moment, it was as if we were two equals, two friends. "I can certainly understand that," he said. "Is there anything you want for, Maddalena? Anything you need?"

"I do not think so, Your Eminence," I said. "Madonna Giulia and Madonna Adriana brought the best of their food stores and wine, and—"

"I did not ask about Giulia and Adriana," he interrupted. "I asked if there is anything *you* want or need, Maddalena."

I paused, taken aback. That Cardinal Cesare Borgia should concern himself with my desires . . . "Oh, I . . . Your Eminence is too kind, but . . ." I mumbled, bowing my head.

"Come, Maddalena," he said, smile back on his face, and once again it was as though I were speaking to a friend, to someone comfortable teasing me and being teased by me in return. "Surely there is something I can do for you. To reward your staunch loyalty in serving my family."

Before I could think better of it, my smile rose to match his, and I said, "If I were to be completely honest, Your Eminence, there is much I would do for some fresh cheese."

He laughed brightly. "Fresh cheese? Then you shall have it. Surely the pope's son can have some fresh cheese sent to the Castel Sant' Angelo for a pretty maid with a smile like the sunrise."

I was struck, almost physically so, by both the compliment and the way his words so closely mirrored my own thoughts of him. "Your Eminence is too kind, truly," I said again. This time I met his eyes and widened my smile, letting him see how happy I was.

He closed the distance between us and took my hand, bringing it to his lips. "A man would do much more than fetch you some fresh cheese for that smile of yours, Maddalena," he said. And, before I could summon a reply, he turned and was gone, descending the stone stairs back into the fortress.

I remained frozen there after his departure, my smile stuck to my lips, face upturned to catch the early rays of the wintry Roman sun. His words had warmed me more than any fire could on this winter day. His words that surely meant more to me than they did to him, to a prince of the Church, the son of the pope. A man of God, I reminded myself. A man who had risen high in the world and in God's eyes and so was not free to treat me as a man treats a woman, a man whom it would be a sin to think of as a man. And I a betrothed woman!

Yet I could not bring myself to extinguish the flame beneath my breastbone. And so I had one more thing to add to the litany of guilt in my prayers.

Chapter 28

CESARE

Even from the window of the papal quarters in the Castel Sant' Angelo, I could see the chaos sweeping the city outside. Smoke rose off in the distance, and groups of French soldiers and mercenaries made their way through the streets, our people trying to flee or hide.

To King Charles's credit—not that I was inclined to give him much—he had tried as best he could to discourage looting in the Holy City, setting up gallows in some of the city squares to serve as an ominous deterrent. He had even executed a few men whose crimes were particularly egregious. Yet, inexperienced in warfare as he was, he was finding out a disciplined army on the battlefield was one thing, and an army at loose ends in a foreign and hostile city was quite another. When the blood of men was raised for battle, they would find another outlet—much to the horror of the people of Rome.

"Damn Charles, damn him," I swore, turning from the window. "We cannot let this go on."

Father's face was pale, haggard. "What would you have me do, Cesare?" he asked. "Accept his outrageous demands?"

"We could at least try to negotiate," I said. "Send him counter-demands."

Father shook his head slowly. "We can wait a bit longer," he said. "Charles needs my support, or at least acquiescence. This fortress is impregnable; we can wait as long as it takes."

"But how much longer can the Roman people wait?" I demanded furiously, gesturing toward the window.

"This is war, Cesare. You cannot save everyone." He sighed. "Eventually Charles will be willing to negotiate. He does not wish to stay here any more than we want him here."

His Holiness was not entirely without resources, and he had spies in the Palazzo Venezia, where Charles was ensconced with his top advisors and that snake della Rovere. Reportedly the men were living in all but squalor, sleeping on dirty straw beds and burning tallow candles that dirtied the walls and tapestries. Charles was apparently so fearful of being poisoned that he had four men assigned to tasting his food and wine.

No, he would not wish to linger in Rome. What I didn't know was what position the pope still thought he had from which to negotiate, other than that he still sat upon St. Peter's throne. For now.

We were interrupted by a knock on the door, and when Father called "Enter!" Michelotto slipped inside. "Holiness," he said, bowing. "Your Eminence."

"Michelotto," I greeted him. "What news from outside?"

"Pillaging and looting, just as we've feared, Eminence," he said. "But I bring dire news of a personal nature, and it saddens me that I must be the one to report it to you."

My blood ran cold at his words. Lucrezia? "Out with it," I said through clenched teeth.

"I've learned that a band of Swiss mercenaries in the employ of King Charles have ransacked the home of Vannozza dei Cattanei, your mother," Michelotto told me. "I went there to confirm the information myself, and sadly it is true."

"What?" I exploded. "They dare?" I seized a crystal glass from a table and hurled it against the wall, where it shattered into a satisfying number of pieces.

"Cesare!" Father said, rising. "Have you lost your mind?"

But I had, no doubt. "Where is my mother? Is she well? Is she safe?" I shouted.

"She is, but shaken," Michelotto said, his calm demeanor

somehow completely unchanged. "I spoke to her myself, and she received me once she was certain I came on your business, Eminence. The mercenaries handled her a bit roughly when she tried to halt their entrance, but they . . ." He hesitated, glancing at the pope. "They did not violate her person. She is a bit bruised but will recover."

"Why did you not bring her here?" I demanded, thrusting my face close to Michelotto's. "Why did you not insist she come to the Castel Sant' Angelo, for her own protection?" I whirled on my father. "Why did you not have her brought here as soon as the French army was at our gates?"

"Your mother and I are no longer a part of each other's lives, Cesare," Father said. "Had she sought protection here I would have granted it, a fact she knows well. She chose to stay in her home, and I cannot say that surprises me."

"With respect, Eminence," Michelotto spoke up, "I did insist she accompany me back here. But she chose to retreat to her house in the country for the time being. I did my utmost to persuade her, but she would not be moved."

"God's teeth," I swore, clenching my fists against the desire to hurl something else at the wall. "Could the woman be any more stubbornly foolish?"

"A trait you might recognize in yourself," my father said tartly. "What happened to her is horrible, but she shall be safe in the country until this is over."

I stalked back to the window. "That they would dare assault the home and person of the mother of the pope's children," I muttered. "They will pay for this, those men that dared lay a finger on my mother," I swore. "I will see to it."

Both of them simply looked back at me in silence. For what could I do to seek my revenge, trapped in the Castel Sant' Angelo like a rat, while the French had the run of the city outside?

I did not know, and that feeling of impotence made me want to put my fist through the very stone walls that hemmed us in. But I would find a way.

Chapter 29

MADDALENA

I was not reassured after my encounter with the Cardinal of Valencia—if anything, I was less so. Certainly the situation must be more dire than we'd known, if it was no longer safe for the pope to remain in the Vatican Palace. When I was not worrying, I was struggling to push Cesare Borgia from my mind—his smile, his kind words, the way his tongue seemed to caress my name. Each fond remembrance was a sin, and even the thought of speaking such sins aloud to my confessor made my cheeks burn in shame.

And so I would turn my thoughts to Federico. It was my fault we were both still in the city and that he was in the way of such danger.

The more I ruminated and stewed in my regrets and my culpability, the more I felt I could not stay safely shielded behind these walls, not when Federico—my friend and, yes, the man I might love—was in danger beyond them.

I had to find him. I had to at least try. Surely there was still someone at the Vatican Palace I could ask. Perhaps he had already fled to the country, and then at least I could rest easy that he was safe.

Or perhaps I would find him, and at last bring him back to the safety of the Castel Sant' Angelo. Surely he would acquiesce, now that he had witnessed what the French were doing to the city.

I slipped from my bed early the next morning, as usual. Isabella, who shared the small room with me, would not think anything of it. Hopefully I could be back before too long.

Hopefully I would come back at all, and not run afoul of some French soldier.

I shuddered as I donned my heaviest cloak against the winter chill, pulling up the hood to conceal my face. Hopefully there would be few of them up at so early an hour; hopefully they were all sleeping off a night of drink and dissolution and so would take no notice of one servant girl slipping through the streets.

Mother Mary, Christ Jesus, blessed and righteous St. Michael, watch over me.

I had discovered, after much idle poking about the fortress these past few weeks, where the secret walkway that led to the Vatican Palace was. I slipped through unnoticed.

It was open to the air, which I had not expected; though the high stone walls hid anyone passing from the view of whoever might be on the street below. My heart beat rapidly beneath my breastbone at the audacity of what I was doing. I hoped fervently that I would not encounter anyone on my way.

Soon I found myself in the Vatican Palace. I huddled in a corner, struggling to steady my breath and get my bearings. Once I had recognized where I was in the palace, I headed for a side servants' entrance that would lead me to the vicinity of the stables. If Federico was well and had not fled, this would be where I found him.

I slipped into the stables and found myself with a sword immediately at my throat. "Who goes there? State your business or I cut your throat," a man barked. He had the Catalan accent I recognized among those members of His Holiness's personal guard.

I let out a squeak of panic. Hands trembling with fright, I lifted my hands and pulled down the hood of my cloak. "I . . . my name is Maddalena Moretti," I said, my voice shaky, much as I would have liked to sound strong. "I am a maid, in the service of—"

He sighed with both relief and annoyance and lowered his blade. "A servant girl," he said, disdainfully. "What in Christ's name are you doing here?"

"I . . . I am looking for someone," I said. "My betrothed. His name is Federico Lucci. He is a footman in the service of His Holiness, but is often in the stables. Have you seen him?"

"I know the fellow, but I have not seen him, no," the man said brusquely. "You had best get the hell out of here and somewhere safe. No doubt your man will come find you if he can, a tasty thing like you."

My skin crawled at these words, and I hurried out of the stables. Yet such a comment was the least of what I had to fear on the streets of Rome.

I hastened to the Vatican servants' quarters next and found them deserted. No doubt everyone who had not fled was in hiding. I thought hard about where else Federico might be if in fact he had not gone home or remained with the horses in the countryside.

He could be dead. I gasped aloud as the thought slithered its way through the shields I had erected in my mind to keep it out.

No, I did not know that. I didn't have any reason to believe it, to believe that he wasn't perfectly safe somewhere.

Then I recalled his friend's wine shop, where he and I had passed so much time. Perhaps he had sought shelter there. If nothing else, I might find someone who had seen or spoken to him.

I set out from the Vatican before I could think better of it. The walk to the wine shop was not a long one, and I tried to stay in the shadows cast by the newly risen sun and out of view of enemy soldiers.

The streets were as empty as I'd ever seen them, and I could not help a shudder at how eerie it was. I pulled my cloak closer, as if hoping it would make me invisible; I was all too conscious of how very conspicuous I was, out on the streets all alone.

In the distance, I heard shouts and breaking glass, and whooping and hollering, as if a fight had broken out. I quickened my pace, crossing myself under my hood, begging God and His saints to see me through this.

Finally the shop came into sight. It was dark and silent, apparently abandoned. As I drew nearer, I saw the windows had been smashed and the furniture splintered within. Broken glass carpeted the floor, as did spilled wine and what might have been—what I hoped wasn't—blood.

I remained stock still, peering in horror at the evidence of violence inside. Dread began to coat the inside of my stomach, heavy as lead. There had been a struggle here. I crossed myself again, murmuring a prayer for the shop owner, Federico's friend whose name I could not manage to recall.

It was not certain that Federico had even been here, been a victim of this horror. He might yet be safe in the country, or somewhere else in the city, somewhere I would not know to check. I must have faith.

I could look around the shop, I reasoned. Perhaps there was something that might help me. I was reluctant to go inside for some reason I could not explain, but having come this far, it would be foolish to turn back now. Lifting my skirts, I stepped onto the threshold and past the broken door.

Suddenly I heard a burst of laughter and shouting from nearby. I turned to find two men walking along the street—French soldiers, judging by their dress and the language they spoke rapidly to one another. I could not be sure, being unfamiliar with the French tongue, but it sounded as though they were slurring their words, still drunk from the night before.

I moved to dart into the shop to hide, but they caught sight of me, and quickly hastened toward me. One caught my arm and whirled me around to face him. He asked me a question in his language, his companion laughing by his side.

"I . . . I do not understand." I struggled against his hard grip. "Let me go, please!"

The men continued speaking to each other, and the one holding me ran a finger along my cheek. "Please, let me go!" I cried. I doubted they could understand my words, but surely the sentiment was clear enough as I struggled against them. They simply had no intention of obliging me.

Rage began to fill me as their fingers poked and prodded, as though I were a piece of horseflesh at market. First Juan Borgia, and now this? Were men animals, all?

The Cardinal of Valencia was not coming to save me this time, but I had been doing a fine job of fighting off his despicable brother even before he arrived that day. And I could do that now.

"Let me go!" I shouted. I drove my knee between the man's legs, and he let me go with a scream of pain. I did not hesitate; I bolted away from them and back down the street from which I had come, toward the Vatican.

I heard shouts and looked back to see the man's companion pursuing me. He wove unsteadily across the cobblestones, drunk indeed, and as I was about to look away, he tripped and fell to the street. He let out a yell of pain, and I ran on. When I glanced back again he was nowhere in sight.

A hysterical burst of laughter escaped me. Those men deserved whatever pain they got, and then some. Perhaps they would no longer prey upon young women in the streets. I could only hope.

I veered down a street that would extend my journey slightly but would likely throw them off should they start to pursue me again. Yet no one followed.

In sight of St. Peter's Square, I had finally allowed relief to flood my blood when I heard hoofbeats coming up behind me. I turned to see a mounted rider pursuing me. "Stop!" he cried.

I screamed and ran faster, futile though I knew it was, and my legs felt like to give out. I could never outrun a man on horseback.

"Maddalena! Please!"

I stopped dead at the sound of my name and turned to face the mounted man. By then, he was almost upon me, and before I knew what was happening he had slowed his horse, seized me by the waist, and pulled me up into the saddle in front of him.

I screamed again, in panic and outrage. "Let me down! Who—" I broke off as I finally got a look at the man's face. "You . . . Your Eminence!"

"Yes," Cesare Borgia said, spurring his horse on. "What are you doing out on the streets, Maddalena? Surely you know it's not safe—why, I saw you running as though you were being chased, and—"

"I was being chased, by two French soldiers who accosted me,"

I said. "I fought them off and ran, and then you came riding up behind me, and . . ." Suddenly all the fight went out of me, and I sagged against his lean body. Only then did I notice how good he felt against me, and just like that, all the thoughts I'd been trying to suppress—as well as, God forgive me, that sinful dream of over a year ago—came roaring back. I drew a sharp breath and quickly recited the Pater Noster in my head. *And lead us not into temptation, but deliver us from evil . . .*

He chuckled. "Fought them off, did you? Well done. But what in God's name possessed you to leave the Castel Sant' Angelo in the first place?"

"I was looking for someone," I explained. "A . . . a friend." If I wondered why I did not use the word *betrothed* with Cardinal Borgia, I did not stop to examine it too closely. "I have not heard from him and do not know if he is safe, and I was worried. I . . . decided to try to find him."

By this time we were back at the Vatican, and Cardinal Borgia directed his horse into the stables. He swung down from the saddle and lifted me down after him. "That was brave of you," he said. "Brave, but foolish. And did you find this friend?"

"No. No, I did not."

"I am sorry to hear that." He led the horse into the stable before drawing me toward the palace. "Come. We must both get back into the Castel. Luckily for you, I decided to ride out to try to find my mother." He gave me that smile I had remembered so many times—too many times. "It seems I have saved you again."

Before I realized what I was doing, I reached out and slapped him across the face.

I could not tell who was more shocked, him or me. No doubt I had not truly hurt him—I was a slight women, with no experience in violence, and he was a man and no doubt trained to protect himself. But the astonishment in his gaze was comical all the same.

I bit back the apology that leapt to my tongue, the horror at my actions that years in service to those above my station had ingrained in me. Instead I said, "I do not need you to save me, Your

Eminence. I managed quite well before you found me. If you need to be a savior to someone, save the people of Rome."

I expected his ire, even anger, in return; but as he had before when I had spoken boldly to him, he surprised me. He took my hand, raised it to his lips, and kissed it. "I shall do as you bid me, Maddalena, avenging angel, Madonna of Holy Vengeance," he said, without so much as a trace of mockery. "I shall do the best I can."

It was my turn to look shocked, to be rendered speechless.

"And I shall start with your friend," he said. "What is his name?"

I shook my head, as if to clear it. "Federico Lucci," I said. "A footman in the employ of His Holiness."

A sardonic smile curled his lips. "Is this man your lover, then?"

"No!" I gasped in shock. "I am not . . . I would never . . ."

"I did not mean to offend you," he said, in earnest. "But it seems plain that this man is dear to you."

"He is," I said. "He is . . . we are betrothed."

He frowned slightly before his expression cleared, becoming neutral once more. "I see. Well, you have my word on this, Maddalena Moretti. I shall have my men find out where he is, and what has become of him, and I shall tell you. I swear it."

Relief and warmth spread through me in equal measure. "I . . . I do not know how to thank you, Your Eminence."

He took my hand and kissed it again, his lips warm against my skin. "It is as I told you before, Maddalena. A man will do a great deal to see that smile of yours. The smile of an angel of holy vengeance."

I struggled to compose myself as he led me back into the Vatican Palace and to the secret tunnel.

An angel of holy vengeance, indeed. Perhaps my dream of him as such an angel had not been so far from the truth, after all.

Chapter 30

CESARE

Immediately upon returning to my rooms at the Castel Sant' Angelo, I summoned Michelotto and directed him to gather whatever information he could about this Federico Lucci—as soon as it could be safely done. I would keep my promise to the magnificent Maddalena, no matter how long it took.

Later that night, I paced restlessly in my chamber, unable to sleep, even having discharged the good deed I'd promised. I could not get Maddalena's face at the moment she'd slapped me out of my head: haughty and imperious in her outrage, like a statue of some ancient Roman goddess. Madonna of Holy Vengeance, I'd called her. By God, but if I was a painter, I would paint her just so, and give the work that title.

I admired her, true, but my admiration was not keeping me awake; rather, I had lust to thank for that. A woman as beautiful and firm-willed as she inspired a great deal more than admiration in a man, after all.

I could seek her out, find where she was sleeping, and invite her to my bed—invite, of course; it would never be anything but her choice. She certainly did not seem the type to be unfaithful to her betrothed, but I could not help but contemplate what it would be like if she was. I had to smother a moan as I allowed my imagination free reign. To have her writhing beneath me in this bed, all that fire and will directed toward me . . .

I got up and began to pace, hoping to make my arousal fade. Because of course I would not seek her out. Not today. Not like this. Not when she had fought off some lechers seeking to demean and violate her, all while trying to find the man she was promised to marry. Christ, was I not a better man than them, at least? Could I not respect her virtue?

But I thought—perhaps only hoped—such an invitation from me might not be completely unwelcome to her. She had melted so deliciously against me when she sat before me in the saddle; and in the past, her smile had seemed inviting and warm; that she even enjoyed my company . . .

Basta, Cesare, I told myself firmly. You, a prince of the Church, would worry over a servant girl's opinion of you?

But I did, and in the dark of night, in the agony of unfulfilled lust, I could admit that much to myself, at least.

Yet now was hardly the time to be distracted by a serving girl, beautiful and righteous and alluring and headstrong as she may be. The French were in our city; it could be none of us would live out the month.

And if I wanted to do something for Maddalena, I could make good on my promises to her: to find her man (though I felt very grudging about it just then) and to do something for the people of Rome. And so I resumed pacing, trying to think of some way the Borgias—and Rome—might emerge victorious from this crisis.

Despite my best intentions, things soon deteriorated far beyond anyone's control. If there was still any belief that God was on the side of the pope and his cause, this belief collapsed on January 10 with a section of the Castel Sant' Angelo's wall. Though the French troops had set up some of their fearsome cannons facing the fortress, they had remained still and silent, ominously so. But no, the wall, insufficiently reinforced, collapsed on its own, leaving a hole large enough for French troops to spill through should they choose.

Leaving guards at the fortress for the women within—and the

Papal Treasury, which had been transported there as well—Father returned to the Vatican, bringing me with him. The hour of reckoning had come. He would receive the French king.

He no longer had a choice. Yet as angry as I was that it had come to this, I was also relieved. The moment had come, and we would face our fate.

I was not permitted to be present during Father's audience with King Charles, nor were any other cardinals or advisors—only a pair of guards for each man, who would stand at a distance. I understood this, even as I resented it. I paced my Vatican chambers like a caged lion. Charles would be sent to the Vatican garden for the meeting, where he would come upon the pontiff, supposedly deep in prayer, and the king would then genuflect three times before the pope raised him up to greet and embrace him. It had all been arranged carefully between the two men in advance via their envoys.

It was not until late that night that I was finally summoned to my father's chambers. I made my way quickly, practically running. The guards outside immediately opened the door to admit me, and I passed through the outer rooms into Father's private chambers.

He was waiting before the fire for me, still dressed in a simple white cassock and skullcap. I assumed that this was what he had worn to greet the French king, and I couldn't help but wonder at the choice. Surely a set of resplendent robes, perhaps even the papal tiara, would have served better to impress and intimidate Charles, who by all accounts was a small, awkward, and even ugly man with a bent and twisted spine. Yet there was brilliance in the choice he had made as well: Charles would no doubt have expected to be greeted with splendor, to be overawed by the Holy Father. And so Father had done the unexpected: dressed in simple, spotless white, as though he were an everyday priest humbly greeting and providing guidance to one of his parishioners.

I was struck anew by the sight of the man before me, just as the first time I had beheld him as the Pope of Rome, the Vicar of

Christ on earth. In this moment, he seemed to me more than a man indeed.

I approached him and knelt. "Holy Father," I murmured.

His hands rested on my head in blessing. "My son," he said softly, real affection in his voice. "I have much to tell you."

"I am yours to command," I said.

"I know," he said, his voice still soft. "Rise."

We both took chairs in front of the fire. "King Charles and I agreed to many things today," Father said at last, after a few beats of silence. "Some of which I could not avoid. And yet it went better than I had expected." He chuckled. "He is an interesting man, Charles. For all the might of his army, he is remarkably ineffectual in person, and so it was not difficult to persuade him to my way of thinking."

Interesting indeed. "What are the terms?" I asked, unable to wait any longer.

"I promised to grant Charles free passage through the Papal States," Father began.

Not that Charles needed any such thing—no one in the Papal States would try to oppose his army. Yet I saw the political value in the pope naming this as a concession, as something he was generously granting the French king. "What else?"

"Charles shall have Prince Djem ride with the expedition, though I shall continue to receive the payments for his keep," Father went on. "He cares only about the prestige of the hostage, apparently. Charles shall also keep the papal fortresses he is already in possession of—I had no way to deny him, of course. And I promised cardinals' hats for a pair of Frenchmen at his request." He grimaced. "And I must forgive and welcome back into the fold the cardinals who betrayed me."

"God's blood," I swore. "Those traitors?"

"I do not like it either, Cesare, but I did not have a choice. Charles insisted, and in granting this I shall be safe on St. Peter's throne."

"Will you be, though, with those vipers at your breast?" I demanded.

"Charles does not seek to depose me; he finds me amiable and agreeable," Father said. "Which is not at all what those cardinals, especially della Rovere, wanted. They've been thwarted and will come back with their tails between their legs. And my forgiveness will hopefully eliminate their desire to rebel again." He sighed. "Forgiveness is always the better course if possible, even if it is not the easiest one."

"And so what do we gain in return?" I asked, my tone short.

"Retain is perhaps the better word. Charles has sworn to protect and obey me, as all the kings of France before him. He will not get the Castel Sant' Angelo, and I have not recognized him as King of Naples—he did not ask it and I did not offer it. Nor have I denounced King Alfonso's right to rule."

Fascinating. Charles had brought an army to the pope's domain, yet he lacked the nerve to insist upon the very thing he had come for. Was the scourge of Italy, Savonarola's fiery sword of redemption, truly so weak a man?

"Naples will not thank you for sending the French to their doorstep," I said.

"Yes, but I withheld formal recognition, so it is left to the Neapolitans to defend their own," Father said. "I have done what I could. The rest is up to Alfonso and Ferrantino."

"I suppose this is the best outcome we could have hoped for, under the circumstances," I said, rising. "If that is all, Father, I think I am for my bed . . ."

"Sit down, Cesare." His voice turned suddenly ominous.

I froze briefly before lowering myself back into the cushioned chair. "What is it?" I asked, dreading his answer.

"I am sorry, Cesare," he said. "But I conceded one further thing to Charles."

"What?" I asked, a part of me afraid I already knew.

"You, too, will be sent to ride with the French expedition to Naples," he said.

I exploded from my chair. "You are giving me to him as a hostage? Without discussing it with me?" I demanded. All the awe I had felt as I beheld him before the fire just minutes ago had vanished. He had betrayed me, his supposed right hand. I was to be given over to the enemy.

"You will be safe, and I will have eyes and ears inside Charles's camp," Father replied.

"You would send me away? With them? When I should be at your side?"

Father rose. "As you said, you are mine to command," he said, his voice low and dangerous. "And so I do command you. You go where I send thee, Cesare."

"I do," I said bitterly, moving toward the door, "but that does not mean I like it or understand it." I banged out of his chambers, storming back to my own rooms and no doubt yet another sleepless night.

"What news?" I asked the next night as Michelotto stood before me in my private chambers. He had been on the streets of Rome much of the day, listening and speaking with his informants. Bodyguard, assassin, spy, spymaster—Michelotto's many talents were worth their weight in gold, I was finding.

"It would seem His Holiness has won a great victory over those who oppose him," Michelotto reported. "Ascanio Sforza has ridden for Milan, and Giuliano della Rovere has reportedly collapsed in a fit of rage and taken to his bed."

"They did not imagine the pope and King Charles would come to such accord," I observed. Earlier King Charles had accompanied the Holy Father to the basilica of San Giovanni in Laterano, that they might pray together. Such a friendship was not why the rebellious cardinals had sided with the French king.

"The looting has subsided as well," Michelotto reported. "No doubt the soldiers have had their fun, and the army is preparing to march again."

"And we shall be going with it," I said bitterly.

"My lord?"

I told him of the demand my father had granted the French king, and was not surprised when he nodded rather sagely. "Ah, yes. I heard a rumor of that. I was not certain it was true, or if you would prefer that I stay in Rome."

"No," I said. "I will need you with me to watch my back in that nest of vipers. Charles may be an easy dupe, but I do not trust him."

"He would have nothing to gain by hurting you," Michelotto pointed out, ever the strategist.

"True, but I had rather rely on your eyes and skills than Charles's good will."

The following night, a banquet was held at the Vatican to celebrate the agreement between pope and king. Charles and his generals were in attendance, as were those cardinals who had stayed loyal to my father, and a few who had not, welcomed back into the fold. I'd had Michelotto arrange for another two food tasters in the kitchens. I did not trust any of these men.

The French king, as my father described him, was a notably unimposing figure. His back was indeed bent and hunched, taking away from a height that was not impressive to begin with, and made for a painful-looking walk. His nose was large, entirely out of proportion with the rest of his features. He had coarse black hair and a beard that looked rather unkempt.

In addition, his table manners were atrocious; he belched loudly and ate with his hands, eschewing the offer of a fork. He hung on the pope's every word, and my father's charm and good will were on display at every turn. Charles was duly impressed, and must be kept that way.

"A pleasure to meet you finally, Your Eminence," Charles said to me at the start of the meal, his Latin heavily accented. "Your reputation precedes you."

I gave him a tight smile. "As does yours, Your Highness," I said. "Or perhaps it is only your cannon that precedes you."

He guffawed loudly, and I wondered if he simply meant to overlook the subtle insult, or if he had not noticed it at all. "My country has many great arms-makers, Your Eminence. I shall be happy to allow you to inspect the cannon, if you are interested."

"Very interested, Highness."

"And you shall have ample time, no? We will soon become much better acquainted, I do not doubt."

"Indeed," I said, finding it hard to retain my brittle smile.

"I hope you will enjoy the journey. Naples is said to be a beautiful place."

"Indeed it is, Your Highness. No doubt that is why you have gone to such trouble for it."

He gave me a curious look. "Yes," he said, somewhat uncertainly.

"And how are you finding Rome, Highness?" I went on.

"Your hospitality is very fine," he said. "I daresay I am not as eager to leave as I ought to be."

"I should think not. You shall not find such hospitality in Naples, after all."

This time Charles glared at me, but I kept my bland politician's smile perfectly in place.

"I hope you enjoy the wine, my son," the pope said to the king then, diverting Charles's attention. "It is the finest vintage I had in my cellars; I have been waiting for an illustrious guest to share it with."

Charles virtually preened at these words. Mother Mary, I thought incredulously, the man is a vain fool. His army's meeting no resistance all the way down the peninsula has no doubt only heightened his vanity. "Your Holiness is too kind, as always, and the finest of hosts," Charles said. He rose from his seat, lifting his golden goblet into the air. "A toast, to His Holiness Pope Alexander! May his reign be long and prosperous, and may the friendship between the Holy See and the Kingdom of France be eternal."

"Hear, hear!" called the assembled company, and we all drank. Father looked exceedingly pleased, beaming as he set down his goblet.

Sitting farthest away from the pope and the king were a few of those cardinals who had embraced the French cause. Their faces were frozen into an expression of uncomfortable disbelief, as though they had sat down upon a bed of thorns. I allowed myself a small inward laugh. It would appear they had not truly believed in the accord between the French king and the pope they'd sought to depose until they had seen it with their own eyes.

The banquet was of interminable length. I stayed quiet through much of it, still struggling with the idea of joining these French barbarians in a matter of days, and that my father was sending me with them. Was I so inconsequential to his plans that he had no better use for me than as a hostage?

Juan would never have been used as such, were he here.

Yet as the night drew to a close, my weary mind remembered my promise to Maddalena. My promise to help save the people of Rome. If the French would not leave without me, would not leave all the innocent Romans in peace until I rode with them, then I would go. I would help in that way. I could only hope it would make her think well of me.

The thought made it easier to smile congenially as the assembled company drank yet another toast.

Chapter 31

MADDALENA

Once again, the household of the pope's women had gathered on the terrace of the Castel Sant' Angelo, but for a much happier reason. Today we were watching the French army ride out of Rome. And good riddance, I thought. May you never come back.

Our lives could return to normal. We could return to Santa Maria in Portico in the coming weeks and leave this cold fortress that had begun to feel rather like a tomb—fitting, for, as Isabella had told me, that was exactly what it once was. She claimed the structure had originally been built by one of the pagan emperors of Rome as a tomb for himself and his wife. It did not surprise me. I had come to feel a bit like a corpse myself, tucked away behind the cold walls.

And once our lives returned to the way they once were, surely I would be able to find Federico myself, if I did not have word from Cardinal Borgia first. My failure to do so, even with the risks I'd taken, had not allowed me to sleep any better. With the French gone, the servants would return to the Vatican—no doubt some of them already had, with the Holy Father again in residence—and someone would know where Federico had gone. And if not, I could hire a messenger to take a letter to his family's vineyard once peace had returned to Rome and its environs.

But I kept remembering the blood in the wine shop. I returned again and again to that image. It was likely Federico had not been there at all, yet it haunted me each time I closed my eyes, my stomach twisting in a sickening mix of guilt and dread.

I pulled myself from my dark musings and peered down at the street below. Cardinal Borgia was riding beside the French king as they left the Vatican Palace and rode past the fortress.

I had not seen Cardinal Borgia since the day I had foolishly left the Castel Sant' Angelo to seek Federico—the day I had slapped a prince of the Church. I still blushed to think of it, but what I blushed at most was the memory of his lips grazing the skin of my hand, and of the words he had spoken to me with such reverence: *I shall do as you bid me, Maddalena, avenging angel, Madonna of Holy Vengeance.* Never had someone spoken to me so before, as though I were to be admired, worshipped.

He had kept his first promise to me: later that same day, several wheels of fresh cheese had been delivered to the Castel's kitchen expressly for me. I had shared with the staff, of course; the cook had baked us a fresh loaf of bread to go with it, and we all practically squealed with delight as we devoured our feast. Naturally, the others had been curious where I had gotten such a bounty; I lied—promising myself to confess the sin later—and said Federico's family had sent it. Gossip would be ruthless if I said it had come from Cardinal Borgia; there would be speculation that was neither wanted nor warranted. We had no relationship beyond that of a maid and a man who far outranked her in the world, even if he was particularly kind to me . . .

He is very brave, I thought, watching him ride past. He rode into unknown danger, into a war that was not of his making, and yet one he would try to stop.

And he had kept his promise to me. With the departure of the French, the people of Rome would be safe. However he and the Holy Father had arranged it, the French were leaving, and the city would rejoice. He had even offered himself up as a sacrifice to see it done. Whether or not he could bring me news of Federico, I considered his promise fulfilled.

He could be killed, I thought suddenly, and the thought forced the breath sharply from my lungs as though I had fallen flat onto stone.

Surely he is in little danger, I tried to reassure myself. He is the pope's son, after all. It would be more than their soul was worth for anyone to harm him. And behind him rode a fair-haired man I had seen with His Eminence before, his bodyguard. He was not alone. He had his man to protect him.

And yet . . . it was war. Horrible and unpredictable things could happen when men have violence in their blood.

I might never see Cesare Borgia again.

This should not have mattered to me. I should have harbored no more feeling for him than the respect due a prince of the Church.

But I did. And wrong and sinful though it was, I could no longer deny it as I watched him ride away and my heart broke.

Chapter 32

CESARE

King Charles had been insistent that I be at his side as he paraded out of Rome, as if I were a captured prince in a triumphal procession. And wasn't that exactly what I was?

Yet as we left the city, he was content to let me fall back, which I happily did, Michelotto riding at my side. I had every confidence that I was actor and politician enough to keep Charles in the dark, but best to avoid his notice altogether.

The night before, my father had finally let me—and Michelotto, as he would be involved as well—in on the full extent of his plans. "So you see, Cesare," Father had said, once he'd finished explaining, "you shall not be a French hostage for long."

We had gone over it again, and again, and one last time for good measure, to ensure we all knew our roles and could execute it flawlessly. We would only have one chance.

Despite my lingering anger, I had laughed when he'd first explained the plan, and I wanted to laugh again each time I pictured what the expression on Charles's face would surely be when he found out what we'd done. But it did not do to look too pleased with myself as I rode along. I was a virtual prisoner, after all. Instead I retreated firmly behind a polite yet brooding exterior, a slight scowl permanently upon my face.

It was not all that difficult to maintain. I only had to dwell upon my father sending me away in the first place—with a plot up the sleeve of his papal robes, yes, but he had sent me away, nonetheless. Our political situation had been largely improved, but that he could part with me at all still did not sit well with me. He did not need me at his side, as he claimed. He had—almost literally—moved Heaven and earth to get me into the Church, and yet still I was not indispensable.

What would it take?

I could start by carrying off this adventure flawlessly. And I would.

He could never have trusted Juan with such a task, I told myself smugly as I rode. Juan would have botched it immediately. No doubt even Father knew that.

If nothing else, at least I had kept my promise to Maddalena, I reminded myself. I couldn't help a smile as I indulged in the memory of how she had looked after she'd slapped me. An angel of righteous vengeance, indeed. Now she—and the people of her city that she loved so much—would be safe.

After several hours on the road, one of the French officers kept glancing over at me—annoyed, it seemed, by my surly silence. It would not do to give too much offense to my temporary hosts; the time had come for a show of casual resignation. "How are you enjoying the ride, Michelotto?" I asked.

Michelotto looked up, far too savvy to betray surprise at the first words I had spoken in hours. "Very much, Your Eminence," he said. "I have never been south of Rome before."

"Indeed? Then you are seeing much of the beautiful countryside."

"I am. I like it very much."

"Naples has some truly beautiful views," I went on. "I look forward to beholding them myself."

"I am eager to see them, my lord. Is there not danger from the volcano near the city?"

"Mount Vesuvio? Yes, I daresay there is," I said. "The faith of the people of Naples must be strong indeed, for them to live constantly in the shadow of such danger."

"Only God's will protects them, no doubt."

"No doubt," I echoed. "The stewards of the city, whoever they may be, must be very careful to always act in accordance with God's will, lest he use the volcano to express his wrath."

The French officer who'd been glaring at me scowled at these words. I doubted his Italian was very good, but he clearly understood enough. It was for that reason that I had addressed Michelotto in Italian instead of Catalan, which we could be safely assured none of the Frenchmen spoke. I did not want them thinking we plotted against them in a language they could not understand—we did plot against them, of course, but it wouldn't do to be obvious about it. And I enjoyed needling them where I could—the type of paltry revenge one could afford to allow a hostage.

That night we camped upon the road, and I took great pleasure in imperiously directing the set-up of a tent for Michelotto and myself, taking great pains to ensure the dozen trunks I'd brought—which, I had said, contained my most valuable possessions and from which I could not be parted—were securely settled nearby.

"Will there be a man assigned to guard my trunks?" I asked of a passing officer.

He grimaced. "You've brought your own man, haven't you?" he asked in broken Italian. "He can guard your things."

I spoke French rather well, of which King Charles was aware, but these men didn't need to know that. "Oh, no, monsieur," I said haughtily. "That will never do. My man must guard my person at all times."

"You're in no danger so long as His Holiness keeps his bargains."

"His Highness King Charles would never dare, not when His Holiness embraced him as a son," I declared. "But His Holiness does have enemies, may God forgive them. And so I must have a guard with me at all times."

"We haven't the men to spare to guard your vanities, Eminence."

"The biggest army Italy has seen in centuries hasn't a man to spare? Must I ask the king himself?"

The man sighed heavily. "Very well. I'll have a man spread his bedroll here, if that will help you sleep, my lord." He spat the last two words.

I smiled condescendingly. "It shall, monsieur. God give you good night."

I went back into the tent to find Michelotto within, contorted with silent laughter.

We had been a few days on the road when a messenger arrived for King Charles.

The messenger burst into the large tent where Charles and a few of his generals dined. I was present by command more than invitation. Like a jewel in a glass case, it was easier for the French king to enjoy his prestigious hostage when I was directly under his eye. I kept a smile on my face by constantly reminding myself of what was to come.

The messenger, breathless and mud-spattered, dropped a hasty bow to the king. "Your Royal Highness," he panted, "I bring urgent news."

"*Oui, oui,* what is it?" Charles barked.

"Word has come from Naples. King Alfonso has abdicated the throne and fled to Sicily."

Gasps and excited murmurs immediately broke out among the gathered Frenchmen.

"He has fled?" Charles asked, almost giddy, rising from his chair.

"He has, Highness. He has left the crown to his son Ferrantino, who is even now mounting a defense of the capital city."

I grimaced. After everything the pope had done for Alfonso: defending his claim in consistory, risking his tiara, conspiring with Ferrantino and the Orsini and being betrayed by the latter as a result, out-maneuvering Charles and refusing to crown him King of Naples. All to support the Aragonese claim, and this was how Alfonso repaid him.

Brash, blunt Ferrantino was now King of Naples. He would have made a good one under ordinary circumstances, no doubt.

Yet this would likely be the final blow to Naples's defense: their king had fled, abandoning them, without a care for his people or his family. The morale of her troops and the disarray of her government would be Naples's undoing.

Charles rubbed his hands together eagerly, as though ready to reach out and pluck his prize between two fingers—his task would not be much more difficult than that now. "Is there more?" he demanded.

"They say King Alfonso was—is—rather mad," the messenger continued. "That he has been driven mad by fear, and that is why he fled."

I remained silent as the men around me crowed with pleasure. Alfonso's father, Ferrante, had no doubt been mad, after a fashion—what other word was there for a man who kept a grisly museum filled with the bodies of his enemies? Perhaps this madness tainted his bloodline.

"Pull up a chair for this fine man! Bring him some wine and hot food!" Charles called. One of the servants hurried to add a chair to the end of the table. "A toast!" the king went on, raising his goblet. "To fair Naples, who lies on her back with her legs spread, moaning for a strong Frenchman to take her!"

The gathered men roared their approval.

Charles drank, and as he moved to sit back down his eye caught on me. "What shall the pope say now, eh?" he taunted. "He shall have no choice but to crown me king, once Ferrantino is dead in battle and my arse is on Alfonso's throne!"

I smiled, tight-lipped, as I picked up my goblet. "His Holiness will do what is right, as always," I said calmly. I raised the goblet slightly in Charles's direction, taking a long sip and ignoring his scowl.

After another two days of riding, we arrived at the town of Velletri, where Giuliano della Rovere was bishop. He was waiting in the grand bishop's residence to welcome the French king, a wide smile that did not quite reach his eyes upon his angular face.

As I stepped into the entryway of the palace, his eyes locked on mine immediately, as a stag will always sense the presence of a wolf. His smile did not dim for an instant as he glided toward me. "Cardinal Borgia," he said smoothly, leaning in to give me the kiss of peace. "You are most welcome to Velletri."

"I thank you for your hospitality, Cardinal della Rovere," I said.

"I would not have thought His Holiness could have parted with your sharp mind at such a time," he said, his grin widening as if he knew exactly how these words would pinch me. "But I am honored to have you as a guest."

"I can see why you must have preferred to come here at this time of year," I said, glancing perfunctorily around the entrance hall. "Rome is a bit chilly for you at present." I met his eyes with mine.

His gaze hardened, but his smile did not slip. "Indeed. I have found Rome's climate rather objectionable for some time now."

"I would not expect an improvement any time soon if I were you," I said.

"I can see why you might feel so," he said. He studied my face carefully. "You've the look of your mother about you," he said. "She must be very proud of her eldest son."

If della Rovere was expecting me to be thrown by the sudden change in topic, he almost got his wish. It took my every effort to prevent my face from contorting into a bitter expression at his words.

Politics had not been the only source of the rivalry between him and my father. Many years ago, Giuliano della Rovere had been madly in love with the young Vannozza dei Cattanei, and she had spurned his advances in favor of Rodrigo Borgia. Della Rovere had had a bastard daughter of his own since then with another woman, but as Roman gossip had it, he had never ceased to love Vannozza.

I met his gaze, my own impassive. "She is indeed," I said. "I would offer to give her your regards, but I know not when I shall see her next. You see, she was forced to flee after the Frenchmen you invited into Italy sacked her house in Rome and did not know better than to injure a Roman gentlewoman."

Shock flitted across della Rovere's features; he could not hide it. "I . . . had not heard," he said, crossing himself. "Terrible. I shall pray for her."

"Oh, you needn't trouble yourself," I said. "The pope, as well as her son the cardinal, pray for her every day. There is nothing she needs from you." I walked past him and out of the entry hall, Michelotto following close at my back.

Snake though he was, Giuliano della Rovere was a fine host, seeing to every comfort of his French guests and keeping them well furnished with wine. The food and drink looked to be the finest available, though I very deliberately did not touch my goblet, and pushed the food about on my plate without taking a bite. Della Rovere noticed, and kept glancing toward me, irritation in his eyes. He spoke to me no more than courtesy demanded, and I was perfectly content to have it so.

After the feasting had ended, a servant showed me to my room: a small, chilly one with damp stone walls and no wall hangings. There were two narrow cots crammed inside, for Michelotto and I.

"His Eminence apologizes most profusely for the lodgings—he knows it is not what you're used to but regrets to say there is nothing more suited to your station available at present," the servant intoned pompously. "What with the French king and his retinue here, the finer rooms are already taken."

I laughed mirthlessly. "You may tell Cardinal della Rovere that I understand completely."

The servant bowed without further comment and left.

I sat down on one of the beds right as Michelotto came through the door carrying a worn leather saddlebag, which he handed to me. "A few hours from now will be best, Eminence," he said.

I opened the saddlebag, smiling slightly at its contents: plain breeches, a shirt, and a hooded cloak. "Yes," I agreed. "Everyone should be asleep by then. We've cause to thank Giuliano della Rovere's generosity with his wine cellar this night."

In the darkest hours of morning, Michelotto and I slipped outside and to the edge of the French camp. I was wearing the simple clothes he had brought for me, and my cardinals' robes and hat were stowed in the bag in turn. We both wore dark cloaks, pulled up to cover our faces.

The sentry guarding the horses straightened upon our approach. "Halt," he said. "What business have you here?"

"We need only two horses, monsieur, and we shall be on our way," I said in perfect French, my voice low.

He snorted. "I am hardly about to give you—"

He broke off, his eyes widening at the two gold coins in my outstretched hand. He took one, bit it, and quickly snatched the other from my palm. "On your way," he said, and turned and melted into the darkness.

It could not have been easier. Michelotto and I each chose and hastily saddled a fine stallion, mounted, and were off, galloping back toward Rome.

Two days' hard riding later, we reached the papal castle of Spoleto, where my father had instructed I go. I had nearly laughed myself hoarse the entire way, imagining the faces of Charles and his men and Giuliano della Rovere when they found me gone. I laughed still further when I thought of them opening the many trunks I had brought, the ones I insisted contained all the valuable things I could not travel without, no matter the inconvenience, and finding them empty.

Chapter 33

MADDALENA

It was not until some three weeks after the French departed—at the insistence of the Holy Father, who counseled caution—that Giulia and Adriana moved the household back into the Palazzo Santa Maria in Portico. It meant a flurry of activity for us maids, packing everything up from our quarters in the Castel Sant' Angelo—honestly, why had these ladies brought so much with them to essentially be imprisoned?—and seeing it all transported back to the palazzo, where everything needed to be unpacked again and put in its proper place.

It was clear the soldiers and mercenaries had been through the palazzo, but they would have found little of value: all the valuables kept here had been transferred to the Castel Sant' Angelo along with the papal treasures. The French had made off with some cheaper tapestries and furniture, as well as a few statues from the garden, but nothing Adriana was troubled to lose. However, soldiers had tramped through the palazzo with muddy boots, had spilled their wine about, and had even urinated in the halls, making for quite a mess that we servants were obliged to clean up.

We were busy for several days, between cleaning and unpacking and brushing out gowns and seeing to the washing of linens. And the whole time, even as I was hauling linens to the laundry or gossiping with Isabella or putting away jewels, my mind was racing like a horse in the Palio, and I, just like one of the bareback riders of that race, tried desperately to cling on.

Ever since I had watched Cesare Borgia, Cardinal of Valencia—whom many Romans had taken to referring to by the Italianized version of his title, Valentino—ride away with the French army, my mind had been scampering about ceaselessly. It did not even pause when I slept, for I was once again dreaming of him, dreams no good woman should have. I would wake up in a sweat, certain parts of me throbbing for him. Eventually I would fall back asleep, only to dream of the cramped dark space of the confessional, and of speaking aloud the sins of which I dreamt and that I carried in my heart. I would awake again, in the early light of dawn, relieved that it had been only a dream, knowing I should confess such things but also knowing that I never would. I could not bear it.

And so my mind continued to churn, both sleeping and waking, one state bringing me my heated desires and fears and another bringing me cool reason and duty. I could not seem to escape either.

Mixed into all these desperate thoughts was Federico. I had not had a moment free to seek him. Part of me hoped he might come to me instead and take me away from this den of sin I had built for myself.

But I did not wait in suspense long. A few days after we returned to Palazzo Santa Maria in Portico, a messenger came for me, telling me that the Cardinal of Valencia wished to see me.

Isabella and another maid were in the hall where the messenger gave me my summons, and both gaped at me. "Our paths crossed in the Castel, and he offered to help me find Federico," I explained. "I assumed he had forgotten."

It would not have surprised me if he had. By then word had spread throughout Rome of Cardinal Valentino's exploits in escaping French captivity, and it was repeated by all with a measure of awe. The pope's dashing son had outsmarted the murderous, rapacious French! He had become something of a hero since his recent return to the city.

Isabella recovered her wits first. "You had best go, then," she said matter-of-factly. "I'll give your excuses if you're missed. Go! No doubt he has found your man!"

As I followed the messenger to the Vatican, I tried to tell myself that this was the only reason for my pounding heart: I was finally to learn what had become of Federico. Yet even that had the ring of a lie.

The messenger led me to a room not far from those occupied by the Holy Father, knocked on the open door, and stepped inside. I followed hesitantly. "Maddalena Moretti, as you requested, Your Eminence," the man said, bowing.

Cardinal Borgia rose from behind an ornate wooden desk and walked around it, handing a coin to the messenger. "*Eccellente. Grazie.*"

The messenger took the coin, bowed, and left.

"Maddalena," he said, turning to face me.

I swept a curtsy. "Your Eminence," I murmured, wondering if he could hear my pounding heart.

"No doubt you have surmised why I've called you here," he said. He motioned to a bench that had been cut into the window across from the door. "Sit, please."

I moved across the room to sit, and to my surprise he sat beside me, as though we were equals. The stone bench was large enough that we were not touching, as was proper, with not even the whisper of clothing brushing clothing; yet my body sprung into awareness at his close proximity.

"I would guess, Your Eminence, it is to do with Federico Lucci, my betrothed," I said.

"Indeed."

"I am surprised Your Eminence remembered," I said. "Much has passed since last we saw each other."

"Yes, a great deal. But I made a promise, did I not?" I glanced up and found his eyes locked on mine, steady and serious. "I am not a man who goes back on his promises, Maddalena."

"I . . . I did not mean to imply you were," I said hastily. "It is simply that . . ."

He waved my clarification aside. "I have taken no offense," he said.

Silence fell, and when I could bear it no longer I asked, "If it please Your Eminence . . . what have you learned of Federico?"

"Ah," he said. "I suppose I am hesitant because, well, I do not have good news, I'm afraid."

Cold spread through my limbs, even as my mind rushed to find some way out of the darkness they implied. "Please," I whispered, through lips that felt numb, "I would know the truth."

He sighed and clasped his hands in his lap. "I will get to the point, then," he said. "I'm so sorry, but I'm afraid Federico Lucci was killed by French soldiers during the invasion."

I closed my eyes, as though to keep out his words. "He . . . he is dead?" I whispered. I could not tell if I meant it as a question or a statement.

"I'm afraid so."

Tears seeped out from beneath my closed lids. *This cannot be. No. Holy Lord Jesus, Blessed Mother Mary, please, tell me it isn't true,* I prayed.

Yet hadn't I known since I had seen those bloodstains in the wine shop? I hadn't let myself believe, but I had suspected, deep down. I had known, somehow, when he and I had said goodbye, that it was our last. That that kiss would be our last.

And it was my fault.

It took me a moment to realize Cardinal Borgia was speaking once more. "I had my best man looking for word of him. It did not take him long to determine what happened. Some French soldiers had set upon a shop owned by a friend of his, I believe—were starting to loot it. He was there with the man that day and tried to fight them off. They cut both men down without a second glance. It was very courageous, I must say. I do not know as it is any comfort, but he died a brave man."

"But a foolish one," I said softly. I finally opened my eyes and was almost taken aback by his expression: full of compassion and sorrow, almost as though my loss was his own.

"An honorable one," he corrected gently.

The blood on the wine shop floor . . . it had been Federico's blood. I had been there, at the spot where he died. Had the bodies of Federico and his friend been inside still? I let out a choked sob.

"He was given a Christian burial," the cardinal offered. "I made certain of it."

I nodded. "I . . . I thank you for that." I could not hold back my anguish, my guilt, any longer. I buried my face in my hands and began to sob, only embarrassed in some tiny part of my mind to be carrying on so before Cesare Borgia.

"Ah, Maddalena." He shifted closer, wrapping his arms around me and drawing me to his chest. "I cannot tell you how sorry I am to have given you this news."

With my face buried against his shoulder, I let out all my sorrow: for Federico and the death he hadn't deserved, the one he would not have had if I had not been so selfish and full of lust and pride; for his friend, a man whose name I could not remember but who had been a good man; and for the life I had so foolishly turned my back on and would never have.

And I cried for the remorse I felt, that would never leave me as long as I lived. I cried for how Federico's death was my fault, as certain as if I had been the Frenchman who had run him through with a blade.

Cardinal Borgia drew me closer, so we were pressed tightly together—indeed, I was nearly sitting in his lap. To my horror, a shiver of pleasure went through me, and my crying stopped as I became more aware of my chest meeting his, his cheek resting on the top of my head as he held me, his breath stirring my hair.

It took me far too long to pull away. But reluctantly I did, pulling one of my handkerchiefs out of my bodice and drying my eyes. "I . . . I am sorry, Your Eminence," I said, my voice still thick with tears—and something else I couldn't, wouldn't identify. "I have behaved most inappropriately."

He took my hand, twining my fingers through his. "Not at all," he said. "You have had a terrible shock. Anything I can do to comfort you . . ."

Our eyes locked again as his thumb caressed my wrist. He

leaned ever so slightly toward me, his lips parted, and I found myself doing the same, as if compelled by some force outside myself.

But I was not compelled, and that was the sin.

Quickly I leapt up, pulling my hand from his. "I . . . I apologize, Your Eminence," I said. "I should go."

"Please, stay," he said, rising as well. "Until you are less upset. You are surely in no state to make your way home."

"You have been too generous already," I babbled. "It was so very kind of you to find out this . . . news for me."

His expression was solemn as he regarded me. "I fear it was not kind at all."

"But now I know," I said. "I . . . I needed to know."

"I am sorry, Maddalena."

I bobbed him a curtsy, not daring to look at him. "Goodbye, Your Eminence," I said. Then I whirled on my heel and fled.

I did not get very far. Some hours later I was still on my knees in one of the chapels in St. Peter's Basilica. I had staggered in and dropped to my knees before the altar. "Why?" I had nearly howled, looking up at Jesus Christ on his cross above the altar through my veil of tears. "Why would you take someone as kind and decent and full of life as Federico? Why? Why?"

I had dissolved into weeping then, and once the tears finally subsided I had risen on unsteady legs to light a candle in Federico's memory. After, I knelt once more, taking deep breaths to calm myself, and I prayed. I prayed for Federico's soul, that he might be admitted to Heaven straightaway; I prayed for God to punish those who had murdered him; I prayed for the soul of his friend; I prayed for God to ease my grief; I prayed for the grief of Federico's family to be eased, after losing a second son so soon after the first.

And I prayed to be forgiven, though I did not see how it could be so.

I could have averted this, and that I must bear the rest of my days. I must bear Federico's death for the rest of my days. Another sin added to the tally that grew ever larger within my soul.

It was a tally that now included the shameless, wanton way I had acted earlier that day. Cardinal Cesare Borgia, a prince of Holy Mother Church, had told me of the death of my betrothed, and I had cried in his arms, pressing myself against him like a brazen slut. I had taken comfort in his embrace, in the embrace of a man of God. While mourning the death of the man I was supposed to love, I was filled with lust for another, a man forbidden by all laws of God and the Church. What forgiveness could there be for me?

There are seven deadly sins, Maddalena, but lust is the deadliest.

On my knees on the hard stone floor, I gazed up at the crucifix and could only beseech the Lord Jesus to tell me what would become of me now.

Chapter 34

CESARE

Rome, March 1495

"Thank you for agreeing to meet with me so quickly, Your Excellency," I said, rising to greet Girolamo Giorgio, the Venetian ambassador.

He inclined his head. "It is an honor, Your Eminence," he said. "I look forward to a productive discussion."

"As do I. Please, sit." I gestured to a chair in my private audience chamber. Once we were seated, I snapped my fingers, and a servant bearing a tray with a decanter of wine and two goblets—Venetian glass, of course—entered the room immediately. The ambassador's eyes widened in appreciation.

I had remained out of sight in the castle at Spoleto for almost three weeks—all a part of Father's plans. Just as I had envisioned, I had nearly been able to hear the French king howling with rage all the way in Velletri. He had written a furious letter to the pope, railing at his and my treachery. Father had responded in a mild and apologetic tone, asserting that he had known nothing of my escape until it happened and assuring Charles he would be reprimanding me for it. Charles, by then having cut his way through Ferrantino's troops and in the process of ensconcing himself in Naples, had little recourse.

Once enough time had passed, Michelotto and I rode back to Rome, for there was work to do.

I had kept my promise to Maddalena and inquired after her betrothed—unfortunate, but in truth what I had expected. There were many such sad stories in Rome from the French occupation. It had pained me to give her such news and cause her such sorrow. Yet—and it was wicked of me—I had rather enjoyed holding her as she wept, feeling the supple curves of her body pressed against mine. I wondered if Federico had known what a pearl he had in her. But I was not so without scruples that I would seduce a grieving woman, a fact I'd acknowledged with a touch of regret.

There were political matters to see to as well. The pope was planning to create what he called a Holy League, between as many Italian and European powers as possible, with the aim of driving the French out of Italy. And when he summoned me directly upon my return to the Eternal City, he made it clear he needed my help in doing so.

It had been a proud moment. I had played my part perfectly, and he trusted I would continue to do so. I was, at last, necessary. Perhaps even, finally, indispensable. If it had taken my adventure in French captivity to prove that, then it had been well worth it.

Hence the meeting I had arranged with the Venetian ambassador.

I raised my goblet in a toast to the ambassador and took a sip. He followed suit. "A fine vintage, Your Eminence," he said. "Very different from the *vino rosso* we get in the Veneto—earthier, a bit heavier. A wonderfully complex flavor."

"I'm glad you like it, Excellency. It comes from the countryside not too far from the Holy City. I'll see that you are sent a barrel."

"Your Eminence is too kind." Giorgio took another appreciative sip and set the goblet down. "I was glad to receive your request to meet with you. I know this meeting would be most welcome to my masters in the Senate and the doge himself. Mother Venice and the Holy See have common aims at this time."

"I perceive the same, Excellency," I said smoothly. "I can well understand Venice's neutrality when the French first invaded—why should La Serenissima concern herself with the crown of Naples, no? But I think the time has come to agree the French have no further business remaining on the Italian peninsula. Who knows what threat they will pose to the sovereignty of all Italian nations if left to run unchecked in our lands?"

Giorgio smiled slightly as he raised the goblet to his lips again. "Those are Venice's feelings precisely, Your Eminence. And war, as you surely know, is very bad for trade. The French presence in Italy has proven harmful to Venice's mercantile interests on the peninsula. Nothing crippling"—he waved a hand casually, assuring me Venice remained the richest nation in Europe—"but certainly it is an unwelcome development for my country. Should the French remain, and thus continually unsettle the region, the damage to our trade will only worsen."

I smiled, pleased with myself for foreseeing this outcome. A Venetian cared about nothing until it harmed his purse. Luckily for the Holy See, the French presence in Italy was doing just that.

And if Venice was hoping to wind up with a chunk of Ludovico Sforza's Milanese territory—which they had always coveted—it would only assist in securing their cooperation, even if it would be impolitic to mention it.

"The Holy Father is certainly aware of these developments, Excellency, and finds them as untenable as does Venice. And so we find our aims are united."

The ambassador nodded. "And what does the Holy See require of Venice?"

"Military support," I said, "and Venice's signature on a treaty to create a Holy League against the French."

"And who shall comprise this Holy League?"

Ah. The delicate part of the negotiations. Venice was still hedging her bets. "The Holy Roman Emperor has already agreed, as has Spain." Well, Spain had not agreed yet—my meeting with the Spanish ambassador was the next morning—but they would. After all, it was their ancestral claim to Naples being uprooted. "And His Holiness expects Milan to join us as well."

Giorgio snorted. "As well Milan should. They got the rest of us into this mess."

"Indeed they did. And between you and I, Excellency . . ." I leaned forward conspiratorially, prompting Giorgio to lean toward me in turn, "His Holiness is most displeased with Milan and its masters at this particular time. And he means to make his displeasure felt."

There. Let Venice think she might end up with pieces of the duchy of Milan, even as I promised no such thing.

"Is that so?" Giorgio said, barely hiding his smirk. "Well, that is most meet and fitting, to be sure. His Serenity the doge will be glad to hear it."

"No doubt. Do I take it, then, Your Excellency, that Venice is in agreement?"

"She is," he said. "I shall write to the doge and senate this afternoon, and as soon as a treaty is drawn up, Your Eminence may expect my signature."

I raised my goblet, smiling, and the ambassador clinked his against it. "Then we are in accord."

Spain needed no urging to agree to the Holy League; indeed, they already had troops on the way. Any chance to strike at their old enemy, France—especially over the right of the Aragonese line to rule Naples—and they would take it. Milan might prove more difficult to convince, and so His Holiness planned to use some of Holy Mother Church's most potent weapons: shame and guilt.

He summoned the Milanese ambassador to an audience before the College of Cardinals and the rest of the papal court. There would be no private meeting for Milan—the pope meant to dress down her and her ambassador before the entire Curia.

I stood to the right of the papal throne as the ambassador entered, knelt, and kissed the pope's slipper and ring. "Your Holiness," he said. "An honor to attend you."

"Rise," Father said in a booming voice. "No doubt you know why we have summoned you."

"I do, Your Holiness."

"Good. We shall waste no time." He looked down his large nose at the ambassador. "We trust your master, Ludovico Sforza, sees now the error of his ways in inviting the French and their war machines into the Italian peninsula."

"He does, Your Holiness."

Ludovico was now officially the Duke of Milan; his nephew Gian Galezzo had died in the Sforza castle in Pavia in 1494 shortly after King Charles had visited there. It was widely rumored he had died at Ludovico's hand, so Ludovico might finally obtain the ducal crown, and was indeed accepted as fact in some quarters. The official story was the poor boy had succumbed to an illness. I was not entirely sure of the truth, but it did not matter in the end: Gian Galezzo was dead, however it had occurred, and his uncle was now Duke of Milan. I could not help but suspect that his finally attaining the ducal crown—and his desire to enjoy it—had played a part in his sudden repentance.

"We should hope so," Father said. "And we further trust that he means to make amends for his rash and foolish diplomacy, if it even can be called such?"

"He does, Your Holiness. Duke Ludovico wanted me to assure you that he, and all his resources, are entirely at Your Holiness's command."

Good. If he was eager to get back into the Holy Father's good graces, it made our task that much easier.

"Very good. No doubt, then, we can expect Milan's agreement to our new Holy League, and the commitment of her troops in driving the French from our peninsula."

"Nothing would give Duke Ludovico greater joy."

"Well, we certainly strive to bring Ludovico Sforza joy," the pope said, voice thick with irony. Several of the cardinals tittered at this, and I allowed myself an unabashed laugh. "Very well. As soon as the treaty for the Holy League is drawn up, we will expect Your Excellency's presence at the signing."

The ambassador bowed. "You may count on it, Holiness."

"Good." The pope rose from his throne. "God give you good day, Your Excellency."

The ambassador left the audience chamber, and I saw an almost imperceptible relaxing of my father's large frame.

On March 31, the Holy League pact was signed and sealed, and the major powers of Italy and Europe were in accord. The French had to go, and should they prove reluctant, there was an army massing to help convince them.

Fortunately Charles would not need much convincing. Naples, though easily conquered, was not easily held, he was finding. After their long march, his soldiers did nothing but loot and take up with loose women. As such, rumor had it a terrifying new disease was spreading. The French called it *le mal de Naples,* while the Neapolitans had taken to calling it the French pox. These factors did nothing to endear the French to the Neapolitan people or barons, who had at first greeted them as liberators from the tyranny of old King Ferrante and his heirs. The French welcome in Naples, it seemed, had very quickly been worn out.

After the ceremony for the signing of the Holy League pact, Michelotto found me outside the banquet hall, where a celebratory feast was being held. "Your Eminence," he murmured, glancing around swiftly. "A word."

I led him into a small receiving room nearby and shut the door. "What news, Michelotto?"

"It is as Your Eminence thought," he said. "Some of them are still here."

A dark smile touched my lips. Some of the troops who had

come with Charles remained in Rome after his departure, ostensibly to keep order in what the French king considered a conquered city. In reality, all they did was drink, whore, and get into brawls in taverns and brothels.

Some, I had suspected, were Swiss mercenaries, more difficult for Charles to control and thus easier for him to leave behind. Swiss mercenaries, the ones who had looted my mother's house and treated her abominably.

"And you know where they are?" I asked.

"I do, my lord. And I know where they will be tomorrow."

"Where would that be?"

"In the piazza outside the Vatican, Your Eminence. I will make certain of that."

My smile widened. "Good. See to it not all of them leave."

"Consider it done, Eminence."

My smile remained in place as I went to rejoin the banquet. Those men would see what befell those who crossed a Borgia.

By the next afternoon, word had spread: two thousand Spanish guards had fallen upon a group of Swiss mercenaries in the Vatican square and massacred them. Twenty-four were killed, many more injured, and still more fled Rome in terror.

According to Michelotto, the gossip in the streets was that the pope's son, Cardinal Valentino, had ordered the slaughter.

The rumors did not bother me. I wanted them all to know. I wanted everyone to know it was me, and to mark it well.

Chapter 35

MADDALENA

Rome, July 1495

Giulia and Adriana were lounging languidly in the July heat, being fanned by us serving girls, when a footman arrived. "His Eminence, the Cardinal of Valencia," the man announced. The words were scarce out of his mouth when the cardinal appeared in the room behind him.

Adriana uttered a cry and straightened in the chair where she had been slouching. "Your Eminence!" she said, rising to her feet and patting her hair. "You should have sent word you were coming! We could have received you properly, and had refreshments—"

He smiled and raised a hand. "Do not trouble yourself, cousin," he said. "I bring excellent news, and it could not keep."

"Nothing can keep in this heat," Giulia said, with a sensuous smile. She snapped her fingers at Isabella and me. "Run to the kitchens and fetch us some chilled wine, if there is any to be had," she said.

We both curtsied and hurried off. I nearly tripped carrying the tray back up the stairs, so eager was I to hear the cardinal's news.

"Steady," Isabella whispered from behind me. I paused outside the sitting room door, took a deep breath, and went back into the room.

". . . realized he had no choice," the cardinal was saying. "He had left his retreat too long already, and he paid for it."

I stopped in front of him and curtsied. "Wine, Your Eminence?" I asked.

"That would be most welcome." He smiled widely upon seeing me. "Maddalena. I hope you are well?"

"Very well, Your Eminence," I said, setting down the tray on the nearby sideboard and pouring him a goblet.

I had not caught so much as a glimpse of him since the day he had told me of Federico's death, when I had cried in his arms. With Lucrezia still in Pesaro, he had not much occasion to visit the Palazzo Santa Maria in Portico. Which made me all the more curious as to his news, and all the more shamefully delighted to set eyes on him again.

It had been many long months since I had learned of Federico's death. My sinful dreams of Cardinal Borgia had since morphed into nightmares of watching Federico die in the wine shop. He lay bleeding, reaching out a hand and begging me to save him as I just stood and watched him bleed to death, unable to move or speak. The nightmares plagued me.

I had confessed my guilt over Federico's death, and the priest had done nothing more than lecture me on the desirable state of marriage, especially for women. A woman needed a husband to curb her naturally sinful ways, inherited from Eve. I should not have hesitated in marrying a good man who had asked me. He seemed less concerned that my doubt had unwittingly led to Federico's death than he was with my hesitation at remarriage. Still, he had assigned me my penance—a week of bread and water once more—and absolved me. Of my feelings toward Cardinal Borgia, my sinful thoughts and dreams and even actions, I said nothing. Not confessing such sins would weigh down my soul enough to drag it straight to hell, but I could not find the words.

Yet the cardinal's presence at the palazzo that day still helped to lift the cloud of darkness and guilt I had been living under since I had heard the horrible news.

"And so?" Adriana prompted once Isabella and I had finished

serving the wine—a crisp white from the Veneto the ladies favored in the hot summer months. "You said there was a battle?"

"Indeed," the cardinal said, taking a sip. "The combined forces of the Holy League met Charles's retreating army at Fornovo and have won a great victory, under the command of the Marquis of Gonzaga. Charles escaped, but there were heavy casualties, and he was forced to leave behind all the plunder he had acquired on his trip across Italy."

A smile slipped across my face. I had pieced together most of Charles's trials in Naples: too much wine and whoring had made Charles's soldiers impossible to command, and the people of Naples had turned on them. Hearing news of the Holy League forming against him, Charles reluctantly set out for home, hoping to reach the northern mountains before the allied forces could meet him. He had passed by Rome—causing much alarm and near-panic; I had hardly slept for days—reportedly hoping that the pope would now bestow the crown of Naples upon him. The pope, however, was not in Rome at the time, having taken the papal court to the hilltop city of Orvieto for a spiritual retreat, or so it was claimed. And so, thank God and all His saints, Charles had ridden by Rome and kept riding.

Giulia clapped her hands together. "So it is over? The French have truly gone?"

He nodded at her. "They are making for France as fast as they can march."

Adriana crossed herself. "Praise God," she said. "This great trial is at an end. And a true triumph for His Holiness."

"And for you, Eminence," Giulia added. "I am given to understand you played a crucial role in the negotiations that brought the Holy League together."

The cardinal smiled. "You are well informed, Madonna Giulia," he said. "I did indeed assist His Holiness in negotiations and am pleased all came to fruition, and to a happy outcome." He glanced over at me, met my eyes briefly, and smiled.

I was sure the naked admiration was quite visible on my face. The dream that God had sent me, of Cesare Borgia appearing like

St. Michael the Archangel, wielding holy vengeance with his sword to save us, had been true after all. And Cardinal Valentino had kept his promise. The cardinal waged his battle in a different way than with the sword, but he had liberated us from the French all the same.

Yet if that dream had been sent from God, what to make of the dreams I'd had since? I shivered and shoved the thought aside.

Their talk turned to other things, news of His Holiness and of Lucrezia in Pesaro and Juan in Spain. Isabella and I were sent to fetch some sweetmeats from the kitchen, and to bring more wine.

"Would you do us the honor of dining with us this evening, Your Eminence?" Giulia asked as the hour grew late.

He rose from his chair. "Much as I would enjoy the pleasure, I am set to dine with His Holiness this evening," he said. "I shall gladly accept such an invitation at another time, though."

Adriana went to kiss her cousin on the cheek. "Thank you for bringing us the news," she said. "Giulia and I shall both be on our knees in the chapel this evening, thanking God for this deliverance."

He swept them a bow, looking more like a young gallant from the streets than a prince of the Church. "It is always a delight to be the bearer of fine news," he said. "I wish you both well, and hope we see one another again soon."

"Maddalena," Giulia called, "see His Eminence out. Isabella, see to the dishes."

I bobbed her a curtsy and followed Cardinal Borgia to the door. "This way, Your Eminence," I said, stepping past him to lead him out. "Though I am sure you know the way."

"I do indeed," he said, but he followed after me.

Upon reaching the entrance hall, I gave him a curtsy as well. "Farewell, Your Eminence," I said, though there was more—so much more—that I wished to say. "May God give you a good evening."

My breath caught as he took my hand, bringing it to his lips for a kiss. "And you, Maddalena," he said softly. "Are you well? I have thought of you often these past months."

"Your Eminence is too kind," I said. I met his eyes, my expression surely wan and drained. I had not been sleeping so well, after all. "I am as well as can be expected."

He nodded grimly. "I am sorry for your grief, Maddalena. None of us are without our scars from these last months, it seems."

I wondered what had happened to him of which he did not speak. I wanted to know. I wanted to know everything, all the thoughts and sins and scars and joys he carried in that unknowable heart of his.

I wanted to know him.

But I was only a serving girl, and he a cardinal. If God in His wisdom had put this man in my way, likely it was only to teach me humility.

"Your words mean a great deal, Your Eminence," I said.

"I hoped it may bring you some comfort that I did as you commanded me," he said, and I looked up to see a slight smile curling his lips. "I did everything I could to drive the French from Rome. Would that I had done it sooner."

I had thought of his promise many a time, yet I'd never imagined he did as well. "You remember that?"

"Of course I do. I remember everything about that morning." He chuckled. "It was, after all, the first time I was slapped by a serving maid."

I let out a giggle and tried desperately to compose myself. "I . . . I truly am sorry about that, Your Eminence."

"No, you're not," he teased. "Nor should you be. I deserved it."

I looked away from the warmth in his eyes, a corresponding warmth spreading through my body. "Your Eminence, there was nothing further you could have done. By then it . . . it was already too late for Federico."

He kissed my hand again, his eyes never leaving mine. "May God grant you relief from your sorrow, dear Maddalena," he said. "And perhaps He will send you another worthy man."

"Perhaps," I said as he turned to leave.

But he can never send me the one I want most.

PART THREE

SANCIA *of* ARAGON

Rome, May 1496–May 1497

Chapter 36

CESARE

It was not quite summer, and still the Roman sun beat down with extraordinary heat upon the Vatican piazza. The heavy crimson velvet of my cardinal's robes was not helping matters. A line of sweat trickled down my back as I stood on the massive marble steps of the palace. Father sat beside me on a throne brought outside for the occasion, but he had the good fortune to be seated beneath the papal canopy and thus shaded from the sun's glare.

Where are they? I wondered irritably, squinting toward the other end of the square. *Surely they have entered the Lateran gate by now.*

We were awaiting the arrival of Jofre and his wife, Sancia. Once the Holy League had successfully met the French in battle and the chaos of the French invasion was over, Father had declared his intention to have his family around him once more. "This crisis has taught me that we never know what misfortune may befall us here on earth, nor when," he had said. "And so I want all my children here in Rome with me, where I may work to assure that each of them has the glorious future to which you are all entitled."

It was understood—but not spoken aloud—that Father's triumph in the French crisis had also helped to solidify his grasp on power. As such, he could afford to flaunt his family in a way even he had not quite dared before.

Lucrezia had arrived last fall, and she and Father and I had had a most joyous reunion. Her erstwhile husband had elected to remain behind in Pesaro, for reasons she could not adequately explain.

Father had not been altogether displeased by this turn of events. "You were right about this Sforza marriage, Cesare," he had admitted shortly after Lucrezia's return. "I should have heeded you. The Sforza family was not brought to heel by their ties to me, and Giovanni Sforza failed to bring his army when commanded. This alliance has brought us nothing, and it would be far better if Lucrezia were free."

The Cesare of a few years prior might have gloated right to his face, but I had learned a great deal since then. "Divorce is always a possibility," I said levelly. "Especially for the pope's daughter."

"Hmmm. I have considered it, of course. It bears further thinking, though."

I had not commented on the matter further. There would be plenty of time to decide what might be done.

Next in Father's quest of reuniting the family had been making arrangements for Jofre and Sancia to come to Rome from Calabria, where they had passed the French invasion thankfully unscathed. I was eager to see my little brother and intrigued to meet my sister-in-law.

Father and I had arranged a great ceremony to welcome them to the Eternal City. Their retinue would be greeted at the Lateran gate by the cardinals and their servants, the head of the Vatican guard and a troop of soldiers, and ambassadors from Spain, Venice, the Holy Roman Empire, and other nations.

And Lucrezia. Or so she had decided the night before.

"You mean to ride out to greet them?" I had asked her incredulously as we'd dined together. "Why not wait at the Vatican with Father and me?"

"No. I shall greet them straightaway," she insisted. "I am excited to see Jofre, and to make Sancia of Aragon's acquaintance. I've already had Maddalena lay out my best dress."

I had jumped slightly at the mention of Maddalena, wondering if Lucrezia had noticed me surreptitiously peering around Santa

Maria in Portico for her. No doubt she was too busy seeing to my sister's wardrobe to make an appearance at that particular moment. "I see," I said. "Well, whatever you like, Lucrezia."

She cast her eyes down. "They say she is very beautiful," she said to her plate.

"Who?" I asked, my thoughts still caught on Maddalena Moretti.

"Sancia of Aragon."

"Yes, they do say so," I said, with an inkling of where this was headed. "I have never set eyes on her, but those who have all agree on her great beauty. Jofre is a lucky man." Still I found it strange—absurd, almost—to refer to my little brother as a man rather than a boy. He was still only fifteen, yet he had ever seemed younger than his years, even as Lucrezia and I had been wiser than ours. Perhaps it was what came of being our mother's youngest.

"Do you think . . ." Lucrezia trailed off.

"What is it, Crezia?" I asked gently, and at last she met my eyes.

"Is she . . . do you think . . . is she more beautiful than me?" she asked.

I wanted to smile at her question, at how young and innocent Lucrezia could still be, despite all that she had been through in her young life. But I knew I could not treat this as anything less than the deadly serious query she meant it as. "As I said, I have never seen her," I said, and Lucrezia's face fell. "But," I went on, "I cannot imagine that any woman in all the world could be more beautiful than you."

She tried to hide her pleasure. "Not even Giulia Farnese?"

"Not even Giulia Farnese," I confirmed. "You are more beautiful to me than she is."

Lucrezia's face lit up.

"And you should not think of Sancia as a rival, Crezia," I went on. "The two of you might become great friends. Your ages are not so different."

"Perhaps," she conceded. "They say she is very proud, and somewhat vain."

"If by vain, you mean she has a care for appearance and for fine clothes and jewels, that seems a common affliction among women," I said, arching an eyebrow at her.

She giggled. "And many men, too."

"And many men," I agreed. "As to pride, she is a king's daughter, after all. She has a right to be proud, to a point." I leaned forward slightly. "But do not forget: you are the pope's daughter, and your place is as first lady of Rome. We Borgias are entitled to our pride as well."

She smiled. "You are right as always, dearest Cesare. However did I get along without you for so long?"

"I'm sure I can't say," I said lightly, pushing down the guilt that always surfaced when I remembered my failed promise to her. My guilt was only assuaged—mostly—by how safe she had been in Pesaro when the French came. Better that she'd been out of the way, so that Charles had not gotten any other creative hostage ideas.

Our talk soon turned to other things: how different Jofre would look, when Father might summon Juan home, and how soon we all might join our mother for a meal together. I could not help but think back to the meal we had all shared just after Father had been elected pope, and how much had changed since. Lucrezia, Jofre, and Juan were all married; I was a cardinal. My three siblings had traveled far afield, and I had been through a war. What—and who—would we see once we all gathered, and looked around at one another at long last?

Whether my words to Lucrezia had ultimately reassured her or not, she had still ridden out to be among the first to greet Jofre and Sancia, no doubt decked out in all her finery. I hoped she had been pleasant to Maddalena as she was readied for the occasion.

I had nearly dozed off in the sun when I heard trumpets and the sound of many hooves approaching. I straightened quickly, and Father leaned forward eagerly in his seat.

"I look forward to finally meeting the famous Sancia of Aragon," Father commented. "And to seeing your brother, of course."

"Yes," I replied, wondering what on earth could possibly be so fascinating about Sancia that she made the members of my family forget Jofre was returning as well. "I'm sure Jofre has grown a great deal."

Father chuckled. "If this wife of his hasn't made him into a man yet, nothing will, I'll warrant."

I frowned at the slight to my little brother, but it would not do to challenge Father over it. Not when the riders were growing ever closer.

Soon the parade entered the square, with the captain of the guard and some of his soldiers riding at the head, where they'd no doubt been clearing the streets. Directly behind them I made out three sparkling figures on horseback, flanked by a soldier on each side.

On the far right was Lucrezia, her blond head shining in the bright sun. Her dress glimmered with gold thread, and diamonds encircled her throat and hung from her ears. I allowed myself a small smile. She was still determined to outshine the famous—or perhaps infamous—Sancia, that much was plain.

Sancia rode in the middle, her head turned slightly toward my sister to speak to her. As yet they were too far away to clearly discern her features, but her hair was a lustrous dark brown, almost black, and her skin was a dark olive. Next to my fair sister and her creamy skin, the difference was especially pronounced. Her gown was of a crimson that allowed her skin to fairly glow, and her fine jewelry sparkled in the sun.

On Sancia's other side rode Jofre, and even at a distance it was easy to tell that he was taller, and his shoulders somewhat broader. I smiled, eager to embrace him.

The company who had gone out to greet them rode at a slight distance behind, and some of the Roman people trailed behind them and into the square, joining the cheering crowds that waited there, eager, as ever, to catch a glimpse of the pope's family.

"Splendid," Father said as they drew near. "Splendid. What a picture the pair of them make, eh? And your sister as well! This is as fine a spectacle as I could have hoped."

And indeed, the spectacle had been important to him. He had wanted to reinforce to Rome, and all of Italy, that the Borgias were triumphant, firm and unshaken in their place atop the heap of Italian politics. He had led the scattered nations of the peninsula through a foreign invasion as well as anyone could have, and as such his position was stronger than ever. He took each opportunity he could to remind the people of that, and this was no exception.

The trio reached the steps of the palace, and grooms appeared immediately to assist them in dismounting and take their horses to be stabled. Lucrezia led the way up the stairs and dropped into a deep curtsy before Father's throne.

"Holy Father," she said, and rose. "I am honored to present to you my brother Jofre Borgia and his wife, Sancia of Aragon, the Prince and Princess of Squillace."

It was a perfect speech, and prettily performed, especially since we had given Lucrezia no official role in the ceremonies. Yet I hardly heard her, for my attention was fixed, totally and inexorably, on Sancia of Aragon as she came up the steps.

My eyes were drawn to her as the head of a flower will follow the path of the sun across the sky, and I could not look away. She knelt before the pope, kissed his slipper and his ring, and he raised her up and spoke words of welcome to her and Jofre, but I heard nothing. I could only stare at this woman whose beauty had been spoken of to such a degree I was certain it had been exaggerated. Yet the praise had not done her justice. Every inch of her, every gesture, seemed designed to captivate: strong yet perfectly balanced features with graceful dark brows; perfect breasts shown off just enough by the neckline of her gown; a tiny waist and generous hips hinted at by the cut of the garment. But it was her dark eyes and the look within them that truly captivated me: one of brilliant and vibrant life, and utter pleasure at the world around her.

I wanted her to show me the world as she saw it, show me how to find such pleasure wherever I looked. And it was pleasure of a somewhat different kind that I imagined as well as I looked at her. Images tumbled through my mind faster than I could try to keep them out, images of things one should never consider doing with a dear brother's wife.

She turned, approaching to greet me as well.

I thought of all the things I wanted to whisper in her ear: *So this is what the poets write of, of what the troubadours sing. This is what Dante felt for his Beatrice, and Petrarch for his Laura. This is what a humble country friar feels for God.*

Of course, I could say none of these things. When she knelt gracefully before me to kiss my ring—Holy Mother preserve me, the sinful images would not leave my mind—I quickly raised her up and spoke the words expected of me, and therefore loathsome: "Sister. I welcome you to the Eternal City, and to our family."

She was nearly as tall as I—we would fit together perfectly. As her eyes met mine, I thought I saw a spark within them as she assessed me. Was she feeling the same things I was? I did not know whether to hope for or dread it.

"Your Eminence," she said, her voice low and with a faint accent of the south; the sound nearly caused my knees to buckle. "I am honored to meet you, and to be welcomed into the family of the Holy Father." She cocked her head slightly and smiled, and the heat of the sun dimmed in comparison. "I am told I owe you a great deal of thanks, for your diplomatic efforts in defending my homeland."

I bowed slightly. "A land from which such beauty hails is worthy of all the defense Holy Mother Church can muster."

Her smile widened at this, and she held my gaze. My blood scorched my veins.

"Brother," came a voice to my right, and I quickly pulled my gaze away from Sancia. Yes, of course. My younger brother, who was married to the woman who stood before me.

"Jofre!" I exclaimed, a bit too loudly. I moved away from Sancia—reluctantly, gratefully, and gave him a brotherly embrace. "You have grown into a fine young man."

He smiled, the awkwardness of a boy lingering in his face. "Indeed. I have learned much these past years—my wife, especially, is wise in the ways of the world, and I strive to be worthy of her."

His voice cracked on the last word, and my heart clenched. The look he turned on Sancia was one of pure adoration—and why would it not be? Surely he felt himself the luckiest man in

Christendom, to have been given such a wife. I was not entirely sure that he was not the luckiest man in Christendom.

Sancia gave him a fond smile in return, but I marked the difference in the way she regarded him. It was a look one would bestow upon a brother, not a husband. Certainly not a lover. She was a few years older than him and had had a much different life. Surviving and certainly thriving in Ferrante's cruel court was not something that happened by accident. Jofre aroused affection in her, but not much else.

Desire roared through me, shouting in my ear of all the ways I could show her what a real man could do for her. As potent—but much quieter—was my shame at the thought of cuckolding my own brother.

And lead us not into temptation, but deliver us from evil. In that moment I prayed silently for such deliverance, the most sincere prayer I had said in years.

Prince of the Church or no, I was not confident God would hear me.

Chapter 37

MADDALENA

The fan I was waving barely stirred the stifling air inside St. Peter's, where Madonna Lucrezia was attending Mass with her family as well as some visiting dignitaries. One of the older cardinals was presiding and—God forgive me—the droning monotony of his voice did nothing to combat the Roman heat and inspire sharper attention.

I did not usually attend Lucrezia outside of the palazzo, but given the heat, she had requested Isabella and I come to fan her and the Princess of Squillace during the Mass. I had happily obeyed, glad to attend Mass in the company of Lucrezia and the Holy Father—and the Cardinal of Valencia—but as the sweat trickled down my back beneath my chemise, I saw my enthusiasm had been misplaced.

Still, I was delighted Lucrezia was back in Rome, and to be serving her again. I had taken up more embroidery work from her, as well as the mending of her finer gowns. After Sancia of Aragon's arrival—she and her husband were residing in Palazzo Santa Maria in Portico—she had noticed my work and exclaimed over it, leading to my doing such work for her as well. I was busy indeed. And Lucrezia had graciously seen to a raise in my wages over the additional work. I was thrilled with the turn of events: more money for doing more of what I loved. Even closer I came to my dream, distant though it often seemed.

The Princess of Squillace leaned over and whispered something in Lucrezia's ear, too quietly for me to hear. Lucrezia giggled and glanced over her shoulder, looking at something behind and above her. "I don't know. Do we dare?" I heard her whisper back.

"I dare if you do," Sancia responded, her eyes alight with mischief.

Lucrezia giggled louder this time, and the elderly cardinal glared in her direction. Without warning, she rose to her feet. Startled, the ladies in her entourage did the same, as did Sancia and her ladies. Whispering and giggling the whole way, Lucrezia and Sancia led the women out of the pews and toward the staircase in the back of the sanctuary that led to the choir left.

Isabella turned a shocked gaze to me, and my mouth hung open in response. As the last of the ladies' entourage filed past us, we quickly scrambled to follow. My face burned with shame and uncertainty. One should never disrupt the Mass, but my place was at my mistress's side, was it not? Surely I could not be faulted for that?

By the time Isabella and I arrived in the choir loft, Lucrezia and Sancia had resettled themselves, their ladies around them, and were talking and laughing openly without bothering to whisper. Below us, the assembled congregation had turned to observe us, some staring with open shock, others outrage—including the cardinal saying the Mass. The Holy Father, however, beamed indulgently at his daughter and daughter-in-law from his chair at the front, and turned back to motion imperiously for the cardinal to continue. The man stuttered and stumbled several times before he regained his place.

"Come, come, you two," Sancia of Aragon said when she spotted Isabella and me, snapping her fingers. "Come over here with those fans. It is beastly hot in here."

We did as she said, and she and Lucrezia immediately settled in to gossip and chatter throughout the rest of the service. My face burned from more than the heat, but if the pope did not disapprove, who was I to do so?

"Blessed Mother, Christ Jesus, forgive us," Isabella sighed late that night as we slipped into the empty kitchen to find some bread and cheese and wine. "Never have I seen such disrespect during Holy Mass, let alone think I would ever be party to such."

"If the Holy Father did not mind, perhaps it is not as blasphemous as it seemed," I said, the mantra I had repeated throughout the day as I wrestled with whether I would need to confess my part in the escapade.

Isabella made a face. "I would never have imagined sweet, pious Lucrezia doing such a thing," she said, finding a half-full jug of wine and two glasses. "It's that Sancia. She's a bad influence on our Lucrezia, and no mistake."

Privately I very much agreed, but I did not feel comfortable saying so out loud. "We should not speak ill of those whom we serve," I said carefully.

Isabella laughed. "Oh, come now, Maddalena. Gossip is one of the benefits of our position. One of the few, I might add." She made a face. "Disrespect for the Mass is disrespect, no matter who you are."

Whatever the pope's daughter did could not be wrong, could it? Not if he approved? Yet did not the Bible call on us to obey God and His laws the same way, no matter who we were or what our station?

And after all, the pope should not even have a daughter. But I would not let my mind wander down that path.

"Lucrezia would never have done that without Sancia urging her," Isabella went on, taking a sip of her wine. "Sancia had better pay mind to her husband and attending to her wifely duties rather than stirring up trouble."

"Poor Jofre," I said. "I can't help but feel a bit sorry for him."

Isabella giggled. "I know, poor lad. He is a lovesick puppy whenever he is around her, yet his voice sounds like that of a boy more often than not! God forgive me, a woman should always cleave to her husband, but he is not much of one, I don't suppose."

"They are not well matched, that is certain."

"Never have I seen a couple so ill-matched!" Isabella exclaimed. "And I have seen many an unfortunate marriage, as I'm sure have you."

I was silent, thinking of my own unfortunate marriage, and of what a good match Federico and I would have been. If only I had been less of a fool.

Luckily, Isabella pulled me from my melancholy before I could sink into it too deeply. "Why, and I think Cook shall quit if my lady Sancia complains about the food one more time." She drew up to her full height, aping a bored yet seductive look. "You Romans eat *so* much meat," she said, mimicking Sancia's southern accent and haughtiness. "All this rich *food,* it is not good for the figure, no? Ah, but then, I suppose it is impossible to get *fresh seafood* here. At the court of my *grandfather,* King Ferrante, in the Kingdom of *Naples,* we had fresh seafood *every day.*"

I giggled. Isabella exaggerated, but only slightly; Sancia's complaints about the food were habitual. She had said something similar only a few days ago.

"Oh, my dearest Lucrezia," I exclaimed, tossing my head. "The color of that gown simply *will not do* for someone of your fair complexion. It would be more suited for *me,* but oh no, *you* must wear this *blue* instead. Honestly," I added in my own voice, as Isabella's shoulders shook with mirth, "after I'd made all the alterations to that gown and added in all the embroidery Madonna Lucrezia requested! All that work, and now she'll never wear it, because Sancia of Aragon told her she oughtn't."

Isabella stifled her laughter and looked up at me, batting her eyelashes ridiculously and tugging the bodice of her dress down so her nipples were nearly showing. "Why, if it isn't His *Eminence,* the Cardinal of *Valencia,*" she said in a breathy voice. "A true *pleasure* to see the *savior* of *Naples.*"

I laughed a trifle uneasily at this. I had noticed Sancia of Aragon making eyes at Cesare Borgia when he came to visit his sister, but tried my best to ignore it. It had nothing to do with me, in any case.

"Really, she has no shame," Isabella said, putting her bodice back in order. "He is a cardinal, a man of God! I should think even one such as her would hesitate at seducing a man of the Church."

"God protect us from such sin," I said, though I did not cross myself.

"Sin indeed! And he her own brother-in-law besides!"

"Surely she would not be that shameless in deed, though she may be in thought," I said before changing the subject. "Now, what to eat, Isabella? I am hungry. What has Cook left for us?"

Isabella turned to the counter behind her to see what could be found.

"But if you cannot find me *fresh seafood,* simply do not bother," I added.

We both dissolved into giggles.

Chapter 38

CESARE

"Your Eminence. What a pleasant surprise."

I looked up to see Sancia of Aragon coming toward me down the hallway. I had just left Lucrezia, having spent a pleasant afternoon visiting her.

She was wearing a gown of dark red—her preferred color—and her dark curls were rather casually pinned up, as though they might escape the pins' confines at the slightest touch. She wore no jewelry—unusual for her—and yet it was plain to me that she did not need it. She looked more beautiful without it, as though the gaudiness of the jewels detracted from her natural beauty.

We had been in each other's company often since her arrival—at family dinners, at public events with the Holy Father, and when I would visit Lucrezia and find her in Sancia's company. The two had become fast friends, for which I was grateful—for Lucrezia's sake, and ashamed though I was to admit it, my own.

It seemed plain our attraction was mutual. We were often catching each other's eye over the dining table, across a room, through a crowd. Each time I felt her gaze would set me on fire. I could only hope no one else had noticed. Indeed, we had never spoken a word to each other that was not perfectly appropriate. Yet that almost made it worse.

Holy Virgin forgive me, but all I wanted to do as I watched her walk toward me was take her in my arms. Her movement was sensual, fluid. The way she would move against me in bed, pressing her body to mine . . .

I forcibly wrenched myself from my sinful reverie as she approached and dropped a curtsy, all too aware this was the first time we had been alone together. "Princess Sancia," I managed, hoping my voice did not sound as strangled to her as it did in my own ears. "Though perhaps, as we are family, we may dispense with the formalities. You may call me simply Cesare."

"Cesare," she said. Her tongue curling around my given name nearly brought me to my knees. In the name of Christ, who was this man I had become, so in thrall to a woman I had never even touched? "Then you must call me simply Sancia."

I gave her a slight bow. "It would be my privilege."

She nodded back in the direction from which I had come. "Visiting your sister?"

"Yes, indeed."

"A pity you must depart so soon, before I have had the pleasure of your company."

"I am set to dine with His Holiness this evening," I said. My next words were out of my mouth before I could think better of them. "But I am not due for some time yet. Would you care to take a stroll through the gardens?"

Interest—and, I thought, desire—flared in her eyes. "I would be honored."

I offered her my arm. I could nearly feel her hip pressing against mine as I led her down the stairs and out into the gardens. We were so close, too close, yet not nearly close enough.

We started along one of the paths. When she did not seem inclined to speak, I cleared my throat. "And how are you finding Rome?" I asked. "Such a change it must be, after Naples." Perhaps if we spoke of mundane things, my thoughts would stay on mundane things.

"It is very different," she said in her low, rich voice. "I am not used to being so far from the sea and its breezes." She wrinkled her pert nose. "There is not such a stench there as there is here in Rome."

"Does Rome have nothing to recommend it, then?"

She laughed, and the sound was like music, like the taste of a fine wine. "No, no. Do not misunderstand me, Your Eminence. Cesare. I confess I merely fall into homesickness for my beloved Naples at times. Rome has much to recommend it, from the lovely architecture of its palaces and churches to the fine society. And it is the Holy City. Anyone who lives here must consider themselves blessed to do so." She looked up at me. "And there is your presence, of course. Perhaps the chief way in which Rome is superior to Naples."

I felt a strange twinge in the pit of my stomach—and lower—at her words. There was no mistaking her meaning, not with those words and the way she was peering up at me through her eyelashes, her head tilted and a slight, almost hungry smile on her face, as though she wanted to devour me. How I responded would determine how we moved forward from here.

I could ignore her words. Ignore them and in so doing say I had no interest in pursuing whatever this was between us. No interest in hurting my little brother. Not even if his wife was the woman I wanted more than any other in all my life.

Yes, that is what I would do.

She pulled me to a stop on a garden path surrounded by high bushes and trees. "Have you nothing to say to such a declaration, Cesare?" she asked, shattering nearly all that was left of my resolve with her repeated use of my Christian name.

"I have many things I wish to say to you, Sancia," I said, not backing away, "but none are in the least appropriate to say to my brother's wife."

"Then do not say them to your brother's wife," she challenged. "Say them to me, Sancia, the woman who stands before you, for I wish to hear them all."

My resistance crumbled at that. I reached out and pulled her against me, my mouth coming down on hers. Her lips opened readily beneath mine, and she made a low noise in her throat that made me hard in an instant. I was pushing her back onto a low stone bench and pulling up her skirts before I realized what I was doing. Abruptly I pulled away from her, and she sat up, breathing hard.

"Why did you stop?" she asked. "I can feel that you are ready." Her gaze moved downward meaningfully, and she reached out to put her hand beneath my robes. I caught her wrist, stopping her.

"No," I said, my voice strangled. "Not here. Anyone could happen upon us."

"That is part of the fun."

"If we are to do this, we cannot be discovered. It would kill Jofre. Do you want that?"

She was silent. Despite her actions, she was fond of my brother; no doubt more like a sibling, as I had surmised. "You are right," she said aloud. She rose and met my eyes. "Where? And when?"

It would need to be as soon as possible, lest I be driven out of my mind. "Tonight," I said. "Do you know of the tunnel that leads from Santa Maria in Portico into the Vatican?"

"I have heard of it, but never seen it."

"Find it. I will meet you halfway down the tunnel at midnight and bring you back to my rooms. No one will disturb us."

She smiled with relief and anticipated pleasure. "A whole night spent with you? It is nearly more than I dared dream."

I wanted to laugh with pure joy that I need not resist this magnificent woman any longer. "And I. We must make sure you are back before dawn, so you are not missed."

She shivered. "Perhaps this shall be as exciting as a tryst in the garden, after all."

She went to move past me toward the palazzo, but I caught her by the arm. "I can promise you will have more excitement than you ever thought possible in my bed."

Her eyes darkened with desire. "I must go inside and pray," she murmured.

Fear struck my heart. Had I gone too far?

"Pray for what? Forgiveness for sins we have not yet committed?" I demanded.

She looked back at me, her gaze bold. "Pray this day passes as quickly as possible." With that she turned and disappeared down the garden path, leaving me to collect myself as best I could before returning to the Vatican.

I should have been asking God for forgiveness for what I was about to do. Instead I could only thank Him for sending me Sancia of Aragon.

I usually enjoyed dinners with my father. It was when we would discuss politics and make plans, and he would often seek my counsel. But that night, it seemed an interminable affair. Father spoke of plans for Juan's triumphant return to Rome, a subject on which I normally would have had much to say, but I barely listened. I could think only of Sancia, and the pleasures that awaited us both.

I left the dinner table as soon as I reasonably could and returned to my rooms, where I paced like a caged beast. I wanted to send for wine, but decided against it. Too much drink could render a man unable to perform, and though it had never happened to me, I could not risk it this night. Not when the woman who embodied all my desires would be in my bed. I would make good on my promise to her if it killed me.

And it may well damn my soul, but I could not bring myself to care.

As midnight approached, I left my rooms without so much as a torch and made my way down to the tunnel. I had dismissed my manservant for the night and told Michelotto to make himself scarce. I was still fully dressed in my cardinal's robes; should anyone happen upon me, some excuse could be easily made. The way back, with Sancia in tow, would take more care. But should anyone see us, I would make sure they were bribed well. I was too consumed with desire to give it much more thought than that.

I moved into the dark tunnel, feeling my way along the damp stone walls. I heard the scratching and skittering of rats and mice, but paid them no heed. As my eyes adjusted, I saw a cloaked and hooded figure waiting up ahead. I approached, and the figure did not move. "Sancia?" I asked, my voice barely above a whisper.

"*Sì*," she said, and stepped closer, removing her hood. "It is I. Your woman."

I stopped no more than an inch away from her, not close enough for our bodies to touch, but almost. "I have not made you mine yet."

Even in the dark I could see the look in her eyes, one of desire and expectation and relief but also . . . something more. "I am yours, Cesare," she whispered. "I have been since first we set eyes on each other." She looked down. "I was afraid you had changed your mind and would not come."

I took her hand, clasping it tightly in mine. She felt something more for me than just lust, then. And I, God help me, knew what I felt was not just lust, either. She fascinated and captivated me in every way, and I wanted nothing more than to be in her presence, always. "Never," I said roughly. "Not pain of death nor threat of hellfire could keep me away from you."

With no further words, I led her back up the passage the way I had come.

Thankfully, the fates were with us, and we saw no one else on our way back to my rooms. I led her into my bedchamber, where a low fire was lit against the slight nighttime chill, and bolted the door behind us. I turned to find her standing by the massive bed, already having removed her cloak. Beneath it, she wore only a shift, and I could not tell if I was disappointed I would not have the pleasure of removing her layers, or relieved I was that much closer to my goal. Watching her across the dimly lit room, I quickly removed my robes until I stood before her only in my long shirt. When she did not move, I quirked an eyebrow. "Now you," I said.

She smiled, that slow, sensuous curling of her lips, and took the hem of her shift between her fingers. Slowly she lifted it off over her head, letting the fabric gingerly trail over her smooth olive skin, revealing herself to me one inch at a time: first her thighs, then the dark patch of thick hair at their apex, then her generous hips, her slightly rounded belly, her ribs, and then her breasts. Finally she stood before me in her naked glory, as perfect and beautiful as any of the statutes sculpted by the ancient Greeks and Romans. They could have had no better model. And indeed, beholding her in her carnal glory, even with animalistic lust roaring through my veins, I could understand what many artists had long said: that the human body was God's finest work of art. Only now, looking at Sancia of Aragon, did I see it was true.

I started to move toward her, wanting to feel her curves beneath my hands, but she lifted a finger. "Aha," she said. "First you must repay the favor."

I had not the patience to move slowly, and swiftly pulled my shirt off in one motion. She beheld me, my body well formed from much time riding and training in the fighting arts with Michelotto. My manhood stood erect, straining toward her, and she studied its length with a lascivious smile.

"May I approach, and worship at your altar?" I asked.

"Oh, you may," she said, and in an instant I had crossed the room to her and was kissing her fiercely as the full length of our naked bodies pressed against each other. My hands roamed over her, first her breasts and then down her back to cup her buttocks. She made that same moaning sound low in her throat, and it took all of my self-control not to climax right then. Even if I had not been driven so completely mad for her, it had been some time since I had been with a woman.

She reached between us and took me in her hand, her fingers stroking, toying. I groaned and broke the kiss. "Christ Almighty, Sancia," I swore. "You would undo me so soon?"

She smiled, her hand continuing its light movement. "I am no shrinking virgin, Cesare," she said. "And I have waited long enough."

That was all it took.

I lifted her bodily and laid her on the bed, thrilling at her gasp of surprise and delight. I covered her body with mine, kissing her mouth hungrily before kissing my way down her body. I took one nipple in my mouth and sucked, then the other. She arched her body beneath me and moaned. "Yes," she gasped. "More. Please."

I moved my hand between her legs, and they opened eagerly. I slid two fingers inside her, feeling the welcome moisture there. She was as aroused as I, even in this short time.

"I am ready," she breathed. "Oh, I am ready." She wrapped her legs around my waist. "Please, Cesare. Please."

"I like it when you beg me," I murmured, kissing and sucking at the sensitive skin of her neck.

"Please, Cesare, please!"

I could resist no longer. I thrust myself into her, and we both cried out at the sweet relief and torture of the sensation. She lifted her hips to meet my thrusts, moaning with each stroke. "Yes, God, yes," she gasped, pulling me even closer. "Yes. Harder."

I obliged, thrusting harder, faster, burying myself in her. Dear God, she was exquisite, tightening around me, her beautiful body welcoming my every stroke. I thrust again, and again, and finally nearly shouted as the most shattering pleasure shook me. Everything else in my life, everything that had been and everything yet to be, would come second to this moment. I heard her cry out my name sharply, her body shuddering around mine, and knew she had reached her pleasure as well. It seemed to go on and on, until finally I collapsed against her body, spent, and she wrapped her arms around me and held me to her chest, both of us breathing heavily with exertion.

After a moment, she laughed. "You promised me excitement in your bed," she said. "And you more than fulfilled your promise."

I laughed, lifting myself off her and turning onto my side to draw her against me. "I am nothing if not a man of my word."

"Then promise me this as well." Her beautiful face turned serious, and she reached up to brush a sweaty curl off my forehead. "Promise me you will never leave me."

I was not able to promise her any such thing: she was married to my brother, and should he wish to leave Rome—or should my father send them away—she would be obliged to go. I had no rights to her, not in the eyes of God nor man. The only rights I had to her were in my heart.

That would have to be enough.

"I swear it," I said. "Never will I leave you."

She kissed me, a long, sweet kiss, and nestled her head against my chest. We dozed off, sleeping lightly, ever aware of each other's presence.

I awoke perhaps an hour later to her hand stroking my manhood, and instantly I hardened beneath her touch.

"I see the excitement has not ended for the night," I said drowsily, opening one eye and looking at her.

"The night is hardly over, Cesare Borgia."

"Indeed it is not." Swiftly I moved her onto her back, causing her to squeal with delight. "But you shall not rush me along this time, vixen."

I let my hands and mouth wander over every curve of hers I had admired hiding beneath her clothes in weeks past, kissing and caressing every inch, taking my time. I made my way slowly down her body, and put my mouth between her thighs, using my tongue to probe and caress that most intimate part of her. She cried out sharply at the first touch of my tongue, and I smiled against her. Her hands wove through my hair, gripping tightly; she was begging and sighing and moaning in the most exquisite ways. Then her climax was upon her, her body writhing beneath my mouth as she quivered and gasped my name. When she was finally still I sat up, gazing down at her, and she smiled with her eyes closed. "Oh, Cesare," she said in a soft, breathy voice, and I was very pleased with myself. That she was experienced in the ways of bed sport was plain, but it seemed no lover had ever been quite this thorough before.

"Are you too tired for more, my love?" I asked, and her eyes snapped open at the word *love*.

"Hardly," she said.

I lowered myself over her and entered her once more, slowly, bit by bit, and she moaned, her voice ragged. "Yes, Cesare, yes. Yes, my love."

I nearly lost all control as she applied the word to me in turn, but I held on, moving deep and slow within her, painfully slow, until she was begging me again, until she could no longer bear it, and I made sure she came to her pleasure before I allowed myself to let go.

I never wanted to leave this bed.

Chapter 39

MADDALENA

I had let Donna Adriana know I would need additional ribbons and thread for some of the work I was doing on Madonna Lucrezia's gowns, so she had counted out some coins and bid me go to the market. Isabella had insisted on joining me, claiming she would not be missed. She had been assigned duties serving mainly Sancia of Aragon—much to her chagrin—and since Sancia and the rest of the Borgia family had been summoned to the midday meal with His Holiness, she had decided to take advantage of her brief leisure time.

"I swear I have not left that palazzo in weeks!" Isabella said, tilting her head up to the bright and unforgiving Roman sun as we walked to the market. "Madonna Sancia is even more demanding than I expected. Every hour of the day and night she needs something, practically."

"You exaggerate, *amica mia*. Surely she must sleep," I teased.

Isabella arched one dark eyebrow. "I am certain she does, but where she sleeps, I do not know."

I turned to face her. "What do you mean?"

"There have been several nights when I have looked in on her after she had retired—lest she accuse me of being derelict in seeing to her every need—and found she was not in her bed."

"Why would you go into her bedchamber when you have not been summoned?"

Isabella flushed slightly. "Well, the first time it was as I said—I wanted to leave her no room to criticize me. But after I became curious to see if she was out of her bed on other nights, so I checked back. And indeed she has been. She was missing more nights than not last week."

"Let us hope you are not caught snooping," I said.

"Maddalena, you are quite missing the point. Where has she been all these nights, at such an indecent hour?"

"No doubt with her husband."

Isabella snorted. "If that is the case, he has more stamina than I gave him credit for. But would it not be more appropriate for him to visit her rooms, and not the other way around?"

"I am surprised you did not check Don Jofre's rooms on those nights to be sure," I said, half-joking.

"I wanted to, but I could not think of a plausible excuse that I could give to his servants. I can hardly say that Sancia sent me, for if she is there it will be an obvious lie, and if she is not, she will not thank me for summoning her husband when she is not in her rooms."

I laughed aloud. "You have plainly given this a great deal of thought."

"What else have I to occupy my mind all day? I do not have fine embroidery to work on, as you do."

I grinned. "Do not act as though you are jealous, Isabella. We both know you would sooner put the needle through your eye than be forced to apply it to fabric."

Isabella shuddered. "God forgive me, but you're right. I had rather scrub Sancia of Aragon's chamber pots all day than sew."

"Then we are perfectly suited to our tasks," I said, giggling.

She sighed. "I do wish I had some special skill like you, though, one that makes me more valuable to these fine ladies we serve." Before I could think how to reply, she added, "Nor would I say no to a private word on occasion with Cardinal Borgia." She winked at me.

"Isabella!" I chastened, feeling myself blush. "He is kind to me because he helped me once, and he appreciates my service to his dear sister. Nothing more. And for shame—he is a prince of the Church!"

"Who is advocating anything shameful?" she said with a grin. "I am speaking only of exchanging a few words, is all."

I fell silent. Surely she could not know of my most secret and disgraceful thoughts about Cardinal Borgia, could she? Surely I had not given such away?

By then we had reached the market, and I sought out the vendors who would have what I needed. As I purchased some thread in several colors—silver, crimson, and a few shades of blue—and tucked them away in my satchel, I heard a voice hailing me from a few stalls over. "Maddalena Moretti! Can it be you?"

I turned to see Fabrizia, a maid from the Vatican with whom I had been friendly. Our paths had not crossed since I'd left for Santa Maria in Portico. "Fabrizia! Lovely to see you. You look well," I said.

"As do you," she said, approaching with a smile. "You are still serving the pope's daughter?"

"I am indeed." I indicated the stall we were moving away from. "I do much sewing and embroidering for her and others in her household. I am here replenishing my supplies. And you are still employed in the Vatican Palace?"

"I am indeed." She gave me a sly look. "Sancia of Aragon lives with Donna Lucrezia in Santa Maria in Portico, does she not? Along with her husband, the youngest Borgia boy?"

"She does," I said, wondering at the shift in topic. "I do embroidery work for her as well. Isabella here," I indicated, "mainly serves Madonna Sancia. Isabella, this is Fabrizia Tortelli."

Fabrizia nodded. "A pleasure, Isabella. I only ask about Madonna Sancia because . . ." She glanced around furtively. "Well, I wondered if you had noticed anything untoward."

"As a matter of fact, I have," Isabella spoke up. "I was just telling Maddalena that for several nights in the last week Madonna Sancia has not been in her bed. I suppose she may be with her husband, but—"

"To be sure she is not," Fabrizia said, her eyes sparkling with gossip. "Here, come away from the crowds, I've something to tell you both . . ."

She drew us off to a quiet corner of the market and glanced around before continuing. "Right," she said, her voice low. "I saw her—this Sancia of Aragon—one night in the Vatican. Very late, it was. Near dawn, in fact—I had just arisen to go about my duties."

"What was she doing there at such an hour?" I asked.

Fabrizia chuckled. "Ah, Maddalena. Still such an innocent. What else would she be doing there at that hour?"

I bristled at her condescension. "Why don't you tell us, as you seem to know so much about it?"

"Oh, I shall," she said, either missing or ignoring the irritation in my voice. She leaned in, lowering her voice to a whisper, and we both moved forward to hear her. "She was dressed in a dark cloak, with a hood covering her face. At one point she turned, and I was able to see her clearly. She did not notice me, I am certain," Fabrizia said with satisfaction. "But she was in the company of none other than Cardinal Cesare Borgia. She was clutching his arm—rather intimately, I might add—and they appeared to be heading for the tunnel that runs beneath the Vatican."

"And to Santa Maria in Portico," I whispered.

"Is that where it goes indeed? I had heard that, of course, but I've never followed it to the end myself." Fabrizia continued. "Now mind you, when I saw her, I did not know it was the lady Sancia. I thought it was some harlot Valentino had smuggled in for his pleasure. Such things happen often enough. It was not until I saw her two nights later, bold as you please, walking into the Vatican all dressed up and on the arm of her little husband to dine with the Holy Father. Imagine! She has no shame, she cannot—she is bedding her husband's brother, a holy cardinal, and still she dines with Pope Alexander himself!" Fabrizia crossed herself, her eyes cast piously toward Heaven.

Arguments rose to my tongue—Fabrizia had not seen them in any sort of a compromising position; Sancia could have been there to seek Cardinal Borgia's help or . . .

The words withered before I could speak them. I did not need

Fabrizia to call me a naive fool again. And why should I make excuses for Sancia of Aragon? Especially when there were clearly none to be made.

Why should I care what she did, or what Cardinal Borgia did? Their sins were not mine. I would not be called to answer for their actions. It should make no matter to me.

But it did. Suddenly I could not rid myself of images of the two of them entwined, the man who was so kind to me and that shameless woman . . .

Quickly I crossed myself, and if either Fabrizia or Isabella noticed no doubt they attributed it to my horror at the thought of such sin. In truth, I was begging God for forgiveness. For had I not committed the same sin as Sancia, in thought if not deed?

I hated her, but not for her sin, as the Church taught us to despise such sin. For I was guilty of not one but two cardinal sins now: lust and envy.

I hated her, and I had no right to do so.

It took me a second to realize Isabella was speaking. ". . . thought it must be something like that." She nudged me. "Did I not say so, Maddalena?"

"Oh . . . yes, you did. Not an hour ago, in fact."

"I think we all must agree, we must keep this to ourselves," Fabrizia went on. "I've no need for word to get out and have it traced back to me, and I'm sure you both feel the same."

Isabella and I both nodded.

"*Allora,* but I'm glad I ran into you, *ragazze*. I simply had to tell someone!" She giggled. "I could not have kept it to myself much longer!"

"Such a coincidence that we should see you," Isabella said. "You have answered my questions, to be sure!"

"Indeed," I said. "It was nice chatting with you, Fabrizia, but I've some shopping to do yet. We must be getting along."

"Ah, very well! God bless you both. Perhaps our paths shall cross again soon!" Fabrizia waved farewell and turned to leave the market.

As Isabella and I returned into the maze of stalls and stands, she was nearly cackling with glee. "It is as I said, Maddalena! Can you believe it? Well, maybe not exactly as I said, for I never speculated on who Donna Sancia was meeting . . . I never imagined she'd be so bold!"

"And what of him?" I asked aloud, cursing myself silently for even responding. I wanted this conversation over as quickly as possible. "What of the vows he made to God and Holy Mother Church? Why is the shame only on her, and not him?"

Isabella shrugged. "Men—even and perhaps especially men of God—can do what they like and always have, Maddalena. It is not fair, but it is the way of the world. They shall have their reckoning with Jesus Christ in the end."

"Well, we can at least acknowledge they both have sinned, instead of placing the blame solely at her feet," I said briskly. "Now come, I've ribbon to find yet, and the ladies will no doubt be back at the palazzo soon."

For the rest of that day, I could not shake an overwhelming feeling of betrayal. And I prayed I might be delivered from temptation, from this cycle of sin I had found myself in.

Chapter 40

CESARE

I was a man possessed. In the weeks following our first tryst, I expected to tire of Sancia. Never had I met a woman who could hold my interest—in bed and out—for more than a few weeks.

Yet Sancia was different. She consumed my every waking thought. Those nights we could not meet, I dreamt of her. And when she was in my bed once more, my entire being was focused only on the pleasure I could give her, and the pleasure she gave me in return.

It was just as well there were no urgent political matters that required my attention just then, beyond the usual meetings with ambassadors and attending audiences with the Holy Father. I could not concentrate on any of it. Even the fact that Juan was en route to Rome from Spain could not spoil my dazed happiness.

I wanted Sancia, and only Sancia. I wanted her by my side always. I wanted to discuss everything with her, each matter that crossed my desk—after making love to her.

And what only increased my ardor was how she returned my passion, fully. She was enthusiastic about pleasing me in bed, and afterward, content to talk for hours—if we did not get lost in pleasure once more. She was a great admirer of the poetry of Dante and had given me a book of his love sonnets I had never read before. She took to reading aloud to me as we recovered between rounds of bed sport, which only served to ready us all the sooner to devour each other again. I took to studying the book when she was not with me, and one night I whispered one of the poems in its entirety into her ear as I moved inside her. The strength of her climax proved my efforts had not been in vain.

I was unsurprised to learn she was possessed of a sharp intellect, among her many gifts. I found she had not been shocked by the French assault on Naples—indeed, she had been expecting it. "We always knew they would try to reassert their false claim to the throne," she told me one night. "We knew it would not be while my grandfather Ferrante lived, though. Everyone feared him, even the French."

"And did you ever set eyes on his . . . museum?" I asked.

She nodded. "Yes. And I was not afraid. He loved me for it."

"Such a bloodthirsty woman," I murmured, kissing her neck.

She was not to be distracted, however. "They were enemies of Naples. They deserved their fate."

I sighed, somewhat reluctantly returning to the conversation at hand. "And no one feared your father, King Alfonso, then?" I asked. "When I met him, he seemed a most capable man. As capable as any can be in such a difficult situation."

Sancia snorted with derision. "He was cruel, but he was also a coward," she said. "And you see the result. King Ferrante was cruel, yes, but only where it was warranted, and he possessed not an ounce of fear in his body." She shook her head. "My father betrayed his country when it most needed him, and I shall never forgive him for it. Nor shall I forgive the rest of Italy, who handed us over to the French when it suited them." She smiled at me then, her quiet rage seeping away. "Not Rome, of course," she said, kissing me. "Not His Holiness and his most esteemed son the cardinal."

"The Holy League came together in the end," I reminded her.

She scowled. "When it suited them, they did."

I laughed. "I do agree with you, you know. It was something my father and I spoke of at the time. Why can Italy not unite against foreign invaders? If we could all put aside our differences, we would be a force to be reckoned with on the world stage, a mighty empire; not scraps to be fought over by the dogs of Spain and France."

She smiled up at me. "And who will be the hero who unites us? You?"

"Find me an army, and I shall. I will bring all of Italy to your feet."

"And I would take it." She grinned. "A true Caesar you would be, my love."

"Mmmph," I groaned. "Say that again."

"Which part, hmmm? The part about you as Caesar, or the part where I call you my love?"

"Either makes me hard."

She laughed. "I can see that. Typical man. Power and the promise of fucking both induce the same reaction." She pushed me down into the mattress and swung her leg over my waist, so she sat astride me. "But in this bed I shall conquer the fearsome Cesare."

"Oh, shall you?" I asked her. "Surely you know that the Church forbids this position."

"So I have heard." Slowly, she lowered herself onto my manhood, and I groaned, bucking against her. "If His Eminence the cardinal tells me to stop, surely I must do so."

"God, no. Don't you dare stop."

"Are you sure?" she asked, going still, my entire length sheathed within her. "I should not wish to invite damnation upon us both . . ."

I shifted my hips, thrusting upward. "Sweet Jesus, no, Sancia, do not stop, please . . ."

"Ahh." She leaned down and kissed me. "I do enjoy hearing you beg as well." With that, she began to move, riding me, and I could no longer harness my thoughts. There was only sensation, only her body moving slickly around mine, only pleasure.

One night we were all gathered for dinner at the Vatican, only our family and Father's most trusted cardinals—as well as Burchard, and Giovanni Sforza, who had finally followed his wife back to Rome. As everyone finished eating, Father clapped his hands and called for music, and musicians were sent for. I expected to be called upon to dance with Lucrezia, as Father always enjoyed seeing us dance, but instead he cast his eyes about the room and decided on a different pairing.

"Lucrezia," he boomed, "and Sancia. Lucrezia, teach our new daughter one of the Spanish dances."

"Of course, Papa," Lucrezia said, smiling prettily as she rose. "You might have told me! Sancia and I could have practiced!"

"There is one Spanish dance we do at the court of Naples which perhaps Madonna Lucrezia knows as well," Sancia said, her southern accent thicker now as she addressed the court. Sancia walked over to converse with the musicians, and they struck up a dance Lucrezia knew well indeed. My father's eyes trailed Sancia eagerly, and I tried to tamp down my burst of jealousy. My father appreciated nothing in life so much as a beautiful woman, but he would never make advances toward Sancia—not his son's wife.

Unlike his son, who is all too happy to bed his own brother's wife, I thought guiltily as the ladies started to dance. There was much giggling as they tried to decide who should take the man's role, and not to my surprise, Sancia did.

As though summoned by my guilt, Jofre came to sit beside me and watch the women dance. "She is beautiful, is she not, brother?" he asked, his eyes greedily following Sancia as she moved. Her sinuous grace as she danced only made me think of her glorious body writhing against mine in bed. I forced myself to give her a cursory glance and look away.

"She is indeed," I agreed.

"I thank God every day that he sent me such a wife," Jofre said. "I still cannot believe I have been so blessed."

I wondered—did he know? But as I turned to look at my brother, his expression was utterly free of guile. He was simply that enamored with his wife and took every possible opportunity to speak of her to others. As he spoke to me, he could scarcely keep his eyes off her.

"You are worthy of many blessings, Jofre," I said. You are worthy of a family much better than this one, I added silently. My shame felt like to drown me, yet perhaps the greatest source of that shame was I knew I would not stop my affair with his wife. Nothing on earth would compel me to give her up. I loved Sancia more than I loved Jofre. And I loved myself more than I loved Jofre.

He grinned at me. "To Sancia," he said, raising his goblet.

"Yes. To Sancia." I tapped his goblet with mine, and we both looked at the woman in question. She saw us watching and threw a wink in our direction. We each assumed it was for us alone.

A few nights later, when she arrived in my rooms, I asked Sancia, "Does Jofre still come to your bed?"

She smirked. "Jealous?"

I did not answer, merely stared at her until she sighed and looked away. "Yes. He does. Once a week or so, twice if he is feeling bold. He greatly enjoys the act, and I cannot say no. He is my husband."

"And you?" I asked, unable to stop myself. "Do you enjoy it?"

"The act of love? I should think you of all people would know how very much I enjoy it."

I was not in any kind of mood for her teasing. "You know perfectly well what I mean, Sancia."

She rolled her eyes. "My, my, someone is testy this evening. Very well, if you must know, no, I do not particularly enjoy it when Jofre claims his husband's right. I am not repulsed by him, certainly, but he has no true skill, nor does he have the patience to learn."

I was far more pleased to hear this than I should have been.

She stepped closer, pulling my shirt off over my head. "Do you wish me to refuse him?" she asked softly. "Should I make some excuse each time? I will if you ask it of me."

I sighed heavily, considering. "No," I said reluctantly. "He might become suspicious. Besides . . . should you become with child, it is best that Jofre believes it is his."

"I do not wish to bear his child," she said, running her fingers down my bare torso. My muscles twitched involuntarily under her touch. "But yours I would bear gladly, and with pride."

I crushed her to me at these words, holding her tightly as I envisioned all I had not dared to imagine: Sancia with my child heavy in her belly; us raising our child together. Sancia as my wife.

"Ah, God, why did Fortuna send you to him and not me?" I murmured against her hair.

She drew back and looked up at me. "But Fortuna did send me to you. I am here with you now." She began unlacing my breeches eagerly. "Enough talk. You are so tense, so angry, Cesare. I know a much better outlet for such feelings than thinking about your brother . . ."

I picked her up and carried her to the bed, not even bothering to remove her shift. I simply hiked it up and plunged into her, hard, her cry one of pleasure and surprise. She reveled in the roughness and haste of it, urging me on between gasps. I thrust into her fiercely, branding her with my body, wanting to erase every other man who had dared try to claim her.

Chapter 41

MADDALENA

In August the member of the Borgia family I had hoped never to see again returned home.

I did not attend the procession for Juan Borgia's return to the Vatican, but Isabella slipped out of the palazzo to join the crowds thronging the streets. She reported back that every member of his entourage was outfitted in silk and pearls, and that the Duke of Gandia was weighted down with so many jewels it was a wonder his horse could carry him. The procession that met him was much larger than the one that greeted the Prince and Princess of Squillace, and the whole piazza in front of the Vatican was trimmed with banners in the colors of the Spanish flag and crests bearing the Borgia bull. There was no doubt who the pope's favorite son was. I wondered, fleetingly, how Cesare Borgia must feel.

Not long after his arrival, the Duke of Gandia came to Santa Maria in Portico to visit his sister. I was in attendance should they need anything, praying fervently he would not notice me. I hoped he had forgotten about me in the years since he had tried to force himself on me.

Lucrezia and her brother immediately started to converse in Catalan. I had learned a few words of the language in my time serving her, but not enough to make out their conversation.

After they had been visiting for a time, Sancia of Aragon happened into the room. "Oh, do pardon me, dearest Lucrezia," she said, glancing at Juan. "I did not realize you had a guest."

Lucrezia and Juan both rose. "Do join us, dear sister," Lucrezia said, switching to Italian. "You have met my brother Juan, but it will be good for you to become more acquainted."

Sancia swept the duke a curtsy, and he kissed her hand, smiling broadly at her. "The pleasure is truly mine, sister-in-law," he said. His eyes roamed lazily up her body before coming to rest on her face.

If she noticed the insolence, she did not comment; in fact, her smile grew even wider. "I look forward to getting to know you better indeed, Your Grace," she said. "Your wife is not here, correct? We should have loved to receive her as a sister."

"I was just telling Juan how I long to meet her, and my little nephew," Lucrezia said.

"Alas, I have left her behind in Spain with our son," Juan said. "She is with child again, so it was not meet that she should make the journey."

"You must be eager to get back to her," Sancia said.

"Indeed, but not before I've tasted all Rome has to offer these days," he said. His eyes flicked over her form once more.

"I am finding it to be a city of many pleasures," she said sweetly.

Honestly, did the woman flirt as easily as she breathed? Married to one brother, bedding a second, and making advances on the third? The handsomest and best Borgia brother was not enough for her? I cast my gaze down, jaw clenched. Of late I could barely look at her and did so only when she addressed me.

The three of them sat down and began conversing anew, talking of who Sancia had met in Rome and the entertainments Juan hoped to take part in while in the city. I remained at my post against the wall and was relieved they did not call on me all afternoon.

Chapter 42

CESARE

Rome, October 1496

Father had been planning this all along. I fumed as I watched Juan make his grand entrance to St. Peter's, the sound of trumpets announcing his arrival. With the young Guidobaldo da Montefeltro, Duke of Urbino, at his side, he processed up the massive aisle toward the altar where Father was waiting, beaming at his favorite son. I sat with the other cardinals, practically gnashing my teeth with envy and anger and not caring who knew it.

For months, Father and I had been plotting our revenge against the Orsini family, they who had schemed—through Virginio Orsini—to stand against the French with us, and at the last minute had turned their coats and surrendered their fortresses to King Charles and his army. The constant feuding between the Orsini and Colonna clans of Rome was ever the proverbial thorn in any pope's side, but the Orsini betrayal was more than a mere annoyance. With the final remnants of the French troops left in Naples at last defeated, Virginio Orsini and his son had been thrown into the dungeons of the Castel dell' Uovo on the pope's orders, and Father had decided the moment to strike was nigh.

I had agreed; with the Orsini clan so weakened, we would not have a better chance. And I longed for revenge myself. We had made the plans, including investing the Duke of Urbino as Gonfalonier to command the papal armies. He would lead men to lay siege to the Orsini strongholds north of Rome, which Father and I were eager to take into our possession. However, only two weeks ago did he let me in on the rest of his plan.

"Juan shall ride out with the duke," Father said one day as we were poring over maps and accountings of weapons and horses.

I snorted. "And do what? Groom Montefeltro's horse?"

Father was silent. I looked up to find him staring at me with a faint look of distaste on his face. "No," he said slowly, as though I were an imbecile. "We mean to make him Captain-General of the Church. He shall share the command with Montefeltro."

"You cannot be serious."

"I am deadly serious," Father said impatiently. "This was the plan all along, Cesare. You are my right hand within the Church, and Juan shall be the sword arm of our family, leading the papal armies against our enemies. This is his first task. It is why I have summoned him home from Spain. His time has come."

"Father, you cannot send Juan," I said. "He knows nothing of military strategy or tactics. Send him with Montefeltro to learn, but do not give him a command position."

"This is his destiny."

"Then he is destined to fail," I snarled, rising to my feet. "He has done nothing since returning to Rome save eat and drink and gamble and carouse with whores, like always. If he is meant to have such a large role, why has he not been joining us in the meetings? Why does he do nothing to prepare himself?"

"He will do," Father said. "He will join us." He rose from his chair in turn. "You have always been envious of your brother, Cesare, to the point of hatred, and nothing in this world saddens me more. Furthermore, your envy and disdain cloud your judgment where he is concerned. You are not able to see his many gifts and talents. Pride and envy, Cesare—those are deadly sins."

"There is no sin, deadly or otherwise, I am guilty of that Juan is not," I retorted. "And pride—I have some right to that. While Juan was off carousing in Spain and barely paying attention to his wife, I was here, at your side, helping to guide the Church and Rome through the French invasion. I was helping drive them out of Italy. I was the French king's captive. And," I added, "at least stupidity is not one of my sins."

"Enough!" Father roared. "Enough. I'll not tolerate this disrespect anymore. You must accept your place in life and accept your brother's. We must stand together against those who still consider us outsiders for our Catalan blood. We must present one unified force. Juan shall learn, you and I shall prepare him, and he will bring great honor and triumph to our family. Now, remind me how many men the Colonna have promised?"

I sat back down, still seething, and tried to refocus on the numbers and figures in front of me. Why did Juan need to be prepared by me for a role for which he was not suited? Why not give that role to me?

I got through the meeting, but could not tamp down my irritation the rest of the day. That night Sancia could tell I was somewhat distant, but I refused to explain when she asked repeatedly what was wrong. I was not about to admit my feelings of jealousy and resentment toward Juan to her of all people. I could not let her know how inadequate I felt.

After that, Juan did indeed begin to join our meetings and councils, contributing nothing of value. He would make suggestions as to strategy only to be contradicted by Montefeltro and myself, until even Father could no longer pretend to consider it. He would praise Juan mightily each time he made a completely obvious point, and my hands itched to punch Juan right in his smug smile. This was the man to whom we were entrusting the papal armies? Montefeltro would provide a more experienced, steadying hand, but it was somewhat disconcerting to realize that the Duke of Urbino would stand no chance whatsoever against Virginio Orsini, were he free.

As Juan was named Captain-General in St. Peter's, swearing his sword to the defense of Holy Mother Church, I could only sit and watch, hardly able to hear the words of the ceremony over the howling question in my head: Did I want Juan to fail, or succeed?

Juan rode out the next day with Guidobaldo da Montefeltro and Fabrizio Colonna to set to their task. At first the news was good: castle after castle fell before the combined papal and Colonna troops, and Father was jubilant. But the castles they were taking were small ones, of little strategic importance, and had hardly been manned. At the sight of the approaching army, the few Orsini troops stationed at each would put up a token resistance, if any at all, before quickly surrendering. The papal forces worked their way through the countryside north of Rome with little to no opposition, scarcely having to fight.

The true test would come with their ultimate target, the Orsini stronghold of Bracciano. They laid their siege at the beginning of December, and it seemed the entire papal court held its breath—especially after Guidobaldo da Montefeltro was wounded early in the siege, leaving Juan to lead the papal troops alone.

"What can be taking so long?" Father demanded one day, pacing angrily in his audience chamber after the last of his meetings was done. "The castle is held by a woman, of all people. Juan cannot manage to best her?"

I remained silent, proud of myself for keeping my laughter within. It had been weeks, and still Bracciano had not fallen. It was being held by the admittedly formidable Bartolomea Orsini, sister of Virginio and wife of one of their best captains, Bartolomeo d'Alviano. The castle's defenses were holding, and they had stocked themselves well, knowing the siege was coming. There was no sign that the people within were beginning to run out of provisions.

Juan, on the other hand, was running out of patience. No doubt waiting out a siege was not the military glory he had in mind. He sent Father long, whining letters, cursing the Orsini (and Bartolomea most of all) and asking for more troops. What good more troops would do him in capturing a castle he could not storm, I wasn't sure, but there were no more troops to send. He resorted to making his unhappiness plain in his correspondence to our father, no doubt hoping he would be recalled.

As Father paced, Michelotto slipped into the room. "Your Holiness," he said, bowing. He turned to me and bowed. "Your Eminence. I've news."

"Very good. Come, Michelotto."

We made to leave, but Father stopped us. "What news? News of the siege?"

Michelotto hesitated. At my direction, he had placed spies within Juan's camp, so I might hear the news first and so I could learn what Juan exaggerated or glossed over or omitted entirely from his communications. I had not told Father, but it did not surprise me that he knew. "Yes, Your Holiness," Michelotto replied reluctantly. "I had planned on giving a report to His Eminence . . ."

Father sat back down on the papal throne. "You may as well tell us both. If it is news from the siege, I wish to hear it as well."

Michelotto shot me an apologetic look, and I shrugged. Neither of us could disobey an order from the Holy Father. Given my captain's reluctance to speak, the news he brought must reflect negatively on Juan. I was both eager and afraid to hear it.

"Very well," Michelotto said. "Bracciano holds firm; there is no sign it is going to fall."

When he paused, Father motioned impatiently for him to go on. "Yes, yes. This is hardly news. We were saying as much when you came in."

"Indeed," Michelotto said, and looked over at me helplessly. I gave him a subtle motion to carry on. He must have poor news indeed. "The Orsini have grown quite confident in their victory and as such rather . . . bold. Just yesterday they . . ." He sighed and plowed ahead. "They sent a donkey into the camp of Your Holiness's and the Colonna troops. Around the donkey's neck was a sign reading 'I am the ambassador of the Duke of Gandia.' There was a letter addressed to the duke tied under the donkey's tail." Michelotto glanced over at me. "I do not know what the letter said, but—"

"Enough," Father said, rising from the papal throne. "Enough. I have heard enough." He descended the steps, and we both bowed as he passed on his way out of the chamber. As he reached the doors, he turned to me. "Are you happy? Are you satisfied now that Juan has been made a fool of?"

The desolation and anger mingled in his eyes made for an expression I could not recall ever seeing on his face before. The entire French army had borne down on us, with more men and weaponry than we could possibly match, and yet I had never seen him look quite so defeated as when his favorite son had disappointed him.

"He may still succeed," I said without conviction. "This is only an embarrassment, not a mortal blow."

Father waved this aside and walked away. If the Orsini were feeling this bold, the cause was all but lost. We both knew that where Juan was concerned, a public shaming and a mortal blow were one and the same.

Within two days, the story of Juan's embarrassment—and, by extension, the pope's, and therefore the Borgia family's—was all over Rome. No doubt it did not take much longer for the tale to spread all over Italy. Even with the season of Advent upon us, Father excused himself from all public appearances. He did not even attend Mass on Christmas Day. He did not send for me. He conducted only what business was absolutely necessary with Burchard or another cardinal.

December came and went and still Bracciano had not fallen.

What with Father's withdrawal, I found myself at loose ends. When not wrestling or sparring with members of the papal guard or Michelotto, I found myself with more time to spend with Sancia—perhaps the only thing that brought me more pleasure than exercising and training in the martial arts. She and I even met a few times in my rooms during the day as that dark winter continued, laughing like spoiled children at our nerve and praying we would not be caught. Michelotto, well aware of our affair, was given the additional task of making sure no one else discovered it.

Much as I had tried to keep my impatience and disgust with Juan—and Father's preference of him—from Sancia, it was inevitable that we should speak of the matter. I could no longer keep my thoughts to myself, and she was the one person to whom I could speak freely who might understand and be sympathetic. The same could not truly be said of anyone in my family, not even Lucrezia.

"I knew this would happen," I fumed to her one night. We had already made love once, and yet I was still agitated. I had pulled on my shirt and was pacing the room. "He sends Juan, a man with no military or political experience, to besiege the mightiest fortress north of Rome. Could Father have truly expected Juan to succeed? Is he really so blind? And as a result, the whole of Italy is laughing at us."

"And you think he should have sent you?"

"Of course. Of course I wanted to go, and exact revenge on those Orsini bastards myself. But if not me, at least someone capable."

"This is what comes of being the best man for every job, no doubt," Sancia said, lying languidly on the bed and watching me pace. I paused to appreciate the sight of the flickering firelight making shadows on her smooth bare skin. "His Holiness cannot send you everywhere, have you do everything. He needs you here." She caught my eye and arched an eyebrow. "I need you here."

Gratifying as this was, I did not respond. What could I do? How could I save our family from this shame Juan had inflicted on us?

Nothing, I realized, and that was what galled me most. There was nothing I could do. Juan would make the Borgia family a laughingstock, and I could do nothing but remain in the Vatican and stew.

"Perhaps this will be the end of it, at least," I said. "Perhaps this will finally show Father that Juan is not fit to be a general. Perhaps he will let us switch places."

"And you think Juan is fit to be a churchman, do you?"

"You think I am?" I demanded, whirling to face her.

She smiled. "I suppose in terms of keeping your vows, you are somewhat lacking. But you have excelled in your position so far. And you would excel as a soldier as well, I've no doubt."

"Yes. And Juan excels at nothing, other than drinking and whoring."

Sancia was silent. "Your sister wishes you to come and visit her," she said finally.

I sighed and sat down on the bed. "Changing the subject, are you? Sick of my frustration with Juan?"

"No. I only just remembered to tell you."

"She did not . . ." I felt sudden alarm. "She did not ask you to tell me, did she? She does not know we are . . ."

"No, no, I don't think so. She only mentioned it in passing yesterday, and I thought I would tell you." Sancia smiled. "I could have told her that I am taking up all your time, but I thought it best not to."

"A wise choice." Lucrezia would never betray us should she know the truth, but I could not bear facing the condemnation in her eyes if she knew what I was doing to Jofre. "I will go see her tomorrow. Provided His Holiness does not need me, which I doubt he will."

"Such tension," she murmured, coming up behind me and running her hands down my back. She lifted my shirt off. "You need an outlet for such tension, methinks."

I smiled, turning to her. "Changing the subject again?"

"No. Tell me all about Juan and how you feel about him." She lay back against the pillows, parting her legs.

"I don't want to speak or hear his name while I am in bed with you," I said, and took her in my arms.

Chapter 43

MADDALENA

Rome, January 1497

I heard the news directly from Cardinal Valentino—one of the many advantages of working for his sister was that I was among the best informed in Rome. No matter who Madonna Lucrezia had visiting—family members, Roman nobility, churchmen or politicians seeking a favor from her or Giulia la Bella—I tended to be present in the room. I was, I had come to recognize with pride, one of her favorite maids, along with Pantasilea, the maid who dressed and undressed her each day.

Juan Borgia's disastrous attempt to besiege the castle of Bracciano was well-known to all in Rome. The castle looked like to hold forever, until a man named Carlo Orsini arrived with Vitellozzo Vitelli—the latter a fearsome name well-known to most in Italy—to break the siege. Or so Cardinal Borgia was saying.

"And so the fool marched north to Soriano and met them in open battle," he was telling his sister. "They had no prayer of winning, not with the enemy's numbers and Juan's incompetence. Poor Montefeltro has been taken prisoner, we have lost all of our artillery, and five hundred soldiers were killed."

"What would you have had our brother do?" Lucrezia asked softly.

"He should have surrendered," the cardinal said bluntly. "If he had half a brain in his head he would have known he could never win, and so he should have lifted the siege and come home. That would have been a far better outcome."

"Is it not shameful, to give up like that?"

"Not if you are preserving yourself and your men and your arms to fight another day," the cardinal replied. He snorted. "No doubt the worst part for Juan is that he took a wound to his pretty face."

I could not help a small smile.

"Oh!" Lucrezia exclaimed. "Is he all right?"

"He'll be fine. From what I hear, he'll have not enough of a scar to ruin his looks, but just enough of one to make him look like an actual soldier," Cardinal Borgia said sarcastically.

Lucrezia shook her head. "You should not gloat, Cesare. He is our brother; his failures are our failures. We are all one family. You should have been praying night and day for his success."

Praying was the one thing Cesare Borgia likely did not have time for at night.

He sighed, looking chastened, no doubt in a way only Lucrezia could effect. "You are right, as always, dear sister. I pray the next time we must bring punishment to our enemies, Father chooses a more worthy instrument."

Lucrezia glanced over her shoulder. "Maddalena, run and fetch us some wine, won't you?" she asked.

I curtsied and left to do her bidding, letting the grin I had been hiding spread across my face.

Finally, Juan Borgia was reaping some of the evil he had sown. I had no doubt that God was punishing him for his pride, for his lust, for all his sins, which were legion. And I well knew what I would pray for that night: for Juan to continue to pay for each and every one of those sins.

Yet my smile was soon enough wiped from my face. As I served the wine, Cardinal Borgia barely glanced at me; and later, when he passed me in the hallway, he gave me no more than a distracted nod. No more kind words or laughter; no more inquiries as to my well-being. Not since Sancia of Aragon had come.

Chapter 44

CESARE

Thanks to Juan's disgraceful defeat at Soriano, Father had no choice but to make peace with the Orsini, which he did in early February. The Orsini could have their castles back once they paid an indemnity of fifty thousand ducats. They accepted these terms and were restored to their status as masters of much of the Romagna as if none of it had ever happened. Money, troops, and weapons all lost for nothing gained in return.

"At least ransom Montefeltro," I said to Father after the truce had been agreed upon. The young Duke of Urbino still languished in an Orsini dungeon after the battle at Soriano, with a high ransom price on his head. No doubt that was how the Orsini were hoping to gather some of the fifty thousand ducats they now owed. "It is our fault he was captured in this folly in the first place." Juan's fault, I added silently, not daring to say it aloud.

Father snorted, snapping his fingers for more wine. We were dining together privately, the first time we had done so since the battle, though he had consulted me on the peace terms. "Let him stay there," he said indifferently. "He was careless enough to get captured, after all. He has proved himself of no use to us."

I swallowed my objections. While it was true the Duke of Urbino was not the greatest of military men—not like his late father—he had hardly been set up for success in this venture.

Still, I reasoned in the days that followed, surely Father had at least learnt his lesson about Juan. Surely there would be no further folly such as this. Father dearly wanted to take the fortress of Ostia: the last stronghold of the French in Italy and a city that was still loyal to Giovanni della Rovere. To that end, he had done what I had advised him to do in the first place to take on the Orsini: he had written to Spanish commander Gonsalvo de Cordoba, then in Naples, to bring his troops north and drive the last remnants of the French from Italy—giving one last thumb of the nose to della Rovere at the same time. Cordoba had obliged, with the blessing of his masters King Ferdinand and Queen Isabella, and was even then on the march.

I underestimated Father's blind spot where Juan was concerned, however, and the lengths to which he would go to make a hero of a man who had no business aspiring to such a title.

When Cordoba arrived in Rome, he was summoned immediately to an audience with the Holy Father. I was surprised and discomfited to arrive and find Juan also in the hall outside the audience chamber.

I had seen him only once since his defeat, at a family dinner Father had held. At the time, he had had bandages bound around his face—more bandages than one would strictly need for what I understood to be a superficial flesh wound. We had not had an opportunity to converse privately, and out of respect for our father and Lucrezia, I had forgone the urge to needle or criticize him. I barely spoke to him all night, could hardly look at him in my disgust, and that suited us both well enough.

His presence at this audience could mean nothing good. He would only have bothered to attend if Father had ordered him directly, and I could think of no acceptable reasons for that.

He had dispensed with the bandages, revealing a healing gash on his right cheek. As I suspected, it would likely heal with just enough of a scar to make him feel like more of a man. When he saw me, he straightened up from where he'd been leaning against the wall outside of the audience chamber, as though he'd been waiting for me. "Brother," he said. "It has been a long time. Are you well?"

"Perfectly," I said. "You look well also. I see you are wearing your defeat lightly."

Anger darkened his features, and I saw the effort it took him to fight it back. "No military man is without defeat," he said. "It is learning from it that counts. I wouldn't expect you to understand, Cardinal Borgia." He spoke my title mockingly.

I chuckled. "Another thing you lost on the battlefield at Soriano, Juan, is your ability to bait me." I walked past him and into the audience chamber.

Father entered via the rear door right as I did and took his seat on the papal throne. I bowed and took my place at his right. Juan entered, his brow slightly furrowed, and bowed as well, taking a spot to Father's left—though, I noticed with petty satisfaction, at a greater distance than I.

Once the rest of the ministers and advisors and cardinals had entered, Father nodded to Burchard. "Send in Cordoba."

Burchard bowed and gestured to a footman, who turned and left the audience chamber. He returned with Cordoba in tow, flanked by two of his lieutenants. "Captain Gonsalvo de Cordoba, Your Holiness," the footman announced, bowing.

Cordoba approached the papal throne and knelt, kissing the pope's slipper and ring. "Rise, Don Cordoba," the pope said, almost fondly. The two lieutenants went through the same ritual, then the three stood before the pope, waiting for him to begin.

"We are very pleased to see you, Captain," Father began, "and thank you for responding so quickly to our summons. We pray you extend our thanks and continued goodwill to your sovereigns, Their Most Catholic Majesties Isabella and Ferdinand."

Cordoba bowed. "I thank you for the honor of your summons, Holy Father, and will extend your salutations to their most Serene Highnesses." His Latin carried a heavy Spanish accent.

"Excellent. You know the task we have set you. We wish for the French to be driven from their last lair on Italian shores, and as such they must be driven from the port city of Ostia. We entrust this to your capable hands."

Cordoba bowed again. "I am honored to accept."

"We do not send you to accomplish this alone, without any support from Holy Mother Church. We shall send with you the Captain-General of the Church, Juan Borgia, Duke of Gandia."

Juan strode to stand beside the Spaniards before the papal throne, bowing to the pope. "I am honored to accept this task, and to go forth and serve Your Holiness against your enemies," Juan said, his voice loud and confident. God's teeth, when had the man not been possessed of confidence that he was in no way entitled to?

I had opened my mouth to object before I remembered where we were. This was a disaster in the making at worst, a huge mistake at best, but I could not question the pope here. It would have to be done in private.

He had already announced it publicly, so no doubt he would never go back on it. But I'd be damned if I did not have my say.

Father was beaming down at Juan. Not a man for politics, Cordoba's face remained stony even as he spoke. "I am honored that Your Holiness would send the Captain-General with me for this expedition," he said. "His skills will come in very handy."

It was a credit to Cordoba that he was able to say as much with a straight face.

"We have no doubt as to the success of this venture and give you our blessing." Father made the sign of the cross over the men. "Go forth and conquer our enemies and return to us when you are victorious."

All four men bowed, and turned to leave, Juan leaning in to say something to Cordoba. No doubt some point of "strategy" Cordoba would be wise to discard. From what I knew of him as a soldier and a commander, he would have no qualms about doing just that. We might actually succeed in this venture.

The audience at an end, those gathered dispersed, and Father retreated back to his private rooms. I followed, though I had not been summoned. If I waited for a summons, I would never get to speak to him.

"Your Holiness," I said tightly, walking into his dressing chamber where one of his servants was removing his formal vestments. "A word, if I may."

"We did not send for you, Your Eminence," he said coolly.

So that was how this was going to go.

"I noticed. I also noticed that once again, you did not discuss this particular strategy with me beforehand."

"That is correct."

"It seems to me quite a persistent pattern. You have sent me into the Church—against my stated wishes—claiming a desperate need for my wise counsel. Yet in certain matters—namely those that pertain to my brother Juan—you feel no need for said counsel."

"I already know what your counsel in such matters will be."

"No doubt. And so it would seem that when you've something planned you know I will disapprove of, you decide against informing me at all. Has it never occurred to you to heed these objections of mine? If you need and trust my counsel so?"

"That is enough," he said shortly. "The announcement has been made, and Juan will be leaving with Captain Cordoba's troops to take back Ostia. It is done."

"After what happened at Bracciano and Soriano? Why? I cannot believe I must even ask the question! What further proof could you possibly need that Juan is unfit to command a nobleman's palace guard, let alone entire armies?"

"Gonsalvo de Cordoba is in command here," Father pointed out. "Do you doubt his abilities as a commander, or the skills and discipline of his troops? They are well-seasoned Spanish soldiers, Cesare."

"I do not doubt him or his men," I said. "But in what way is Juan going to be a help and not a hindrance?"

"He will learn from one of the best," Father said. "Cordoba will command, and Juan will see how it is done, how one might be successful in such a role. It will be good for Juan—and more importantly, the Borgia family—to have his name attached to a successful venture. He shall recoup some of the honor lost at Soriano, and he shall further his education in the military arts."

"So you are using Cordoba to restore Juan's reputation?"

"I am sending Cordoba to accomplish a task that will benefit us as well as his monarchs and native land," Father said, his impatience beginning to get the better of him. "There are benefits all around."

I threw up my hands. "If you say so, Father."

I turned to leave, but as I reached the door, he called out to stop me. "Cesare. He is my son, just as much as you are. I cannot cast him aside without giving him a chance to redeem himself."

I stayed silent, struggling with what to say. Was there ever anyone less worthy of redemption than Juan?

"You must pray for his success," Father added. "His triumph will be the triumph of the whole family."

God's teeth, how sick I was of our family name resting solely on Juan's incompetent shoulders. And in that one awful moment of rage and envy and spite, deep down, I wished Juan would never return. That he would fall on the battlefield. For surely that was what would be best for the reputation of the house of Borgia.

I turned and left.

In early March, with Juan headed for Ostia with Cordoba and his men, it was time to turn our attention to other matters. Chiefly, one Giovanni Sforza of Pesaro.

Despite the fact that Sforza had reluctantly raised his men and joined the army marching to Ostia upon the pope's rather forceful suggestion, it was plain he had reached the end of his usefulness—not that he had ever been particularly useful in the first place.

"Sforza must go," Father said bluntly as we settled by the fire with our wine, mulled with spices and warmed against the chill in the air. "The French will be back, no doubt. They have not fully given up on Naples. And eventually the French royal family will remember they also have an ancestral claim to Milan, if they have not already."

I snorted. "And when that day comes, it will not do for us to be bound in any way to Ludovico Sforza."

"Precisely."

"Divorce, then?" I asked.

Father leaned back in his chair, stroking his chin. "What would be the grounds?"

"Non-consummation? He did not consummate the marriage, as we directed, for months after the marriage."

"You are certain?"

"Yes," I said. "One of Lucrezia's maids confirmed it, at the time." Pretty, sweet Maddalena. Sancia had largely driven her from my thoughts, but it was still a pleasure to see her when I visited my sister. Likely for the best. She did not need to be entangled with one such as me.

"But since, he has taken her to his castle," Father pointed out. "And the date we asked him to wait for has long since passed. Do you really believe she lived with him in Pesaro for all that time and he did not exert his rights as a husband?"

"No," I admitted. "We can ask her, of course, but I'm certain he did. To say Sforza resented your directive would be putting it mildly." The son of a bitch had probably consummated the marriage as soon as she stepped into the entrance hall of his castle. My blood boiled at the thought.

"What, then?" Father mused. "What are our other options?"

"There is always poison," I said offhandedly. After all, it may have worked for Ludovico Sforza.

Father considered this. "I am the Pope of Holy Mother Church, the Vicar of Christ on earth," he said softly. "I cannot be party to any such thing."

"It could be done without your knowing." No one would know what had happened or who had carried it out; I would see to that. I might even enjoy doing it myself.

He shook his head. "No. That cannot be the way we do this."

"As you wish."

"It must be divorce," Father decided. "We must make it work."

"How? How, when the marriage has surely been consummated? Who will believe it has not?"

"I am the pope, Cesare," Father said tersely. "The truth is what I say it is."

This gave me pause. "Perhaps," I allowed, "but—"

"Who will believe Sforza if he says it was consummated, if we say otherwise? Especially since she has not conceived a child."

"Lucrezia will know," I pointed out.

"Lucrezia will do as we tell her," Father said. "She knows her first duty is to her family, not to her husband. I doubt she would be upset to be rid of him. It does not seem as though she is that fond of him."

I was silent. Sforza was not the dashing, handsome prince of any young girl's dreams, and though she'd never said as much to me, I knew Lucrezia was disappointed with him. Still, she was always attentive to him and his needs. She took the Church's directive that wives must be loyal and obedient to their husbands very seriously and saw it as her duty.

But did she love Sforza? No, I was quite sure she did not. While she might be a bit chagrined at the thought of divorce initially, I had no doubt she would come around.

As if thinking the very same thoughts, Father said, "We will find her someone she will like better this time. A younger, more handsome man, with more useful connections."

"Yes," I said, excited by this discussion. "Yes, whatever it takes, Sforza must go."

Father nodded. "I shall have Burchard direct the canon lawyers to begin looking into annulments, and what would be necessary. Discreetly." He took a sip of wine. "Say nothing to Lucrezia. Not yet."

Chapter 45

CESARE

Ostia surrendered to Cordoba and his forces on March 9, after a short struggle. Juan was of little help in the final outcome, or so my spies reported back to Michelotto.

You would never know it, I thought bitterly as I watched the triumphal parade enter the piazza in front of the Vatican, by the way Father carried on, and the way Juan—very much alive and well—was being honored. Since we'd received the news, Father had crowed about the victory to anyone within hearing, and about Juan's (practically nonexistent) part in it. "The French are finally gone from Italy, Excellency," he said to Girolamo Giorgio, the Venetian ambassador. "You have no doubt heard about the triumph we have effected at Ostia, where our son, the Duke of Gandia, took it back from the last of the French troops." Or the day before, when he'd met with the Mantuan ambassador: "We expect our son, the Duke of Gandia, home tomorrow. He's just won a great victory at Ostia. You will be present at the triumphal parade, yes?"

Father's explanation that Captain Cordoba was the true leader of the expedition, with Juan attached to it simply as a means for the Borgia family to score political points, had been a good one, much as I hated to admit it. It spoke of sound political strategy, which any other use of Juan in a military situation did not. Yet it was as if he had forgotten his reasoning altogether, and genuinely believed Juan to be responsible for the capitulation of the French at Ostia.

Judging by Gonsalvo de Cordoba's face as he rode beside Juan into the piazza—beside him, not at the front of the procession, as the commander had every right to do—he had heard at least some of what Pope Alexander had been saying.

The two men reached the Vatican steps and dismounted, walking side by side up to where the pope waited, enthroned with much of the Vatican court around him. Lucrezia was there, beaming in our brother's direction. Her feckless husband was also part of the procession, due to his presence at Ostia, and she would be reunited with him soon. Beside them stood Jofre and Sancia. Jofre had leaned in to whisper something in Sancia's ear, and while she was nodding attentively, her eyes wandered over the crowd. She caught my eye and let a slight smile spill onto her lips, winking at me. My blood heated at her small gesture, but it was not the time to lose focus. Later tonight, while I was inside her, I would tell her how I felt looking at her in that gown with its low-cut bodice, trimmed in fur, and how even before all of Rome I was hard-pressed to stop the stirrings in my cock . . . *damn, Cesare, pull yourself together.* As if knowing the danger I was in, Sancia's eyes left mine and fastened on Juan as he and Cordoba approached, reminding me where my attention ought to be. I refocused just as the Holy Father rose from his throne, and they knelt.

The pope spoke words of welcome and praise, speaking highly of Cordoba's skill as a soldier and a commander. Next he spoke of Juan's skills as a leader and in all matters military, and I watched the pride on Cordoba's face vanish into stony anger. For the love of all the saints, Father, stop, I thought beseechingly in his direction. The man has won us a victory, and you would antagonize him so?

It got worse at the banquet held in the Vatican after the procession. Juan was seated in the place of honor at the pope's right hand, with Cordoba beside him. Father pronounced many toasts as the night went on, to victory, to the glory of God who had granted such a triumph, and to Juan by name. Gonsalvo de Cordoba, the true hero of Ostia, was never explicitly mentioned, and though he tried to maintain a pleasant and grateful demeanor, it was clear as the night wore on how further injured his pride was. Father did not notice in the least.

"What news, Michelotto?" I murmured as he came up toward the end of the feasting. With the return of the army, he had gone to speak to his spies, wanting to find the latest information.

"Nothing much of import, Eminence," he said quietly. "There was a rather violent disagreement during the campaign between the Duke of Gandia and the Lord of Pesaro. Some matter of pride and strategy, apparently, and the two men nearly came to blows."

Our eyes moved to seek out Giovanni Sforza, seated farther down the table beside his wife. Lucrezia was laughing with Sancia on her other side, while Sforza simply sat and stared stonily, arms crossed over his chest. His wine goblet was empty and there were some traces of food left on his plate. He looked to be wishing the festivities were at an end.

"Perhaps that is why he is so surly," Michelotto commented.

I smirked. "No doubt it is not that he is offended over the slight to Gonsalvo do Cordoba's honor." I took a swig from my goblet, eyes fixed on Sforza. "No, he always looks like that, Michelotto. At least when he is around us Borgias. He acts as though we are beneath him, even his wife, instead of thanking God for his good fortune each time he even thinks about touching her." I took another sip of wine; I had consumed more than usual this evening, and it was making my tongue loose. "Ah, well. No matter. He will not be around much longer in any case."

Sancia came to my rooms that night, and despite all the drink I'd had, I was ready. I practically threw her on the bed and plunged into her immediately, with no preliminaries. Her cries and urging told of her equal desperation for me. We reached our pleasure quickly, and the force of my climax nearly stopped me breathing. Never had it been like this for me with any other woman. Never would it be again.

"It is torture, night after night, when we are all together, to watch you and know you are mine in all the ways that count, but not in the eyes of God and the law," I said to her afterward, once we had caught our breath. "I wish things were different," I whispered against her neck. "I wish you were my wife and I need not ever be apart from you or see you with another man."

"Or see me dance with Juan?" she teased, referring to earlier that night.

Fury ignited in my breast, but I tamped it down. I had just cut open my heart for her, and she responded by teasing me? "Yes. That is a sight I need never see again."

"He is a fine dancer."

"I mean it, Sancia," I said. "Do not try to make me jealous with him. I speak in earnest. If . . . if I were someday free, free to marry, would you agree to be my wife?"

"What about Jofre?"

I waved aside her words and my guilt. "We will have your marriage annulled. He was so young when you were married—is still so young—that no one would find it hard to believe it was never consummated."

She was silent, her eyes wandering over the ceiling above the bed, as though she could see the future I painted for her. "And I would be at your side as you ride out to conquer Italy?" she asked. Her habitual seductive, teasing tone was still there, but lesser now, and filled with more wonder, as though she were as enamored with the idea as I.

"Yes. I will make you a queen."

She smiled. "And I would consent to be queen."

I kissed her fiercely, kissing my way down her body, using my mouth and tongue on every inch of her until she was writhing beneath me and nearly screaming my name. Just as I liked her.

God Almighty, what rotten turn of the wheel of fortune had made me the eldest Borgia son, instead of the youngest, the one married off without a care to Sancia of Aragon? For if I could not achieve the destiny that I had been born for, what more did I need than this?

Chapter 46

MADDALENA

"Maddalena! Oh, Maddalena, you must help me!"

I dropped the embroidery I was working on at my usual post in the public receiving room and quickly stood as Madonna Lucrezia burst into the room. Tears were streaming down her face, and she was nearly shaking with despair. "Madonna Lucrezia! Whatever is the matter?"

"Come with me," she choked out between sobs, grabbing my hand and pulling me after her down the hall and into her rooms. She slammed the door behind us and sank down onto a daybed in her private sitting room, dissolving into tears.

I hovered beside her, uncertain of what to do. "What is it, Madonna?" I asked hesitantly.

She looked up at me with swollen, red-rimmed eyes. "He's gone," she choked out.

"Who? Who is gone?"

"My husband."

Shock filled me. "But . . . gone? Madonna, are you sure?"

"Of course I'm sure!" she cried, sounding like a spoiled child, which she so rarely did.

"But . . . and I mean no disrespect, Madonna, how do you know he has not gone off for a ride or a hunt or some such thing?"

"Because I asked one of the grooms!" she exclaimed. "I had not seen him since the day before yesterday, and when I went to seek him he was gone, along with all of his things. So I went down to the stables, and one of the grooms told me he had ridden for Pesaro with a few of his men the night before last." Her voice hitched as another sob forced its way out. "Without even saying goodbye! Without even telling me he was leaving!"

Moved beyond propriety by her distress, I sank down onto the daybed beside her, hesitantly rubbing her velvet-clothed back. "He did not even leave a note or . . . ?"

"No, he did not. I looked and asked the groom if he had left a message. He had not."

"Perhaps there was an emergency in Pesaro that he needed to tend to immediately?"

"So immediately he could not even take his leave of his wife?" she countered. "Had that been the case I would have gone with him. Of course I would have! A wife's place is at her husband's side. And I know my duty." She looked up at me earnestly. "I know my duty as a wife, Maddalena, I swear I do! I have tried to be a good and dutiful wife; I have tried as best I can. Lord knows he has not made it easy . . ." She trailed off and drew a shuddering breath. "But I have tried. I promise I have tried; I would swear it before God and Christ Jesus and His Blessed Mother and all the saints . . ."

"Shhh, shhh," I soothed, rubbing circles on her back. "He knows, Madonna. God in His infinite wisdom knows how hard you have tried, and He knows what is in your heart."

She gave me a teary smile. "Thank you, Maddalena. You know just what to say."

These words reminded me how inappropriate it was that I should be so comforting my mistress, in such a familiar way, about such an intimate topic. "Shall I fetch Donna Giulia for you, Madonna?" I asked. "Or perhaps Donna Sancia? Surely they would like to sit with you and offer you advice."

Lucrezia scowled. "Giulia is with Father at the Vatican, Adriana is off visiting some relatives in the city, and Lord only knows where Sancia is. I could not find her." She impulsively seized my hand. "You will stay with me, won't you, Maddalena? I do not wish to be alone."

I covered her hand with mine, feeling like an older sister must—in that moment, at least. "Of course, Madonna. I shall stay with you as long as you need."

She smiled, even as another tear trickled down her cheek. "Thank you. I do not know what I would do without you." Her face screwed up as she began crying anew. "I do not understand why he would leave without a word . . ."

Not sure if she wanted advice or just a friendly ear, I nevertheless ventured, "Perhaps you should write to him, Madonna. No doubt he will reply with an explanation."

"I will indeed. But what explanation could there be? What could I have done to drive him away like this?"

This went on for some time, and I simply murmured my agreement and sympathy every so often. No doubt she only needed a friend, and I could be that for her.

Suddenly there were voices in the hall outside, and Lucrezia stopped crying to listen. "Your Eminence, you can't . . ." I heard, a voice I recognized as Isabella's.

"Of course I can," came Cardinal Borgia's rich, confident voice. "She is my sister, and I need to see her." The next thing we knew, he had flung open the door and stood before us.

Lucrezia rose to her feet. "Cesare! What are you doing here?"

The cardinal remained in the doorway. "Is it true?" he asked, without greeting. "Is he gone?"

"Who?" she challenged.

"You know very well who. Your husband. Giovanni Sforza."

She laughed mirthlessly. "Nothing escapes you, does it, Your Eminence? I see your spies have already informed you."

He sighed. "Lucrezia . . ."

"Yes! Yes, he is gone, without a word to me, and I've no idea why! No idea what I might have done—"

"It was nothing you did, dearest sister. Trust me."

"How do you know?"

The cardinal's eyes flicked to me. "We should discuss this in private."

Anger flickered to life in my veins. After all that had passed between Cardinal Borgia and me, was I still someone to be dismissed so thoughtlessly?

"No." Lucrezia sat down defiantly beside me and firmly took my hand. "Anything you wish to say to me can be said in front of Maddalena. She has been by my side since I found out."

I felt a surge of self-righteous pride at these words and faced the cardinal defiantly.

He sighed again. "Very well." He looked at me. "You can hold your tongue about what you might hear, yes?"

"Of course, Your Eminence," I bit out indignantly.

"Good." He slammed the door shut behind him and came to sit in a chair at Lucrezia's right. "It does not matter that he left," he said.

"It matters to me!" she exclaimed.

"It doesn't matter," the cardinal said again, "and I don't want you to trouble yourself more over it. We are arranging a divorce for you."

There was a shocked silence at this, though I could not tell who was more shocked, Lucrezia or me. Only that her grip on my hand tightened almost painfully.

"You are . . . what?" she asked in a whisper.

"We are arranging a divorce for you," her brother repeated. "You will soon be rid of him. Do not let it trouble you that he has left."

"Who is we?" she spat. "You and Father, of course."

"Yes. Who else?"

"Who else indeed," she said scornfully. "And why are you doing such a thing, or need I not ask? I suppose my marriage is no longer politically expedient, is that it?"

"You know very well that that is why, Lucrezia. You are an intelligent woman. You can see for yourself the state of politics in Italy, and why—"

"And what of my happiness?" she spat. "Have you considered that?"

This gave the cardinal pause. "You are happy with Sforza? Truly?"

"He is not the husband I would have chosen for myself," she said, "but have you thought of the shame, the embarrassment I will endure should you and Father proceed? A divorce? You both, who claim to love me, would inflict that upon me?"

"It is necessary," he said bluntly. "For the family, and for your happiness, Lucrezia. We shall find you someone better, someone who—"

"My happiness," she said irritably. "Do not fool yourself into thinking this has anything to do with my happiness, Cesare."

"It is necessary, Lucrezia," he said again.

"Ugh!" she cried in frustration. "And on what grounds shall you arrange for this annulment, Cardinal Borgia? Non-consummation?" She laughed sharply. "I hate to be the bearer of bad tidings, but the marriage has been consummated. Many times. He took me to live in his house in Pesaro; of course he took me to his bed."

"It does not matter. It will be our word against his."

"And if I refuse to lie?"

"Lucrezia, you must be rid of him! Why can you not see—"

I was rising to my feet before I realized it. "Enough," I said.

Both Borgias turned to face me, eyes wide with surprise.

My throat went dry at my own temerity, but I urged myself on, locking eyes with Cardinal Borgia. "Enough," I repeated. "Your Eminence, your sister has had quite a shock—two shocks now, in one day. I pray you leave her be so she has time to reckon with both."

They continued to stare at me, and a small thread of panic stitched itself into my stomach. Would this be when I had finally gone too far?

Yet the cardinal rose. "You are quite right, Maddalena," he said, his voice soft and full of chagrin. "Quite right. You have my sister's best interests at heart, and I should, too. I have forgotten myself." He moved toward the door. "I shall leave you, Lucrezia, as your stalwart maid has commanded," he said. "But please, I beg of you, think on what I have said." With that he opened the door and departed, closing it softly behind him.

We both stared after him, myself with no doubt the greater share of surprise.

Lucrezia let out an enormous sigh and rose to her feet, embracing me. "Thank you, Maddalena," she whispered in my ear. "Thank you."

Chapter 47

CESARE

Rome, May 1497

It was a small family dinner, Father and I venturing to Santa Maria in Portico this time. Father enjoyed dining with us this way; for when he hosted his children in the Vatican, he still had to be the pope, and stand upon a certain amount of ceremony. So sometimes he preferred to come through the secret passage into Palazzo Santa Maria in Portico, dressed as a nobleman rather than the pope, to dine with us there in ease.

Neither Sancia nor Giulia Farnese were present, out of respect for Lucrezia's husband having vanished—it was only Father and his children (though Juan, true to form, snuck out early, saying he had an "appointment" to attend to). We had all been especially attentive to Lucrezia of late, upset as she was by her husband's departure—and by our plans for her. Father had been somewhat annoyed I had revealed the plan to her before he could, but understood why I had done it.

I caught a glimpse of Maddalena Moretti flitting past the door, assisting in the service of the meal that evening. I still could not believe I had been cowed by a serving girl more than once now, but mostly I admired her for her kind heart, and her steadfast loyalty to my sister. Maddalena had been right that day, and I wrong. I would have resented anyone else who put me in such a position, but for some reason, unbeknownst even to me, she was exempt.

As the meal was coming to a close, with Juan already departed and Lucrezia and Jofre still at the table with our father, laughing and recounting old family stories, I excused myself and said I meant to retire early. In truth, I meant to seek out Sancia. It had been some time since we had been able to meet, and I was aching—both in my heart and other parts of my body. I was hoping to ask her to come to my rooms that night.

I would often wonder, afterward, what would have become of us all had I not gone to find her.

I first checked the sitting room where Lucrezia, Sancia, and Giulia often spent part of their days, and where they received visitors. She was not there.

Since I was nearby, I went to her rooms and asked her maid if Sancia was within, but the girl would only say she was not. Where could she be? Perhaps she and Giulia had been invited out somewhere, though no one had mentioned it.

I went back down to the ground floor, puzzled and frustrated and intending to see myself out. Yet as I passed one of the smaller receiving rooms, I heard noises within. Something I recognized, but that seemed wildly out of context for that moment and place.

I suppose I thought—if indeed I had any conscious thoughts about it at all—I would open the door and surprise a pair of servants, who thought they might take their pleasure in one of the finer rooms while the household was distracted. What I never imagined was the scene that greeted me as I opened the door to the room.

A man's back, clothed in a crimson velvet doublet that looked awfully familiar, faced me. His hose had been lowered so I could see his pale buttocks, heaving as he thrust into the woman who was seated on a daybed and had her legs wrapped around his lower back.

I could see the woman's face over the man's shoulder, her eyes closed in ecstasy, her breath coming in sharp, short little pants that she was trying to keep quiet. Sancia.

And Juan.

Juan must have heard the door open, for he turned his head to glance over his shoulder, all without ceasing his thrusting. Upon seeing it was me, he merely grinned and turned away, back to the task at hand.

My hands clenched into fists, and had I been possessed of my dagger or sword, I would have dragged him off her and killed him, cutting off his manhood for good measure. I had half a mind to pull him off anyway and beat him to a bloody pulp. Yet then Sancia opened her eyes, and when the haze of her passion faded and she saw me standing there, she gasped aloud in consternation, even as Juan kept pumping away between her thighs. "Juan," she gasped, pulling on his sleeve. "Juan, we must . . ."

I did not stay to hear more. I turned and left the room, letting the door bang shut behind me, and left the palazzo by the main entrance and began to walk back to the Vatican. I walked as quickly as I could, my body so rigid with fury I felt as if I might shatter into a thousand pieces. I walked away from Santa Maria in Portico as fast as my legs could carry me, so I did not return to that awful, hellish room and do something I would regret.

PART FOUR

CAIN *and* ABEL

Rome, May–June 1497

Chapter 48

CESARE

I did not sleep that night. I could only keep replaying the moment in my head, a scene I knew would haunt me all the way to my grave. The woman I loved more than life, more than my very soul, more than all my ambition, fucking my brother Juan, the person I hated most. He had to have known what Sancia was to me—that mocking grin on his face as he met my eyes while he was inside her told me as much. Did he even love her? Care for her at all? Or did he only want to take what was mine, and watch me suffer?

And yet that Sancia was willing had been perfectly plain. Juan's behavior, as singularly horrible as it was, was no better than I expected from him. He lost no opportunity to remind me he was the favored son and had everything I coveted—including my lover. But Sancia had professed to love me.

She was the traitor.

How could she? After all the words of love we had spoken, after all the things we had done in my bed? Could it be possible Juan was a better lover than I? No. No, it could not be. I could not believe Juan worshipped her body in the same way I did, that he had the patience and devotion and stamina necessary to . . .

No. God's teeth, no. I could not picture it. And so my mind returned to the scene I had witnessed, both more and less torturous than my imaginings of what else might take place between them. Of what else they might be doing to each other, even now.

How could she? And after I had so recently spoken to her of marriage, and she had said yes. Though not, I recalled, as enthusiastically as I might have expected. Not without reservations. Could it be . . . oh, God, how long had she and Juan been fucking one another? Since his return? I could not have been bedding her at the same time as him and not known it. Could I?

I had been thinking of how I might convince Father to annul Sancia and Jofre's marriage, and finally allow me to leave the Church. A new Neapolitan marriage for Lucrezia, and one for me, to Sancia, to strengthen our ties to Naples and send a strong message to Milan and France alike. He would have come around to it. Eventually. And Sancia would have been my wife, borne my children, and I would have had her in my bed every night.

And she had betrayed me. And betrayed me with the one person she knew I could never forgive her for.

I got very drunk that night. I could not bring myself to care about the gossip in the kitchens as His Eminence the Cardinal of Valencia called for more and more wine. Around dawn I finally fell into more of a stupor than a sleep and did not care whether God or the devil took my soul—or what was left of it—before I woke.

I woke around noon with a splitting headache and had my secretary cancel all my appointments. There was nothing on my schedule that could not be taken up another day. I forced myself into breeches, a shirt, and a leather doublet, and went out to the barracks where the papal guard was housed, and where they had a practice arena right outside.

I took up a practice sword and went out to the ring, where a few of the men were sparring. "Who wishes to try their hand today?"

One of the men—a tall Spaniard named Enrique that I had fought before—stepped forward. "I'm game, Your Eminence," he said in Catalan. "Been looking for a rematch since you thrashed me that last time."

The men around him chuckled good-naturedly, as I would have on any other day. Instead, I merely nodded grimly and moved to the center of the ring. The other men quickly dispersed to the sides of the ring and gathered to watch. I almost felt sorry for Enrique, who I knew to be a good man, as we crossed swords.

"Begin!" one of the men shouted.

Immediately I charged forward, on the attack. Enrique stumbled back, not expecting my speed, but he quickly recovered and parried my thrust. Before he had time to strike back, I had surged forward again, following up with an overhand strike, then a reverse. Enrique moved backward, barely able to block each of my attacks, never mind go on the offensive. I hacked away, wanting the satisfaction of the dull blade meeting flesh or at least the padded armor he wore, but he continued to block me.

Apparently I had settled into a rhythm without realizing, for Enrique was able to break the pattern. In the split-second pause between blows, he thrust his sword at me, and I barely managed to jump aside in time. Incensed, I recovered and swung my sword over my head, meaning to bring it down on his skull. He raised his own sword in time to block, and I bore down. Though he was the larger man, I forced him to his knees. Once there, I kicked his sword away. Instead of placing the dull tip of my practice sword to his throat, to indicate a kill and thus the conclusion of the match, I backhanded him across the face, the blow leant an additional strength from the pommel of the sword still in my hand. I hit him again, and again, his nose streaming blood and his lip splitting. He tried to get up and stumbled back against the fence at the edge of the ring. I dropped my sword and kept punching. I no longer knew what I was doing or who I was hitting, I only knew this rage within me had to go somewhere, had to get out, no matter what, lest it consume me, kill me . . .

I had drawn my arm back for another blow when someone grabbed my forearm in an iron grip. I struggled against the grip and whirled around to see Michelotto behind me. Immediately I remembered myself. "I think you have well and truly bested Enrique here, my lord," Michelotto said softly. He nodded behind me. Enrique had slumped to the dusty ground, his face a mess of blood. He spat two teeth into the dirt and groaned.

"God. My God. Enrique, my friend, I am so sorry . . ." I reached out a hand to help him up, but he flinched away.

"See to him," Michelotto barked, and one of the men ran off to get some water and a cloth.

"Yes, yes. I will send my personal physician, I swear it," I said. "I . . . I am sorry, Enrique."

My God, what had I done? I had been so afraid my rage would kill me that I had almost allowed it to kill another man, one I had considered a friend. What kind of monster was I?

I followed Michelotto out of the practice ring, my head held high. My rage was gone, replaced by shame, but I could not let it show.

I made good on my promise to send my personal physician to see to Enrique, and when he returned I had him wash and bandage my knuckles, bloody and raw from my explosion of temper. I had my supper sent up to my rooms and drank two more glasses of wine to dull the pain. Then, as dark fell and most people had gone to bed, I made for the underground passage to the Palazzo Santa Maria in Portico.

I did not know what I meant to do when I found Sancia. Did I mean to rail at her or beg her?

I supposed I would know when I saw her.

I made my way through the darkened hallways of the palazzo, not seeing anyone, not caring how I would explain my presence should anyone see me.

I was passing Lucrezia's wing of the palace on my way to Sancia's rooms when I saw a familiar slender, auburn-haired figure. Maddalena Moretti.

Beautiful, sweet Maddalena, so kind and with such a good heart. Maddalena, who was afraid neither to strike me nor to cry in my arms.

Maddalena. The one woman who had rejected my brother. The one person who had cause to hate him as much as I did.

She could be mine. All mine.

And suddenly I knew what I had come for.

Chapter 49

MADDALENA

I started at the sight of the cardinal in the dim hallway. "Cardinal Borgia," I said, once I'd caught my breath. I curtsied. "Forgive me, you startled me. Is there something I can help you with?"

He did not reply.

"I have just assisted your sister in readying for bed," I told him. "She is not dressed to receive anyone, but if it is urgent I can tell her you are here." Or perhaps he was attempting to sneak into Sancia of Aragon's bedchamber? Oh, dear Virgin, should I have pretended I had not seen him?

He stepped closer, into the light of one of the candle sconces on the wall, and I was taken aback when I saw his face. His handsome features looked drawn, haggard; his eyes were red, as though he had not slept of late. Surely he had not been weeping?

I had never seen him like this, so wretched and forlorn. "Are . . . are you quite well, Your Eminence?"

He snorted. "Am I well," he repeated dully. "No. I think it is safe to say, Maddalena, that I am not."

"I . . . I am sorry to hear that, Your Eminence." I twisted my fingers together nervously behind my back. How could I assure him that I only wanted to help in whatever way I could? That his secrets would be safe with me? "Is there . . . anything I can do for you?"

At this, he drew nearer, stroking my cheek lightly with his fingers. I froze, scarcely able to believe what was happening. If his touch were not sending sparks throughout my entire body, I would have thought I was imagining it. He tucked a strand of hair that had fallen from my cap behind my ear. "There is something you can do for me, Maddalena. I am sorely in need of company this evening, and I confess that I have craved yours for some time."

My breath came shorter, more ragged. I was under no illusions as to what he meant by "company." And what was more, he had just confessed that he desired me, had desired me as I desired him. Had he had the same dreams as I? The same fevered imaginings?

Had he realized it was not Sancia of Aragon he wanted, but me?

I could have what I'd long wanted, what I had tried to tell myself I did not want, must not want.

"I . . ." I ran my tongue over my lips to moisten them, my mouth suddenly so dry I could not speak.

He let his hand trail down to my waist and drew me closer to him. He gave my hip a squeeze and sighed, drawing back. "Forgive me, Maddalena. I should not say such things to you. You are a maiden, are you not? I would not despoil you, and I should not have asked."

I swallowed once. "I . . . I am no maiden, Your Eminence. I am a widow."

The meaning of my words was plain.

Surprise crossed his features. "Is it so? And you so young?"

"I swear it. I . . . I have not been a virgin for years."

"Then . . ." He cupped my face in his hands. "Would you join me, Maddalena? I swear, I do not mean to coerce or force you. I am not my brother." A shadow crossed his face at these last words.

"I . . ." I struggled for a moment. Yet what I was truly struggling with was that it was no struggle at all. Besides the endless reasons that I should say no—he was a cardinal, a man of the Church; it was a sin to lie with a man not my husband; lust was a deadly sin; *there are seven deadly sins, Maddalena, but lust is the deadliest*—I knew that I would not. Not after all this time dreaming of him, wanting him.

All these years of guilt, of repentance—for Federico's death, for sinful dreams and thoughts and desires . . . and where had it gotten me? I had been merciless with myself, as the Church demanded of sinners, yet it did not make me feel any more righteous. It certainly had not made me happy. If I was going to feel guilt, and repent, why not at least do the deed, have the pleasure? I had already committed the sin of lust by desiring him—I might as well see it through to its conclusion. "I will, Your Eminence. I will come to your bed, gladly."

A smile touched his features. "Good. Follow me."

He took my hand and led me through the dark, quiet palazzo; down to the lowest level and to where the fabled tunnel was.

I stayed close to him as we walked, body tight with nerves and anticipation and excitement.

We emerged into the Vatican, and he led me up to his rooms. I followed him into the bedchamber, where a fire was burning despite the relative comfort of the spring evening.

Once the door was closed behind us, he wasted no time. He spun and took me in his arms immediately, kissing me. His mouth opened hungrily over mine, and I let his tongue slide into my mouth, thrilling at the contact, my whole body coming alive with delicious shivers. All my imaginings paled beside the physical reality of my body pressed to his, of his mouth on mine.

He drew back, fingers undoing his cloak, then his doublet and shirt. "Undress," he said, softly but firmly.

I removed my cap and set about untying my apron, dress, sleeves. I stood before him in my shift, and he stepped forward, twining his fingers in my hair and undoing the pins and braids that held it back. He kissed me once and stepped back, arching an eyebrow in invitation for me to continue.

Hands trembling, I reached for the hem of my shift and lifted it off. I stood, waiting as his eyes swept over me from head to toe. "To the bed," he said, his voice rough.

I did as he said, getting into the bed and pulling the sheet over me as he removed his breeches. Nerves assailed me. It had been so long since I had been with a man. What if I did not remember what to do? It had not taken all that much to please Ernesto, in truth; even my half-hearted attempts at kisses and caresses had seemed to sufficiently rouse him. But surely Cesare Borgia was used to more . . . skilled bedmates. Surely Sancia of Aragon knew exactly what she was doing . . .

But she was not here in his bed. I was. That was what mattered.

He got beneath the sheet with me and took me in his arms. His lips found mine once more and trailed down to my neck as he ran his hands over my body. Heat sprang up wherever he touched, the soft, tender skin that had been untouched for so long. And that had never been touched in love, not truly. I had not known being touched by another could be like this. I could scarcely breathe with delight, with anticipation; I could feel my heart beat between my legs. "You are beautiful, my sweet Maddalena," he whispered in my ear. "You are not afraid, are you?"

I struggled to speak. "Not afraid, no. I just . . . I wish to please Your Eminence—"

He cut me off. "Say my name. That shall please me." He was smiling as he kissed me, our naked skin pressed against one another.

"Cesare," I said, more of a gasp than anything else.

"Again." He reached down to part my legs, his hand trailing up my inner thigh, and I opened them willingly.

"Cesare." I closed my eyes, all thoughts vanishing, every nerve of my body so alive and awake as my skin brushed against his that it was almost painful. I could scarcely breathe.

He positioned himself atop me, bracing his weight on his arms, and lowered his hips onto mine. I gasped as he pushed inside me, opening my legs wider, wrapping them around his waist. He was much larger than Ernesto had been, and I felt he would split me into pieces—and yet that somehow the shattering would be magnificent.

He groaned as he slid fully inside me and began to move within me. I gasped at the slick pleasure of it, lifting my hips to meet his, and he began to thrust faster, his breath coming in short pants.

"Maddalena," he gasped. "Yes. So sweet. You are so sweet."

I wrapped my arms around his neck, drawing him closer. "Yes. Oh, yes, Cesare." I could scarcely form the words, was barely conscious of having spoken them. All was sensation, sweat and skin and the hardness of him inside me, filling me.

I felt the hitch in his breath as I said his name, and he began to thrust harder still. The strength and force of it felt so good, and pleasure crept up through my core, causing me to gasp.

"Yes, Maddalena. God, you are good, so good . . ."

I felt as though I was going to die, or burst, and suddenly it was though I had been plunged into a dark, warm wave, and I cried out with surprise and pleasure, sure I was being ripped apart.

When I surfaced, Cesare called my name, then with one last, hard thrust collapsed against me, body shuddering as his pleasure came upon him. I clasped him tightly, my body wrapped around his, until he went still. He withdrew and lifted himself off me, the sticky warmth of his seed trickling out between my legs.

"Oh, Maddalena," he said, once he'd caught my breath. "You are exactly what I needed. You have pleased me indeed."

"And you me, my lord," I said, grinning at him boldly. What need was there for shyness now, after all?

He laughed and reached over to push strands of sweat-dampened hair out of my eyes. "Good. It is good you should have pleasure, too."

"I have never known such pleasure before," I confessed.

He smiled, pleased. "Your husband was not a very good lover, then? Too stupid to know and appreciate what a jewel he had, I'll wager."

I laughed. "I think you are right."

Soon he was asleep beside me, but I was too awake—in every sense—to do the same. I could only look at him, at his handsome face, at his hard, muscular body, and marvel that I had, for perhaps the first time in my life, gotten something I so desperately wanted.

Chapter 50

CESARE

I awoke slowly the next morning, as though surfacing from a deep dream that had held me captive all night. When I was finally awake, I saw Maddalena asleep beside me, her red-tinted hair spread out over the pillow.

As I had fallen asleep the night before, I had expected to regret this in the morning. I was distraught over Sancia's betrayal, and so I went and debauched my sister's maid? What way was that for a nobleman to act?

But Maddalena had been forthright; I had not taken her virginity, and she had come willingly. I had given her a choice. And she had certainly seemed to enjoy herself in my bed.

I smiled at the memory of what she'd said, that she'd never known such pleasure with her husband. Poor woman. Well, now she knew of the pleasures of the flesh that she'd been denied in her marriage bed. I grew hard again as I recalled how she'd gasped when I entered her, how her hips had met mine . . .

I had no regrets. None. I had done what I had done, and I would do it again.

She stirred beside me and opened her eyes. They widened in something like surprised happiness when her gaze fell on me. "It was not a dream, then?" she said, her voice raspy from sleep.

"No, my Maddalena."

She smiled. "For I have dreamed of such a thing before."

That startled me. "You had dreamed of . . . me? Of this?"

She blushed but nodded. "I knew it was wrong," she said. "But I . . . could not help my thoughts where you were concerned."

To think, all the times I had seen her in Lucrezia's rooms, admired her beauty—above that of many noble ladies in Rome—and mused idly of what it would be like to bed her, she had been thinking the same. "And was it as good as you dreamt?"

"Better."

I grinned. No guile, no flirtation; she was as unlike Sancia as it was possible to be.

The thought of Sancia pierced like a blade, yet a slightly duller blade than the day before. The rage was still there—leashed, but there—but the place where my love for her had been had begun to harden. And why waste my thoughts on such things when I had a beautiful woman in bed with me? "Well," I said, reaching a hand between her legs. "Perhaps we had better make absolutely certain I compare favorably to your dreams."

We made love again, and it was just as satisfying as the night before. When we finished, I directed her to get dressed. "My sister will no doubt be looking for you soon," I said, kissing her as she looked about for her clothes. "And I can no longer hide from my duties."

She gave me a quizzical look at that, but I did not want to elaborate on Sancia's betrayal, and how I had wasted the day before. I dressed and sent her back in the direction of the tunnel. "I shall no doubt see you soon, my Maddalena," I said, kissing her one last time at the door.

And surely I would, I thought as I watched her walk away. She was a willing bedmate, beautiful, eager to please. I would send for her again.

Chapter 51

MADDALENA

Thankfully, I got back into Santa Maria in Portico without being detected, and after quickly washing up and brushing the wrinkles from my clothes, I went about my duties attending to Madonna Lucrezia and reattaching the lace on a set of her sleeves. If anyone noticed the small, quiet smile that refused to leave my lips, no one remarked upon it.

Later that night, though, things felt somewhat different as I lay on my pallet, seeking sleep, which was not inclined to come. I tried not to toss and turn, so as to avoid waking Isabella. But now, in the dark, while the rest of the world slept, I was forced to confront what I had done.

When I had followed Cardinal Borgia—Cesare—to his rooms, I had known that I was committing a number of sins, foremost among them that he was a prince of the Church and therefore sworn to celibacy. Did that not make what we had done his sin, though? No, I certainly shared in the blame, for woman was always a temptress, just as Eve had tempted Adam to taste of the apple in the Garden. I was certainly guilty of the sins of lust and fornication, of wantonly going to a man's bed and letting him have me . . .

I turned onto my back and stared at the ceiling. Sin though it had been, I could not help but relive what it had felt like to be in his bed, to feel his hands and lips on me . . . even now I could feel the weight of his body on mine, the length of him pushing inside of me . . .

A slow throbbing began between my legs, and I swallowed audibly in the silent room. I was damned, I knew I was damned, but I would do it all over again. And again, and again, and again . . .

Who knew sin would feel so good, so delicious?

Of course it did, I reprimanded myself. That was why it tempted us. If it was not pleasurable, we would not have to work to resist it. That was how Satan entrapped us.

Yet why must pleasure be a sin? Why could it not be a virtue, to seek it out?

Quickly I crossed myself. That was blasphemy, and I knew it.

My mother's voice arrived unbidden: *You went off to Rome and turned into a despicable whore, like I knew you would. What else could become of a girl like you there, with such sin in your heart? But to sleep with a cardinal, a man of God . . . that is a disgrace not even I could have imagined. Can you feel Lucifer's fire even now, you filthy slut? For you shall fall into it soon enough . . .*

Tears crept into my eyes. No, I protested, as if speaking to her. I am not a whore. I am not a slut. I did not go to his bed with evil in my heart. For is that not what sin is? To wish to do ill? Why should taking some pleasure for myself be so wrong? Why?

Suddenly I realized there was one thing that did not seem to fit into what I had been taught my whole life: if what I had done was wrong, unforgiveable, why did I feel so happy? Why did I feel as though there was light inside of me, a light that had been kindled where previously there had been none?

Was this what it felt like to finally have something you've yearned for, hungered for? Warmth and tenderness and passion?

My mother would say such light was naught but a trick of Lucifer, but did I agree?

A tapping at the door interrupted my relentless thoughts, and a man poked his head in. "Is there a Maddalena Moretti here?" he asked.

I sat up. "I am she." I glanced over at Isabella; always a sound sleeper, she only muttered in her sleep and rolled over.

The man opened the door wider. He was dressed in Borgia livery, a crest with the bull on his chest. "I am sent to fetch you by His Eminence the Cardinal of Valencia," the man said.

I didn't hesitate.

Chapter 52

CESARE

My second night with Maddalena was as pleasurable as the first—more so, as she had shed some of her shyness. "I know something that shall please Your Eminence," she'd said coyly, having undressed and seated herself on the bed.

I raised an eyebrow at her. "Oh?"

"Yes." She pushed me down so I lay flat on my back, and before I knew what was happening, she had bent her head and put her mouth on me. "Christ, Maddalena," I swore, gripping the sheets as her tongue moved over me. "Yes. Christ, yes."

Afterward, she straightened up, looking pleased with herself. "My husband used to ask me to do that," she said. "I was always rather disgusted by it until now."

"Your husband was a sinful man," I said, trying to catch my breath. "Such things are forbidden by the Church, you know."

"So is my presence in your bed," she pointed out.

"Ah. Well, then." I flipped her onto her back, and she squealed in delight. "For both our sakes, I pronounce you forgiven of these sins."

The next day, as I walked the halls of Santa Maria in Portico to visit Lucrezia, I stifled a yawn. I might need to forgo the lovely Maddalena for a night or two, lest I lose my stamina. Yet it was true that part of the impetus for my visit to Lucrezia was in hopes of catching a glimpse of her captivating maid.

As I approached Lucrezia's suite of rooms, all such enjoyable thoughts were chased away by the sight of Sancia of Aragon, coming toward me.

My entire body tensed in anger as she approached, but I refused to acknowledge her. It was best for everyone, though God and all the saints knew what effort it would cost me to do so.

Sancia, damnable woman that she was, could not leave well enough alone. As I strode past her, my jaw tightly clenched, she stared after me. "Not a word for me, then, Cesare?" she called.

I stopped and turned, praying I could keep my temper under control. "You would not like the words I have for you, Sancia," I said tautly.

"Is that so?" she taunted, like a bullfighter waving her cape before my eyes. "Or are you too much of a coward to face me?"

With that, I snapped. I charged toward her, grabbed her arm, and hauled her off to the nearest empty room—a largely unused receiving room of some kind, though not, thankfully, *that* particular room—and slammed the door behind us. Once we were alone, I whirled on her, advancing toward her slowly. "You would dare call me coward, after what you have done?" I demanded. "Going behind my back to Juan's bed?" I laughed mockingly. "Or to whatever room where he can pull your skirts up fastest, I see. No doubt he has not the stamina for much more."

"How dare you," she spat. "I need not answer to you."

"I think that you do," I said, moving closer. She did not back away; instead she raised her chin and glared back at me, defiantly. I was impressed and it only infuriated me more. "You were mine, Sancia. We both said as much, the night you first came to my bed. We loved each other. Or so you said. Was that another of your lying whore's tricks?"

"How dare you insult me so," she said. "You knew of my past

when you first bedded me. I take my pleasure where I find it, and—"

"Your past was none of my concern," I interrupted. "It still isn't. It was your future that mattered to me."

She laughed bitterly. "And what future would that be, Cesare?" she demanded. "Your fantasies of leaving the Church, of marrying me, of conquering Italy? You need not have spun such tales to win me; I was already in your bed. You cared more for your ambition, for what you saw in your dreams, than you did for me."

"They were not fantasies," I snapped. "I meant every word."

"Then you are an even bigger fool."

"Why, you—"

"We took our pleasure together. It need not be more than that," she said. "I did not need, want, or expect more."

"You knew there was more to it for me than that," I bit out, my anger growing with everything that she was forcing me to admit. "And you acted as though there was more to it for you, too."

"There was not," she said.

"You are a lying, deceitful bitch."

"Why, because I will not bend to your every whim, Cesare Borgia? Because I will not be your slave? Juan does not want nor expect anything from me other than bed sport, and that is how I prefer it."

"Don't you dare say his name to me," I said through clenched teeth. "Two Borgia brothers was not enough for you, Sancia? You needed the third as well?"

"Oh, listen to you," she said scornfully. "So high and mighty, as though you did not immediately take a serving wench to your bed after learning about me and Juan."

An almost deadly stillness settled over me. "What did you say?" I asked, almost calmly.

"You heard me," she said. "I know what you did. So you can refrain from your holy, moral recriminations. You are no better than me."

I'd be damned; was that hurt I saw in her eyes? As though she had any right to be hurt if I fucked every woman in Rome. And maybe I would, just to spite her. "I do not see how you could possibly know who has or has not been in my bed, since you are no longer in it," I said.

"I have my ways. I have my own eyes and ears in the Vatican." She laughed harshly. "To think. A servant girl. And you think me disgusting? At least I do not choose my bedmates from the slums."

"In fact, that is exactly what you've done, Sancia."

Her hand snaked out and slapped me across the face. My head snapped to the side, and my cheek stung where her palm had struck it. "I dare you," I spat through gritted teeth, "to strike me again."

"I know exactly which little bitch it is, too," she went on, as though she had not heard me. "She serves Lucrezia. One of your own sister's maids! Maddalena. A fitting name, I suppose, for a woman who has come to a man who thinks himself Christ—"

"If any harm comes to Maddalena, Sancia," I cut her off, "rest assured that I will know who to blame. And you will be sorry."

"I am not afraid of your hired thug Michelotto," she flared.

I took a step closer, and this time she took a step back. "Perhaps not. But you should be afraid of me."

This time I was ready. As her hand lashed out to strike me again, I caught her wrist in a tight grip, and I saw her wince in pain. "Now, I am going to see my sister. I suggest you make yourself scarce." I released her.

"Perhaps I shall go see Juan," she spat.

"Do that. I care not whether you go to his bed or directly to hell."

"Enjoy your low-class slut," she sneered. "No doubt she knows lots of whore's tricks."

"No more than you, Sancia."

With a scream of rage and frustration, she yanked the door open and left the room, slamming it behind her.

That night my cock prevailed over my wisdom and I sent for Maddalena. I made love to her hard, fast, urgently, thinking not of her pleasure but only of my own. I wanted to erase every last trace of Sancia from my body, to burn her from my flesh. And Maddalena, as if knowing just what I needed, as if we had been lovers for years, drew me in and held me tightly within her body, meeting me and moving with me until ecstatic oblivion claimed me.

Chapter 53

MADDALENA

Lucrezia's divorce soon became common knowledge, at least among those associated with the Vatican and the Borgia family. It was an open secret that the pope was seeking to annul her marriage to Giovanni Sforza, and this had become a great source of distress to Lucrezia, who hated the gossip as much as, if not more than, the idea of her marriage being annulled.

"I don't understand how Papa can do this to me," she wailed to Donna Adriana as a few other maids and I assisted with her bath. "Does he not know what people will say about me?"

"What could they possibly say? What would anyone dare say about you?" Donna Adriana asked. "You are the pope's daughter."

"You know perfectly well what they will say, pope's daughter or no," Lucrezia huffed. "That I am a bad wife. I could not make my husband happy. I am a failure as a woman. They already speak ill of us because we are Catalan, and—"

"Psh," Donna Adriana scoffed. "The ignorant with nothing better to do will say such things, perhaps. But anyone who matters knows that marriages among families like ours are about politics, and nothing more. Wifely virtue does not signify."

I had to hold back a snort. Who better to know such things than Adriana de Mila, whose son was sent off to the country just after his own wedding with cuckold's horns affixed to his head at the behest of the man who would become pope?

Donna Lucrezia went on about marriage in the sight of God and duty, but I was no longer listening. I yawned, trying my best to hide it as I washed Donna Lucrezia's long tresses. I had not been getting much sleep of late.

Yet as tiring as my nights were, I would not trade them for anything. Sleep was for the girl I had been, who had needed to dream of such things as now happened to me in my waking hours. To be desired by a man such as Cesare Borgia, to revel in his touch and watch how he thrilled at mine . . . it was worth any sin. It was worth the exhaustion, and the looks of wrath and disgust I fancied Madonna Sancia had been sending my way of late. Each time I caught her glaring in my direction, I would simply lower my eyes but keep my chin up. Even if she somehow knew that I had taken her place in Cesare's bed, what right had she to be angry? She had cast him off. And there was nothing she could do to me in any case, not while I was effectively under Valentino's protection.

I pushed aside thoughts of Sancia and returned to much more pleasurable recollections of my lover. Why, the night before, he had . . .

"Maddalena?"

I started and looked up to find Donna Lucrezia and Donna Adriana both looking at me questioningly. Donna Lucrezia looked somewhat irritated, as though it were not the first time she had called my name.

"My apologies, Madonna," I said. "I . . . I did not hear you."

She raised her eyebrows. "I asked you to get the cloth, so I may step out," she said.

"Of . . . of course." I hurried to grab a clean length of cloth and unfurled it, holding it out for Madonna Lucrezia. She rose from the tub, wet hair streaming down her back, and stepped out. I wrapped the cloth around her, proceeding to help dry her. Once she was dried off and dressed, she would sit out in the garden for a few hours to help her hair dry. It was all quite an ordeal.

She resumed her conversation with Donna Adriana, and I was free to fall back into my dreamy, preoccupied haze.

"Where were you last night?" Isabella hissed later that night, once we were relieved of our duties and heading down to the kitchens to find something to eat. "I awoke in the middle of the night, and you were not in your bed."

"Donna Lucrezia needed something," I said.

"A fine attempt, Maddalena, but I know better," Isabella said, folding her arms across her chest. "You have been out of your bed several nights of late. Madonna Lucrezia is not that demanding, especially given that Pantasilea sleeps just outside her bedchamber."

I sighed. I had been dying to tell Isabella the truth, but was not sure if I should. Now that she had found me out, I might as well. "Very well. But you must not tell anyone."

Her eyes sparkled at this hint of something salacious. "I promise!"

I dragged her out to the garden, and we huddled beside one of the hedges. I lowered my voice to a near whisper after ensuring that we were alone. "I have been with His Eminence. Cardinal Valentino," I confessed. Now that I had begun the tale, I found I could not stop. It all poured out of me. Isabella's eyes grew wider and wider as she listened, and when I finally finished, she was silent for a long time.

"Well?" I demanded. "Haven't you anything to say?"

Isabella shook her head. "I scarcely know where to begin." She regarded me with a mixture of surprise, wariness, and admiration. "You truly have been bedding Cesare Borgia these weeks past? The handsomest man in Rome?"

I could not help preening at those words. "Yes, he is, isn't he?"

"But he is a prince of the Church! And I know you, Maddalena, to be a good Christian."

"I . . . I am. I try to be." Indignation crept into my voice. It was one thing for me to wrestle with such guilt and misgivings, but it was a great deal more uncomfortable to hear the same from someone else. "You've had no trouble making suggestive comments about him in the past, saying you wished he would have private conversation with you and I know not what else."

"I was speaking in jest," Isabella argued. "I never meant to imply . . . I never truly thought . . ." She shook her head. "And you had such harsh words about Donna Sancia when that woman at the market—Fabrizia?—told us they were having an affair. And here you go, doing the same thing." Understanding dawned on her face. "I see now. You were jealous. You desired him even then."

Blushing, I nodded.

She sighed. "Oh, Maddalena. I . . . I do not mean to judge, I swear it. I am shocked, is all. I never expected . . ."

I clutched her arm. "I know. Believe me, I know. But I . . . you must believe me when I say I am happy. It is a strange and impossible situation, but I am." My face heated up. "I . . . sin or no, I enjoy being in his bed. I cannot help it. I have desired him, it is true, and he desires me. That is all there is to it."

"Oh, Maddalena," she said once more. "You will take care, won't you? What you are doing is dangerous. These people, these powerful nobles and churchmen, they are not like us. Their world is not ours. He is dangerous. He would hurt you as soon as he breathes and think nothing of it. And I do not wish to see you hurt."

"I understand," I said. "I do. And I expect nothing from him, Isabella. Truly I don't. He cares for me, he does, but I know there can be nothing more to it than this."

"Hmmm. Mind you remember that."

"I will."

"I mean it. There is no more foolish creature than a young woman in love. Take care, Maddalena. Mind that you do not become caught up in their Borgia games."

"I will not," I replied.

"*Buono.*" She smiled. "And so? Is he as skilled in bed as he looks?"

I laughed. "Oh, yes. That I can tell you for sure."

She giggled. "Well, good. Good that he cares for your pleasure;

many men don't. Take whatever happiness you can from it, while it lasts."

"I plan on it."

"But, Maddalena," she said, her face growing serious again, "you will be careful, won't you?"

"I will, *amica mia*. I promise it."

We embraced, and when we stepped back she had a thoughtful look on her face. "I suppose it all makes sense," she said. "Madonna Sancia is now bedding the other Borgia brother. The Duke of Gandia."

I blinked in surprise. "She is?"

"Oh, yes. You hadn't heard? They are quite blatant about it. He comes into her bedchamber bold as you please, no shame." She considered this. "So Sancia of Aragon tossed aside Cesare Borgia, and he has picked you up in her stead."

"I suppose," I said uncomfortably. "No doubt she broke his heart, and he came to me for comfort."

Isabella chuckled. "If he has a heart to break. Just mind, Maddalena, that he does not break yours."

Chapter 54

CESARE

Rome, June 1497

Before long, all of Rome knew Sancia of Aragon and Juan Borgia were lovers. Michelotto said people gossiped about it openly in the streets. He heard no rumors of my and Sancia's relationship, so at least I was spared the public embarrassment of losing my lover to Juan. That did not mean no one had ever found out; I knew servants gossiped, and there was no telling who might have heard, or seen us. But in the wake of this newest scandal surrounding the Borgia family, my name was not mentioned, and for that I was grateful.

However, even if I was not being laughed at, the same could not be said for Jofre. The entire city knew the cuckold's horns had been affixed to his head, and by his own brother. Worst of all, Jofre knew. At least I had been discreet about bedding his wife, though this reasoning often proved cold comfort.

At one family dinner at the Vatican, the tension seemed obvious to all, save for Father. I did not deceive myself that he knew nothing of what was going on; he simply did not wish to acknowledge it. Sancia sat between Juan and Jofre and spent most of the meal speaking quietly to her lover beside her, the two of them giggling like country peasants in love. Jofre would try to win her attention every chance he could, and each time she responded perfunctorily to him and turned back to Juan, he looked as if he'd been slapped. Lucrezia, every so often, would glance at the two of them and purse her lips disapprovingly. She loved them both, but she too could not countenance the pain they were clearly inflicting on Jofre.

I sat at the table fuming, draining my goblet of wine nearly as fast as the servants could fill it, and for once I did not care if anyone noticed. Let them think I was angry on Jofre's behalf—strangely enough, that was part of it—or let them guess the whole truth. It no longer mattered to me.

"I've two appointments to make in consistory tomorrow," Father said one evening in early June. He had summoned me to his private apartments before I retired, and I had obeyed, hoping it would be a quick meeting. I had not been sleeping much of late, albeit for pleasurable reasons.

I had expected something like this. The consistory was to be secret, so no doubt he had something ambitious in mind.

"I am appointing you papal legate for the coronation of Federigo of Aragon," he said, eyeing me with a pleased look.

I blinked in surprise. I had hardly expected this honor, being one of the youngest and newest cardinals in the college. But when had such a thing ever stopped Father?

Poor Ferrantino had recently died, quite unexpectedly, of an illness, and so his uncle Federigo had succeeded to the throne. Wanting no half measures or ambiguity should the French decide to invade again, Father had announced he would be sending a legate to Naples to crown the new king, making the blessing of the pope—and therefore God—on the new ruler unquestionable.

I was delighted to learn it would be me, once my surprise had waned. "You honor me, Holy Father," I said, bowing my head. "I shall endeavor to represent the Holy See with all the honor and dignity it deserves."

"I have no doubt," he said.

"And the second appointment?"

"Yes," he said. "I shall bestow upon your brother Juan the duchy of Benevento."

In an instant, I had leapt from my chair. "The duchy of Benevento?" I demanded. "Have you taken leave of your senses?"

"I have not." He arched an eyebrow at me. "I hope this is not the 'honor and dignity' with which you will be representing the Holy See in Naples, Cesare."

But I would not be cowed by his scolding. "Father, believe me when I tell you that I say this not out of jealousy," I said. Though what, indeed, had Juan done to deserve such an investiture? I wondered bitterly. But that didn't matter; I needed to convince my father that he was making a grave political error. My initial response should have been a more measured one, but it was too late. "Think about it. Benevento has long been a papal fief, not in the keep of any one man or family. If you gift it to Juan, you will be seen as stealing it for the benefit of your family. No other pope has dared to give away the papal lands like this before. It will be a great scandal."

"I am the pope. I can do as I wish with the lands in my keeping."

"Not this," I argued. "You cannot do this. Politically, it will be a disaster. Everyone will say we have reached too far. That we have risen too far."

"We have risen far," he thundered, drawing himself up to look at me eye to eye—as I'd entered my twenties, I had finally become as tall as he. "And shall rise farther. I'll have none question our power. This is what my ascendency to the papacy has been for, Cesare. To make our family great."

"They can question us, and they will," I asserted. "Have you forgotten the ring of cardinals who allied themselves with the French, with the hope of dethroning you? Do you wish them to try again?"

"They would set themselves against God's chosen over a parcel of land in the south of Italy?" Father asked scornfully. "To what end?"

I stared at him uncomprehendingly. Had he truly forgotten all the politics and scheming, the money changing hands that had put him on St. Peter's throne? Not for the first time, I wondered if he had fooled himself into believing it had truly been God who put him there.

"To protest the overreaching of the papal power," I said. "The papacy is not dynastic, and they will resist any attempts to make it so."

He snorted. "That is precisely what we are doing," he said. "We shall make of the papacy a Borgia dynasty. First it was my uncle, then me, and someday it shall be you."

"Perhaps, but you cannot show your hand," I said. "There will be outrage, and it can only be harmful to us."

"Let there be outrage. Let them try to harm us."

I threw up my hands in futility. "Has your foolish adoration of Juan so blinded you?" I exploded. "You would risk your position and the position of our family just to further ennoble him?"

"I risk no such thing!" he shouted. "You are once again blinded by your malice and petty jealousy."

"Not this time, Father," I shot back. "This time, you know I am right. You just cannot admit it, not to yourself, and especially not to me."

I stormed from the papal chambers without waiting to be

dismissed. Michelotto had been lounging against the wall outside, and he stumbled to attention as I came bursting out.

"Send a man to Santa Maria in Portico," I told him tersely. "Have Maddalena Moretti come to my chambers directly."

"Of course, Your Eminence."

He peeled off to do my bidding—a more menial task than I usually entrusted to him, but he did not complain—and I walked to my rooms, slamming the door behind me when I reached them. I paced angrily in my bedchamber, the blood pounding through my veins, waiting for Maddalena to come to me.

And sooner than I would have thought possible, as though she had sensed my desperate need, there she was in the doorway. I stopped dead in my pacing and beheld her, her auburn hair tumbling loose about her shoulders, her cloak just barely closed over her thin shift. And I realized how much I had come to depend on her, as other men depended on alcohol or potions to dull their minds. She was the only thing that could take my mind from my troubles.

We did not speak, merely removed our clothes and fell to the bed together, where I lost myself in her, and enjoyed the losing.

Chapter 55

MADDALENA

"Will there be anything else, Madonna?" I asked Lucrezia, turning to face her where she was tucked up in her large bed.

She hesitated. "In fact . . . yes, there is, Maddalena." She crooked a finger, motioning me to come closer. Glancing furtively over my shoulder, as though expecting Donna Adriana to come in, Lucrezia reached beneath her pillow and pulled out a folded square of parchment. "I need you to deliver this for me," she said, her voice so low I had to lean in to hear her. "To one Pedro Calderon, one of my father's chamberlains. He also goes by the name of Perotto."

"To . . . who, Madonna?"

"He'll be waiting in the stables at the Vatican," she said. "He is a few inches taller than me, almost bronze skin, dark curly hair, dark eyes."

"Who is he, Madonna? Do you need something from—"

"Never mind why," she said impatiently. "Pantasilea usually carries messages to him, but as she is ill, you will need to do it."

I took the parchment, deciding it did not matter much. Cesare had wanted me to come to him that night. I was going to the Vatican anyway, though Madonna Lucrezia need not know that. What was an errand for her on my way to my lover's bed? "Of course, Madonna. I will find him. Am I to wait for a reply?"

"No," she said. "No reply. Only see that he gets it."

"Very well, Madonna. Consider it done."

She smiled sweetly. "Thank you, Maddalena. You take such good care of me."

I curtsied. "I do my best, Madonna. God give you good night."

"And you, Maddalena."

I shall have a good night, but whether it comes from God or the devil, I do not know, I thought, with a mix of guilt and giddiness. I curtsied and left her bedchamber, proceeding to my own room to fetch my cloak, but thought better of it. It was damnably hot, and I only wore the cloak to better shield me when I went to Cesare's rooms. Tonight I was on an errand for my mistress, and so had a legitimate purpose for being at the Vatican.

I removed my apron, tucked the parchment into my bodice, and made to leave. Just then, Isabella came into the room. "*Madre di Dio*, but Madonna Sancia shall be the death of me," she declared, flopping onto her bed. "I am starving, Maddalena. Come to the kitchens with me to see what we can find. Or better yet, treat me to something fresh from the market. I know you are paid well, with your embroidery."

"I am on my way out," I said apologetically, "or I would. Some other time, *amica mia*, I promise you."

She sat up and eyed me suspiciously. "Are you going to him?" she asked.

"Yes," I admitted. "But first I have an errand for Madonna Lucrezia."

She looked at me carefully. "And . . . everything is still fine?" she asked. "He treats you well?"

"Yes, of course," I said. "Why do you ask?"

She shrugged.

"Why, Isabella? You've heard something. Tell me."

"They say Valentino nearly beat a man to death in the practice yards not long ago," she said, staring hard at me. "A soldier, a man from Spain who had long served the Borgia family. He almost killed him, Maddalena."

"Yes, I heard that in the market."

"And so?" she asked. "That does not give you pause?"

"It was an accident," I said. "He trains with the soldiers all the time. All of Rome knows that. I'm sure he did not mean to hurt the man so."

"That is not how I heard the tale."

"You know how gossip is in this city, Isabella."

"You may be right," she said, unconvinced. "But he has never hurt you, has he? Never harmed you in any way?"

"Of course not," I said. "He would never hurt me."

She was silent.

"He would not, Isabella. Truly." I thought back to two nights ago, when had he made love to me hard and fast, so much so that I almost could not breathe but delighted in the breathlessness. Afterward, he had held me in his arms as he fell asleep. "Maddalena *mia*," he had whispered in my ear, a slight Catalan accent I had never heard from him before curling around his words. "*Mia bella* Maddalena."

She sighed. "As long as you are sure, Maddalena. You know him better than I."

"I do. And certainly better than any gossipmongers at the market."

"I would imagine so. I only want you to be safe, that is all."

"I am," I told her. "I am safe with him."

With Isabella's fears assuaged, I set out to find this mysterious Perotto Calderon. I had never heard his name before, but it did not matter. Madonna Lucrezia had given me a task to carry out, and carry it out I would.

I went directly to the Vatican stables, remembering with a quick pain in my heart the last time I had come to seek Federico here. Yet the pain had dulled, as though it had happened not to me, but to someone I had once been. I supposed that was true.

The stables were quiet this time of the night, with only two grooms currying horses. My eyes probed the warm darkness as I looked for the man I sought. I soon made him out at the rear of the long room, standing near some hay bales, arms crossed over his chest. I moved toward him hesitantly; he fit the description Madonna Lucrezia had given me, but what if it was not him? "Perotto?" I asked uncertainly.

He straightened and peered at me through the dim. "Who asks?" he said suspiciously.

Relieved that I clearly had the right man, I removed the letter from my bodice. "Madonna Lucrezia sent me." I extended the parchment to him.

He did not take it immediately. "You are not Pantasilea," he said.

"No. She is ill. Madonna Lucrezia sent me instead."

"Hmmm." He did not sound convinced, but he took the letter and unfolded it. His face relaxed as he beheld the words on the page. He was in truth quite handsome. "This is indeed her hand." He glanced at me. "Thank you."

"Always happy to serve my lady. God give you good night, Master Perotto."

"And you," he said distractedly, already turning away from me, absorbed in the message.

My duty done, I could now turn my thoughts to more enjoyable pursuits. Moving quickly, I entered the Vatican Palace via the servants' entrance and made my way to the apartments of my lover.

It was only after the rush and spark and burn of lovemaking that I finally wondered what Madonna Lucrezia's message had been to this Perotto. He had seemed suspicious of me, as though he had something to hide. Indeed Madonna Lucrezia had made it clear that the message was a discreet matter, usually entrusted to only one person. Was . . . was he her lover?

For shame, Maddalena, I scolded myself, even as my eyelids drifted closed. To think one such as Madonna Lucrezia would take a lover while still married.

If she had, I was hardly in a position to judge. And it was none of my affair in any case.

Chapter 56

CESARE

Father's announcement of Juan's and my appointments was met mostly with silence. Michelotto brought word from his spies that many of the College of Cardinals were upset at my own appointment as papal legate over the older, more experienced cardinals, but the true outrage was at the gifting to Juan of the duchy of Benevento, as predicted. The general feeling was that the pope had largely overstepped the bounds of his secular authority. Yet no one knew quite what might be done about that. So the grumbling remained just that. I instructed Michelotto in no uncertain terms to bring me word if he got wind of anything changing in that regard.

In the meantime, Father threw a grand banquet to celebrate Juan's investiture, and even those who complained mightily about the matter did not see fit to abstain from the Holy Father's sumptuous table. Hypocrites, all, I thought contemptuously that night, watching two of the cardinals in question working their way through large plates and leering appreciatively down the bodices of the serving girls who poured them more wine. I had caught sight of Maddalena at one point—no doubt there attending Lucrezia—but she was not serving, thank heavens. If any of these men had looked at her like that I likely could not have stopped myself from plucking out their eyes.

Meanwhile, Juan and Sancia behaved more shamelessly than ever. She was seated beside him at the table, and no one could have failed to notice his hand on her leg, or the way she often whispered in his ear, placing a hand possessively on his chest or shoulder. When the feasting was over and the dancing had begun, they were the first couple to take to the floor, their bodies pressing almost obscenely close as they danced together.

I had danced a few turns with Lucrezia, but soon lost the stomach for it. Instead I was back at my seat, drinking more wine as I furiously watched Juan and Sancia make fools of themselves, and of me. I was incapable of looking away; as though this was hell and watching them was the punishment God had devised for me, that I might pay for my sins in the most excruciating way possible.

As I stewed and drank, Jofre came to sit in a chair beside me. He, it was plain, had had more than his share of the wine as well.

He did not speak at first, but his eyes were fixed on the same sight as mine. I remained silent; he would say what he wished when he was ready.

"I used to think myself the luckiest man in the world, to have such a wife," Jofre said eventually, his words slurring.

"And so you are," I said, knowing what was coming but wishing to forestall it if I could.

"No. I am not. Anyone would think that to have such a wife would be enough, but it is not. I have learned that the hard way, brother." He took another drink and said morosely, "My wife does not love me."

"Surely she—"

"I love her, but she does not love me. Our marriage is torture for me," he said, as though I had not spoken. "And Juan . . ." His voice broke, yet I saw only rage in his eyes. There was a resemblance to me, and perhaps to Juan as well, in his face, but his features were softer, more blurred, as if in his case water had been mixed in with the Borgia blood. "He is my brother," Jofre went on, teeth clenched. "I thought he loved me, as I always loved him. How could he do this to me? How?"

He did not know, then. He did not know I had bedded his wife before Juan. Yet his question felt like an accusation all the same.

"They must hate me," Jofre said. "They must hate me fiercely, to so shame me before all."

"I am sure that is not true," I said, the first honest words I felt I could speak. I had nothing but enmity for both Juan and Sancia, but I was certain they did not mean to hurt Jofre, nor bore him any ill will. They were both simply too selfish to see the harm they were causing him. Or to care.

Just as I had been too filled with mad love and desire for Sancia to care.

"Then what must they think of me?" Jofre demanded, turning to face me.

"I do not believe they think of anyone save themselves."

Jofre laughed mirthlessly and lifted his goblet to his lips. "How nice that must be, to think only of oneself. I find I cannot think of anything or anyone but the two of them."

Chapter 57

MADDALENA

"Let me help you with that," I offered when I came into the kitchen, seeing that Pietra, one of Donna Adriana's maids, was attempting to lift a heavy tray.

She straightened. "I do not need your help, thank you," she said shortly.

I drew back, surprised. "Very well, then," I said.

She struggled to lift the tray, and even as she staggered away under its weight, I heard her mutter "*Puttana.*"

I froze, staring after her. Had I heard her correctly? Had I just imagined it? No, I was certain. She'd said *puttana*. Whore.

She knew.

And if she knew, who else knew?

I glanced around the kitchen and saw Lucca, one of the cook's assistants, watching me. When I caught his eye, his lip curled in a sneer, and he turned back to chopping spinach.

It was safe to assume my secret was no longer a secret.

I resolved to ask Isabella about it when I saw her. She would never have said anything, so how had I been discovered? Who had seen something?

I did not see her until later that night, when we'd both been dismissed. She looked puzzled when I mentioned the incident in the kitchen to her. "I have not heard anyone say anything, no," she said. "Are you sure you did not mishear Pietra? She's always grumbling about something under her breath."

"I suppose I could have," I said, beginning to doubt myself. I'd been so sure before, especially with the way Lucca had looked at me after . . .

"If there was gossip about you, it might be I would not hear it right away," Isabella offered. "Everyone knows you and I are close friends, so anyone speaking ill of you would no doubt not do it before me."

That seemed likely. But perhaps I was simply imagining it all, and I said as much to Isabella.

"Perhaps," she agreed, but she looked troubled all the same.

"What is it?"

"It is just that . . . you know how everyone talks around here," she said. "It may be no one knows about you and Valentino yet, but they will. They will eventually, Maddalena, and you know it."

I did know it. But there was nothing I could do about it. I could not stop people from talking. I was equally powerless to refuse Cesare. As long as he sent for me, I would go. I could not resist him.

The next day, I received more strange looks from other servants, and that night when Isabella and I went to find something to eat after we'd been dismissed, the cook—who usually teased us and shook his head indulgently when we asked for a taste of the best wine—only slapped a few plates down in front of us with the leftovers from that night's meal and disappeared without a word, though he did toss a glare in my direction. Isabella and I exchanged uncomfortable looks, but did not speak of it.

What was there, really, to say?

The following day, Donna Adriana sent me to the market for some thread to mend a gown of hers, and one of her maids, a girl about my age named Nina, went with me to be sure I got the right color.

I rolled my eyes at Donna Adriana's fussing—surely I could be trusted to secure the correct color thread—but knew better than to protest.

Nina fairly skipped alongside me as we left the palazzo, clearly thrilled to be out and about rather than at Donna Adriana's beck and call.

Yet all too soon it became clear that Nina's excitement was less about being away from Donna Adriana than it was about me.

The palazzo was just out of sight when I noticed her looking at me out of the corner of her eye, a smile on her lips. "What is it?" I asked.

"I'm glad we've been sent out to the market," she said.

"Yes. It is a nice day for a walk."

"Not that," she said, waving a hand. "I have been wanting to have a private word with you."

"With . . . me?" I asked, baffled.

"Of course!" She leaned closer. "You've quite a reputation these days, you know."

Dear Lord and Mary Virgin, preserve me. My body tensed even as she spoke.

"So . . . what is it like?"

"What is what like?" I asked, determined to feign ignorance for as long as I could.

Her grin widened. "Oh, you know very well what I mean." She lowered her voice. "Bedding Cesare Borgia, the not-so-holy cardinal. What is it like?"

I quickened my stride. "I don't know where you heard such a thing, but—"

"Do not deny it, Maddalena Moretti," she said, catching up with me. "I know it's true. Everyone does. The entire palazzo is talking about it. Hadn't you noticed?"

I quickened my pace still further, as though to outrun her questions. "This is none of your affair," I said curtly.

She laughed. "Oh, come, Maddalena. I bear you no will ill. I do not wish to call you a slut or a whore. I admire you. However did you catch his eye? He is the handsomest man I have ever seen,

I think. What is it like with him? I imagine it must be quite delicious." She grinned wickedly.

"I do not wish to discuss this, Nina."

Her smile faded. "You are not better than the rest of us because he fucks you once in a while, Maddalena. Don't forget that."

"Thank you for the lesson in humility," I snapped, and after that we did not speak the rest of the afternoon.

That night when I arrived back in my room, the story of my walk with the insufferable Nina almost spilled from my lips as soon as I saw Isabella was already within. Yet she held up a hand to stop me. "I have something to tell you."

"I have something to tell *you*."

"Me first," Isabella said in a tone that booked no argument.

I sighed and sank down onto my bed. "Very well. What is it?"

"Everyone knows about you and Cardinal Valentino," she said.

"Everyone? Do you think . . . Madonna Lucrezia knows?" I could not bear her disappointment in me.

Isabella shook her head impatiently. "I mean all of the servants," she said. "The high and mighty pay no attention to our gossip. I doubt they have heard anything."

"How did they find out?"

Isabella sat down beside me on my bed. "Apparently Anita saw you. That maid of Donna Sancia's she brought from Naples?"

"Saw me where? What did she see?"

Isabella gave me an impatient look. "She was at the banquet at the Vatican last week with her mistress, the one honoring the Duke of Gandia. She saw Cardinal Valentino take you off into another room, and she followed, and . . . she saw."

I groaned, putting my head in my hands. I had been present at the banquet attending Lucrezia. Cesare had been upset—I still did not know why. While the dancing was going on he had stormed out of the room where the festivities were taking place and had come upon me in the hallway. "Maddalena," he had said, sighing my name as though it were a prayer and answer all in one. "Come with me."

"Where?" I asked, but he had simply grabbed my wrist and pulled me into a nearby room. He had pushed me up against a wall at the back of the room, some drapery and hangings shielding us somewhat from the doorway, and kissed me, hard, pinning me to the wall with his body.

When his hands began lifting my skirts, I had pulled away from the kiss. "Here, my lord?" I gasped. "What if . . ."

"Do not call me 'my lord,'" he breathed against my mouth. "Call me Cesare."

"Cesare," I murmured, and he kissed my neck, even as his hands continued their exploration beneath my skirts. "Cesare . . ."

Suddenly, he'd drawn away, releasing me. "I am despicable," he said, more to himself than to me. "I am no better than my brother, trying to take you against a wall . . ."

I struggled to catch my breath. "No, Cesare," I said, my voice low. "You are not your brother. I have chosen to give myself to you, remember."

He looked up at those words, and I drew him to me and kissed him. He needed no further convincing; he hiked up my skirts and had me there against the wall. It was over quickly but pleasurable in its rough haste all the same, and I had to return to the banquet on weak legs and trying to hide my silly smile.

Now I wished I had let him walk away; that I had not seduced him. For apparently Anita had seen it all—or enough to leave her in no doubt as to what I was to the Cardinal of Valencia. His whore.

"That was stupid of us. Of me," I whispered.

"Yes, it was," Isabella said. "For now everyone knows. And they think you either an irredeemable slut or that you are Valentino's spy. A few are jealous. None of which wins you any friends among the rest of the servants. Quite the opposite."

"And you?" I asked, raising my head to look at her. "Into which group do you fall?"

She slid an arm around my shoulders. "I am your friend," she said. "As ever. I know you do not spy for him, and you mean no one else ill will. What then should I hold against you?"

I returned her embrace, and when we drew apart she added, "I only wish he had never looked twice at you, Maddalena. Truly I do."

"You should not."

"Why? Is being in his bed truly worth all the rest?"

What had I truly lost but the good opinion of people I did not know well? Many of whom I did not much care for anyway. How much could that actually change my life? Was I not better off with Cesare than without him? "Yes," I answered. "It is."

Chapter 58

CESARE

I could not avoid Juan, much as I wanted to. Our mother invited us—along with several other Roman nobles and churchmen—to dinner one June night at her villa in the country. Despite Juan's loud and largely false stories bragging of his exploits in battle, it was a pleasant enough night. I had not seen much of my mother of late, and it was a joy to speak to her at length, though she was much occupied by her guests.

"You are not working too hard, are you, Cesare?" she asked after the meal had ended. "I know you wish to be a help to your father, but you are making time to enjoy life as well, yes?"

I smiled, thinking of Maddalena. "I am, Mama. I promise."

"Good." She kissed my cheek, sighing. "I worry about you and your brothers, Cesare. And Lucrezia. Is she much upset about the divorce?"

"She is . . . coming around to the idea," I said. Lucrezia had grown weary of trying to resist, and had ceased arguing. She was still not happy, but she would be once she had a new husband who could truly appreciate her—and his connection to the Borgia family. "You must come and visit her soon."

"I shall. It has been too long." She paused. "And what of you and Juan? Word in Rome is you are quite at each other's throats."

"They gossip about this?" Michelotto had either omitted this deliberately, or simply thought it beneath my notice.

"You know how Romans are, Cesare. And the two of you hardly make any secret of the enmity between you." She sighed again. "It wounds me, my son. I am sure your father feels the same."

"He does," I said tightly. "But we are grown men, and Juan continues to make decisions I cannot help but despise. We are too different, Mother. I am sorry this pains you."

"I can only pray someday you will both feel differently."

"If God wills it," I said, wanting to placate her.

She smiled. "My son, the cardinal. Who could have believed it?"

I laughed. "You doubted it? When it was what Father planned all along?"

"I suppose I should have long ago ceased to be surprised at the force of Rodrigo's will," she said. "But what is most important to me, my son, is this: are you happy?"

Happy. What was happiness?

Could I ever be truly happy watching Juan receive every accolade and honor—including our father's highest regard—I had ever craved for myself? Could I ever be happy knowing the one woman I had ever loved had left me for him? Had betrayed me with him?

Could I ever be happy knowing I would never lead armies to victory in battle, as I was certain I'd been born to do?

I thought of Lucrezia's smile when I came to visit her, the way she called me her favorite brother in the words of our native Catalan. Of the power I wielded with cardinals and statesmen and ambassadors. Of Maddalena and the pleasure she gave me, the way her touch could rouse me, and the satisfaction I got from pleasing her in return. And how, with her, I found more than simple physical release—there was an emotional one, too, a clarity when I was with her that I could not find anywhere else.

"I am happy enough," I answered.

As dusk was falling, Juan and I rode back to Rome together, Michelotto a few paces behind us. "It was lovely to see Mother," Juan said. "She is looking well."

I was somewhat surprised at this overture of civil conversation from him, but mindful of my conversation with our mother, I decided to reverse my previous decision to ignore him all night. "She is indeed," I said. "Country life suits her, though I miss when she was closer to us."

"Who could blame her for escaping the stench of Rome in summer?" Juan asked.

"True," I agreed. "She spoke of coming to visit Lucrezia soon."

"Ah," Juan said fondly, and I was reminded that, for all his faults, he did truly love our sister. "She will be pleased. I visited her yesterday, and she has been missing Mother."

We rode through the streets of Rome, and when we reached the Ponte Sant' Angelo—the Castel Sant' Angelo looming above us in the growing darkness—Juan pulled up his horse. "This is where I leave you, Cesare."

"What, here?" I asked. "Where are you going?"

"I've an appointment to keep."

"Michelotto and I can ride with you, if you like."

He laughed. "I am a man grown. I do not need my elder brother's protection. And this is an appointment I must keep alone."

"Do you truly think it wise to roam the streets of Rome alone at this hour? A man in your position, richly dressed, who clearly has coin on his person?" And given the number of enemies you've accumulated, I thought.

"I will be fine."

"His Eminence is right, Your Grace," Michelotto said, pulling up next to us. "At least return to the Vatican with us and fetch one of your men to go with you."

"Gentlemen, I thank you for your concern, but I am late. I must be off." Juan tipped his cap to us and rode off in the direction of the Jewish Ghetto.

Michelotto and I exchanged uneasy glances. "Does his foolishness know no bounds?" I asked.

"It would seem not."

"That was a rhetorical question."

"Of course, my lord. Where do you suppose he is going?"

"To meet some woman, no doubt." Suddenly I was struck with inspiration. I should follow and catch him in the act. It would be amusing, at least, to throw in Sancia's face. "I'm going to follow him."

"Is that wise, my lord?"

"Why not? I want to know what he is doing." I turned my horse in the direction Juan had just gone. "Follow me at a distance. If he looks back he might get suspicious to see two men behind him. He may not look too closely at one."

"Yes, my lord."

I set off after Juan at a distance. He led me through narrow, twisting streets, until we were in the depths of the Ghetto, no place for a young nobleman after dark.

I soon lost sight of him, cursing myself for a fool. Michelotto caught up to me. "My lord?"

"Here," I said, dismounting and handing him the reins of my horse. "Wait here. I will try to follow on foot."

"My lord, I don't know if—"

"Just wait here!" I called over my shoulder, walking off toward where I thought Juan might have gone.

I had walked perhaps two minutes when I heard a scuffle in an alley up ahead. I quickened my pace and turned down the alley toward the sounds.

I squinted against the darkness, barely making out the shadowy shapes of a few men. A struggle was ensuing.

I drew near cautiously, aware of the danger. This may have

nothing to do with Juan. Yet as I got closer, the scene before me resolved itself. My body tensed.

A group of men, wearing dark cloaks and masks, had fallen upon Juan. They had pulled him from his horse—the beast had panicked and run off—and had borne him to the ground, where they were struggling to subdue him even as he shouted and fought to get away. But there were too many of them.

I saw a flash in the dim light as one of the men drew a dagger and I heard Juan's scream as it was plunged into his flesh. The other men—I counted four total—had drawn their daggers and were stabbing them into whatever part of him they could reach.

One of the men shifted, and I saw Juan's face, twisted with screams and crumpled in agony. He opened his eyes and saw me standing there, watching the horrific scene before me. "Brother, help me!" he called. "Please!"

I started toward him but stopped. I saw my mother's face, pleading with me to end my feuding with Juan.

I also saw Juan mocking me, insulting me; Juan failing at every task set before him and being honored anyway. I saw our father beaming with pride at everything Juan said and did. I saw Juan trying to rape Maddalena. I saw Juan making love to Sancia, the woman I had thought I would love forever.

I saw Juan taking everything I had ever wanted for himself, as though it were his right. I thought about what it might be like if he no longer stood in my way.

Juan's eyes, locked on mine, widened in shock and despair, as if he knew what I was thinking. "Brother! Cesare! Help me!" His cries were weak, and blood bubbled from his mouth, muddling his words. He began to choke on it.

I turned and walked away.

Chapter 59

MADDALENA

The summons came after nightfall. I was already in bed, but I rose and dressed quickly, going with the messenger back to the Vatican. I was somewhat puzzled. Of late Cesare arranged ahead of time for me to come to him, rather than wait until such a late hour to summon me from my bed and to his.

When I arrived, we spoke little. We made love vigorously as ever, but something was troubling him. He seemed distant, even as he moved inside me. Afterward he lay still, holding me tightly, before he withdrew and sat on the edge of the bed, running his fingers through his hair.

"Cesare," I said softly, sitting up. "Is something wrong?"

He laughed shortly, a weak, dark sound. "Either everything has gone wrong, or everything has gone right."

"What do you mean?" I moved closer to him.

"It is nothing I would burden you with. It is better if you do not know."

His tone was cool, yet underneath it I detected a note of concern. He truly thought I was better off not knowing whatever it was that was troubling him.

With a creeping sense of confidence, I felt certain I could persuade him to tell me, whatever it was; that I could persuade him to tell me anything. As I had told Isabella, my relationship with Cesare Borgia could never be anything more than this, could never exist beyond the four walls of his sumptuous bedchamber. Yet whatever this was was more than simply sex, more than lust, more than the need for physical release. He enjoyed my company, not just my body. He did not merely fuck me and send me away; I spent the better part of the night in his arms. And that, perhaps far more than anything else, was something I would never have dreamed could come to pass.

My fingers were nearly touching his skin, close enough to feel the heat of his body, when I stopped myself from touching him.

I knew the rumors about Cesare Borgia, about what kind of man he was and what he was capable of. I knew what kind of power he wielded, and the ways in which he had influenced the politics of the Italian peninsula and all her nations. But more than that, I knew things beyond the rumors, things that the gossips hadn't even guessed at.

So whatever this was, whatever had happened this night that he sought to protect me from . . . did I truly want to know?

I lowered my hand to my lap. I did not. I did not want to know.

As though sensing my withdrawal, he said, "You may go," his tone even more distant than before. "I shall not be good company this night."

I rose from the bed and dressed quickly, donning my cloak even in the summer heat. I moved to the door and looked back at him. He had not moved. "May God give you good night," I said softly.

"God or the devil shall see me through this night, and I know not which," he said. I hesitated for a moment and simply slipped out the door to return to my room.

Chapter 60

CESARE

I thought I would never sleep that night, but after I sent Maddalena away I fell into a sleep from which I did not wake until morning. Once again she had soothed me and calmed my mind when I needed it most.

As I rose and dressed for the day ahead, I knew it would be much waiting: waiting for someone to ask what had become of Juan; waiting for someone to discover what had happened. I was not concerned anyone would know of my part—or rather, lack thereof. There were only two people who knew I had been there. One was dead and the other would not betray me.

It was not until evening that I received the summons I had been expecting all day. I went to the pope's apartments and was admitted immediately.

"Cesare," Father said, pacing in his private audience chamber. Burchard was present, as were a few servants. "I have heard something most disturbing."

I made sure my face was neutral. "What might that be, Holy Father?"

"Two of the Duke of Gandia's servants came to me," he said. "They have not seen their master since yesterday afternoon. He never returned home last night and is nowhere to be found."

"I trust they've checked his usual . . . haunts?"

"Yes, and he has not been seen at any of those establishments."

He looked questioningly at me. "Did you return to Rome with him from your mother's villa? When was the last time you saw him?"

"We did ride back into the city together, and at the Ponte Sant' Angelo he said he had an appointment to keep and insisted on riding off alone," I said. It was the truth, after all.

"And you let him go off alone?"

I spread my hands in a gesture of helplessness. "Michelotto and I both tried to persuade him otherwise, and suggested he at least ride back to the Vatican with us to get a guard to accompany him. But he insisted he was late and must go alone. How was I to stop him?"

"Hmph," Father snorted. "At times I think that boy hasn't any more sense than God gave a common rabbit in a field."

Finally, we agreed on something where Juan was concerned. "He will turn up," I offered. "Likely he is ensconced at the house of some Roman lady and can't be bothered to stir forth or send word to his household."

"Hmph," Father said again. "No doubt you are right, though my understanding is that he has not needed to stray far from home in order to find such companionship."

It was the first time I'd heard him acknowledge the affair between Juan and Sancia. "My understanding is the same," I allowed.

"If you hear from him, let me know, won't you?" he said. "I shall be sure to give him a good dressing-down when he returns, for worrying us so."

I wondered whether Father would be quite so unsettled if I disappeared for a day, but it didn't matter. Not anymore. "Of course, Holy Father," I said, bowing. "Should I hear anything, you will be the first to know."

When there was still no trace of Juan the next morning, Father sent men to every corner of Rome to search and inquire. Michelotto reported that the city was buzzing with news of the Duke of Gandia's disappearance. Shops had been closed and the Orsini and Colonna had fortified their palaces in the city, fearing violence would break out.

For the first time I pondered: who had arranged Juan's death? Clearly he had been lured there so he might be assassinated, but who was behind it? The Orsini seemed likely. They had particular reason to hate our family after the military campaign that had been launched against them, and no doubt knew the best way to strike against Pope Alexander would be through his favorite son, who was certainly stupid enough to be led to his death. That the Orsini had the money, connections, and influence necessary to carry out such an assassination was not in doubt.

His body would be found eventually, I was certain. And my part in the matter would remain unknown. While many would likely suspect me of my brother's murder, and while they would not perhaps be entirely wrong, I had not sent the hired thugs after him. That culprit would be found, and attention would be turned away from me.

I was a Borgia, and the pope's son. What could truly be done to me?

On Friday afternoon, the members of the papal court were hastily summoned to the audience chamber. The pope's agents had found a man who had seen something the night Juan had disappeared, and they were bringing him to the Vatican to make his report to the Holy Father in person.

The man looked nervous as he was escorted in before the papal throne, and after he paid the pontiff the proper respects, Father waved a hand eagerly. "They tell us you have news of the Duke of Gandia, good sir. Pray, tell us your name and what you know."

"I am Giorgio Schiavi, Your Holiness," he said, looking uncomfortable. "I am a timber dealer, and many a night I keep watch on my wares as they are unloaded from the boats to prevent theft. That is how I came to be out on the Tiber on the night in question."

"And what did you see?" Father pressed.

"At about the hour of two, I saw two men come out of an alley at the point of the river where refuse is thrown in. They looked around and retreated back down the alley. Two more men appeared, and when they did not see anyone, either, they signaled to their companions. A rider on a white horse came, with a body slung across the saddle behind him."

There were gasps from those assembled, and Father's knuckles whitened as he gripped the arms of the throne. When he did not speak, the man went on.

"The horseman turned so the rump of his horse faced the river, and one of the men took the body by its hands, the other by its feet, and they flung it into the river. The man on the horse asked if the body had sunk, and they replied it had. Then saw what appeared to be the man's cloak floating on the water. He asked what it was, and his companions said, 'Sir, the cloak,' and so the man on the horse threw some stones at the cloth to make it sink. Then they all retreated back up the alley the way they had come."

Father's face had gone white as a slab of marble. He was struggling for words. "Good sir," I asked, "why did you not report this incident to the authorities as soon as you witnessed it?"

He bowed in my direction. "Your Eminence, in my life I have seen more than a hundred bodies thrown into the Tiber at that same spot, and no one had ever troubled themselves about any of them before."

"Thank you for bringing this information forward," Father managed, his voice sounding slightly strangled. He rose and looked over at his captain of the guard. "Captain. See that the river is searched. I want the fisherman, all the tradespeople with boats to be out searching the Tiber for the Duke of Gandia. Tell them there shall be a reward for whoever may find something."

The captain bowed. "Right away, Your Holiness." He left swiftly to carry out his order.

"You are all dismissed," Father said abruptly, and left the chamber with me on his heels.

"You heard this man Schiavi," I said, once we were safely in Father's private rooms. "He sees bodies thrown into the Tiber all the time. We do not know that it was Juan." Except it must be. Schiavi had seen four men, and one on horseback. I had seen four men setting upon Juan. No doubt the horseman had been waiting at another spot to help them dispose of the body and ensure the task was done. If I was right and the Orsini had ordered Juan's murder, the man on horseback may well have been a member of that family.

Father turned to me, haunted and grief-stricken, as though he had seen something he could never forget. "But if Juan is not dead in the river, then where is he, Cesare?" he pleaded. "If he was alive and well, he would surely know by now that I am tearing the city apart trying to find him." He shuddered. "If this body in the Tiber is not Juan's, I am afraid it is only a matter of time before his body turns up elsewhere. And I . . ."

He trailed off and sank into a chair, burying his head in his hands. I sat beside him, in silence, ready to offer comfort, and all the while wondering if it would be better or worse if I told him the truth. At least then he would no longer need to wonder.

Before long Juan's body was found. A fisherman pulled him up in his net, fully dressed, and with his purse containing thirty ducats still attached to his belt, making it clear that robbery had not been the motive for his murder. Whoever had hired these men for the deed wanted it known that Juan had not been a random target. A total of nine stab wounds were located on his body, from his head to his legs.

His body was taken to the Castel Sant' Angelo to be washed and dressed, and Father locked himself in his rooms and refused to see anyone. Not even me. Maybe especially not me.

Chapter 61

MADDALENA

Madonna Lucrezia paced restlessly in her bedchamber, still dressed in her night things, though it was past noon. She had refused to get dressed, refused to leave her bedchamber, and refused to eat or drink. Early that morning she had received the news of her brother Juan's death, and she was devastated.

"Who would have killed him?" she cried as Donna Adriana tried to take her hand to soothe her. "And why? Who would have wanted to kill Juan?"

For once, Lucrezia's innocence grated on me instead of charming me. He was her brother and she loved him, I understood that, but did she truly not know what kind of man he was? He had no shortage of enemies in Rome, from political opponents of the Borgia family to men he had personally offended or had quarrel with. The only ones likely to miss the Duke of Gandia, aside from His Holiness, were in this palazzo.

The door burst open to reveal Sancia of Aragon. Her eyes were red, and tears streaked down her face, but unlike Lucrezia she was at least dressed in a day gown. "Have you heard?" she wailed. "Oh, it is so awful!"

Lucrezia nodded, her tears starting anew, and she opened her arms for her sister-in-law, who rushed into them. The two young women held each other, sobbing.

Lucrezia did not approve of Juan and Sancia's romance and worried over the harm it was causing to her brother Jofre. Yet in this moment of grief, she had put aside her judgment and was happy to comfort and be comforted by someone else who had loved him—however unworthy I thought him of that love.

I would never say so aloud—not even to my confessor—but the Duke of Gandia had gotten what he deserved. God had finally seen fit to punish him for his sins, his evil, and though it might cause pain to a few, justice had been served. I had no doubt of that.

My mother's voice piped up: *And what will you say when God decides to punish you for your sins? Lust, fornication, seducing a man of the Church . . .*

The difference between Juan Borgia and me is I have not sinned with evil in my heart, I argued. I have not hurt anyone, nor have I sought to. I had repeated this to myself so many times I was at last starting to believe it.

Something more pressing was troubling me: who had been the hand to wield God's justice unto the Duke of Gandia? Would any of us ever know? And what if the day came when I found that what I suspected was correct?

I was no fool. By now everyone knew precisely upon what night he had been slain. And so a possible explanation for Cesare Borgia's strange behavior on that night had been presented to me.

Isabella sidled into the room after her mistress. She caught my eye and gave me a look, full of weight. She had something to tell me. Fortunately, Donna Adriana noticed the two of us. "Maddalena, Isabella, please go fetch some bread and broth. These ladies must eat something."

We curtsied and departed. Making toward the kitchens, Isabella pulled me down an empty hallway, looking around to make sure no one was near. "What is it?" I asked her.

"I know you've been with Madonna Lucrezia all morning, but there is much talk in the streets, and among the servants, about the Duke of Gandia's murder," she said.

"As I would expect," I said. "Perhaps now they can stop gossiping about me."

Isabella gave me an exasperated look. "You do not know what they are saying."

"I can guess."

"Can you?" She arched an eyebrow. "I will tell you anyway. The opinion of many is that the Duke of Gandia was murdered on the order of his brother, Cardinal Valentino. That their hatred for each other, and the cardinal's jealousy, drove him to have the duke killed, so the duke would no longer stand in the way of his ambitions."

"That . . . does not surprise me," I admitted.

"And?" she demanded. "Is it true?"

"How would you expect me to know?" I asked. "Do you think that, if he indeed sent assassins after his brother, he would tell me?"

"But you . . ." She drew back. "You believe that he did."

It was what I had been trying to avoid thinking all morning. Yet I could not do so any longer, not when Isabella was forcing me to confront the question.

The fact remained that I was glad Juan Borgia was dead. I was glad I did not need to attend him when he came to visit his sister, that I need no longer become so rigid with tension in his presence that I felt I would crack into a thousand pieces. That I would never again need to look at his hands and remember them holding me so I could not escape, feeling violated all over again as I remembered how he had touched me.

God and His Son taught us we must forgive, but I was no divine being; far from it. I had never forgiven Juan Borgia and never would. Given the depth of my other sins, this one troubled me not at all.

"And what if he did?" I replied, finally. Isabella's jaw dropped open in horror. "I do not know if he had his brother killed or not, but it makes no difference to me."

"Maddalena," Isabella said, her voice hushed with horror. "You cannot mean that."

"Can't I? Did I never tell you, Isa, how I came to work at Santa Maria in Portico?"

I told her the whole sorry tale, and this time when she looked on me with horror and shock, it was mixed with sympathy. "Oh, Maddalena," she said. "I didn't know. Why did you never tell me?"

"I was afraid," I confessed. "I knew you would not speak of it if I asked you not to, but I did not want word getting back to the duke that I was talking about him. I did not even want him to know I was here. So I said nothing. But now he is dead, and it matters not." I wanted to spit on the marble floor. "And good riddance."

"I am so sorry," she said, hugging me quickly. "Yes, I am glad that he is dead, too, after hearing this. But . . ." She looked at me pensively. "To kill one's own brother is no small thing, even so. Does that not . . . scare you, if it is true?"

Why did Isabella have such a knack for asking the questions I did not want to ask myself? "Cesare would never hurt me," I said. "And however it happened, I am glad the Duke of Gandia is dead."

Chapter 62

CESARE

Even after Juan's funeral procession, Father stayed locked away, refusing to eat or drink or see anyone. I had tried multiple times to gain admittance to his chambers and was turned away every time.

"He must be made to eat, Your Eminence," Burchard said to me at one point, peering owlishly up at me from his small height. "We all understand his grief, but he cannot put his health in jeopardy like this."

"I agree, Burchard, but what would you have me do? He will not see even me."

"If I may be so bold, Your Eminence must continue to try. If he will not listen to you, I do not know that he will listen to anyone."

Despite the circumstances, this pleased me—I had become known throughout the Curia for being the one man whose counsel the Holy Father sought. I had finally become indispensable, as I had always hoped to be.

And if I were not yet, I soon would be.

As another day passed and still he did not emerge, I began to wonder in earnest if I should tell him the truth. But I did not know with certainty who had laid the trap. All I would really be able to tell him was that I had watched my own brother be murdered and had done nothing to stop it. And what would be the point of that?

Still I could not stop thinking about telling him, and I realized that for the first time in my life I felt the urgent need for confession and absolution. Yet this was a sin no one could absolve me of. I had known that when I had weighed my options in the alley and decided to walk away. I did not deserve absolution.

Juan's desperate cries—*Brother, help me!*—would echo in my ears until the day I went to my own grave.

And yet if I had the choice to make again . . . God forgive me, I would not have chosen any differently.

I went to see my sister, who was devastated. As she wept in my arms, I felt the guilt truly eat at me. But I also became angry that someone as useless and cruel as Juan should be mourned so. He had not been worthy of Lucrezia's love, of our father's love. Yet they wept for him all the same.

I stayed with Lucrezia late into the night, wanting to comfort her as much as I was able. One thing was clear: she must never know what I had done.

As I was leaving, I came upon Jofre returning home. He was drunk, swaying on his feet. He'd taken up with a band of young ruffians of late. Father had been most disapproving—why such behavior had been forgivable in Juan but not in Jofre I did not know—but recent events had distracted Father from the reprimand he'd been planning to deliver to the youngest Borgia. Jofre roamed the streets unchecked, for now.

"Brother," I said, steadying him. "You do not look well. Shall I help you to bed?"

He wrenched away from me, stumbling back. "Don't need your help," he said sullenly.

I shrugged. "Very well," I said. "I bid you good night, then."

I turned to go, but he called out to me. "Wait!" he called. "I have to tell you something, Cesare," he slurred. "God help me, I must tell someone."

"What is it?" I asked.

"You must promise not to tell anyone."

"Very well, I promise," I said. Surely Jofre's big confession would be no more than visiting some whores, and he did not wish Sancia to know. As if Sancia cared.

He glanced around to make sure we were alone and said softly, "I did it."

"Did what?"

"Juan. I had Juan killed. It was me."

I took a step back in surprise. "You . . . did what?"

"I hired the assass-assassins," he said, stumbling over the word. "I sent them after him. It was me."

"If this is a jest, it is a poor one."

"It is no jest," he snapped petulantly, and began to giggle. "You all, none of you," he said through his drunken laughter, "none of you see me as a true Borgia. I am not one of you, not really. You do not believe I could do it, do you? That I could have my own brother killed?"

I did not believe it, did not want to believe it: that the boy Juan and I had wrestled with and taught to play chess, the boy Lucrezia had read stories to, would order the assassination of his own brother. But there was a hardness in Jofre's gaze, a coldness I had never seen before. He was telling the truth.

There had always been a rumor that Jofre was not a Borgia, that he was the perfectly legitimate son of our mother and her husband.

But Father had never said so and had seen to it Jofre was raised just as we were. Yet it was plain he thought of Jofre only after Juan, Lucrezia, and me. I knew all too well how it felt to be treated second best, but perhaps not in the same way that Jofre knew it.

What have we done to you? I wanted to scream at him. What did you let us do to you?

What had ambition and lust for power done to us all?

I would have paid and sent out the assassins myself, if only to keep Jofre's hands clean.

"But . . . why?" I asked, afraid I already knew.

"He was fucking my wife," Jofre slurred. "I love her, and he took her from me. She went to him willingly. I had to. I could not bear it."

Dear God. This, too, was my guilt to bear. For I had done the same as Juan, only I had done it first. Juan was dead for a sin I had committed. The only difference was Jofre had never known of my betrayal.

I might as well have killed Juan twice over.

God, but we were like a family of spiders, weaving our webs and entangling one another and devouring each other without a care.

"So now," Jofre was saying, not noticing the horror-stricken look on my face, "no one can say I am not a true Borgia. I have taken back what was mine, have I not? Is that not what Borgias do? We take what is ours." He began to laugh hysterically, until he dissolved into tears. He peered up at me, eyes rimmed in red. "You will not tell, will you, Cesare?" he whispered. "You promised not to tell."

"I . . . I promise," I said. It was the least I could do, was it not? Keeping Jofre's secret, no matter how it weighed me down.

He began to laugh once more. "It does not matter if you tell anyone, come to that," he said. "Tell the world. Tell them all. Let everyone see that Jofre Borgia is not to be trifled with."

He did not resist as I helped him up to bed, giving him over to the care of his servants. He was snoring before I could leave his bedchamber. Who knew if, in the morning, he would even remember what he had told me. That he had confessed all.

But I would. I would never forget.

Before I could think better of it, I went downstairs and made my way to the kitchens. I did not know where Maddalena Moretti might be found at this hour, but someone there surely did.

Yet as though she'd known I would come seek her—that I needed her—I entered the kitchen to find her standing beside a large wooden counter, speaking with another maid in low voices. Judging by the crumbs on the counter, the two women had been eating their evening meal.

Her companion was facing the door, and as I stepped inside she caught sight of me, and her eyes widened. "*Che?*" I heard Maddalena ask, and the woman silently pointed toward me. Maddalena whirled around, surprise flitting across her face.

"I need you," I said, my voice ragged and cracked. "Come. Please."

She gave a quick nod and cast an apologetic glance at her friend. The other woman nodded in return. Maddalena hurriedly crossed the room and took my arm, leading me out of the kitchen and down into the secret tunnel.

We did not speak a single word all the way back to my rooms. Once inside, I bolted the door and strode to the bed, intending to rip off my clothes and hers as well, so I could bury myself in her as quickly as possible and forget, if only for a while, the horrors I had learned that night. Yet I did not, could not. Instead I kept walking to the window, before turning and pacing as I always did when I was agitated. I could not stay still, not even for pleasurable purposes. I had not brought her there for sex. Not that night.

Maddalena came farther into the room and stood beside the bed, calmly watching me pace. After a minute or two passed, she finally spoke. "What's wrong, Cesare?"

I started slightly at the sound of her lovely, melodious voice, though I had hardly forgotten she was in the room with me. "What's wrong," I repeated, continuing my pacing. "What's wrong." I could feel her eyes closely watching my every movement. "I have committed a great many sins in my life," I said at last, stopping and facing her. "Which you either know or can no doubt imagine. Yet never before have I truly felt as though I have imperiled my soul."

She considered this. "What is your sin, Cesare?" she asked softly.

I resumed pacing. "You do not want to know."

"Did you kill your brother Juan?"

The question came out quietly, but quickly, as if before she could think better of it. Yet when I stopped and looked at her, she met my eyes almost placidly, so that I thought once more what a painting of the Madonna she would make. Her gaze held no fear, no judgment. And I realized why I brought her here: that I might confess. For there was no one else on earth to whom I was willing or able to make this confession.

I crossed the room and knelt before her, taking her hands in mine, and gazing up into her beautiful, serene face. "Yes," I said. "I as good as killed him. And that is the truth."

And I told her all. I told her everything.

Chapter 63

MADDALENA

I did not know what shocked me most: the truth of what had happened to Juan, Duke of Gandia; that Cesare told me all of it and then some; or that he knelt before me when he made his confession.

He rose to his feet and continued pacing as he told me everything: his lifelong jealousy of and rivalry with his brother; his frustrated ambitions; his affair with Sancia; his discovery of Sancia and Juan's betrayal; his witnessing Juan's murder and turning away; and how his younger brother, Jofre, had been behind the deed.

I do not know for how long he spoke, could not say how long the telling of the entire tale took. I did not move once, merely stayed where I was, holding on to one of the massive carved bedposts for support, watching and listening as he talked and paced. As I heard his confession.

When he finished speaking, he turned to look out the window into the darkened courtyard below, one forearm braced against the stone wall, almost as though he could not bring himself to face me. He remained there, silent, spent, for a long time.

I, too, was frozen. I did not know what to say. What was there to say to such a confession? My heart ached, and I could not entirely say why. "Cesare," I whispered.

He turned back to me, and his face bore an expression I had never seen upon it before, nor ever would again, and would never forget: as though he was afraid, deathly afraid. "Maddalena," he said. "Would you . . . do you condemn me, for all these things I've done?"

I wondered if it was truly me from whom he sought absolution. And yet I could see from the utter wreckage in his eyes that it mattered to him what I thought. It mattered desperately.

If he sought absolution and forgiveness from me, he would have it. For I knew the truth, and I was still glad Juan Borgia was dead.

"No," I said. I drew a deep breath, trembling slightly. "I do not condemn you. I don't. But it is you who must forgive yourself." Tears sprang to my eyes as I remembered what Juan had tried to do to me. Justice had been served. My uncle would have reminded me that vengeance belonged to the Lord, but perhaps the Lord had used Cesare Borgia as his instrument. It seemed so to me, a woman who had been assaulted and need not live in fear of that man ever again. "I do not judge you, Cesare. I do not condemn you."

He crossed the room to me and took me in his arms, crushing me to him. He buried his face in my hair, and tears slid down my cheeks. I could not be certain that he was not weeping as well.

I drew him to the bed and lay down beside him. Neither of us removed our clothing. He held me tightly to him, his arms wrapped around me and mine around him, and we did not move the whole night long.

Chapter 64

MADDALENA

"Maddalena, come," Lucrezia hissed when I stumbled into her room in the early dawn. The sun had scarcely commenced rising. "You must help me."

I blinked, trying to banish sleep from my eyes. Pantasilea had shaken me awake moments ago, saying Madonna Lucrezia needed my help at once. "And keep quiet, whatever you do," she admonished in a whisper, casting her eyes to where Isabella slumbered on.

Pantasilea had disappeared as I dressed and went to present myself to my mistress. "What do you need, Madonna Lucrezia?" I asked, trying to stifle a yawn.

Lucrezia was pulling linens and gowns out of her wardrobe and out of drawers, tossing them onto the bed. "Help me pack these," she said, gesturing to three trunks at the side of the room. Pantasilea was already packing some of Lucrezia's jewels and placing them in one of the trunks.

I rushed to obey, taking up the things she had flung onto the bed, and began folding them as neatly as I could. "Where are you going, Madonna? Do I need to send to the stables to—"

"No," she cut me off. "You are not to say a word. Pantasilea has already made arrangements for a litter. No one is to know I have gone until after I've left."

I looked up at her, my hands ceasing their folding. She was agitated, pacing the room—much like her brother did when he was distressed—opening and closing drawers without seeing what she was looking at. I was overstepping, but still I softly asked, "What is wrong, Madonna? Are you quite well?"

She crossed the room to me, taking my hands in hers. "I am with child," she whispered.

I gasped. "No! You are? But . . ." I thought back; it had been over three months since her husband had fled. "Surely . . . is it your husband's?"

"Of course not," she said. "How could it be? I have only just found out."

"Who . . ." I began, before realizing how inappropriate such a question was.

She rolled her eyes at me. "Honestly, Maddalena. I am surprised you do not know. In any case, I am taking myself off to the convent at San Sisto. I will remain there until the child is born." Her eyes filled with tears. "I have to. I have no choice. If I can keep Father from finding out, all the better."

I did not think she was likely to keep a secret like this from her father—to say nothing of her brother—but I did not say so. "Where will you say you have gone, Madonna? What should I—and the other servants—say if we are asked?"

"You may tell anyone who asks where I have gone. I will not be able to keep that a secret. Only say I am deep in mourning for Juan and I wished to seek solitude and seclusion." Her eyes filled with tears again. "It is not untrue, at that."

"Did you wish me to accompany you, Madonna?" I asked, returning to folding her garments. Much as I loved Lucrezia, I prayed she would say no, for how was I to go to Cesare if I was shut away in a convent with her?

"Thank you, but no. Only Pantasilea will accompany me," she said. "The fewer people who know, the better." She took my arm, forcing me to look at her. "You must not tell anyone what I have told you, Maddalena. For my sake and your own. It can be . . . dangerous in Rome to know too much."

This chilled me. Did she truly think I would betray her? Or someone might harm me, for knowing what I should not? Oh, if only she knew all the things that I knew and should not. "I will keep your secret, Madonna."

"You promise?"

"Yes, of course."

"Good. Good." She released my arm and resumed her pacing. "Pantasilea, if you are done with the jewelry, come help me dress," she said. "I shall not need too many jewels where I am going, after all."

Pantasilea did as she was told. I continued folding and packing the clothes Madonna Lucrezia had chosen, as well as some personal effects. The three trunks quickly filled up, and soon they were shut and ready for transport to the convent.

Not two hours after Pantasilea had roused me from my bed, Lucrezia was gone.

Chapter 65

CESARE

Father rose from the throne, his hands trembling as he took in those assembled in consistory. His face was pale and gaunt, and he had clearly lost weight in the few days he'd been shut up in his rooms. Still, he stood as tall as ever, and his voice, as always, commanded the attention of everyone in the room.

"The Duke of Gandia is dead," he announced, "and nothing could have given us greater sorrow, for we loved him above all things. Had we seven papacies, we would give them all to have the Duke alive once more."

He paused after this pronouncement. Shocked silence filled the room. "God has done this," he continued, "perhaps to punish us for some sin, not because the duke deserved to be so cruelly killed. We do not know who murdered him and tossed him in the Tiber like so much trash. But we will find out. Rest assured, we will find out."

After that, he seated himself, and the business of the consistory continued on as usual, with petitions and audiences and other church business.

Toward the end, the Spanish ambassador, Garcilaso de la Vega, approached the papal throne and bowed. "Your Holiness," he asked, his voice ringing throughout the room, "can you put paid to the rumors that you blame the Sforza family for the murder of the Duke of Gandia? Specifically Giovanni Sforza and his cousin, Cardinal Ascanio Sforza?"

There were whispers throughout the room at this question, but not any true surprise. I had heard murmurings that the Sforzas were suspected of the murder; certainly they had no more cause to love Juan than anyone else, and what with Lucrezia's impending divorce—now fairly common knowledge—it was not altogether out of the question that they might want to strike at us.

But according to the gossip Michelotto had brought me, the favored suspect in the streets and fine houses of Rome alike was me.

"I would assure Your Excellency that we know the Sforza family to be innocent of such a crime, whatever the gossip might say," Father responded without missing a beat. "Lord Sforza is not in Rome at present and has not been for some time. And God and all the saints together forbid that we should ever entertain such horrible suspicions of Cardinal Sforza. We have always looked upon him as a brother, and he shall always be welcome in our presence whenever he sees fit to come."

De la Vega bowed. "Well said, Your Holiness, if I may say so."

Hushed voices broke out again among those assembled, and it seemed certain that this rumor, at least, had been put to rest. It had been some time since Ascanio Sforza had been comfortable in the halls of the Vatican, but I had no doubt as to why my father wanted to lure him back: he needed Sforza on our side in the matter of Lucrezia's divorce.

After the consistory, I followed Father into his personal chambers. "We know for certain it was not the Sforzas?" I asked, careful to avoid any hint that I knew more than he did.

Father snorted. "Hmph. 'Tis a foolish rumor, which is why I put it to rest. They would have nothing to gain from it—quite the opposite. Ascanio Sforza knows his way back to power lies in working at my side once again."

"And no doubt such a return to Your Holiness's good graces can be bought at the price of a divorce from Cardinal Sforza's cousin," I said.

"Precisely. With the Sforzas looked upon with much suspicion by the rest of Italy after the French debacle, Ascanio and Ludovico cannot afford to lose the support of the Holy See by standing behind their cousin. They will tell him to do whatever we ask and hope that we will thank them for it."

"Indeed," I said. Lucrezia would be divorced and remarried before a year was out. "Let us give your verbal olive branch time to reach Ascanio's ears. Then I shall send him a friendly letter inviting him to meet with me to discuss the matter at hand."

Father smiled and clapped a hand on my shoulder. "An excellent plan." He drew back and his face fell slightly, became haggard and a decade older in a mere moment, as though he had forgotten his loss for a few seconds only to have it come crashing back down upon him anew. "This business must proceed apace, but . . . Christ's wounds, Cesare, I cannot rest until I know who killed Juan. I shall not."

Father sent agents out into the city again, questioning people, scouring for any trace of who may have been behind Juan's assassination. As the days passed and nothing was found, I grew more and more uneasy. Surely someday soon, someone would trace the murder back to Jofre. Or someone would come forward who had seen me. Then what?

My confession to Maddalena had lifted some of the weight

from my soul, but not all of it. Not when my father could never know the truth.

As I was returning to my rooms one night, my father's chamberlain approached. "Your Eminence," he said, bowing, "His Holiness has sent for you."

"Thank you," I said, sighing inwardly. "Let me wash up quickly, and I shall attend him."

"With respect, Your Eminence, I think you should come now," the man said. "He is in quite a state, pacing his rooms and muttering. It is like it was in the days . . . right after," he finished uncomfortably.

I frowned. "Very well," I said. "I shall come directly."

I followed the chamberlain back to Father's rooms and stepped into his private sitting room, closing the door behind me. He looked up, startled, at the sound of the door closing. "Cesare," he said. "You are here."

"Father," I said, taking a few steps closer. "What is amiss? Your chamberlain told me you were in a right state. It is late. You should get some sleep."

"I cannot," he said. "I cannot sleep, damn it. Do you know what happens when I sleep?"

I waited.

"In my dreams, every night, I see Juan," he said, tears filling his eyes. "I see him standing at the foot of my bed, silent and pale, stab wounds and blood all over his body, his face. He simply stands there and stares. He does not speak, but he does not need to. I know what he means to say, what he would say if he could. He cannot rest until I find his killers. He cannot rest until I have punished those responsible. And because he cannot rest, I cannot rest."

"Father," I said, gingerly taking his arm, "these are ravings. Nightmares and evil dreams, nothing more. You need to pray, and sleep, and then you shall not dream such things."

He wrenched away from me. "No! You do not understand, Cesare." He began to weep. "My son, my son, they took my son! How could anyone be so filled with malice?"

I said nothing.

"You will help me, Cesare, won't you?" he demanded, ceasing his crying. "You will help me find those responsible. I know you and your brother were often at odds, but he must be avenged, surely you can see that?"

When I spoke, I spoke softly. "That would depend upon whom would be suffering your vengeance."

He froze, facing me, a look of almost comical horror and disbelief on his face. "You . . . no," he whispered. "You . . . could not have. Tell me it isn't true, Cesare. Tell me what they are saying is wrong, is spiteful rumor, nothing more."

I bowed my head.

"Did you kill your brother?" he suddenly shouted, his voice echoing off the high ceilings.

"I am responsible for his death," I said quietly, "but I did not kill him."

"What . . . what the devil can that possibly mean?" he demanded, sounding as though the very words were strangling him. "You are responsible . . . you . . . who killed him, Cesare? Who? Damn you, tell me!"

"I am responsible," I said again. "That is all you ever need to know. You wished to know, so you might have peace? Now you do."

He took a sudden step back, all color draining from his face until it was as gray as ash. "You . . . you are protecting someone," he whispered. "Who?"

I said nothing.

"Who was it, Cesare? Who are you protecting?"

Still I did not respond.

He sank wearily into one of his large chairs. "Never mind," he said. "Never mind. I do not want to know."

The next day, Father recalled all his agents who were scouring the streets for any mention of Juan or his killers. I do not know what he thought, who he believed was behind it all, but he never spoke of it again.

PART FIVE

CITY *on* FIRE

Rome and Florence, June–August 1497

Chapter 66

CESARE

Rome, June 1497

Though Father's grief over Juan's murder had not abated—and likely never would—there was no lack of pressing matters that needed attending to. Lucrezia's divorce, for one—she had shut herself away in the convent of San Sisto in mourning for Juan, and Father and I had agreed she might be left alone for the time being. What better place, after all, to help establish her as the most virtuous of women as we negotiated an end to her marriage?

But that was not all. Girolamo Savonarola, the doomsday Dominican of Florence, had been a thorn in Father's side nearly since he'd been elected pope. Father had excommunicated the little friar some months ago, for speaking against the Church and ignoring repeated summons to Rome to explain and defend his prophetic doctrine. Among one of the many prophecies attributed to him, besides the invasion of King Charles of France, whom he'd called "the scourge of God" sent to punish and reform Italy and the Church, was his prediction of the deaths of Lorenzo de' Medici, King Ferrante of Naples, and Father's predecessor Pope Innocent VIII. All had indeed died in not too short a span.

"Ridiculous," Father had scoffed years before, early in his papacy, when word of this so-called prophecy had reached him. "It needed no divine vision to predict the deaths of those three. Ferrante and Innocent were old men, and Lorenzo was known to be in exceedingly poor health. Prophecy, indeed."

I had refrained from pointing out Father had been older when he was made pope than Innocent had been when he'd died. Nevertheless, his point was well taken; Innocent had been rather sickly and unwell toward the end, so any such "prophecy" had a decent chance of success, divinely inspired or not.

Yet things with the friar had taken an interesting turn of late. Though he had, as far as anyone in the Holy See knew, obeyed the excommunication and ceased preaching his sermons, he was still a source of mighty power and influence in Florence. He had followers at all levels of society, from the most impoverished to those within the circle of intellectuals and artists who had once congregated around the brilliant Lorenzo de' Medici. Lorenzo's eldest son, the ousted, dim-witted Piero, had been hanging about Rome, trying to gather support for an invasion to retake his home city and re-install himself as ruler—when he wasn't drinking himself into a stupor or carousing with whores. Father had taken to implying such support, depending upon what his policies toward and needs of Florence were at any given moment, but thus far the time had not been right for us to back an actual uprising.

Following the expulsion of the Medici, Savonarola had turned Florence into something of a theocracy. Word had reached us in February of a so-called "Bonfire of the Vanities" the friar had held, in which Florentines were encouraged—or extorted, by some accounts—into bringing out their luxury items such as fine clothing, jewelry, artwork (especially that of a sensual nature), cards and dice, lavish furniture, secular books, and so forth, to cast into a massive bonfire in the city's main piazza. It was said to have been a spectacle, with a large amount of "vanities" burned. Whether Savonarola's hold on the population was entirely voluntary on the part of all Florentines was almost beside the point, for it was a strong hold either way.

However, he had broken his silence toward the Vatican and written the Holy Father an admittedly lovely letter of condolence upon the death of the Duke of Gandia. Rodrigo Borgia, man and father, was moved by the gesture. Pope Alexander VI, head of Christ's Church on earth and consummate politician, was suspicious.

"What can he mean by this, truly?" Father said, having shown me the letter on the day it arrived. "He has spent hours' worth of sermons preaching against me, against my mistresses and children, and he would console me on the death of my son? What does he hope to gain?"

Not for a second did either of us consider Savonarola was in earnest, that he was a true man of God capable of extending Christian sympathy even to those with whom he vehemently disagreed. No doubt this was how he presented himself to his legions of followers, but the stakes of the game he was playing were too high for that. There was power—a great deal of power—in play, and his every move had at least one layer of meaning beyond the obvious.

"Being in accord with you can only be to his benefit," I said bluntly. "No doubt he means to start preaching again and reject the excommunication. He cannot maintain his power over the people of Florence otherwise."

Father snorted. "If he hopes to accomplish all that with one simple letter, he is even more deluded than I thought."

"Or this is just his opening salvo," I replied. "With him, it is damnably difficult to say which."

"It is at that. Damn it, but we need better eyes in Florence. We need better information about what he may be planning." He looked at me speculatively. "I would send you, if I could spare you, but I need you to assist with arranging Lucrezia's divorce and remarriage. And you would attract far too much attention once it was known that you were there, of a kind not conducive to gathering information."

"I had already thought of going myself, albeit in disguise," I said. "But you are right; that won't do."

"What of your man, Michelotto?"

I laughed humorlessly. "I need him here no less than you need me in Rome."

"One of his men, then. I know he has a vast network of spies. Surely he—and you—can spare one."

"Perhaps. With Florence in the state it's in, I worry that there would be too much suspicion of a foreign man. Michelotto is trying to find a Florentine to recruit, but has had no luck so far." In truth, I had been putting my mind to this puzzle for some time and had yet to come up with a satisfactory answer. What type of person could appear in Florence, pose as a member of Savonarola's faithful flock—the *Piagnoni*, or "wailers," as they were called—and then disappear just as easily, all without attracting too much notice?

And then it came to me.

Chapter 67

MADDALENA

"I am sorry for my delay," I said, breathless, as I arrived in Cesare's rooms at the Vatican. "I had not expected you to summon me and was finishing some tasks."

I had been in a secluded corner of the garden, working on a few embroidery designs for my own enjoyment while there was still light. I had not known I was wanted until I'd slipped back into the palazzo and found his messenger waiting.

He waved a hand. "No matter. You are here now."

I cupped his face in my hands. Smiling, I stood on tiptoe and gave him a long kiss. It seemed I would never tire of the taste of him, of his mouth on mine, of the warmth that spread through me, knowing what was to come . . .

And now there was the intimacy that had grown between us

since he had confessed his part in his brother's death. I was more than a body to him. And he was more than that to me. Too much more, perhaps.

My face fell as he took a step back. "Not yet, *carissima mia,*" he said. "There is something I must ask of you first."

I froze, taken aback by his use of the endearment—*dearest one.* So surprised was I that I was slow to react to the rest of his sentence. "What is it you must ask?" I said, a bit cautiously.

"There is a task I need you to undertake for me," he said. "A very important task." He sat me in a chair near the cold hearth. He sank into a nearby chair in turn and leaned toward me, his elbows resting on his knees and his eyes focused on mine in the dim light of the candles. "I would sooner not ask it of you, but there is no one else who can accomplish this in the way you can, and immediately. And no one whom I trust more."

Our eyes met, acknowledging all the things between us of which we would never speak again. "Whatever it is, tell me, I pray you."

He sighed, as if unsure how to begin. "I do not know how much you know of political matters, or of what is going on elsewhere in Italy."

I laughed again at this. "As I am in the bed of a cardinal and employed in the house of the pope's mistress, I know more about it than most."

Such frank speech did not offend him; he merely smiled. "Forgive me; of course, you of all people would be well informed." His expression grew serious again. "What do you know of Girolamo Savonarola, the Dominican friar of Florence?"

I knew some things of him, one of which was that he had preached on many occasions against Pope Alexander and the corruption of the Church. I needed to be careful in my answer. "He is considered by many to be a holy man, a prophet," I answered. "He has indeed seemed to foretell several things that have come to pass. He has a great following in Florence, and much power and influence there."

Cesare nodded. "Good. You know the salient points, then. He

is Ferrarese by birth, a brilliant theologian, and currently holds the position of Prior of San Marco, a monastery once closely associated with the Medici family, who were its benefactors for many years."

"I had heard that as well," I said. "But I confess, I do not understand what this has to do with the task you have for me."

A reluctant smile appeared on his sensual lips. "It has everything to do with that task, Maddalena *mia*. For I must ask you to go to Florence, to pose as a member of Savonarola's loyal following, and pass on any and all information you learn to me."

It was so silent for a moment that I fancied I could hear the crackling of flames on the candlewicks.

He watched me carefully, obviously wishing to see my reaction. "You . . . Your Eminence . . . Cesare . . . you cannot be in earnest," I said once I found my voice.

"I am in deadly earnest."

"Why . . . why me?" I asked. "I am no spy. I have no skills in such matters." I looked hard at him. "Spying is what you are asking of me, is it not?"

"To put it bluntly, yes."

"Surely there are others in your family's employ who are much better suited to this task than I."

"Not in this case," he said. "A man with a foreign accent appearing in Florence just now would be cause for much suspicion. All of Italy wishes to know what Savonarola may do next; every state, every ruler. Such a man would likely not be allowed to get too close to any of the friar's followers, or to the friar himself. A woman, on the other hand . . ."

I shuddered at these words. "Surely you do not mean for me to . . ."

He rose quickly from his chair. "Good Christ, Maddalena. Of course not. Is that what you think of me? That I am the sort of man who would send his woman to bed another for information?"

His woman. I shook my head slightly to rid myself of the spell of those words. "It was the way you said it," I said hastily. "Of course I do not think such of you."

He knelt before my chair, clasping my hands in his. "I would kill any man who dared touch you," he said, his eyes deadly serious. "I mean that."

And I well knew that he was capable of murder. Yet I thrilled at his protective words.

"I believe you do," I said. "What is it you would have me do?"

He rose to his feet and began pacing, all business. "I indeed phrased myself poorly, and I beg your pardon." He gave a wolfish grin. "Seduction would do us no good in any case; the friar is said to have a horror of women in the carnal sense. What I meant to say is there are many women amongst Savonarola's loyal following, women of all classes. They go to hear his sermons, and some have sought his private counsel, so I hear. You need only pose as a well-to-do widow from the countryside. If and when he starts preaching again, you will attend his sermons and report back what he is saying. Try to learn what you can of his plans; even if it is only gossip, I wish to hear it. Should you have opportunity for personal conversation with the friar, take it. Take it and suss out what you can of his motives, of what kind of man he truly is.

"Most importantly, I wish to know the mood in Florence. Whether most of the people are truly in Savonarola's thrall, or secretly hoping for a return of the Medici family. The latter can be arranged easily enough if such is the case. But as of now, we do not have enough information to know how to proceed."

My head was spinning as I struggled to take it all in, the expectations and implications. The scale of the matters he was placing into my hands. "Proceed with . . . what, exactly? Forgive me, but I still do not understand . . ."

"We must move against Savonarola eventually," he said. "But we do not know precisely when or how would be best. You will help us determine that."

I was silent.

"He cannot be allowed to continue to oppose the Church," Cesare went on. "He cannot continue to challenge the pope's authority and inspire Florentines to do the same. If he were some backwoods preacher in a little village in the Kingdom of Naples, he would not matter. But he all but controls one of the greatest and wealthiest cities in Italy. He must be curtailed. Or, more likely, silenced."

He paused, and when I still did not speak, went on. "I have thought long and hard on it," he said, "and it can only be you. There is no one else who fits our needs like you, no one else whom I trust enough to accomplish this. You are the only one, Maddalena."

He finished speaking and looked at me expectantly. I was conflicted, truly so. I had heard much gossip from all quarters about Fra Savonarola. Many of them thought him a true holy man, even a saint. He had assisted in driving out the corrupt Medici and reestablishing republican rule in Florence. And I had yet to hear of anything he had said of the pope that was not technically true.

The thought of opposing such a man was frightening. The thought of bringing about his downfall—of bringing about a coup, if Cesare's comments about restoring the Medici were to be taken seriously—was frightening. The thought of influencing the politics of Italy was frightening.

But it was a powerful feeling.

Cesare Borgia, gifted political operator as he was, was entrusting a large, crucial task to me. Maddalena Moretti, a maid from the countryside of the Romagna. He trusted me. He valued me. I was indispensable to him.

"Very well. I will do it."

Chapter 68

MADDALENA

Florence, June 1497

In only a few days I was ready. Cesare had procured for me clothing befitting a gentlewoman—nothing too ostentatious, but much finer than anything I owned—and a fine trunk to carry it all in. We went over and over what I was to do in Florence, where I was to go, the types of people I was to speak to, what information I was on the lookout for. I was to write down anything and everything of interest and send the news on to Cesare as I had it, in code. He was sending a few of his men along after me to serve as messengers and would be providing them with the fastest horses he could find, so they could make the ride from Florence to Rome in three days. There was a house in Florence where I would stay, a small one not too far from the city center. One of Cesare's men, a young guardsman who served under the terrifying Michelotto da Corella, was to accompany me for my protection, posing as my groom. Lucrezia was still in the convent of San Sisto; no excuses would need to be made to her for my absence. I was to tell no one of where I was going or what my task was, though I whispered to Isabella the night before I left that I was going away on an errand for His Eminence and could not say more. Eyes troubled, she had pressed me, but I had refused to tell her more. "Be careful, Maddalena, won't you?" she bade me. "I hope you know what you've gotten yourself into."

My guard Rodolfo Ubaldini and I departed early one morning, with him driving a cart bearing our luggage and me. It took us four and a half days to reach Florence at the speed of the cart. Rodolfo did not speak much, though he was respectful enough. I had no fear he would take untoward liberties with me, seeing as Cardinal Valentino had tasked him with protecting me with his life. No doubt Rodolfo knew exactly who I was to the cardinal. So I was quite certain that I was as safe as the cardinal himself.

The afternoon of our arrival, we settled into the house Cesare had directed us to, unpacking our few belongings and eating a meager meal of provisions we'd brought with us for the road. The next morning I would have to find the market and see what I could procure—how much nicer it would have been to have someone posing as my maid instead of my groom, I thought grumpily. Yet Cesare had given me a purse full of florins for any expenses. We would eat well, even if I had to be the one to cook.

And, I thought, as I drifted off to sleep that first night, if Florence was anything like Rome, the market is where I would certainly hear some of the best gossip. No doubt most cities were alike in this regard.

I had spent much of the journey to Florence fretting as to how, exactly, I would accomplish the mission Cesare had entrusted to me. What did I know of being a spy? The fear of failing—of failing Cesare—was a very real one.

Yet as it turned out, information about the "little friar," as many referred to him, was not so hard to come by.

My first full day in Florence, I rose early and went to the market to get whatever could be found fresh. Tomatoes, spinach, fresh bread, and why, I may as well spend my Borgia coin on a freshly slaughtered chicken.

"You new around here?" asked the woman selling vegetables as she counted my coin.

I smiled. "Yes, indeed. I've just moved into Florence from the countryside."

"Thought so. I know most of the women and servants in the

neighborhood." She nodded at me. "Maria Bati. My husband and I have the best vegetables in Florence, and don't let anyone tell you different. And you are?"

"Maddalena Valenti." Cesare had said I might use my true Christian name—it wasn't so uncommon—but advised me to choose a false surname, should anyone ever come looking for me, unlikely though that was. Valenti had a certain romantic appeal to me, being a take on his own title, Valentino.

"Good to meet you." She handed over the produce, which I placed in my basket. "I'm sure I'll see you most mornings, eh?"

"No doubt." In a flash of inspiration, I spoke again. "Pray tell me, if you would . . . where does everyone in this neighborhood go to hear Mass? I am still hopelessly lost in all these streets . . . so different from the country, you know. Perhaps you may point me in the right direction?"

"The parish church is just there," she said, pointing over my shoulder. Between the canopies of the market stall I could see a small dome and campanile that looked to be in the next street. "Of course, most were cramming into the Duomo to hear Mass for a while, what with the friar preaching his sermons."

"Friar?" I asked, my eyes wide with innocence.

"Fra Girolamo Savonarola. You've not heard of him?"

I shook my head. "We get so little news in the country," I excused myself. "At least I did, since my husband passed."

Maria crossed herself. "God bless his soul. Well, all the way to Rome, and beyond, they've heard of Fra Savonarola, make no mistake. His sermons used to draw thousands."

"And they do not anymore? Does he no longer preach?"

Maria snorted. "He's been excommunicated, he has. Seems he offended the pope. I've not heard him myself, my husband and I living outside the city walls on our farm as we do."

"I see," I said. "I do not know whether to be disappointed or not that I cannot hear him myself."

"From what I hear, he'll be back in the pulpit sooner than later, excommunication or no," she said. She turned away to assist another customer, and so I wandered away with my basket.

At the next stall, where I purchased the chicken, I overheard a group of women gossiping. Judging by their dress, they were who I was pretending to be: women of good families, whose husbands had respectable trades or owned their own shops, perhaps. "This Sunday, that is what I heard," one said in a low whisper.

"Does he dare?" another wondered.

"How can he not?" interjected a third, who seemed to be the self-proclaimed leader of this group. "How can he not return to the pulpit, when God himself speaks through him? He has a responsibility."

"I will believe it when I see it," the second woman said.

"Come to the Duomo for Sunday Mass, then, and you shall see the friar take the pulpit with your own eyes. My husband heard it from one of the men in the Signoria. They do not wish to anger the pope, but they fear the growing displeasure of the people if they do not allow him to preach."

I paid for my chicken and walked away, heart racing. The Signoria was part of Florence's governing body. If they were not forbidding Fra Savonarola from preaching, then preach he would.

I returned to the house, left my purchases in the kitchen, and ran immediately into the small study. Pulling out ink and parchment, I wrote, *It is as you suspected. Fra Savonarola will preach again this Sunday in the Duomo.*

I wrote down the rest of what I had heard, folded and sealed the letter, and went off to find one of the messengers, who would take it to Cesare.

That Sunday I went to the Duomo to hear Mass and, more importantly, to see if the friar would preach.

Florence's Duomo, properly called Santa Maria del Fiore, was a hulking, enormous structure that dominated the other buildings of the city. Built of green and white marble on the outside, it was capped by a massive reddish-orange dome. That Sunday was the first time I had seen it up close, and I could not help but gawk upward at the mammoth church. Even St. Peter's Basilica in Rome was not this impressive, especially in the state of disrepair it was in. As I traversed Piazza del Duomo and approached the main entrance, a man to my right crossed himself. "Every day that it does not collapse is a miracle," he murmured.

I arrived early, and it was a good thing, for while I was able to get a seat at the back, those who came later were forced to stand, and even started spilling out the doors of the cathedral into the piazza. Clearly word had spread about Fra Savonarola's rumored return to the pulpit.

None of us were to be disappointed.

I did not know the friar on sight, but as soon as he took the pulpit, the congregation burst into a kind of hysteria, immediately beginning to sing the hymn "We praise thee, O God." A woman at the end of the pew to my left, dressed in shabby and torn clothing, burst into tears, covering her face with her hands and rocking back and forth as she sobbed. Bewildered, I looked about and beheld similar behavior from many of the congregants, hysterical weeping and shouting and calls of thanks and praise to the Lord.

He has not even spoken a word yet! I thought, almost indignantly. I waited for the congregation to quiet so the friar could speak, bowing my head piously, but not so much that I could not glance up and study the man of whom I had heard so much.

He was a small figure, nearly swallowed within the cowl and robes of his black-and-white Dominican habit. He had a hooked nose and thick lips, with deep-set eyes that were very dark from this distance. Had I passed him on the street I would never have looked twice at him, so undistinguished a figure did he cut. Yet the moment he opened his mouth to speak, I understood everything.

"Lord," he said, his voice booming and authoritative, powerful enough to fill the massive cathedral and carry to the people outside, "I who am but dust and ashes, wish to speak to Thy Majesty."

His voice was so commanding that even as he spoke to God directly, one could not help but imagine his was what the voice of God would sound like. Who could help but believe he spoke for the Lord himself?

I had but a moment to wonder whether he would speak of his

excommunication, of what he was risking by preaching this day, before he immediately delved into that very topic.

"A governor of the Church is a tool of God, but if he is not used like a tool of God then he is a broken tool, and he is no greater than any man. You may say to him, 'You do not do good, because you do not let yourself be guided by the supreme Lord.'

"What was the purpose of those who lied so I might be excommunicated? Once my excommunication was announced, they once more abandoned themselves to consorting with concubines, and to all manner of lies and wickedness."

I hoped the veil I wore hid my face, for it went red with shame. He could not know it, but he referred directly to me. I was indeed the concubine of a prince of the Church, one who had no doubt played a part in his excommunication. It was as the friar said, and I was proof.

"On whose side will thou be, O Christ?" Fra Savonarola went on. "On the side of the truth or lies? For Christ says, 'I am the truth.'"

The friar went on, and I was rapt, listening to his every word, letting it fall on my skin like a stinging rain that might cleanse me of my sins. If such was even still possible for me.

When I returned to the house after Mass, I dutifully went to my desk and wrote everything down. It was everything Cesare needed to know and had hoped I could tell him: Fra Savonarola had indeed returned to preaching, and his sermon directly challenged Pope Alexander and those powerful members of the Church hierarchy. I described the mood of the congregation, their hysterical ecstasy, and the power with which the friar spoke. All of that knowledge was necessary for those who would oppose Savonarola.

For the first time, I wondered if I was doing the right thing.

Chapter 69

CESARE

"It is as we feared and expected," Father said.

I had just reported to him what was in Maddalena's letter, and he was as displeased as he was unsurprised. "It was only a matter of time before he returned to the pulpit."

"Do none in Florence fear the power of Holy Mother Church? Of the damnation they could be cast into for disobeying us?" Father ranted, pacing angrily across his private chamber. "We are the pope. We are the representative of Christ on earth. Not some fanatical Dominican spouting doomsday prophecies!"

"Your commission looked into this," I pointed out. "Everything he has preached is technically in line with the Bible."

He rounded on me. "You would take his side?" he spat. "You would prattle on about technicalities? Next you will become one of those sniveling *Piagnoni*—"

"I merely point out," I interrupted calmly, "that if we wish to take down the little friar, heresy may not be our strongest argument."

"Then find me another one!"

"I will," I assured him, soothingly. "I need more information as yet from my spy in Florence, and then we shall know how to proceed."

Maddalena was doing an excellent job, better than even I had expected. She was just where I needed her to be, doing just what I needed her to do, and yet there were times when I had to stop myself from picking up a pen and writing her two simple words: *Come home*. By which I meant, come back to me. Come back to my bed.

It took me a few nights after her departure to remember I could not summon her easily from nearby Santa Maria in Portico; she could not come to me whenever my whim demanded it. She was indeed the perfect person for the task I'd set her. This fine logic, however, did not make it any easier at night, when I ached for her touch, for her body beneath mine.

I went with Michelotto to what had formerly been my favorite brothel in the city. There was a woman there Michelotto favored, and so I told myself I was merely seeing to it that he was able to enjoy himself. He certainly deserved it. The woman the proprietress had chosen for me, though beautiful, simply did not captivate me as Maddalena did. I bedded her, of course—it would not do to have rumors get out about my supposed lack of prowess—but I did not enjoy it. All I could think was how her hair was too dark, not the reddish auburn of Maddalena's, and that she was a bit too thin, without Maddalena's soft, enticing curves.

Still, there was other work to be done as I waited for Maddalena to report back. Lucrezia's divorce remained the principle item on the pope's agenda, and therefore mine. I threw myself into that; it was not, after all, in my nature to sit about like some lovesick swain and pine for a woman.

I met with Ascanio Sforza in my rooms at the Vatican in early July to discuss the matter further with him. As I had predicted, he had been relieved to have himself and his relations publicly cleared by the pope of any involvement in Juan's murder. He was eager indeed to get back into the Holy Father's good graces, for both his sake and his family's. It was plain he knew his cousin's marriage to the pope's daughter was a lost cause, and though he made token attempts at trying to preserve the alliance, it was all too clear that both he and his brother Duke Ludovico were most willing to facilitate the divorce in any way they could.

Ascanio Sforza had never liked me much, nor had he made any secret of it; therefore it was immensely entertaining to watch him battle between that dislike and his nearly desperate desire to accommodate the pontiff in whatever way possible.

"And the grounds, Your Eminence?" Ascanio asked, his nose wrinkled with disgust as he addressed me by my title. "Infidelity, I suppose?"

I arched an eyebrow at him. "What is it precisely that you are implying of my sister, Cardinal Sforza?"

"Not on her part, of course," he hastened to assure me. "No, on my cousin's part. What with being on campaign with his men here and there over the years . . . well, he is a man, with a man's needs, as I no doubt do not need to explain to you. Certainly there were other women along the way."

I leaned back in my chair, allowing myself a smile. "Were there? The problem with infidelity as grounds for divorce is it is damnably difficult to prove. Not to mention that such might set a precedent that men across Christendom will hardly thank us for."

Ascanio's smile was strained. "What did Your Eminence and His Holiness have in mind, then?"

"Granting divorce on the grounds of non-consummation will be easiest for everyone."

Ascanio nearly choked on the sip of wine he had taken. "Non . . . non-consummation?" he gasped, once he'd ceased his coughing. "Surely not. Certainly the marriage has been consummated."

I spread my hands in a gesture of doubt. "Has it? Several years of marriage, yet my sister has never conceived. It would seem Giovanni is . . . unable."

"Unable?" Ascanio asked incredulously. "His first wife died in childbirth, as you know well. It was the pope himself who decreed my cousin could not consummate the marriage for some months. And may I point out that he and his wife have been apart for a good deal of their marriage, partially because he was . . . unwelcome in Rome."

I chose to ignore the last bit. "Yet they dwelled together in

Pesaro for some time," I pointed out. "My sister is young and healthy, and of fine stock. If he was frequently exercising his husbandly privilege, why did she not fall with child?"

"Does she say that he did not consummate the marriage?" Ascanio demanded. "I cannot believe it to be true."

"She will swear to it."

That did not quite answer the question, but it was all Ascanio needed to know.

"My cousin will not agree to this," Ascanio said, shaking his head. "This will be the equivalent of declaring himself impotent in front of all of Europe."

"I do not expect him to agree to it straight off," I said equably. "After all, that is why you are here, Your Eminence. You—together with your esteemed brother Duke Ludovico—must persuade him that this course of action is best for all of you. For the House of Sforza."

With my last statement, I had summed up everything that was at play here but that neither of us would speak outright. The pope and the Curia were far more useful and valuable allies to the Sforzas than Pesaro. An alliance with us was worth the shame of a cousin who ruled an insignificant principality on the Adriatic coast.

Cardinal Sforza rose. "Your Eminence has made your meaning plain," he said. "I will relay this to my brother, and we shall convince our cousin Giovanni to see things our way."

I raised my wine glass to him. "Most wise of you. His Holiness will be most grateful and appreciative."

With the Sforzas in line, things could finally move ahead. All that was needed now was to inform my sister of the happy news and get her out of that blasted convent.

Chapter 70

MADDALENA

The week following Fra Savonarola's return to the pulpit saw a hectic energy descend upon the city of Florence. I went to the market every morning and took to visiting local shops in different corners of the city—apothecaries, cloth merchants, butchers, any place I could find an excuse to visit—and spoke to shopkeepers and customers alike. I cultivated a few acquaintances that would always stop to speak to me in the street. One woman, Anna Landucci, wife of an apothecary, invited me to her home for lunch one day, and I gladly accepted.

"What thought you of the friar's sermon on Sunday?" she asked over the meal, leaning forward as she spoke. There was the fire of a zealot in her eyes. She and her husband were followers of the friar, but I was only beginning to see the true depth of her devotion. "I know you did not have the opportunity to hear him before this."

I took a bite of my vegetable soup as I considered how best to answer. "I found it . . . very moving," I said honestly. "Very inspiring. I can well see how so many regard him with the highest of esteem."

"Indeed we do," she said, clearly satisfied with my answer. "We are blessed, truly blessed, that he came to Florence to establish the city of God here."

My ears pricked up at this. "City of God?" I asked.

Her eyes shone. "Oh, yes," she said. "He seeks for the lives of all Florence's citizens to be reformed, so we might live more in line with simple Christian values, as Christ himself taught. None of this pagan learning so popular here in recent years. He has even been advising the Signoria and Gonfaloniere on their laws, so we might become a more Godly city. And, of course, he seeks to discourage us from such luxury and sinful decadence as the pope and cardinals require." She made a face of derision. "And once Florence is a true and Godly city again, Fra Savonarola shall reform the Church." She leaned closer once more. "Did you know that Pope Alexander keeps a mistress?" she asked, in a near whisper. "And he is not the first! He not only has illegitimate children, but allows them to live with him in the Vatican! Can you imagine?"

My face grew hot and I hoped it wasn't visible to Anna. Technically only Cesare lived in the Vatican, but I wasn't about to betray such knowledge. "I . . . I had heard rumors of such," I said. "But I did not know how true they were. I got so little news, you see."

Anna nodded sagely. "Ah, yes." She crossed herself quickly. "I must pray for the soul of the wicked pope, for Scripture teaches us that we must love our enemies. Yet I cannot help but hope he gets his just rewards when his time comes. But that is not for me to say; God will deal with him in his own time."

"Yes," I managed to say. "No doubt."

As we continued our meal and our talk turned to other things, I was already composing the letter to Cesare in my mind.

Much of what Anna had told me was further verified by others. That the Signoria was consulting with Fra Savonarola on matters of government was proven to be true. Rodolfo had made friends with a young man whose father was a member of the Signoria, and he confirmed as much. This got out to Cesare as soon as I could write it, along with everything else.

If all this was not plain enough, I soon experienced the little friar's influence first hand.

One day as I walked home from the market, I was accosted by a group of four boys, the oldest of whom was perhaps fourteen, while the youngest could not have been more than nine. All were dressed in robes of pure white.

I had heard of these bands of boys; they were referred to as Savonarola's "angels" and roamed the streets of Florence, chanting prayers and singing hymns, often knocking on doors and asking those within to give up their worldly vanities, that they might be sold so the money could be donated to the poor.

Until then, I had only seen them at a harmless distance on occasion. They arrayed themselves in my path, and I stopped, smiling pleasantly. "*Buon giorno,*" I said in greeting.

"*Buon giorno,* madam," the oldest boy, clearly the leader, responded. "What are you doing out on the streets alone?"

Puzzled—for it was morning, not some dangerous hour of night—I responded, "I have just been to market for my household." I held up my basket as proof.

"Women should not be out on the streets without a male escort," the boy replied, frowning with displeasure.

I began to feel uncomfortable. "I am a widow," I said by way of explanation. "And I have no servants to do the marketing for me. I must do it myself."

The boy's gaze fixed on the gold cross I wore at my neck. Cesare had given it to me; it was the sort of adornment a woman of my assumed station might wear. In truth, I had grown very attached to it and planned on keeping it when this was all over—my first and only gift from my lover.

"If that is all," I said stiffly, and made to move past them. But one of the other boys stepped into my path, blocking me.

"That is a fine necklace you wear, madam," the leader said. "Gold, is it?"

"Yes," I said shortly.

"Surely you know the holy Fra Savonarola has spoken out against such vain adornments."

"It is a cross," I protested. "To show my devotion to our Lord and His Son, Jesus Christ."

"The Lord Jesus cares only for your soul, not how you adorn

yourself," one of the other boys interjected. He held out a hand. "Give it to us, and free yourself from sin."

My hand reached up and clasped the cross in my palm. "It was a gift," I said. "I am loathe to part with it."

"When you part with such vanities, you part with sin," the leader said. "But you may yet turn that sin into virtue. Give it to us, and we shall sell it and see that the proceeds go to feed the poor."

The boys closed ranks around me, so I could not flee. The oldest boy was taller than me, and the next oldest not much shorter. I swallowed hard.

I reluctantly reached up and unclasped the gold cross and set it in the boy's outstretched hand. Just like that, they melted from my path and continued up the street. I walked the rest of the way home on shaky legs.

Chapter 71

CESARE

"He sends children into the streets to rip jewelry from women's necks?" Father asked incredulously. "How can this be?"

"It is true," I said tightly. I had been enraged when reading Maddalena's most recent report, describing how she had been accosted and essentially robbed by a gang of Savonarola's minions. I wanted to ride to Florence and give the little monsters the thrashing they deserved, before turning the force of my wrath on their master, but that would not help matters at all, satisfying though it would be.

No, Maddalena with her eyes and ears and sharp mind would

give me all we needed to take down these heretic thugs. Maddalena, my angel of holy vengeance. "They spout nonsense about vanities and giving the money to the poor, and such things," I added.

Father snorted. "I wonder where the money really ends up."

"Likely not with the friar, or his monastery," I said reluctantly. "Apparently it is known on the streets of Florence that he lives austerely, often fasting, and encourages his brother monks to do the same. He has removed all fine paintings and furniture from the monastery."

Father shook his head. "Whoever your man in Florence is, he is a wealth of information. We must make further use of his talents in the future."

I was silent. I had not told Father who I had sent to Florence, that it was a woman and a maid in his daughter's house. I had simply not disillusioned him when he assumed it was one of Michelotto's men. Yet Maddalena's newfound talents reflected well on me in Father's eyes—he had given me charge of this entire thing, more or less, and thanks to her I was being acquitted well—and that was what mattered.

"Still," he went on, "I am more concerned that the Signoria consults him on policy."

"As am I," I said. "But they hold elections often in Florence. And if the Signoria can be advised by him, they can be advised against him, as well."

A few days after my conversation with Ascanio Sforza, I went to the convent of San Sisto to speak to my sister.

Seated at the grille in the convent's visiting parlor, Lucrezia on the other side—apparently even a prince of the Church could not have a face-to-face conversation with a convent resident, even one merely boarding there—I told her what I had discussed with Cardinal Sforza, and how her husband would be convinced to agree to the divorce in short order.

"You must return to Santa Maria in Portico," I finished. "You'll need to appear at a hearing, to swear that the marriage was never consummated, and we'll be looking for a new husband for you. It is time to rejoin the world."

Lucrezia, who had been silent throughout much of my visit, now said quietly, "I can't."

"Certainly you can. We can have some servants come and move your things back before the end of the day."

"I can't," she repeated. "Not yet."

I paused and studied my sister through the wrought iron grate between us. She looked tired, pale and drawn. "I know this has been a very difficult time for you," I said gently. "You are mourning. Father is, too. It would do him a great deal of good to see you, in fact. But if you need more time alone with your grief, I'm sure another month can be—"

"Another month will not be enough time." Her voice was flat, emotionless, so unlike the vibrant, vivacious Lucrezia I knew and loved.

"Why ever not?" I asked. "I know Juan's death has affected you greatly, as well it should, but—"

"This isn't about Juan," she cut me off. "I do mourn for him, but . . ."

"But what? What is it?"

She was silent.

"Lucrezia? When do you think you will be able to return to Santa Maria in Portico?"

"By my count, I can emerge no sooner than March. Perhaps a bit later."

"March?" I exploded. "But why? What nonsense is this, Crezia? What could possibly require you to spend the better part of a year locked away . . ." I trailed off in shock as I calculated how many months that was. "No," I said under my breath. Then, louder, "No. Christ Almighty, Lucrezia, tell me it isn't so."

"Don't take the Lord's name in vain," she said in that same lifeless voice. "And yes, it is true. You and Father needed to know at some point. It may as well be now."

I leapt up from my chair with such force that it toppled over, crashing to the stone floor and making Lucrezia jump on the other side of the grille. "God in Heaven, tell me that is not Giovanni Sforza's child."

"Of course it isn't," she spat. "He ran away from me and fled back to Pesaro long before this child was conceived."

That was somewhat better, but still nothing short of a disaster. "Then whose?" I demanded. "Whose is it? Who dared defile you?"

"No one defiled me," she shot back. "I gave myself to him in love. And I—"

"Unless he comes with a kingdom, he cannot marry you, whoever he is," I told her.

"I know that. Do you think I do not know that? He is not someone who can marry me. We loved each other, that is all. I do not expect you to understand. I know how you are with women, Cesare."

First Sancia, then Maddalena flashed through my head. I shook my head slightly. "I understand better than you could possibly know, Crezia."

She did not reply.

"But that is neither here nor there," I said. I kicked aside the chair and began pacing in front of the grille. "How could you be so foolish? You know we are trying to get your marriage annulled on the grounds of non-consummation, yes? I told you this long ago. And yet you have gotten yourself with child. So now you will have to go before a council of churchmen and swear yourself to be a virgin while you are carrying some bastard." I laughed mirthlessly. "We shall be a laughingstock."

"You have no idea what it was like," Lucrezia burst out, rage simmering in her voice. "Father married me off to a man twice my age, without giving me any say in the matter. I did not expect any. I did as I was bid; did as my family expected. I never loved Giovanni Sforza, never particularly even liked him, but I tried my best to be a good wife to him. I knew my duty, and I did it as best I could. Even so he despised me. He despised me without ever getting to know me. I went to his bed and endured the marriage act—I did, Cesare, and I will not let you erase that, even if I only ever speak it aloud to you—and hoped to please him, even though I hated doing it. But still he did not care for me. Then he abandoned me, shaming me before all of Italy, as if the rest was not enough. All I ever wanted was to know love and passion, so I found a man who gave me both. A man who enjoyed my company and loved me for who I am, not for my family name or for what I could do for him. And he showed me the marriage act could indeed be an act of love, and very pleasurable—something men need no one's permission to discover for themselves, I notice. So no, Cesare. I will not allow you to shame me further for finding what little joy I could while you and Father prepare to shame me before all of Italy—again—and use me as a pawn in your political games—again. I am not sorry, and I do not regret any of it."

I am not often struck speechless, but my sister's passionate monologue reduced me to just that. I touched the grate between us and, startled, she placed her fingers against mine.

"I am sorry, little sister," I said softly, the words conveying so much more than I could ever say. Yet I knew she heard all the apologies I could not make in so many words. "I am sorry. I love you. I will speak to Father."

Her face softened; her eyes were filling with tears. "Thank you, Cesare. I love you, too."

I drew away from the grille. "Stay here as long as you need. All will be well. I promise."

To say Father was not best pleased when I brought him the news was an understatement. He ranted and raved and threw things, all while I stood calmly and endured his wrath, so that it might not be directed at my sister.

"Lucrezia seemed unhappy, when I saw her," I said, once he had calmed. "This whole mess—plus Juan's death—has taken a great toll on her."

This caught Father's attention. "She is not ill, is she?" he asked.

"No," I said. "I do not believe so, other than whatever ailments come with her . . . condition. It would do her good, and ease her anxiety, to hear from you."

"Hmph," he said. "Hear from me she shall! A letter with a searing reprimand, I should think."

"What did you expect?" I asked him. "What did either of us expect? She is a young girl, head full of ideas of romance, and she was bound in marriage to that ogre Sforza. Of course she took some pleasure and happiness where she could find it. She is a Borgia, after all."

Father paused. "I suppose you are right," he said grudgingly. "Damn it if this whole divorce mess has not gotten infinitely more complicated, but I suppose I cannot fault her for doing as we've all done at one time or another."

And so Lucrezia was forgiven. Father had never been able to be truly angry with her, and neither had I.

Chapter 72

MADDALENA

As July wore on, two things happened.

The first was elections were held in Florence, and a new Signoria and Gonfaloniere were elected. As I soon learned, the men who were newly taking office were of the faction that opposed Savonarola and his supporters. They were sick of being at odds with Rome and the pope over the mad friar and his prophecies. All of which I reported to Cesare.

The second thing I reported was that plague had appeared in Florence.

It was only a few cases at first, in the poorer sections of the cities, where the cloth-dyers and their families lived. Yet, as it often does in the summer in cities where so many live in close quarters, it began to spread.

You can return to Rome soon, Cesare wrote. *I don't want you at risk of the plague, though there are a few cases here in Rome as well. The Holy Father is in contact with the new Signoria. It will not be much longer now. All thanks to you.*

Though he did not say explicitly what "it" was, I had a good idea.

A part of me glowed at his words of gratitude, yet I still stubbornly questioned whether I had done the right thing in all of this.

I had continued attending Fra Savonarola's sermons every Sunday. And though I dutifully wrote a report on each one, which I dispatched to Cesare, what I left out of those reports was how I was genuinely moved by what the friar said. His criticisms of Pope Alexander and his advisors were, as I knew firsthand, completely true. But beyond such departures into the political, much of what he said made sense to me. He spoke of living simply, of having true repentance, of looking to the teachings of Christ before looking to the Church. It seemed so much simpler to me than the world I'd known, the decadence and opulence and power of the Church.

It made me feel both ashamed and like I could truly be forgiven.

But terrible things flowed from Savonarola's power. Unrest in the city, quarrels among families, neighbors turning on neighbors and denouncing one another for sins real and imagined, women accosted and shamed in the streets, personal belongings all but stolen. This happened with the friar's permission, if not his active participation. What to make of it all?

Trying to make sense of it kept me awake at nights, but in the end, I need not make anything of it. I had only report what I learned.

And so the day after I received Cesare's letter, when Anna Landucci showed up at my door, eyes shining with excitement, I listened with interest to what she had to say. "You'll never believe it," she said, stepping inside and grasping my hands. "I've an appointment tomorrow to go make confession to Fra Savonarola!"

I was surprised. "He is hearing confessions again?" He had

done so before being excommunicated, but though he had since returned to preaching he had not heard confessions that I was aware.

She nodded excitedly. "You must come with me!"

I shrank away from her. "Oh, he will not meet with me as well, I am sure . . ."

"Why not? I shall tell him you are a newcomer, and much impressed with his preaching. He will want to hear your confession!"

"I do not know . . ."

"It will be good for your soul, Maddalena," she said encouragingly.

I paused. If only the good Anna Landucci knew of the things that truly ate away at my soul. She could never even imagine.

"Very well. I will go with you."

The next day, I found myself at the monastery of San Marco.

I waited outside as Anna went into the room where the friar would speak to her—not a traditional confessional, but a small cell in the monastery where Fra Savonarola received visitors and counseled those who came to speak to him. I was still not confident he would even see me, and I could not decide if I hoped he would.

Nearly a half hour had passed before Anna emerged from the small room, her face wreathed in a radiant smile. She took my hands in hers. "Go see him," she whispered. "I told him of you, how you had accompanied me here, and he will see you and hear your confession."

I squeezed her hands. "Thank you," I said softly, surprising myself with how much I meant those words.

Hesitantly, I stepped into the room, and immediately the friar's voice, so well-known to me by then, drifted out. "Shut the door behind you, child."

I obeyed, and only after I had completed the task did I turn to face Fra Savonarola.

He looked slightly larger here in a small room than he did in the pulpit, dwarfed by the immense size and space of the Duomo. He was dressed in his black-and-white Dominican robes, his cowl cast down so his tonsured head was bare. He gave me a small smile and gestured to the hard wooden chair across from him. "Please sit, my child."

I did so, smoothing my skirts fastidiously about me. I had worn one of my own dresses, a plain one of rough, dark cloth that I usually wore under my apron when tending to Lucrezia Borgia. Such attire would more endear me to the friar more than anything Cesare had given me, but more so than that it felt right, somehow, to wear my own clothes to this audience.

"Anna tells me you are newly come to Florence," Fra Savonarola said. His voice was the same voice of the prophet who preached in the cathedral, and yet not. It still had the same deep timbre, the same resonance, but here was gentle and intimate, his words for my ears alone, and not for the whole massive congregation. "What is your name, child?"

"Maddalena," I said. And because I could not lie to this man, I said, "Maddalena Moretti."

"Maddalena. A saint's name, a woman who received mercy and grace from Our Lord's own hand. Welcome to Florence, Maddalena."

"I thank you, Friar," I said respectfully. "I have been to hear you preach in the Duomo. I am . . . much moved by your sermons."

"Ah." He smiled beatifically, as if I were the first person to say such to him. "You do me too much honor. My words come straight from the Lord God. All credit is to Him alone."

"I have never heard His voice so clearly as when you speak," I said.

"If I can be the pathway through which you grow closer to Him, then my work on Earth has been worthwhile," he said. These were not empty platitudes, such as the politician-churchmen I had grown so familiar with would say them. He meant every word, deeply. And suddenly I was reminded of my Uncle Cristiano, and how he and I had had so many conversations of faith and the nature of God. And I realized how bereft I had been of true spiritual counsel since he had died. He would have liked Fra Savonarola very much. "I will hear your confession, my child, if you've one to make."

In that moment, all thoughts of why I was there fled from my mind. There was only Fra Savonarola and me, and the feeling, like a thorn from Christ's crown digging into my flesh, that I had grown so far away from the God I had once feared and revered above all else. "In truth I have much to confess, Fra Savonarola."

He nodded encouragingly. "Tell me. God in His mercy sees all and forgives all."

"I am guilty of lust, Friar. Lust and fornication."

I peeked upward at him, waiting for him to condemn me in the righteous fury for which he was known, but his serene expression did not change. "Many more than you are guilty of such sins. Go on, my child."

"It is more than that, I fear. I have lain with . . . with a man of the Church. I have desired him, and I have gone to his bed." My face burned with shame as I spoke the words aloud, and to this man of all people.

"Do you think this surprises me, my dear? So many who claim to be men of God are similarly weak in their resolve and break the vows they have made unto Him. The sin is yours, and his as well, but the difference is that you are here confessing in a true spirit of contrition, and he is not."

Inappropriate laughter bubbled behind my lips at the thought of Cesare Borgia confessing anything in a true spirit of contrition, let alone sins like lust and fornication. I doubt he ever lost a night's sleep over the sins I would spend my life confessing.

Yet the friar's last words snagged my attention. A true spirit of contrition. Was I? Is that what I had in my heart, truly? For a true spirit of contrition surely meant that one would not commit the same sin again. Would I tell Cesare Borgia that I would not come to his bed, once I returned to Rome?

No. I was not that strong.

But perhaps, I thought—and it was as if the sun broke free from the clouds after a storm—perhaps that is the true greatness, the true mercy of God that we, his flock, can never truly understand. He made us as we are, He knows we sin and shall sin again, and yet He loves us anyway.

Perhaps that is the secret.

"Tell me," Fra Savonarola said, his voice gently intruding into my thoughts, as though he knew I had been in the midst of a personal revelation, "in going to this man's bed, did you bear any ill will against the Lord God?"

"No," I said vehemently. "No, I swear it."

"Did you desire to break His laws?"

"No," I repeated, my voice breaking in a sob. "No. I have been in a torment of guilt, Friar. I have."

"Then why did you lie with this man?"

"Because I love him!" I cried. The words seemed to ring within the plain walls of the small room.

Because I love him. I love him.

I had never spoken the words aloud to anyone. I had never spoken them even to myself, even in the quiet and darkness of my own heart.

But they were true.

And so, in confessing to Fra Savonarola, I had made a confession to myself.

"Ah," he said, smiling once more. "Love is something different altogether. Love is the greatest gift God has given us. But we must allow that love to raise us above sin, not tempt us into it. That is what God requires, in giving us this gift. Do you see the difference, my child?"

I nodded, tears trickling down my face. "I do, Fra Savonarola. I do."

"I believe that you do indeed."

I nodded again.

"Kneel, my child."

I slid from my chair and knelt before him.

He placed a hand on my head. "I absolve you of your sins, in the name of the Father, the Son, and the Holy Spirit. Amen."

"Amen," I murmured, crossing myself.

"Rise," he said.

I did so.

"For your penance, you must eat only bread and water for two weeks, and give alms to the poor," he said.

I thought of all the florins Cesare had given me, more than I would ever need to use, even should I stay in Florence for months on end. "I will, Friar. I will."

He smiled again. "My blessings on you, Maddalena Moretti. Your namesake was a sinful woman as well, and Our Lord forgave her and loved her all the same."

I smiled in return. "Thank you, Fra Savonarola. You have given me more peace than I have known in some time."

"It is the Lord who gives you such peace, sister Maddalena. Go with my blessing."

I turned and left the room, shutting the door quietly behind me. Anna was waiting for me in the narrow stone hallway. "Is he not truly a man of God?" she asked rapturously. Then she noticed the tear marks on my face, the tears still falling. "Maddalena! Are you quite well?"

I nodded, smiling at her. "I am well. Better than I have been in a very long time."

Chapter 73

MADDALENA

I served out my penance to the letter. I ate naught but bread and water for the following two weeks, though I still went to the market daily for gossip as well as heartier fare for poor Rodolfo. And the day after my confession, I returned to the monastery of San

Marco with a purse of coins—about half of what remained—and entrusted it to one of the brothers there, telling him that these were alms intended for the poor. He thanked me profusely and assured that he would personally see it done.

Unlike the priests and bishops and cardinals of the Vatican, who said one thing and meant another, I believed him entirely.

Yet the situation was rapidly deteriorating in Florence. The new anti-Savonarola Signoria was encouraging those in Florence who opposed the friar and his methods to cause trouble in the streets, and as such gangs of young men who identified as *Compagnacci*—largely upper-class youths who resented the puritan strictures Savonarola had imposed upon Florence—began to pick fights in the street with known *Piagnoni,* throwing rocks and insults alike at them. The friar ever preached nonviolence and turning the other cheek, but human nature being what it was, fights often broke out between the two factions. It became safer, most days, to stay indoors and off the streets. All of this I duly reported to Cesare, as I could not see any way to excuse ceasing to send him reports.

And, of course, the Signoria was encouraged by the pope, which very few in Florence knew, other than me.

The tension in the streets of Florence was thicker than holy oil; and, like oil, all it needed was one spark to set everything alight. And soon enough, that spark came.

I never knew for certain what caused the events of that fateful night. I heard it was a simple fight between the *Compagnacci* and the *Piagnoni,* commonplace in the city of late, which started it all. I also heard a rumor it was an attack on Fra Mariano Ughi, one of Fra Savonarola's brother monks, as he made his way to the cathedral to preach. Perhaps it was some combination of those things. Yet the cause mattered little. However it happened, someone had set a match to the tinderbox that was Florence, and before long the whole city was on fire.

Soon, there were gangs, small armies, running through the streets, and even within my house I could hear shouting; I could see, even with the curtains drawn, the flicker of torches being carried past my windows. I donned my light summer cloak and pulled up the hood, walking out into the dining room to find Rodolfo eating. "I am going out," I announced, "to see what is happening in the streets. I will not be gone long."

"Wait a bit, Maddalena, and I shall accompany you," he protested. "It may not be safe for a woman alone. It is late, besides."

"I shall be just fine," I said. "I must report to His Eminence, mustn't I?" With that I was gone, out and through the door, following the streams of people passing the house to see what the commotion was.

It was not long before I realized where everyone was headed, where the explosion of tension had centered itself: the monastery of San Marco, not far from the house where I was staying. "Oh, no," I murmured as I rounded the corner onto the street where the monastery sat, only to see a huge crowd gathering in front of it, the shouts and screams deafening. It was a scene out of hell itself, lit by the dim, flickering lights of torches. "Oh, no. No!" I ran the rest of the way, pushing past curiosity seekers until I was at the edge of the crowd in front of the monastery. From within I could hear screams, the sounds of doors being broken down, and loud booms that seemed to be shots from an arquebus—or, likely, more than one. People stumbled away from the crowd, faces bloody, clutching wounds on their arms and sides and legs.

San Marco was under siege.

My legs grew weak underneath me, and I staggered, using all my strength to stop from falling to my knees, for doing so would surely mean being trampled. Had I done this? Had I set this in motion?

There was nothing I could do to help matters; only injury and perhaps death awaited me inside. Yet I felt compelled to bear witness. To bear witness to what I had wrought.

I began shoving people out of my way, shoving through the crowd to get to the entrance of the monastery. I had the urgent desire, nonsensical as it was, to find Fra Savonarola in the fray, to beg his forgiveness for what I had done, to confess everything I had left out when I'd met with him.

I had to make sense of it. For my own peace of mind and soul.

Soon the crowd parted to allow armed men through into the monastery, and from the calls of those around me, these soldiers had been sent by the Signoria to maintain order. Even as those outside were quieted by the arrival of organized troops, still I tried unsuccessfully to fight my way through to the monastery. At one point, I tipped back my head and howled at the night sky in futile rage and frustration, a sound completely swallowed up by the chaos around me.

Suddenly, I felt strong arms around me, pulling me backward, wrestling me away from the riot. Instinctually, I struggled. "Let go of me!" I growled, flailing and kicking as my assailant lifted me bodily and carried me away from the crowd.

"Maddalena! It is me!" a familiar voice said, setting me down some distance from the crowd. I turned to find Rodolfo. "I must get in there!" I cried, making to run back. "I must see . . ."

Rodolfo caught my arm in a vise grip, preventing me from running back. "No," he said. "His Eminence charged me with your protection, and I mean to do my duty."

He pointed ahead. "There is nothing more you can do or see. Look."

I watched as, emerging from the crowd, Fra Savonarola came, marched between two armed guards, with more to the front and back of him. "He has been arrested," Rodolfo yelled in my ear, so he might be heard above the shouts of joy and cries of dismay and pain. "It is over."

I made to take another step forward, and Rodolfo seized me again, spinning me to face him. "It is over!" he shouted, shaking me once.

I began to sob.

Rodolfo released me, gently draping one arm around my shoulders. "Come. We are going home."

He did not mean our borrowed house in Florence.

The next morning, I sent a report on ahead to Cesare. There was no time for me to bid farewell to Anna Landucci, or to Maria the vegetable seller. I would be gone as if I had never been there, just as Cesare had wished. Rodolfo and I packed up our belongings, loaded the cart, and followed the messenger—albeit at a much slower pace—back to Rome.

Chapter 74

CESARE

Rome, August 1497

I sent a message to Palazzo Santa Maria in Portico, to be left for Maddalena. As soon as she had returned and rested, she was to come to the Vatican to see me.

I paced my rooms restlessly on the night I expected her to arrive; it had only been a matter of weeks since I had last seen her, yet it felt like a lifetime. I wanted to take her into my arms, whisper to her how well she had done. She had done everything I had hoped she would, and more. She had made a mark on the history of Italy forever. Even if no one else ever knew, she and I would.

And then I wanted to remove all of her clothing and take her to my bed, to bury myself inside her until I found the relief and ecstasy that had been eluding me these long weeks since her departure. I grew hard just thinking about it and had to do my best to calm myself. There was business to attend to first.

Finally, as the sun had begun its descent, she appeared. She looked weary from her days on the road, though judging by her appearance she had washed and changed her clothes before coming to see me.

"Maddalena." I crossed the room to her and took her in my arms, claiming her mouth with mine. Her small sigh nearly undid me, and it took all my self-control not to pull her to the bed.

Reluctantly I drew away, and led her to a chair, the same one in which she had sat when I had first asked her to take on this task, all those lonely nights ago. "You are back, and safe, praise God," I said.

She let out a weary laugh. "I am."

I plucked her hands from her lap, taking them in my own. "You did beautifully, Maddalena. Better than I dreamed, my angel of holy vengeance."

She made a strange sound, almost a sob. I paused, waiting for her to speak, but when she did not, I continued.

"Savonarola is being interrogated by the Signoria," I said.

She looked up. "Tortured, you mean."

"Yes, I suppose so. The Florentines have certain . . . rather effective methods at their disposal, I am given to understand." I decided it was best not to describe these methods. She seemed suddenly fragile, as if she were a very different woman from the one who had left Rome. No doubt she was, with everything she had seen, including the siege of San Marco, tales of which were already making the rounds of Italy and would soon move beyond the peninsula.

Guilt gnawed at me. She is different because of you, Cesare, some little voice inside me said spitefully. She is changed because of what you sent her to do.

I shook the voice away. I had done what I had to do, and so had Maddalena. She had gone willingly.

"Already, the Holy Father has sent a Papal Commission to Florence to oversee the interrogation and trial of Fra Savonarola, to make sure all is done in accordance with Church law. Normally a man of the cloth can only be tried and convicted by an ecclesiastical tribunal, but we all appreciate that this is something of an . . . extraordinary circumstance."

"And then what?" Maddalena asked, in a near whisper.

"He will be executed. For heresy, most likely. For claiming to be a prophet."

"It is already decided? Even without a trial?"

"Of course. That is how matters such as this go." I frowned. "You knew this, Maddalena. You know that we—that the Holy Father—needed him removed. He could not go on preaching against the pope and the Church. You know that."

"I know," she said quietly.

"You do not . . . sympathize with him?"

At last she looked up and met my eyes. "Certainly he challenged the pope and Holy Mother Church," she said at last. "But I cannot help but think of . . ." She drew a deep, shuddering breath and looked away. "I cannot help but think of the desperate poor in Florence, who found such solace in his words, and were seen by him as no one else had ever seen them before," she said in a rush. "They have lost their protector, their benefactor."

"The Church will help them," I said easily. "They should not have placed their trust in a false prophet."

Maddalena was silent.

I rose from my chair, discomfited by her quiet, subdued nature. "Come. To bed, *mia bella*." I moved behind her chair and brushed her loose hair aside, kissing her neck before whispering in her ear, "I have missed you. Let me show you how much."

To my surprise, she drew away and stood up. "Begging your pardon, Your Eminence, but I should like to retire," she said. "I am most weary from the journey."

I forced myself to hide my great disappointment. She had been several days on the road, after all. And God only knew what horrors she had witnessed during the siege of San Marco, all for my—the Church's—benefit. I had waited this long; I could wait another night or two. "Of course," I said. "Forgive me. Of course, you must rest."

Without another word, she turned and left.

Chapter 75

MADDALENA

The day after my return, I was back to my duties at Santa Maria in Portico. No one commented on my absence; I wondered what story Cesare had put about to explain it. I found I did not care.

I tried to forget everything that had happened in Florence; tried to forget the friar's words, his voice, his call to be better Christians. I tried to forget what he had said to me when I made my confession, the confession that haunted me still. *Because I love him.* I tried to forget what had happened to him, what I had brought about. What I had done to the man who had granted me absolution for my worst sins. Who had shown me God's love and mercy once again.

Perhaps the worst part was how often I succeeded in forgetting. I went about my usual tasks and forgot about the peace I had felt in Fra Savonarola's presence, about the fear and love of God his sermons had stirred in me. And, when I remembered again, it seemed like a travesty that I had ever forgotten. Yet I could not go about my life serving the Borgia family if I did not forget.

I longed to confess my confused feelings to, of all people, Cesare. Especially after he had trusted me with his own anguish, his own secrets. And yet I knew he was the last person I could tell. He would never intentionally hurt me or cause me harm, but I knew—on a deep, instinctual level—that for me to remain safe in this world, I could not give him any more power over me than he already had.

I was more lost than I could ever recall feeling, even after Federico's death.

When I heard, a few weeks after my return, that Fra Savonarola had been burned at the stake in the Piazza della Signoria, along with two of his brother monks, I pleaded illness so I might be released from my duties and slipped out to the church of Santa Maria in Trastevere. I spent the day on my knees in prayer for Fra Savonarola's soul and for my own forgiveness, though I doubted such a thing could be accomplished. I had assisted in bringing about the death of a man whose voice, forever after, would sound in my head as the voice of God. I knelt beneath the glorious mosaics depicting the life of the Blessed Mother and beseeched her to hear me, to take pity on me as a flawed and mortal sinner. She knew the hearts of women, and if she could not understand and forgive me, who could?

I returned to Cesare's bed, for I had never planned to do otherwise. I had greater sins on my soul than this, so I might as well take solace and pleasure where I could find it. I did not feel capable of saying no to him. Even after everything, I did not want to.

Because I loved him.

A few nights after my return, when I arrived in his rooms, he had a gift for me. "Open it," he said, presenting me with a velvet box.

Smiling in anticipation, I opened it and gasped to behold a gold cross set with diamonds and rubies and threaded through a gold chain. "You . . . you cannot mean to give this to me," I whispered, raising wondering eyes to his.

He grinned. "I surely do." He removed it from the box and spun me around, so he could clasp it about my neck. "It is to replace the one those thugs in Florence took from you. Yet this one is better and more beautiful still. It befits your own beauty, *mia bella* Maddalena."

I smiled, sighing as he kissed my throat, now adorned with jewels the likes of which I had never so much as dreamed of owning.

What Cesare Borgia did not understand—could never understand—was I could never wear such a thing, ever. I was a maid; my employers or fellow servants would assume I had stolen it and punish me, or I would be robbed should I wear it in the street. I did not have a litter and armed guards to take me about Rome, after all.

But I did not say any of this to him. That night, he made passionate love to me, and I wore nothing but the jeweled cross.

PART SIX

DEADLY SINS

Rome, November 1497–March 1498

Chapter 76

CESARE

Autumn came to Rome, and I returned from my errand of crowning King Federigo in Naples. Yet I returned to the prospect of a very different life than the one I had left.

Things in Italy had changed. Things for the house of Borgia had changed. And so, things for me would change. At last. At long last.

"Carlotta of Aragon," Father said, leaning back in his chair. "Federigo's daughter. And you think he would give her to you in marriage?"

"He was quite coy," I admitted. "He said he could not discuss the matter while I am still a cardinal."

"Hmph," he said. "And I suppose you assured him that that would soon no longer be the case?"

"I did, but he refused to discuss it until such time as I am in a secularized state."

"I do not like removing your cardinal's hat without the assurance of a good marriage and an estate," Father said.

"Is it not worth the gamble? Carlotta will be heiress to the Kingdom of Naples. And if she were my wife, I would be king." I had to fight a thrill of pleasure at the words.

Father had not lost his dream of establishing a Borgia dynasty; but with Sancia and Jofre yet to produce any children and Lucrezia unable to pass on the Borgia name, he'd had to reckon with the inevitable: I must leave the College of Cardinals, marry, and take up arms for the Church in Juan's place. He was still determined to have his third Borgia pope, but it would not be me. Perhaps one of my sons, of which I hoped to have many.

Juan no longer stood in my way. No one stood in my way. I was close, so close, to having what I wanted. What I had wanted my entire life. And I would have it all.

Before I could leave the Church, Father had commanded me to keep my post as papal legate to King Federigo's coronation. And so, at the end of the summer—once the business with Girolamo Savonarola was satisfactorily concluded—I had gone to Naples and done just that. My time in the kingdom had been productive; while there I spoke to King Federigo of a new marriage for Lucrezia and one for myself. For Lucrezia he had pledged his nephew Alfonso, along with the title Duke of Bisceglie, which would make my sister a duchess upon their marriage. He was less eager to pledge to me his legitimate daughter Carlotta, however.

Still, much business had been concluded, and I'd had time to sample the many delights of the kingdom as well. In the process I had come down with a case of what the Neapolitans called the French pox, a most uncomfortable sickness. However, thanks to my physician—who had prescribed treatments of ointments and hot baths to sweat the disease away—I had returned to Rome with no further sign of it, for which I was grateful.

"Perhaps," Father mused. "Perhaps it is worth the gamble. Or perhaps Federigo is merely putting us off and will continue to be obdurate."

"Perhaps I might go to the court of France myself, to woo the lady in person," I suggested. Carlotta of Aragon was currently at the court of Queen Anne of Brittany. I was confident that, should I present my suit to her in person, she would not resist for long, and would surely talk her father around if he continued to be hesitant.

"Perhaps. The first step is Lucrezia's divorce. It all must follow from that."

At the end of November, I went to see Lucrezia in the convent of San Sisto. A church commission had pronounced that the divorce between her and Giovanni Sforza could go forward, due to Sforza's impotence. Sforza, however, despite my cultivating of his odious cousin Ascanio, was not proving cooperative and refused to put his signature to the document attesting to non-consummation of the marriage.

"And he will not sign it?" Lucrezia asked, through the grille in the convent parlor.

"No, damn him," I said, running my fingers through my hair.

"But you said all went well with the commission that examined me," she said. "They have claimed I am a virgin."

A virgin who is with child, I thought wryly to myself. But after all, who but churchmen could be persuaded to believe such a thing? "They have, but Sforza is understandably reluctant to sign anything attesting to his own impotence," I said.

"As well he might be," Lucrezia muttered. "As he is not impotent any more than I am a virgin."

"Lucrezia, hush!"

"Why?" she demanded. "I am in a house of God. I cannot tell lies here. And in any case, it does not matter what the truth is, does it? You and Father shall arrange all to best suit your own wishes, as you always do."

"I have not come here to argue with you, Lucrezia. It shall happen either way; Ludovico and Ascanio Sforza are finally making themselves useful and are convincing Giovanni to sign the decree. As it happens, I have come to bring you good news."

"And what might that be?"

"Father and I have decided on a new husband for you."

She snorted. "I thought as much. You waste no time, the pair of you, do you?"

"You know your marriage is important for—"

"For the family. I know."

"I have met him, and I think you will be pleased. It is King Federigo's nephew, Alfonso of Aragon. He is—"

"Not Sancia's brother?" she interrupted.

"Yes, in fact."

"I see," she said slowly.

"He is a comely man, young, fit, intelligent, and well-read. He seems kind as well. I met him in Naples at Federigo's coronation. You shall like him, Crezia, I know it."

"Well," she said slowly, "Sancia has always spoken highly of him. She loves him very much."

"He seems to be a fine man. That is why we have chosen him for you." I put my fingers up against the grille, and she put hers to the other, so tiny sections of our skin might touch. "I want you to be happy, Crezia. Really I do. Now tell me: would you not rather have a handsome Neapolitan prince your own age than Giovanni Sforza?"

She giggled, sounding like her old self. "I suppose I would."

"And so you shall," I said, rising to leave. "All will be well, Crezia. I swear it."

"You have never let me down, brother," she said. "That I know."

"God and His Blessed Mother forbid that I should ever do so."

"Does he . . . does this Alfonso know . . ." She trailed off uncomfortably.

"That you are with child?" I asked, a bit of an edge creeping into my voice. "No, he does not, and we will make certain he does not find out."

She had still not said who the father was, and I had since ceased to press her.

Lucrezia sighed and closed her eyes. "You are right, Cesare," she murmured. "All I want is a fresh start. For this horrible year to be behind me."

"I want the same," I said. "For both of us. I wish I could kiss you goodbye, sister. I love you and will come again soon."

"I love you, too, Cesare," she said. "Godspeed."

As I went to leave, a young man in the papal livery came into the visiting room. "Oh," he said, startled to see me there. He bowed quickly. "Your Eminence. I did not expect to see you here."

"And who might you be?" I asked.

"This is one of Father's chamberlains, Cesare," Lucrezia said, from behind the screen. "Pedro Calderon. I am sure you have seen him before."

Indeed, he did look familiar. "And what are you doing here, Calderon?" I asked. "What business have you with my sister?"

"Deliveries, my lord," the man said, sounding uncomfortable.

"He carries letters to Papa for me," Lucrezia interjected. "And brings me anything else I might need, from the outside world."

"Indeed," I said, studying the young man. He nearly squirmed under my gaze. Why Lucrezia could not have someone from her own household accomplish these tasks for her, I knew not. But Father was writing her copious amounts of letters, so I supposed it was easier this way. "Well, good day to you, Calderon. I hope you bring my sister no ill tidings."

"To be certain I do not, my lord," he said. With that, I took my leave.

Back at the Vatican, Michelotto was agitated when he appeared in my chambers. "A word, Your Eminence," he said, closing the door behind him.

"What is it, Michelotto?" I asked, distressed by the frown on his face, more emotion than he usually showed.

"Some very distasteful gossip has made its way into the streets of late," he said. "All due to a very unfortunate comment Giovanni Sforza was heard to have made. I thought it best that you hear it from me first."

"I can only imagine what that man has to say about our family," I said darkly. "Well, out with it."

"He was overheard to have said that you and your father are so keen on a divorce for Lucrezia so . . . so the two of you may have her all to yourselves."

I did not understand his meaning at first. Then, slowly, I arrived at their true intent, their malevolence. "He said what?" I asked, my voice low. "For his sake I hope he did not mean what I think he meant."

"I am afraid he did, my lord," Michelotto said. "Or at least his words are being interpreted as such, and they have now spread to the common people."

"Incest." I spat the filthy word. "He would accuse me of incest with my sister. And Pope Alexander of incest with his daughter."

"That is how his remarks seem to have been intended, and how they are being understood. He was also heard to say that he has never seen a family so unnaturally close."

"He dares!" I shouted. I seized a glass decanter from the table and hurled it against the wall. Michelotto did not flinch at the shower of glass. "He dares speak such disgusting words about me, about my sister, about our family. He is lucky we are merely arranging his divorce and not his murder."

"That *could* be arranged, my lord. And with a great deal less trouble, if I may say."

I looked at Michelotto's calm, impassive face, and knew that if I sent him after Sforza the scum would not live to see another sunrise. And God's teeth, was it tempting. I could not think of anything I wanted more at that particular moment.

"No," I said reluctantly. "It is not worth the scandal it would cause. Everyone would know the culprits, and as of now we have Milan right where we want them: doing our bidding. Murdering Ludovico's and Ascanio's cousin, as gratifying as it would be, will do us no good."

Michelotto nodded. "As you wish, my lord."

"I suppose I should thank you for telling me of this gossip, for it is something I should know, yet I find that I cannot," I said through gritted teeth.

Michelotto bowed. "I understand completely, Your Eminence."

"You are dismissed."

Chapter 77

MADDALENA

Rome, January 1498

"Soon you shall have your mistress back at the palazzo," Cesare said to me as we lay in bed. "In a few weeks she shall give birth to her child and be back at home. Then perhaps the gossip will stop."

"You do not need me to tell you that Romans will always find something to gossip about," I said, running my hands lazily over the muscles of his chest.

His expression darkened. I had hit a nerve. "Yes. I know it well. But as long as they are not gossiping about my sister, I don't care what they say."

There were other rumors circulating of late about Lucrezia and Cesare. I wondered if Cesare was aware of those. Yet that was something I didn't wish to ask him.

He sighed and turned over onto his back, drawing me against his side. "At least now her marriage is annulled. Soon this whole debacle shall be behind us."

It had happened in December; Sforza had finally given in to the pressure being applied to him by both the Borgias and his own cousins, Ludovico and Cardinal Ascanio. He had signed the decree attesting to his impotence, and the divorce was made official. I had been sent for to accompany Lucrezia to the Curia the day she appeared there and made a brief speech before the College of

Cardinals, in Latin, expressing her gratitude to be rid of her false marriage. Heavy with child, her clothes had been adjusted in the days leading up to her appearance—by me, at the request of both Cesare and Lucrezia—to hide her pregnancy as much as possible. I had done the best I could, and if one did not know the truth one would imagine she had merely gained weight—or so I hoped. Still, there was bound to be gossip and speculation. There was no avoiding it, however much Cesare might wish it otherwise.

"I wish I knew who the father was," he wondered aloud. "I know it was not Giovanni Sforza, of course, but she never would say who it was."

"It was not Lord Sforza," I agreed.

He lifted his head and looked at me. "Do you know who it is, Maddalena?" he asked.

I hesitated. I remembered the letter I had once carried to Perotto Calderon, how secretive Lucrezia had been, how furtive he had been in accepting it. How, the day she had confessed to me she was with child and I had asked who the father was, she had looked at me impatiently and said, *Honestly, Maddalena. I am surprised you do not know.*

It had to have been Calderon. Who else could it have been? What else could she have meant?

Her divorce was official; her family knew she was pregnant; what difference did it make if I told Cesare who I thought the father was?

Because you are betraying your mistress's confidence, a voice in my head whispered. She swore you to secrecy when you carried that letter. It is all of a piece.

But was not my first loyalty to Cesare now? Did I not owe him more than I did Lucrezia?

What harm could it do?

"She had me carry a letter to a man for her, once," I said aloud, my decision made. Cesare went very, very still beside me. "To whom?" he asked softly. "To what man?"

"A groom in the service of His Holiness," I said. "A man named Pedro Calderon. Called Perotto."

Cesare was silent. "Only once?" he asked finally.

"I was sent to him the once, yes. She said Pantasilea usually carried messages to him, but she was ill that day, so she had me do it."

He was silent for so long that I thought he'd fallen asleep. When I sat up and looked over at him, I saw he was in fact still awake, staring up at the bed canopy, thoughts tumbling through his head.

"I did not mean to distress you," I said softly.

He pulled me to him, kissing me deeply. "You have not distressed me. Not at all," he said. "Quite the contrary, my Maddalena. Do not think any more of it."

Chapter 78

CESARE

Rome, February 1498

"Yes, Your Eminence?" Michelotto said, bowing as he stood before my desk.

"I've a task for you," I said.

"Your wish is my command, my lord."

"Do you know of a chamberlain in His Holiness's service named Pedro Calderon?"

Michelotto thought about it. "Perotto?"

"Yes. That is the man."

"I do indeed, my lord."

"Good. And there is a maid in my sister's service by the name of Pantasilea. Do you know her as well?"

"Yes, my lord."

"Good. This shall be easy enough then. They need to be silenced."

Michelotto did not flinch. "Permanently?"

"Yes," I said, without hesitation. "It seems this low-born Perotto is the father of my sister's child, and Pantasilea has been aiding and abetting their affair all along. They cannot be allowed to tell anyone of this."

Michelotto bowed. "Understood, my lord. Consider it done." He moved to leave, but hesitated.

"What is it?" I asked.

"Does anyone else know of this?" he asked. "Their affair?"

"They are the only ones with proof of it," I said. "Satisfying as it would no doubt be, I cannot do away with everyone in Rome who speaks ill of my sister. These two are the only ones who could prove anything, if they were driven to it. If they were offered the right price."

"Are they?" he asked. "What of the little maid, the one you take to your bed?"

"What of her?" I bit out.

"I assume she is how you found out this particular information. I did not tell you of it."

I rose from my chair. "Maddalena Moretti is not to be harmed, for any reason," I said, speaking each word slowly and clearly. "Indeed, you will consider her safety as paramount as my own. Is that understood?"

"Yes, my lord. If you are certain."

"I have never been more certain of anything in my life," I retorted. "Maddalena will keep what she knows to herself. And I will not have her hurt, under any circumstances."

He bowed. "Of course, my lord. I should never have mentioned it."

"Indeed. Now go. You have work to do."

Michelotto turned and left, and I sank back down into my chair and closed my eyes. Maddalena. No, I would protect her with all the powers at my disposal, especially now, after everything we had been through together. I needed her. We could not have brought down

Savonarola without her. And she was beautiful and kind and faithful and somehow without bitterness—everything I was not. I did not know when my desire for her body had morphed into something else, into this compulsive necessity, but it had. And I could not go back.

Chapter 79

MADDALENA

Rome, March 1498

It was at the marketplace that I first heard the news. I was on an errand for Donna Sancia—with Donna Lucrezia still in the convent, Donna Sancia and Donna Adriana had put my idle hands to work—and was trying to hurry back as quickly as possible. It was cold for March, and the sooner I could be back beside a fireplace in the palazzo, warming my fingers for my embroidery, the better.

"Yes, that's right," a woman at one of the stalls said. "They were two of the pope's servants. Or perhaps one was his daughter's maid? Anyway, they fished both bodies out of the Tiber two days ago. Both dead, of course."

I froze, cocking an ear toward the gossips beside me, straining to hear more.

"No doubt they did not end up in the river accidentally," the woman's companion said.

"I shouldn't think so. I heard they both had wounds around their necks. They'd been garroted."

"Excuse me," I said, turning toward the two women, unable to bear it any longer. "But do you know their names?"

"Whose names? The names of the servants?"

"Yes," I said.

The second woman screwed up her face, thinking. "I don't know as I've heard."

The woman who had been telling the tale spoke up. "The woman's name was something odd, I know that. And the man's name was something Spanish—Caldera?"

"Calderon," I whispered.

The woman snapped her fingers. "Yes! That's it! And the woman's name began with a *P*, I'm sure of it . . ."

"Pantasilea." She had gone to the convent with Lucrezia, so I hadn't noticed she'd been missing.

"Yes, I believe it was!" she crowed. Her smile faded as she studied me. "Not friends of yours, were they?"

"I . . . I had met them in passing before," I managed. "Excuse me."

I pushed my way through the crowd and headed back for the palazzo, my errand abandoned. I would simply have to tell Donna Sancia that they did not have what she needed, I thought dimly, in the part of my mind that was still coherent.

The rest of it was screaming denials, shouting in disbelief, crying excuses. I wanted to put my hands to my ears, shut out all the noise, except it was coming from inside my head and I would never be free of it.

Cesare had done this. He must have. I remembered the dark look on his face as he'd said that he did not care what Romans gossiped about, so long as they did not gossip about his sister. I thought of her pregnancy, right when she'd been declared *virgo intacta* and been granted a divorce. I thought of the new marriage Cesare and his father had already arranged for her. Anyone who knew of the child was a danger to their plans. And Perotto and Pantasilea knew everything there was to know. So the Borgias had to make certain they could never tell what they knew.

Cesare had done this. He'd had two innocent people murdered.

No. No. I had done this. I had told him my suspicion that Perotto had fathered Lucrezia's child, and how Pantasilea had carried their messages. I began to giggle, almost hysterically, as I remembered what I'd been thinking: what difference did it make if I told Cesare? What harm could it do? I laughed harder and harder, until passersby began giving me alarmed looks.

I had done this.

Oh, God, but I was a fool. How had I learned nothing from my spying in Florence? How was I still so naive when it came to the Borgias, specifically to Cesare Borgia? He—they—had used me before, sending me to Florence and using me to destroy a holy man. How did I not know better? Why had I thought I could tell him the truth and he would do nothing with that knowledge?

When would I learn?

No doubt Cesare, with his power and money and network of spies, would have uncovered the truth anyway. Eventually. I tried to tell myself this, and while I believed it readily enough, it could not wash the blood from my hands. It could not clean the stain from my soul. My soul, which was now further comprised by my association with the Borgias. With the man I loved.

I had to find a church, any church, and prostrate myself before the altar. I had to confess, so I need not bear this hideous burden alone.

I stopped walking, pressing my hands over my mouth as a sob escaped me. I could not confess. I could tell no one, not even a priest, less I put him in danger as well.

Oh, God, oh God, what hell was this? Was this the punishment for my sins? That this guilt should burn within me for all my days, unconfessed and unshriven?

I should have married Federico, and gone to the country, and forgot all about Rome and the Borgias and lived a quiet life among the grape vines and run a farm and borne my husband lots of children. I should have taken the chance to leave this place and its sin and temptations behind me when I had had the chance. For what had staying brought me in all this time but wickedness and suffering? Had the pleasure, the intimacy, been worth this?

Forgive me, Fra Savonarola. I sought to end my sinning, and only mired myself deeper in it. You were wrong to believe me worthy of mercy, as Maria Maddalena was.

When I got back to the palazzo, I threw myself on my knees in the chapel, silently begging God for forgiveness. *I did not know what it was I did, oh Lord, even as those who crucified Your Son knew not what they did. And still he forgave them. I pray that you may still forgive me.*

Yet even as I prayed, tears streaming down my cheeks, I knew I might better pray for protection than forgiveness.

For I, too, knew the secret of Lucrezia's pregnancy. She had told me herself, and all but confirmed the identity of the father. I knew everything that Perotto and Pantasilea had known. Why was I alive while they were dead? Or was I to be strangled and thrown into the river next?

Surely if he had wanted me dead, Cesare would have sent his kept assassin Michelotto for me as well. Surely if any of those merciless Borgias wanted me dead, I would even now be rotting in the river Tiber.

But Cesare . . . he cared for me. Perhaps it was not love, but he cared for me. I knew that by now; it was plain enough. If he wanted nothing more from me than a quick fuck, he would take his pleasure and send me on my way. But it had never been like that between us. Never.

Surely it was enough to protect me.

Wasn't it?

That evening, as the sun set, a servant wearing Cesare's livery came to seek me out. I was to come to his master that night. He found me in the kitchen, where I had just deposited some dishes from upstairs.

I looked at him with hollow, wan eyes and said, "Tell His Eminence I am ill and cannot come."

He nodded agreeably and departed. I looked wretched enough

to appear ill. And in truth, I was—ill in my mind, my soul, my spirit.

And if I was deadly wrong, and whatever Cesare felt for me was not enough to protect me from their Borgia games, let them come for me. I would not go willingly. Not this time.

PART SEVEN

DUKE VALENTINO

Rome, July–August 1498

Chapter 80

MADDALENA

Again I helped my mistress prepare for her wedding.

It was different this time. There was no torn lace, no panic, no last-minute mending. I was not needed to save the day.

Lucrezia was not nervous. She was relaxed and smiling, twirling before the mirror in her new gown, yellow and trimmed with gold. She gave birth to a son in March—a son she named Giovanni, after her brother, she specified—and who was being raised, discreetly, in Rome. He was brought to her when it was deemed safe. Already she had regained her figure, as slim yet shapely as ever.

And she was happy. She was free of the husband she never loved, and this day she would marry a man she did love.

When she had returned to Palazzo Santa Maria in Portico from the convent, she had been exhausted from the ordeal of childbirth, and devastated by the deaths of Pantasilea and especially Perotto. She must have truly loved him, if the way she grieved was any indication. She did not eat for days, and Donna Adriana and I nearly had to force food down her throat to ensure she did not make herself ill. No doubt that was how she'd gotten her figure back, though I would as soon have had her a little plumper and spared us all the ordeal.

Even once she was eating regularly, she was still listless, prone to fits of weeping, liable to take to her bed. If she knew the truth of what had befallen her lover and her maid—if she knew that her beloved brother was behind it—she never spoke of it.

She surely did not know of my part in the incident, and I prayed she never would. I had watched her grief those months and let it scald me, let it dig its claws into my flesh, and accepted it as my penance. My penance for what I had done, and how I had gone back to Cesare's bed anyway.

Surely this was how a drunk must feel, I had mused one night as I made my way to his bedchamber. They drink and drink even though they know how sick it will make them, and yet they do it anyway. And the next day they hanker for the drink all over again, as though their sickness had never happened.

That was how it was, for me, with Cesare. I could not stay away, even though I knew it might well destroy me. He might destroy me.

When he had next sent for me after my refusal, I had gone. I no longer wanted to be scared and hiding. If I was to be punished in some way, let it come, so that I no longer need dread it. Yet when I had arrived in his rooms, he had folded me tenderly in his arms and murmured in my ear, "Maddalena *mia*. You are well? I was worried when you said you were ill." And I had melted into his arms, I had made love to him, and I had reveled in the knowledge that I was right. He would protect me.

For now.

Yet when we were in bed together, we were only a man and a woman, and he was my lover who knew how to bring me pleasure, and I was his, and knew just how he liked to be touched and stroked and kissed, and where. He craved the things I could do to him, and I knew it.

And so I went to his bed whenever he called, and I hated myself for it.

But when I first thought that he might have killed his brother—and after, when I learned the truth—had I not rejoiced anyway? Had I not been glad that so evil a man as Juan Borgia was dead?

Did I not trust Cesare Borgia because he was a killer? Or because he had once killed someone I did not feel deserved to die?

I was complicit in his sin, in all of it. And so where else was there for me to go?

Isabella knew something had happened. She could tell I was changed. Yet I could not tell her, for her own safety. And so, while our friendship remained, there was a hole between us that we had to skirt, lest we both fall in.

Madonna Lucrezia had come out of her depression upon meeting her new bridegroom, Alfonso of Aragon. He had arrived in Rome earlier this month, and already she was smitten. He was about her age, and handsome—a male version of his sister Sancia—with a brilliant smile that he was not shy about bestowing upon her. And best of all, he appeared to love her on sight as well. My mistress was perhaps the happiest I had ever seen her.

As one of the other maids put the finishing touches on her coiffure, Lucrezia clapped her hands and squealed in delight, staring at her reflection in the mirror. "I am ready, am I not?" She turned to me. "What do you think, Maddalena? Will he find me beautiful?"

I gave her an honest smile. "Of course he will, Madonna. You are radiant. He will not believe the vision before his eyes."

She giggled girlishly and picked up her skirts. "Well, then, let us go! I am most eager for my wedding, and especially my wedding night!"

I picked up her train and followed, praying she would be this happy always. Praying she did not let her Borgia blood steal her joy and love of life.

I did not know how she had lasted this long.

Chapter 81

CESARE

Lucrezia and Alfonso are a handsome couple, I thought as I watched them dance. This wedding had been a long time in the making, and no one was more pleased than I. They'd been married in a small ceremony in a chapel in the Vatican, and the enthusiasm with which the couple said their marriage vows was plain to all.

As their dance ended, I rose and went to the floor, smiling as I approached the newlyweds. "May I steal the bride for a dance, good sir?" I said to my new brother-in-law.

He bowed and grinned amiably. "Of course, Your Eminence."

"None of that," I said, clapping him on the shoulder. "We are brothers now. You must call me Cesare."

"I shall, brother!"

Alfonso turned to escort out his sister in turn, and we all took our places for the next dance.

"Oh, I do hope you and Alfonso shall become great friends, Cesare," Lucrezia said as we danced. "I love both of you so."

I smiled. "I am happy you are happy, Crezia. More than I can say."

I had been alarmed when I'd heard of her depression after the death of her lover Perotto. I knew she would be upset, but I'd thought that surely she'd come to see that it was better this way. She could live her life with her new husband and not fear any threat. However, that had not been the case. And I lived in fear that one day, she would learn it had been me who'd had Perotto killed.

But I had tried to put it behind me. Lucrezia was happy, and never again would I have to hurt anyone she loved.

"You were right all along, brother," she said as I spun her. "This was the right path for me. The divorce and the new marriage . . . all of it."

"That will teach you to doubt your elder brother," I teased.

"It will indeed."

When the dance ended, the musicians struck up a slower one in its place. "One more, Crezia," I said, holding on to her hand.

She beamed up at me. "Of course."

As we danced, I asked her, "Do you remember the promise I made to you, when we were both very young?"

"You promised me many wonderful things, as a good elder brother should."

I laughed briefly, but grew serious. "Yes, but I mean: do you remember the day I swore I would never let you be parted from your family? From me?"

She laughed. "Of course I do! I was so small and fearful of what marriage and being a woman might bring. You were so sweet to reassure me, Cesare, as always."

"And," I said, drawing her closer, "I have kept my promise. You and Alfonso shall reside in Rome, and you need never leave us."

She smiled merrily. "Oh, Cesare. I would follow Alfonso anywhere."

The dance ended, and she curtsied and I kissed her hand. I watched her walk back to her husband, positively radiant with joy, and wondered why I suddenly felt so out of sorts.

Chapter 82

MADDALENA

This time, as I watched the wedding festivities, I was allowed to be there. I had been asked to attend should Madonna Lucrezia need anything. But if her happy, carefree glow all the evening long was any indication, she had everything she needed. As before, I was content to simply watch.

It was a much smaller affair than her first wedding, only family members and high-ranking nobles and church officials. Yet everyone was dressed splendidly, and the feast was as sumptuous as ever.

I watched as Lucrezia danced first one dance, and a second, with her brother Cesare. They danced close together, smiling and laughing, moving together as if they had done this their whole lives. And no doubt they had.

I thought of the rumors I had heard, that Lucrezia and Cesare committed incest together, that they had known one another in unholy ways. Watching them dance like this, at ease with one another, so loving, it was easy to see where the rumors had come from. I had never before seen siblings so close and affectionate.

Yet I could not believe it was true. If it was, I of all people surely would have seen evidence to give it credence, and I had not. Cesare Borgia might be guilty of many terrible deeds, but this was not one of them. He loved his sister protectively, fiercely—perhaps too much so—but not in such an unnatural way. The evil he had done had been out of love for her. As unforgivable, as misguided as what he had done had been, had he not thought only to protect his sister?

Could the intentions still be good when the act was so horrible?

As the night wore on and guests began to disperse, Cesare beckoned, discreetly, to me. I followed him out and up to his rooms. Lucrezia was not likely to look for me that night.

Yet when we got to his bedchamber, he did not seem eager for my company, as he often was. Instead he looked down into a darkened courtyard from the window. "Perhaps you should go," he said at last. "It has been a long day for us both."

I crossed the room and slid my arms around his waist, laying my cheek against his velvet-clad back. "Is something troubling you, Cesare?" I asked.

He shook his head. "Nothing I could name."

"I am happy to stay."

"I do not know as I will be very good company."

I could easily convince him otherwise. Perhaps other women might not have dared, but he continued to send for me and not for any other women, even after all this time. Even in the festering nest of gossip that was Rome, I had not heard any rumors about him and any other lady. Not since Sancia, before he had first taken me to his bed. I was sure I was not the only woman he had bedded in all this time, but I was certainly his favorite. His lover. His mistress. The keeper of his secrets.

I slid my hands lower, to his manhood. "I shall go if you want me to," I murmured, brushing my fingers against him. He was hard beneath his breeches. I drew back, as though to leave.

He caught my wrist and spun to face me. "No," he said. "Stay."

I smiled, and went to work removing his clothing, then mine. We went to the bed, and I pushed him down and straddled him, lowering myself slowly onto him. He lifted his hips, thrusting himself deeper into me. "Oh, Maddalena," he groaned.

I began to move atop him, his fingers digging into my hips as he arched beneath me. When he reached his ecstasy, I looked down at his face, my eyes hazy with my own pleasure, and took in his expression, twisted with exquisite agony. I smiled, enjoying the sight.

A week or so after Lucrezia's wedding, Cesare sent for me, and I went eagerly, as I always—still—did. When I arrived that night he was sprawled in a chair before the cold fireplace, idly toying with the goblet of wine in his hand. He scarcely noticed my arrival. "Cesare," I said, and moved to stand behind him, running my hands down his shoulders and over his chest. I bent forward and kissed his neck.

He sighed, turning his head and catching my lips with his. But then he turned his gaze forward again, toward the cold stone of the fireplace. "There is wine there on the table, if you would like some," he said, somewhat offhandedly.

I served myself from the jug he had indicated and took the chair next to his, studying him carefully as I sipped—a good red from Tuscany, if I wasn't mistaken. God forgive me, but being a cardinal's mistress had given me an appreciation for fine wine, finer than I had had any occasion to taste before in my life. "Are you well, Cesare?" I asked finally, when he did not speak further.

He turned to face me at last, and the smile that crossed his face, while weary, was genuine. "Perfectly well," he said. "Only tired." He ran his fingers through his hair. "I was in negotiations with the French ambassador much of the day."

I went still at this. "Oh?" I asked, prompting him to go on, even as I both did and didn't wish to know more.

Everyone in the Borgia circle had heard the rumors by then, even if they likely hadn't reached the rest of Rome yet. Pope Alexander was seeking an alliance with the new French king—the same nation that had invaded us just a few short years ago—and would use his son to seal this alliance. His son Cesare's marriage, which of course would involve said Cardinal Borgia leaving the Church, something almost unheard of.

I suspected it was not so much Pope Alexander using his son to get what he wanted as it was the other way around.

"Yes," he said. "He assures me his king is agreeable to everything, and that our accord shall be a mutually beneficial one. Finally, there shall be no more obstacles. I shall have what I want. What I've always wanted."

I was rather puzzled at the flat tone of his voice. "And does this not make you happy?"

He laughed shortly and took another swig of wine. "Of course it does."

"Forgive me, but you do not seem happy."

"It shall be strange, to leave Rome. To leave Italy." He looked up at me. "To leave you." He spun the stem of his wineglass between his thumb and index finger. "I had not thought very long on any of those things before."

Will you truly miss me, when you go off to conquer the world? When you marry your royal wife? I wanted to ask. But I didn't. Not because I did not dare, but because I did not wish to hear the answer.

He drained the rest of the wine from his glass and stood up. "Never mind," he said brusquely. "As I said, I am only tired." He reached out and pulled me to my feet. "But not too tired for you, my Maddalena." He kissed me deeply and drew me over to the bed.

Enjoy this, Maddalena, I told myself as he unlaced my dress, shivering as his fingers brushed my bare skin. This is all you can ever have of him.

Chapter 83

CESARE

I burst into my father's rooms, jubilant. "I have the agreement, Father," I said, holding up a roll of parchment. "Louis has agreed to it and signed."

"Has he? Excellent! Let us see," Father said, holding out his hand.

I unrolled the parchment and placed it upon the desk before him.

The last months had been a flurry of negotiations between the new King of France, Louis XII, and I. King Charles had died suddenly in April—oddly enough, another event Savonarola had prophesied—and to our surprise and delight we found the new French monarch eager to reverse his predecessor's stance and become as friendly as possible with the papacy.

Our old allies in Spain certainly hadn't been any help. Ferdinand opposed the prospect of my match with Princess Carlotta and had been heard to mutter about the Borgias lusting for the entire Italian peninsula.

He was right.

In addition, Their Most Catholic Majesties made no secret of their shocked disapproval at my leaving the Church. Spanish though we might be, Father and I had no interest in creating a puppet papacy for the Spanish monarchs, and so we had decided to look farther afield for allies. The new French king, in need of our favor if he wished to press his claims to Naples and Milan, was a perfect candidate, and an alliance with France might serve to bring Ferdinand and Isabella back in line.

The situation was perfect, because the French king wanted something from the Holy See—namely, to set aside his barren wife and marry Charles's widow, Anne of Brittany, so he might keep Brittany under the jurisdiction of France. Only the pope could give him this.

The king would have his divorce; I'd made sure of that. And we would have what we needed in return. Impatient to see it all done, and done according to my specifications, I'd conducted most of the negotiations myself, consulting with the pope along the way.

"It is as we discussed," I said as Father read over the agreement. "We shall see to his annulment and provide him with a dispensation to marry Anne of Brittany. In return, once I have put aside the cardinal's hat, he shall bestow upon me the duchy of Valentinois and welcome me at the French court. He will also support my bid for the hand of Carlotta of Aragon."

Father's eyes continued to skim down the page. "And an army," he said quietly. "He shall put an army at your disposal. And mine."

"Yes," I said. "We can begin to forge of Italy one nation, as we always said. I shall start by subduing the barons of the Romagna, who spit on Rome's authority as their overlord."

He waved a hand. "Sit, Cesare." I took a chair beside his desk. He glanced at me. "You must not be too hasty. The first step is to go to France, take possession of your estate, and find a wife. Everything else will follow."

"It will," I agreed. "I do not mean to get ahead of myself. But know I shall achieve all that I stated I would. It all starts now. I finally have the tools at my disposal."

"You do indeed," he said. "Very well. Next month we shall have you announce in consistory that you are renouncing the cardinalcy. And soon after, you shall go to France."

I left the room, exultant, to find Michelotto waiting for me. "So, Your Eminence?" he asked. "Are we bound for France?"

"We are, soon enough," I said. "And shortly you shall no longer need to address me as Your Eminence."

"All went well?" he asked, nodding toward the papal apartments.

"Yes. He has the agreement. The die is cast. And when I return to Italy, it shall be at the head of an army, as a conqueror."

"And His Holiness is in support of your aims?"

I thought of Father's reluctance, his desire that I slow down in my ambition. But it did not matter. Not anymore. For I would be the one at the head of the army, not him. "This is what he has always wanted our family to achieve. His Holiness shall continue to keep the keys to Heaven, and I shall have the keys to his earthly kingdom. The much more immediate kingdom."

Michelotto studied me. "And what do you call the keeper of the one who keeps the keys?"

My lips curled into something that I was sure was more a sneer than a smile. "God."

Chapter 84

MADDALENA

Rome, August 1498

I lay in bed beside Cesare, breathing heavily from our lovemaking. It had been tinged with sadness for me. The next day, he would announce he was leaving the Church, and he would be off to France, to find himself that wealthy and important wife he needed so badly.

And I would be here, in Rome.

He turned toward me, brushing my hair off of my face. "I shall miss you when I am in France," he said. "I wish you could come with me." He brought my face toward his and kissed me.

No, you don't, I thought, even as his tongue tangled with mine, and his hand lazily stroked my breast. For what man wished his lover present while he was attempting to woo a wife?

And where did that leave me?

Perhaps an hour later, we made love again, and I tried to enjoy it as best I could, to revel in it. It might be the last time. I was going to have to live without him. But how would I live? How might I live?

Did it have to be in Rome?

His arm tightened around me. "You will be here when I return from France, won't you?"

My back was pressed to his chest, and he could not see my face. "Where else would I go?"

He kissed my neck and lightly stroked my hip, my belly, appearing satisfied with my answer. He did not seem to realize that it was not truly an answer at all.

He soon fell asleep, but I found I could not. I slid out from under his arm and sat up, looking down at his face in the flickering light of the single candle beside the bed. He looked so much younger when he slept, like the young man he was instead of a would-be monarch who was trying to put the world on his shoulders. I shivered, for though it was summer, it felt to me like the deepest of winter.

If I were ever going to leave Rome, this was my chance. He would go off to France, claim his new title and new bride, and have no further use for me. He might well gather his armies and ride off to conquer Italy and never think of me again. Yet if he did, he would never find me if I did not want him to. The poor can disappear in ways people like him can never conceive of. It is our curse; it is our blessing.

I could go somewhere else and make a living with my needle. I knew I could. I could live a new life, one where I did not have to carefully parse through every word I spoke to be sure I was not condemning anyone to death. To be sure I was saving the right lives. Though there was a kind of power in that, too.

I could start over, and begin to truly atone for my many, deadly sins.

There are seven deadly sins, Maddalena, but lust is the deadliest.

Or I could stay, and wait for him to come back someday, addicted to the pleasure he could wring from my body, to the look in his eyes when he said my name, to the measure of power I held over him. Because I did have power. Not much, but more than he was aware of. That was the thing with powerful men: they only ever thought about what power they stood to gain, not the power they gave away.

I could stay and test the limits of my power.

Or I could leave, and let him come back someday to find me gone.

I could leave, and save what remained of my soul.

Chapter 85

CESARE

I waited in the antechamber, the attendees for the consistory gathering in the audience chamber next door. I had just removed my cardinal's robes and hat for the last time and dressed in a rich doublet of black velvet trimmed in gold, with gray hose.

The day had finally come. I would go into the consistory and announce my desire to renounce the ecclesiastical state in favor of a secular one, with the blessing of His Holiness. Many of the cardinals had not wanted to attend, afraid of the political repercussions, particularly from Spain. The pope had been forced to write them, not so subtly commanding their presence. And so, at last, most were here. I would leave this room the Cardinal of Valencia and reenter it as the Duc de Valentinois. Or, as the Italians were already calling me, Duke Valentino. I would go to France, leave behind my family—and Maddalena, and damn me if she would not be the hardest to leave—and come back a married man, and a man with an army. I could wield power as I had always longed to, and all Italy would fear and admire me.

Yet I found myself remembering my mother's words to me just after Father's election: *It is a simpler life that I would wish for my children, if it were within my power to wish anything for them . . . the day will come when you will remember my words and realize I was right.*

And as I looked in the large Venetian glass mirror that hung on the wall, I saw that simpler life. One where I had not been born a Borgia, or to a family of any importance. I was a man who was free to marry Maddalena Moretti, a woman so good and kind and who soothed my heart and soul even as she excited my body. What more did any man need than that?

Perhaps my mother was right.

But then I blinked, and refocused on my reflection in the mirror, and that impossible vision was gone. Instead a secular prince looked back at me. The man I had always wanted to be. The man I had always been destined to become.

I had expected to feel pride as I looked at my reflection, once I'd removed my cardinal's robes and donned the clothing of a warrior, of a prince. A feeling of satisfaction and even elation at having finally accomplished the one thing I'd always wanted. Instead I felt hollow.

Was this happiness?

Father did not choose you to be his general because he feels you are the best man for the task, a malicious little voice—one I had not heard in a long while—whispered. He chose you because you are the only one left. Because there is no one else.

I was getting what I wanted. Why wasn't that enough?

Maybe it would be, once I had been received at the French court and had wedded and bedded my royal wife. Once I returned to Italy at the head of an army, bent on conquest. When I proved to the world, to my father, and to myself that I could be another Giulio Cesare.

Yet all I could see in the silvery glass was the pain of the past and the doubt of the present, of too many futures dreamt, both possible and impossible, and I could not tell the difference between any of it. I had not been chosen. Father had not chosen me. But did that matter? Truly? A man could take his destiny into his own hands and forge it himself, forge it in blood and fire and steel and ruthlessness. A man did not wait for permission to conquer.

This was what I had always wanted. I was happy. I would be happy.

Maddalena's words returned to me. *Forgive me, but you do not seem happy.*

I was. I would be, even if I had to allow her face to fade to the back of my mind.

I would do what I had set out to do. What I was meant to do. I would do it no matter what it cost. Whatever the price, I would pay it.

I would show them all.

And what if you can't?

My hand slammed into the mirror, smashing it into hundreds of shards that cascaded onto the marble floor. And as I looked down, I saw my reflection again, mingled with my blood. This time the reflection was shattered into pieces.

You were not chosen.

Author's Note

While Maddalena Moretti is a fictional character (as are most of her fellow servants, with the notable exceptions of Perotto Calderon and Pantasilea), the Borgia family, and most of the figures mentioned in connection with them—from those within the Vatican to political players in the other Italian city-states—are very real. In addition, the historical events described in this novel all really happened: Cesare Borgia's rise through Church ranks and eventual departure from the Church altogether, the French invasion and Pope Alexander VI's handling of it, Lucrezia Borgia's marriages and divorce, the arrival of Sancia of Aragon and her relationships with both Cesare and Juan Borgia, the military campaigns against the Orsini and the French, Juan Borgia's murder, and Pope Alexander's involvement in removing Girolamo Savonarola from power in Florence being the main ones. I have tried to depict the varied politics and personalities of this era as accurately as possible based on my research. Some of Pope Alexander's speeches in conclave, as well as the sermon Savonarola preaches in the Duomo when Maddalena attends, are all factual. This being a novel, however, I have of course taken some artistic liberties in my portrayal of the people and events involved.

The Holy League created in 1495 to drive the French from Italy is also known as the League of Venice, as it was in fact signed and sealed in Venice. As Cesare Borgia did take part in those negotiations, I simply moved the whole process to Rome, for both my own convenience and that of the reader in having all the main players stay in the same place.

The murder of Juan Borgia remains unsolved to this day, though suspects abound. Intriguingly enough, Pope Alexander did abruptly call off the search for the assassins with no explanation, leading many to assume that Cesare was in fact the culprit—a popular theory at the time, and one of which a figure no less than Queen Isabella of Spain was apparently convinced. The most likely culprit, or so many historians seem to feel, was the Orsini family, out for revenge after Pope Alexander's military campaigns against them and the death of Virginio Orsini in a Neapolitan prison, held on the pope's orders. How better to exact their revenge than by murdering the pope's favorite son and leader of the ill-fated expedition against them? For dramatic purposes, however, I have made Jofre Borgia the mastermind of the assassination, and indeed he was considered as a possible suspect at the time, due to Juan's relationship with Sancia.

While Girolamo Savonarola's rise and fall happened much as described here, I did take some liberties with both the events and timeline leading to his arrest. As Maddalena is herself fictional, so is her involvement in the entire affair, though certainly Pope Alexander had informants in Florence keeping him abreast of events as they unfolded. The siege of San Marco really happened, although for purposes of length I have left out the event that sparked it: a proposed trial by fire in which both Savonarola and a friar from the Franciscan order, who challenged the Dominican's teachings, were to physically walk through a bed of flames, the idea being that God would protect whoever held the most righteous beliefs. Both parties—and most of Florence—turned out for the event, but after much dispute as to the terms of how the ordeal could proceed it never, in fact, happened, leaving Florentines on both sides of the argument frustrated, disgruntled, and primed for a fight. I have also shifted forward the dates of Savonarola's arrest and execution: in reality, he was arrested at the siege of San Marco in April of 1498 and executed, after torture and trial, in May of that year. I moved these events to the summer of 1497 in order to be able to focus on the other events that took place in spring of 1498 in the Borgia world: the murders of Perotto and Pantasilea, and the negotiations for Lucrezia's second marriage. In addition, Cesare actually went to Naples as papal legate in August of 1497 (where he reportedly contracted the syphilis that would plague him the rest of his life), but I have moved that event back to the fall of that same year.

One of the most infamous charges laid against the Borgia family is that of incest—that Lucrezia Borgia had a sexual relationship with her father and brother Cesare (and, as some versions of the story have it, with Juan as well). However, the general consensus among historians is that there is no truth to this. The incest rumor was started by a comment attributed to Giovanni Sforza to the effect that the pope and Cesare wanted Lucrezia all to themselves, as I've described in the novel. The rumor was fueled by the fact that the Borgias—especially Cesare and Lucrezia—were extremely close. However, there is no evidence whatsoever of an actual incestuous relationship between Lucrezia and her father or brother, and given that Giovanni Sforza absolutely had an ax to grind with the Borgia family—for forcing him into a divorce in the first place, and then essentially declaring him impotent before all of Europe on top of it—his words should very much be taken with a rather large grain of salt.

However, the Roman public—and later much of Europe—took the rumor and ran with it, which is why it has been passed down to us to this day. It is worth noting that the evil reputation of the Borgia family has been rather overblown—especially in the case of Lucrezia, who simply was not the villainess she is often portrayed as being in different media. While Pope Alexander VI and Cesare were both certainly guilty of a multitude of sins—from corruption to murder and a great deal in between—none of their actions were truly out of character for powerful families of the Italian Renaissance. This does not excuse their deeds, of course, but it does raise the question of why the Borgia family has long stuck out as being the most notorious. My personal opinion is that much of it has to do with the fact that they were Spanish in a city which was accustomed to seeing power primarily in the hands of Italians. To this day, of the 266 men who have been elected to the papacy in total, 196 have been Italian. Rodrigo Borgia was in fact a brilliant politician and administrator, yet many opposed his rise to power simply on the basis of his nationality. In our own era, where xenophobic rhetoric sadly continues to appear in our political discourse, it does not take too much of a leap to imagine that a foreign family who rose to power on the Italian peninsula in a very turbulent political time would be especially denigrated.

A brief note on names: I have generally tried to stick to the Italian spellings of names in this book. There are a few exceptions to this, this most notable being Juan Borgia. He is most often referred to in sources I consulted as "Juan" as opposed to "Giovanni," which is the Italian version of the name, so I chose the Spanish spelling. I also wanted to avoid any confusion between him and Giovanni Sforza. Jofre, too, is a commonly used spelling of the name of the youngest Borgia, as opposed to Goffredo, which would be the Italian spelling. In addition, King Federigo of Naples is sometimes referred to as King Federico (Italian) or King Frederick (English), but I chose to use Federigo as the novel already had a Federico, and an English spelling would have seemed out of place.

When researching the lives of domestic servants in Renaissance Italy I found—perhaps not surprisingly, given power structures and who was able to leave written records—that little information is available about the lives of the people who formed one of the largest industries in Rome at the time. Specifically, one thing I was never able to confirm for certain is whether or not women were employed as servants in the Vatican Palace, as Maddalena is in the early chapters. I am inclined to think so—one source I consulted outlined a task in the papal household that was performed specifically by a male servant, which would suggest that there were also female servants, hence the need for differentiation. However, in the absence of solid proof (that I could find in English, anyway) I thought it not out of the question that Maddalena's initial place of employment could have been the Vatican.

Cesare Borgia has always been the member of the Borgia family who most fascinated me, the undisputed bad guy in a notorious family. I've long wanted to write his villain origin story, so to speak, and am thrilled that you now hold that very book in your hands. The addition of Maddalena's point of view seemed like a no-brainer as well. What better way to explore questions of power and politics than through the eyes of both one of the powerful and one of the powerless? These questions of power, corruption, and complicity with which the novel grapples made it a challenge to write, but a worthy challenge. My favorite kinds of novels are those that entertain, teach, and provoke thought. I hope I have done all of those things in this book.

As to what happened to Cesare after he left the Church, well, that information is out there, if you're interested in seeking it out. Maybe someday I will get the chance to write that story as well.

For further reading on the Borgias and Renaissance Italy, below is a selection of sources I consulted while writing this novel.

Bradford, Sarah. *Cesare Borgia: His Life and Times.* New York: Macmillan Publishing Co., Inc., 1976.

——*Lucrezia Borgia: Life, Love, and Death in Renaissance Italy.* New York: Penguin Books, 2004.

Brown, Meg Lota, and McBride, Kari Boyd. *Women's Roles in the Renaissance.* Westport: Greenwood Press, 2005.

Cloulas, Ivan. *The Borgias.* Trans. Gilda Roberts. New York: Barnes & Noble Books, 1989.

Cohen, Elizabeth, and Cohen, Thomas. *Daily Life in Renaissance Italy.* Westport: Greenwood Press, 2001.

Frieda, Leonie. *The Deadly Sisterhood: A Story of Women, Power, and Intrigue in the Italian Renaissance.* New York: HarperCollins, 2013.

Hibbert, Christopher. *The Borgias and Their Enemies, 1431–1519.* Boston: Mariner Books, 2008.

Meyer, G. J. *The Borgias: The Hidden History.* New York: Bantam Books, 2013.

Partner, Peter. *Renaissance Rome 1500–1559: A Portrait of a Society.* Berkeley: University of California Press, 1976.

Sabatini, Rafael. *The Life of Cesare Borgia.* Boston: Houghton Mifflin Company, 1924.

Strathern, Paul. *Death in Florence: The Medici, Savonarola, and the Battle for the Soul of a Renaissance City.* New York: Pegasus Books, 2015.

Acknowledgments

This book has been many years in the making—almost half my life, really, given that my near obsession with the Borgias began in my teenage years and has culminated in the book you are now holding in your hands. As such, bear with me, as I have a lot of people to thank.

First, as always, I must thank Lindsay Fowler, who was the first person I told when the idea for this novel finally, finally crystallized. I sent her a long series of texts outlining the idea, and the last one said, *This feels important.* She agreed, and in talking it all out with me helped start me on the long and difficult journey that was this novel. She also read the hot mess of a first draft, gave me her notes, and didn't think too badly of me afterward! Thank you, Lindsay, for everything. For all of it.

All of the thanks to my wonderful agent, Brianne Johnson, for getting as enthusiastic about this project as me, and for agreeing that it was the right project at the right time. Thanks as well for all the spot-on feedback on this one—you can always see the things that elude me.

So much gratitude to my stalwart editor, Vicki Lame, since I'm sure that editing this beast was akin to dragging an army's worth of cannon over the Italian hills! Thanks for zeroing in on *exactly* what this book needed, for responding immediately to all my way-too-excited emails with revision ideas, and for brainstorming titles (omg, *so many titles*).

Thanks to Lauren Humphries-Brooks, copy editor extraordinaire, for saving me from embarrassing mistakes. Copy editors are publishing's true heroes.

Many thanks to the marketing, sales, publicity, and art teams at St. Martin's Press for spreading the word about my books and getting them into the hands of readers all over the world.

My eternal gratitude to fellow authors Crystal King, Meghan Masterson, Kris Waldherr, and Heather Webb for reading an early copy of this novel and providing such kind words. I am honored to have the support of each one of you!

Thanks to friend and fellow writer Caitie McAneney-Klimchuk, who also read that notoriously messy first draft of this book and provided excellent feedback. Many thanks to Mike Slish, for answering all my research question texts, no matter how random! See you at the next Most Solemn Feast.

My everlasting gratitude to Dr. Mick Cochrane at Canisius College, who didn't bat an eye (not that I know of, anyway) when I turned in a dark and murder-y short story about a maid who becomes involved with Cesare Borgia. And for helping to make me the writer I am today.

Thanks to Talking Leaves Books in Buffalo for their continued support of me and of the Buffalo literary community at large.

Thanks for everything, always, to my writing group: Dee, Kate, Jenn, Sandi, Adrienne, and Claudia. I love seeing all the places this writing journey is taking all of us!

Thank you to the wonderful staff of the lovely Hearth Hotel in Rome for an amazing stay and lots of tips as I was researching this book.

Special shout-out to Jen Hark-Hameister for letting me drag her into my Borgias obsession, and for listening to me rant about historical inaccuracies throughout multiple seasons of the TV show.

All my gratitude and love, as always, to my dear friends and family for your continued support throughout this bananas writing career of mine: Amanda Beck, Bob and Marcia Britton, Alex Dockstader, Sandy Hark, Andrea Heuer Bieniek, Mike and Kathy

Zimmerman, and Tom and Mary Zimmerman. It truly means the world to me.

As always, I must acknowledge all the amazing bands and musicians whose music inspired and fueled me while writing this novel: Kamelot, Halsey, Nightwish, Lacuna Coil, Evanescence, Epica, Chevelle, The Murder of My Sweet, Mayan, Stream of Passion, The Dark Element, Letters from the Fire, Timo Tolkki, Meg Myers, Within Temptation, and Delain. Special shout-out to Kamelot for helping me get inside Cesare's head.

Huge thanks and many espresso shots to my brother, Matt Palombo, for letting me drag him around Rome and babble at him about Renaissance history while I researched this book, and for not complaining when I made him hang out in the Borgia apartments with me for, like, an hour. You're a good sport, dude. And hey! This book has a whole war and also murder! They're getting more exciting as I go!

Thanks and lots of cookies to Fenway the silky terrier, the most ferocious and sleepy of writing buddies.

Eternal gratitude and so much love to my parents, Tony and Debbie Palombo, for all their love and unyielding support, no matter what corner of the world or of human nature my books take me to. Dad, thanks for all the long conversations about Renaissance history and politics, and Mom, thanks for promoting my books to everyone you meet and always being up for watching a good costume drama.

Last but never least, thanks to all my readers near and far. Thank you for reaching out to me via email and social media to let me know what my books have meant to you. Your words have kept me going on many occasions. Thank you so much for making it possible for me to continue doing what I love.

About the Author

Jennifer Hark-Hameister

ALYSSA PALOMBO is the author of *The Violinist of Venice, The Most Beautiful Woman in Florence,* and *The Spellbook of Katrina Van Tassel.* She is a graduate of Canisius College with degrees in English and creative writing. A passionate music lover, she is a classically trained musician as well as a big fan of heavy metal. When not writing, she can be found reading, hanging out with her friends (and her dog!), or traveling. She lives in Buffalo, New York, where she is always at work on a new novel.